From the

Book 14 of

This one is for Walter Scott,
with love and a million thanks

With love as always to Ben

From the Mists of Time

Book 14 of "Circles of Light"

E.M. Sinclair

From the Mists of Time, Book 14 of *"Circles of Light"*
First published 2021

Cover design and formatted by W.J. Scott
Published by Murrell Press
© E.M. Sinclair 2021

E.M. Sinclair can be contacted via **Circles of Light** Facebook page.

Chapter One

He found himself in a courtyard garden. This came as a surprise, as he had pictured a study crowded with books and scrolls, chairs and small tables. He expected to find that was where he would arrive and yet, here he was, in a garden. Turning slowly he saw some plants he recognised but many more he did not. There was a nursery bed, the soil freshly turned, and the familiar scent of earth rising from it. Looking up, he saw only a diffused light, not sky, but even as he wondered, rain sprinkled gently onto his upturned face, accentuating the smell of soil and flowers here.

Reluctant to leave this place, he nonetheless looked for a way out of the white walled courtyard. An archway framed with climbing vines was tucked in a corner and he walked beneath it. He discovered he was now in a wide passage and a door directly opposite suggested a familiarity. Straightening his shoulders, he hoisted his pack more securely and went across to knock on the door.

'Come in, Endis.'

The young man opened the door and stepped inside.

'Come in,' the Ancient Augur repeated, her tone gentle. 'Come and sit down.'

Endis moved towards the armchair where the Augur sat and chose the chair opposite her, putting his pack on the floor at his feet. Only when he'd sat down did he look across at the occupant of the chair. She wore her cloak but the hood was pushed back, revealing her face for the first time. Her hair was of the purest white, as were her brows and lashes, her eyes a clear blue, almost as though they were made of glass or crystal. They stared at each other for a moment then her face, pale as her hair and wrinkled beyond belief, changed shape and Endis realised she was smiling at him.

'There is tea in the pot beside you. I would like some. Perhaps you would too?'

'Of course.' Endis saw two bowls beside the tea pot and carefully filled them. He took one bowl across, placing it on the table close to her chair, and resumed his seat.

'I thought you'd like to see the garden, that's why I sent you there this time,' the Augur continued. 'You are an earth mage, as I recall. You have enjoyed working with Lorak, in Iskallia?'

'I have. Very much.'

'There are rooms beside that garden that you may use. Tell me if there is anything you need.' The Augur gave a faint smile. 'Food will be provided. It will be real food, child, not illusion as Pakan Kelati offered you.'

'Tika and Lorak were worried about that,' Endis admitted.

The Augur waited.

'I thought I was eating stew everyday, but I wasn't,' Endis elaborated. 'Lorak was annoyed.'

'You like Tika?'

Endis gave her a look of surprise. 'Indeed I do. She saved me from the mage fevers. She took me to the safety and peace of Iskallia. She sent me to stay with Lorak and Fenj, who are the kindest of souls.' He stopped before he said more but the Augur finished for him.

'And she has preserved your mother's words forever.'

The young man's hazel eyes filled with tears. He just nodded.

'We all have some treasures we hoard, child. You have your first. There will be more, I'm sure. Pour me some more tea then go and find your rooms. Arrange them as you like. I will let you know when to visit me. You can wander where you wish, but it is easy to lose your way, so be cautious.'

Endis poured her more tea, picked up his pack and bowed. Reaching the door, he heard the Augur murmur again, a tone he couldn't identify in her voice. 'I appreciate your manners, child, but there is no need for such formalities here.'

At a loss for a reply, Endis simply left the Augur's rooms and crossed the passage to the courtyard garden. He looked in both directions but could see no doors in the white stone of the passage walls. He had to assume the rooms the Augur said he was to use were accessed from inside the garden. Endis wandered along a narrow stone path and found the courtyard was larger than it had first seemed. He was about to pass a willow tree when he paused, moving the long streamers of leaves a little apart. He shook his head when he saw a small table and a bench, tucked close to the tree trunk. Endis's expectations had already been proved quite wrong. He had thought to stay in some meagre room and be given constant instruction. A garden such as this was balm to his spirit and it delighted him beyond measure.

He found a tiny building smothered in several sorts of sweet scented blooms. Inside he found garden tools, pots, and seeds. Half hidden behind that place was a door which he opened cautiously. He entered a room the size of the Augur's room and saw a bed set against the further wall, a table and two chairs and a couch. A small stove stood against the back wall and he discovered a washroom beyond another door to the right of the entrance. Endis studied the stove. Flames flickered behind the glass of the door but so they had in Pakan Kelati's kitchen. He stretched out a hand, touching the top of the stove and jerked back as it burnt his fingertips. That hadn't happened in Pakan's kitchen so Endis decided this was a genuine fire.

Looking into cupboards, he was surprised to find food. Had the Augur put these supplies here? Where did she get the food? Were there servants here? He stared for a while then concluded it would be best just to accept food was somehow there. A good amount of light came into the room from two windows he would have said were too small, one above the table and the other above the bed. The small building holding gardening tools blocked any further view of the courtyard but the masses of flowers pleased him well enough.

He took his clothes and notebooks from his pack, putting the clothes in a box by the bed, the notebooks and pens on the table. He spent the rest of the day exploring the garden, slowly realising the light was fading regardless of the fact that he sensed no real sky overhead. Cleaning the few tools he'd used, he went inside again and washed his hands. Peering in the food cupboard, he chose not to cook anything tonight. He took the loaf and a large cloth wrapped cheese, making a meal from those.

Lighting a lamp on the table as the darkness deepened he wrote a report of his first day in the home of the Ancient Augur, wherever that home might actually be. Then he slept, a long, dreamless sleep, waking refreshed and relaxed. He was putting away the dishes he'd used for his breakfast when he felt the lightest tug in his mind. He dithered briefly, wondering if he should take his cloak, or a notebook. Deciding the Augur would tell him if he needed either, he left the room and walked through the garden, aware of the soft busy drone of insects fading behind him as he crossed the passage to the Augur's rooms.

Regardless of her comment yesterday, Endis bowed when he reached her chair, waiting for her to suggest he be seated. The Augur remained silent for a few moments then she sighed. 'I had intended to start by teaching you some history, child, but Menan visited last night. I think I must speak of her today.'

'Does Menan know I'm here? Did she come to learn from you?' Endis asked.

'I summoned her, long ago. She was shocked to find herself brought here. There was little I could teach her. She has a talent for Seeing but absolutely no control or understanding of that talent.'

Endis considered her reply. 'So your power is stronger than hers?'

'Endis, there are those with talent and there are those with true power. The one you call Tika has real power.'

Endis frowned. 'Everyone calls her Tika.'

'They do. That is the name the Great Dragon Kija gave to her when they first met.'

After a few moments trying to make sense of that, Endis had another question. 'Menan has a talent you say. Does Pakan also have only talent?'

'No. He has a dangerous power which he has never been taught to control. His power is great.'

'As great as yours? Or Tika's?'

This time it was the Augur who paused before replying.

'His power is great,' she repeated quietly. 'Let us hope we never have to find out whose is the stronger. As long as he remains in his lands of snow and is uninterested in the people of this world, all will be well.'

A chill slithered down Endis' spine. 'And if he doesn't?' he barely whispered the words.

The Augur's blue eyes took on the appearance of ice, as Tika's had on occasion. 'Then he would have to be destroyed, but such an action would cause a great deal of damage to the land and all creatures.' The Augur spoke calmly.

Endis swallowed. 'Menan's madness has grown more rapidly of late,' she continued. 'It is unlikely, but if she tries to contact you, you must refuse her. I think Tika instructed you how to block your mind?'

'To a certain extent,' he replied, alarmed. 'Only so that I couldn't feel people's pain if I touched them. I don't think that would be enough to keep someone like Menan out of my head.'

'No. It would not,' the Augur agreed. 'So I will show you how to defend yourself rather than just protect yourself. Then we will speak more specifically of Menan Kelati.'

Endis was pleasantly surprised to find he could follow the Augur's directions and understand how to deflect even a sudden mind probe she sent at him. 'You learn quickly, child, but it is no more than I expect of you.'

'Do you instruct all Seers?'

'All? No, Endis. Once there were more Seers born but fewer and fewer through all the ages.'

'Why is that?'

'Too many became crazed too soon, before I became aware of them. Many were killed. The elders of their villages or towns proclaimed them possessed of evil demons and had them killed.'

Endis listened, time passing almost unnoticed. The Augur nodded at a blackened kettle hanging to the side of the hearth. 'Make us some tea, child, my throat grows dry.'

While he waited for the water to heat, Endis thought of many questions but he decided he should be sparing. The Augur was telling him many new things and he should not

9

sound over eager. One thing he did allow himself to ask. 'Tika said she was unsure if Pakan and Menan Kelati were actually people like us. She said she didn't think they could be because they didn't understand about food, and Pakan had told her they did not use a ship to come here across the star fields. So how might they have travelled?'

'They do not have bodies such as you do Endis,' the Augur replied slowly. 'They put bodies around themselves to speak with you and with Tika, believing you would accept them better. I will not say more of them now because I need to concentrate on Menan. The visions and Seeings she experienced are an extremely tangled confusion.' She paused. 'This is not the only world they have visited, Endis. Much of what she Sees are twisted memories of things she actually witnessed but which she has - forgotten. I mean, she forgets they are images she saw in another reality. As far as I have discovered, she has 'Seen' barely a handful of events here. I believe it is unlikely she will ever see more, which is as it should be.'

Endis frowned over the Augur's words. 'Where did she take me then, on all those strange visits to scenes, usually of horror and violent deaths? To other worlds?'

The Augur's gaze sharpened as Endis's voice rose, hinting at sudden panic. 'That is probably correct, child, but you are here now, safe as you can be, with me. Why fret over those visions she took you into?'

Too confused to respond, Endis remained mute.

'What do you know of the stars, of those other worlds?'

With difficulty, Endis focussed on the Augur's question. 'Very little. We know we came from such a place but it was forbidden to speak of where that place was, or what our lives, our society, had been like before we reached this world.'

'Do you understand what the stars are?'

The young man's blank expression was answer enough.

'So much must have been lost,' the Augur lamented. 'Kingdoms, empires, some filled with such knowledge, some with such ignorance, all gone as though they had never been.' She sighed. 'Each star you see shining in the night sky, is in fact a sun, Endis. Just like the sun that

10

warms and lights this world. Our world spins round the sun and other worlds spin around all those other suns.'

Endis listened, shocked by her words but struggling to make sense of them.

'I'll show you another day. It's easier than trying to explain,' the Augur continued.

Endis paled and the Augur clicked her tongue. 'I have a room here I call my infinity room. *That* is where I'll show you what I'm talking about.'

Hoping to change the subject to something a little more understandable, Endis asked how big this house, or palace, or castle, of hers might be.

'It's quite large. I'll show you the library in a day or two.'

'Where does the food come from?'

The Augur gave a vague shrug. 'It is provided. Now. Menan Kelati.'

The time passed quickly, so Endis thought, while the Augur spoke of her concerns over Menan Kelati, until finally she sent him away. 'Return here tomorrow,' she said. 'I would know more of your life in the Asataria.'

Again, when Endis rose, he bowed respectfully as he took his leave. Back in his rooms, he made hasty jottings of certain things the Augur had spoken of, tore a chunk of bread from a new loaf he found in the food cupboard and went out into the garden. The small pots holding seeds had labels on them which he'd thought indecipherable yesterday. Today, he found he could read them. Working quietly on his knees by the nursery bed, his thoughts drifted from the seeds to the Augur's words and back until the light began to fade around him.

This evening, he cooked a proper meal and ate hungrily before settling to his notebook. It was only as he got into bed that a certain phrase struck him. Endis had asked what natural form the Kelatis might have. The Augur had said: "*They do not have bodies such as you wear.*" *You* wear. Why had she not said, such as *we* wear? Before he could worry the thought further, he was asleep.

In her room the Augur sighed. She must be careful with her

words, she chided herself. She had realised her slip even as she spoke but hoped Endis wouldn't notice it. The Augur leaned her head back on her chair. She had known how intelligent the boy would be. It had been so long though, since she had Seen him in her visions, and had longed for the time when he would be here, actually in her presence. He had to be brought to the full knowledge of his life's path so carefully. He was still so young, she thought regretfully. On the heels of that thought, came her own memory: that *she* had been even younger when she had understood how her existence must be spent.

Yet childhood was a mixed blessing for so many human children, the Augur thought. She couldn't remember a time when she *hadn't* known the vague shape of her own future. No. The Augur caught her thoughts back. It was not yet time to recall those memories. It would be hard enough when the moment came to tell them to Endis. Her mind drifted across the world, then returned to check that the boy still slept without dreams. Drawing her hood over her head, the Augur settled back deeper in her chair and sank into a state of resting awareness.

The next day, Endis was confused by the Augur's first question when he'd made her tea and seated himself across from her. 'Tell me of your friends in the Asataria, Endis. Were there many children with whom you played childish games?'

Endis noted the question sounded almost uncertain, as though the Augur was unfamiliar with the behaviour of children. 'No. I had few friends.' He spoke with no hint of self pity, merely reporting facts. 'Tokala and I were the only two of our year to be invited from the lesser school to study in the Academy. Tokala was clever with figures, numbers, shapes. My gifts were with the natural sciences. At least, that's what I guess. I was never that good with numbers.'

'Did you not make new friends in the Academy?' Those clear blue eyes remained fixed on Endis's face.

He smiled. 'No. No one ever forgot I was of a lesser family. Tokala stayed close because she knew me, she

12

knew I regarded her as almost family. She is very beautiful. The other students, particularly the boys, tried to get close to her but she was afraid of them. Naresh was the worst. He was trapped outside in the lesser precinct when the Academy and Assembly sealed itself off.'

'What of the friends from your first school?'

Endis looked puzzled. 'I never played games as they did. It seemed a strange way to spend time.'

'You are fond of Tokala?'

'Oh no. I mean I like her well enough. She was very quiet. We studied together. People in the outer precinct rarely spoke to us once we started at the Academy. It didn't seem to worry Tokala any more than it did me. I think she was probably better with people than I ever was and I'm glad she seems to have made friends in Iskallia.'

'You don't like people?'

Endis frowned in thought. He'd never considered whether he liked folk. 'I think I might like them, but I don't truly understand them,' he finally replied. 'They laugh at things I cannot see are amusing. They smile with their mouths but their eyes say otherwise. They pretend many things and I always took their words as true, only to discover it was some kind of joke.' He shrugged. 'My mother tried to help me understand some of it and taught me that it was best if I kept quiet. I said what I thought if I was asked anything. I didn't understand that most people don't do that.'

The Augur took her time replying. 'Soon you will see their hearts, their spirits, child. Even if you have no vision with your physical eyes, your mind will see who people truly are, and will read the truth in them.'

'Are you sure? How will I learn to do that? Tika could read people's hearts.'

'Your gift is growing, even as the plants in your garden are already responding to your care. I have to tell you, there will be times when you see your Seer's talent as a curse rather than a pleasant gift, but it is in you, it cannot be removed.'

Endis shook his head. 'Why me? Tika had no information about Seers. I know she tried to find any mention of such a talent in her library, and from the Dark Realm. My mother had no mage gifts as far as I know. None at all.'

'Your talent comes through your father's blood, Endis. He was a man of Gaharn but his ancestors were among the earliest true humans to settle in those lands. They remembered the days of the gods and they sang of how they were made. Such songs and stories have been forgotten for millennia, child, but I will tell you of them, as I can.'

'Gods? I've read of gods, in books from Iskallia's library. They were dismissed by my tutors in the Asataria. We were taught only that the land is, the stars are.'

'That is true as far as it goes, child, but it is a very simplistic statement. I suppose it sounds enigmatic enough to appear profound. I think your leader when you arrived here, Jerak, he was the one who came up with that adage. He's the one who made all the rules you've lived by all this time.'

'He was the father of Lady Emla and Lord Rhaki,' Endis agreed. 'He was held in the highest regard. We were constantly told of his bravery and his wisdom.'

He was surprised by the Augur's snort of derision. 'I apologise, child. He was an unbearable bore, so fond of his own dignity and importance. He may have been brave, I wouldn't know about that. But wise? Oh dear me, no. There have been many truly wise ones throughout the long, long life of this world. Jerak would be seen as a simpleton beside any of them.' The Augur's voice had altered as she spoke, a ringing echo around each word.

Endis stared at her, his eyes wide, mouth open. Her hands, roped with veins, tightened on the arms of her chair and she shivered. 'I ask your pardon, Endis. Some things remain irritations in my memory and Jerak of Asataria is one such irritant.' She relaxed her hands with a visible effort and closed her eyes briefly.

Endis rose in silence, moving the kettle above the fire and setting about making more tea. Having been taught all his life to revere the memory of Jerak the Founder, he was shocked by the Augur's words. Waiting for the water to heat, he realised his mother had rarely, if ever, spoken of

Jerak. She often mentioned Discipline Senior Ryla, and clearly held her in highest esteem, but Jerak? No. In the last years, she only spoke of Lady Emla and her closest friends briefly in tones Endis now saw were more scornful than respectful.

He made the tea, understanding just how drastically his world had been shattered, disrupted. Putting a bowl of tea beside the Augur, Endis resumed his seat. 'Forgive me child. Some things still anger me even when I, of all people, should understand there is no point whatsoever in sifting through cold ashes.' She sipped her tea, watching him as she did so. 'You have a question?' she asked.

'I have so many questions,' was his rueful reply.

'Ask one, for now,' she suggested.

'Who *are* you? How many Seers are there?'

She drank more tea before she responded. 'That is two questions, child. The first I will soon explain to you, but it will be a long explanation. The second I will answer at another time. Now, refill my bowl and tell me what you know of gods.'

Chapter Two

Endis was nonplussed by the Augur's request, then he had a thought. 'I saw Mistress Ferag. Tika said she was the Mistress of Death. I wasn't sure if she was a god, or goddess I mean.'

'Did you ever hear of Simert? Or Feshni? Meru? Youki?'

Endis shook his head then blushed.

'Well?' The Ancient Augur sounded intrigued.

'Erm, I think I've heard the name of Simert but none of the others.'

'In what context have you heard of Simert?'

'Well, one of Tika's Guards, she erm, said "Simert's balls". She was annoyed at the time.' The blush reached Endis's ears.

'I see. You say you saw Ferag?'

'Yes. In Far, in Sapphrea. At Lord Seboth's house. She visits his children I understand.'

'She does.' Yet again the Augur's voice changed. Endis felt a great sorrow permeate her words. 'She has lost so many. I'm glad Lallia is happy to share her children with Ferag. Well, clearly you know little history, child, or did your tutors not understand much of this world, how it came about, and so on?'

'It was made?' Endis stared at her.

The Augur sighed. 'As I said, this will take some time to explain but I will show you my infinity room later, which may help.' She settled back among the cushions lining her chair and drew a breath.

'Before the time of mists there was only infinity. Then the Vortex appeared. The Vortex was a spinning mass of matter. Rock fragments from who knows where, whirling in the vast emptiness that is infinity. When I say "fragments" Endis, some of them were the size of this world and some as small as river pebbles. Out of the blackness of infinity came Mother Dark. I never heard where she came from, how she came into existence. None of us knew. With her arrival, the Vortex changed. The fragments it had contained, flew out, in all directions, blazing with colours as a crystal refracts sunlight in your world.

'Some of the fragments caught fire as they hurtled away from the Vortex and many burn still. They are the suns that you call stars, still scattered throughout infinity. Some burnt themselves to a cinder, some shrank to a glowing ember, some changed from fire to gas vapours, but most of them still burn. Mother Dark spent millennia drifting among these stars, seeing pieces of the scattered rocks melting into each other and starting to circle each star to eventually become worlds.

'There was no *time* then, Endis, as you would understand it, no hurry, no rush. Mother Dark saw tiny sparks of life start to emerge on many of these new worlds but although she found them of interest, she chose not to make any one of them her home.'

'Until she came here,' Endis whispered.

'Until she came here,' the Augur agreed. 'No one knows what Mother Dark is, or if she actually has a physical appearance. There is often discussion about this, but in my view it is pointless. Her *voice* has been heard from the earliest times, so it is recorded, but she has never been seen. She caused three other beings to come into existence when she chose this world as her home. The first was Lerran, the second, Hanlif, and the third, Darallax. They had no form when Mother Dark first made them, that came much later. They watched this world grow, change, and observed the creatures that slowly, so very slowly, became people.

'Lerran was the most like Mother Dark, but the two males were different. Darallax was quieter, less adventurous. Hanlif was inclined to a wildness. All three took various forms, copying many of the creatures they saw developing on the world. Hanlif created his own creatures, variations on the ones he watched. Lerran too, made other life forms, and all three created other beings like themselves who became the lesser gods. They lived and fought, like many siblings do, while Mother Dark watched the world. She was fascinated as some animals in this chosen world

17

developed an increasing intelligence, able to remember, to learn, to speak.

'The lesser gods too were intrigued as humans built houses, made what the gods considered ridiculous rules and began to fight each other. Several gods joined in, taking one side or another, causing more trouble, encouraging one group to kill their neighbours. Some chose to mate with the developing humans, then watched to see if their magical powers, gifted from Mother Dark, appeared in any of the offspring that resulted from such matings.

'Mother Dark was distressed to notice that humans lived such very brief lives, the spark of their spirits winking out so soon. She created two more beings, Simert and Ferag, and instructed them to collect up those sparks and return them to her. Those two followed Mother Dark's wishes completely, taking human form for most of the time, and gathering up the precious life force to return to her.'

The Augur at last fell silent for a moment. Endis too, sat quietly. He had seen what the Augur described in his mind's eye as she spoke; strange beings taking any shape they chose. A chaos of colour and forms.

'I tire too easily Endis. Enough for today. Tomorrow I will show you the infinity room, and perhaps speak more, but I must gather my strength again now.'

Endis felt her exhaustion and rose. 'Shall I make you more tea before I leave you?' he asked.

'No, child. You go to your garden and return to me tomorrow.'

When Endis left his garden the following morning, the Augur was just leaving her door. Cloaked and hooded, her bowed figure limped towards him, a walking stick in her left hand clearly a necessity. She took his arm without speaking, turning left from her rooms along the passageway. After a few moments, Endis asked a question. 'What happened to the three who Mother Dark first created?'

'Hmmm? Oh. Hanlif was killed. He did love fighting. He wanted to be lord of the world. He turned on Lerran and Darallax and there was great loss of life among humans and the ones those three had brought into existence. Darallax hid away with his few remaining followers. Lerran also retreated, to let her people recover. Both of them were greatly damaged. Lerran returned to Mother Dark a few years ago.' The Augur limped on while Endis pondered her reply.

'Hanlif was killed?' he asked finally. 'So even gods can be killed?'

'Indeed they can. There have been occasions when Mother Dark has removed one of the lesser gods who has annoyed her. She confines them to infinity, not allowing them access to any worlds. But human creatures can kill them. Sometimes. There is a rule Mother Dark insisted on: that all the lesser gods must wear human form when they interact with the humans here. There have been instances, few admittedly, when a god has killed one of his or her siblings. Then Mother Dark snuffs them out. Here we are.'

Glancing up, Endis saw an arched doorway, the door set back a little and made of white wood. At the Augur's nod, he lifted the latch. The door swung open without a sound. They crossed the threshold and a slight click told Endis the door had closed at their backs. Light began to glimmer faintly, revealing a large, high ceilinged room, windowless and empty. As he looked around, he saw, from the corner of his eye, the Augur raise her hand from his arm and wave it vaguely towards the empty space in front of them.

Endis gasped. Round shapes, some large, some tiny, some moving fast, others slowly, filled the room, all circling a glowing golden sphere in the centre.

'Just study them for a while,' the Augur told him. 'There is a bench just along here. Sit with me.'

Unable to take his gaze from the dizzying display, Endis let the Augur tug him a few paces. He felt a bench at the back of his knees and sank down, still staring at the sight before him. Slowly he began to see how differently many of the spheres moved. Three close to the centre seemed to race in their circles round and round. Others moved in long ellipses, moving out almost to the wall of the room then coming close to the golden globe at the heart of the display. After a considerable time, Endis sighed. 'It's amazing that none of them collide with each other.'

'Some have, long ago,' the Augur replied. 'But this has remained steady longer than many others.'

'What are the small pieces that move among the larger ones?'

'Just leftover fragments. They usually destroy themselves or vanish from here out into the infinity which lies all around.'

'It's very beautiful.'

'That is the sun, that gives warmth and light to your world.'

'It is? Then one of those spheres is this world?'

'Of course. It is the fifth world out from the sun.'

Endis counted carefully and marvelled at the idea of being on a lump of rock, moving eternally in its set path. How could it be? Surely he should feel something, some sense of movement? 'Are there people on all these worlds?'

The Augur took her time replying. 'There are forms of life on most, except for the three worlds nearest the sun. They are too close and the sun is too hot for life that you might recognise.'

'And all the stars we see in the night sky are suns like this, with worlds around them?'

'Some have more worlds, some have less. Some suns are bigger by far, others smaller.'

'But there are thousands of stars!'

'Millions, Endis, not thousands.'

'Do you know where my mother's people came from? Or the Kelatis?'

The Augur turned her head towards him but he could see only the quick gleam of eyes in the depths of her hood. 'I do, child.'

After another pause, during which Endis wondered if she would tell him how far those worlds might be, she spoke once more. 'Mother Dark forbade the gods to breed children with humans after that Last Battle when Hanlif was killed and Lerran and Darallax were so nearly destroyed as well.'

He turned to her, puzzled by the apparent change of subject.

'There is a natural magic in the world, Endis, but when

20

the gods bred children with human females, and the other way about, those children showed strong powers. Unlike the gods themselves, those offspring were not under the command of Mother Dark. Very few humans knew of her then, or even now. But their talents made them too powerful when they used them against one another. There were even more wars between humans. Great cities turned to ruin and dust, people cast out of devastated lands, the very land ripped apart in places.'

'I think I read something about a Last Battle in one of the books in Iskallia. I thought that was only two thousand years ago. Surely such wars would have been remembered, recorded? There was something to do with the Dark Realm, too. Oh.' Endis stopped, ideas connecting in his brain. 'The Dark Realm has to be connected to the Mother Dark you speak of?'

'Lerran ruled the Dark Realm, Endis, and the Last Battle was fought far, far in the past.' The Augur fell silent again, watching the coloured globes in their endless circling, while Endis struggled to make sense of her words.

'The gods breeding with humans, that's what gives people mage talents now? It is passed on through the blood?' He followed that thought when the Augur made no reply. 'That is why the Asatarian people's mage talents were so much weaker than those of people who have always lived here? I was taught that Asatarians reached this world barely two thousand years ago; that would have been long after Mother Dark forbade the gods to mate with humans. Forgive me, but although I truly find this more interesting than anything I've ever been taught, but what has it to do with being a Seer?'

'I do understand your confusion, child, but it is of the greatest importance that you learn all I am able to teach you of the past, to ready you for your own future. I'm sure you must be impatient with my history lessons already.'

'No, oh no. I am really interested in all you've been telling me. I just couldn't see how all those long ago events could possibly help me.'

They sat, watching the globes moving smoothly through the air before Endis spoke again.

'You said it happened both ways: that gods fathered children with human women and human men really fathered children on female gods?'

'That is correct.'

'What happened to them? The ones whose mothers were gods?'

'They became lesser gods as well.' The Augur sounded a little surprised by the question. 'There were fewer born that way though.'

'So there is human blood, perhaps human characteristics, in some of these lesser gods?'

'There is, but it isn't strong enough to overcome the *gods'* blood. Never think that, Endis.'

'Why does no one know of these things? The way the worlds fly around a burning star?'

'There have been humans who discovered the ways of infinity, but many were killed for their discoveries. Many civilisations have risen and fallen, child, in the life of this world.

'There is nothing left of them. No ruins, or histories. Not even stories.'

'It is the way of humans, so I have concluded. They seem unable to work together in peace for any length of time before they fall to petty squabbles and then to war.'

'You said the lesser gods come here. They encourage trouble between people?'

'Some of them do, yes. They've grown bored with that recently. Humans are too predictable they say.'

Endis pounced on the Augur's last words. '*They* say? How do you know what the gods say? Do you *See* them?'

The Augur raised a hand and the glittering display faded from sight. 'Sometimes,' was her only reply before she struggled to her feet. 'You can come and look at the worlds, whenever you wish,' she added as Endis rose beside her.'

'How can *I* make them appear?'

'Oh.' She paused. 'Just think of them and command them to show themselves. They will appear.'

They walked back the way they'd come, more slowly. Endis was aware of the Augur's trembling through the hand that gripped his arm tighter. Stopping at her door, she released him. 'Again, I apologise, child. I must rest. I will summon you later.'

'Let me make you some tea. Or some food,' he offered.

He heard a smile in her voice when she answered. 'I need nothing but rest just now, thank you.'

Endis waited until her door closed then hurried back through the garden, to his room. He wrote as swiftly as he could, trying to find words to describe the astonishing sight of worlds, spinning fast and slow, as they whirled round the sun. Opening another notebook, he wrote all he could recall of the Ancient Augur's talk of gods, lesser gods, Mother Dark. Reading back over what he'd written, he nodded to himself. There were enough important points from which he could expand later.

He was too agitated to eat so he went outside and let the garden soothe him. He spent time removing dead flower-heads and redirecting some of the more exuberant tendrils of vines, keeping his thoughts focussed on his work. The light was still bright when he felt the slight tug in his mind. Brushing soil from his fingers, Endis went to the Augur's door. Entering, he saw she had pushed back her hood again, exposing her face, and he also noted that tea steamed from two bowls.

'Before you tell me more, may I ask why I must know all this about gods and infinity? And when the gods aren't here among us, where do they live?'

'I must teach you "all this", child, because you have to know *everything*. The gods live in their own place, between this world and the infinity. It would probably seem an ordinary enough place to you. As I told you, they are free to travel elsewhere should they so wish, but Mother Dark brooks no interference in other worlds.'

'Only this one?'

The Augur watched him. 'I believe Mother Dark regrets the amount the lesser gods have provoked humans here. What's done is done. Their influence has been greatly curtailed since the Last Battle.

The Augur waited but Endis asked no more. 'The purpose of a Seer now is to try to ease this world back to the way Mother Dark first imagined it. She understands there are squabbles among all families but she believes such squabbles can be calmed rather than growing into violence.'

Endis met the Augur's blue gaze. 'So you, we, do the bidding of Mother Dark?'

'We do Endis. In time, not yet, you will descend into the dark where you may speak with her yourself. Many of Lerran's people still take that step, although many also find it frightening.'

'Will I find it frightening?' Endis sounded curious rather than afraid.

'I don't believe you will, Endis, no.'

'Why not?'

'Because of your blood, child, your father's ancestry.' She smiled, waiting for another question.

'The Kelatis. Are they gods? They travelled through the star fields, without a ship, as you say the gods are able to do.'

'They are life forms from a far distant world. They can manifest solid bodies for a time, never for long, but mostly they are just - energy. You can feel a gust of wind but you cannot see it blow against your face. That is how to think of the Kelatis. Now. I shall explain more of some of this world's past. Questions can come later, child.'

When Endis left her rooms much later, his head felt crammed to bursting with information. Much of it sounded like the wildest of stories, made up to terrify the wits out of children. But he understood though, in his very bones, that every word she'd spoken had truly happened. The light had faded by the time he hurried through the garden and he went straight to the table to write down all he could remember.

It felt very late to Endis when he finally laid aside his pen. Even so, his stomach growled loudly and he got up, preparing a meal from food he discovered in the cupboard. When he'd tidied away his plates he stood at the open door for a while. The garden was dark although he could just make out some plants close by. Above him was only darkness, a complete blackness, with no hint of stars or moon. Undressing, he slid into bed, his mind still full of the things he'd seen and heard today. He turned onto his side, convinced he wouldn't sleep at all tonight, and he slept at once.

When he woke he lay a moment, sure he'd heard voices, laughter, but if he had, all was quiet now. He wandered the garden until he felt the Augur's summons and walked across to her rooms. He bowed, as he always did, and set about making tea. 'I don't seem to have dreamt since I've been here,' he remarked.

'No. There is so much for you to learn, I have blocked dreams for now.'

Sitting down, Endis thought back. 'It was the pirate captain I Saw, or dreamed of, last I think.'

'Yes. You must keep watch on him, throughout his life. He has his part to play.'

'I might die before he does,' Endis pointed out with a chuckle.

The Augur smiled back. 'Oh child! Have you not realised how you are changing? You will *not* die before him. If there had been hint of that happening, I would have brought you here sooner.'

Endis frowned. 'The Asataria just vanished into the earth. I could have been lost with all the others there?'

'No. The event caused you to realise your powers, but if it hadn't, I would have intervened. I admit I did not foresee how you would suffer from the mage fevers. Forgive me for allowing you to have to experience that.'

'How long have you been watching me? I really don't understand why you would?'

'Not just you, child. Your line. Your father's line. When he made your mother pregnant, an Asatarian woman, I was surprised.'

'I don't even know his name,' Endis said very softly. 'He was a man of Gaharn, working as an Asatarian Guard. He died before he knew my mother was carrying me.'

After a moment, the Augur held out her bowl for more tea. 'His name was Andis, child. He was a good man. Your mother named you as close as she dared for him.'

'If he was just an arms man, why were you watching him?'

'His blood, Endis.' The Augur watched while Endis mulled over her words, trying to fit them into the great

25

amounts of information he'd absorbed in the preceding days. His hazel eyes met hers, widening as he reached a conclusion. 'One of my ancestors was a *god*? Is *that* what you're saying?'

'Of course, child.'

'Do you know which god?'

'Indeed I do but that is not something you need to know now.'

He nodded. From all the Augur had told him of gods, and lesser gods, he could well imagine there must have been a lot of them. That led him to another thought. 'When gods die, are they replaced? Why *would* they die though? I understand you said one of the first three was killed in the Last Battle, when he was in human form, but why would they die otherwise?'

'Some become so bored they ask to return to Mother Dark, to lose their identities and merge with her great all encompassing self.'

'Bored?'

The Augur snorted. 'Immortality is not such a wonderful thing, child. To watch the friends you've made grow old and die while you continue unchanged? No, Endis, not so wonderful at all. Now, enough of gods. Today I will tell you more history.'

Again, Endis thought his mind could hold no more when he returned to his rooms as the light faded around him. Again, he wrote all he could of the Ancient Augur's words. After he'd made a meal, he sat eating, going over and over certain things the Augur had spoken of. He poured himself a mug of water and stared at the dark window. He wondered what she'd meant when she said he was changing. How might he change? Frowning, he lifted the small lamp from the table and went through to the tiny wash room. He leaned close to a looking glass above the basin, holding the lamp up as he peered at his reflection. There seemed no alteration in his appearance as far as he could see. It was simply the lamplight that made the gold flecks in his hazel eyes seem more pronounced. Shrugging, he returned to clear away his dishes and prepared for bed.

The Augur waited until the boy slept then she sighed softly. She had so very much to tell the child and she feared time was short. The telling took its toll on her though, making her walk back through memories which in turn, woke even older memories. The Ancient Augur drew her hood over her head, hiding her face from any watcher. Between one slow breath and the next, she slipped into her earliest existence, her earliest memories, her earliest friends.

Chapter Three

Laughter rang through the halls. Lahi's laugh was a high silvery sound; Feshni's was deeper, warmer. Ashri tried to follow the sounds but echoes misled her time and again. She just knew they'd both cheat and change shape although they'd promised to stay as they were when they suggested the game. Ashri stopped running and considered what form she could take that might give her a chance to find one or other of them. It was definitely against their rules to become invisible so what could she be? Birds whistled and called in the gardens beyond the halls and Ashri transformed herself to a tiny brown speckled bird, darting on in pursuit of her friends.

She flew high above a group of shimmering figures then flitted into a twisted bush covered in black leaves as a crowd of different beings walked by, their voices raised in argument. Ashri waited, hunched tight among the leaves, as sparks flashed and splattered from two of the group. She was about to spring into the air again when a voice nearby made her freeze.

'Of *course* Mother Dark will approve. Has she not shown *I* am her most favoured child?'

'I thought Lerran was her most cherished,' another voice replied calmly.

The first speaker snarled. 'Surely you're not serious? Since Lerran took such a liking to that lesser male she must have forfeited Mother's approval.'

'If you plan to hurt those whom Lerran has been nurturing, I believe you'll find more trouble than you think.'

'I thought you'd be eager to join in the sport.' The first voice held a note of scorn.

'I'm happy enough to join you when it doesn't involve upsetting your sister. I'm not stupid, Hanlif.'

The voices drifted further from the bush where Ashri hid. She shivered, her speckled feathers rippling over her back. She hoped none of them had sensed her there or she

28

would be in trouble. All thought of trying to find Lahi and Feshni was gone now. No one else was close by she sensed, pushing clear of the black leaves. Still in her bird shape, she flew fast, back the way she'd come, darting along corridors and wide hallways until she reached her quarters. Transforming to the shape of a spindly girl, she stood by a window, staring out over the gardens.

A ball of light shot into the room behind her, melting into Feshni's form even as Ashri turned to face him. 'You gave up,' he accused her.

'Did not. Something distracted me, so I came back here to think about it.'

'What?'

'Nothing to do with you.'

Feshni sat cross-legged on the large bed and watched her. 'We're friends. You should tell me things that worry you.'

Ashri folded her arms. 'I said something distracted me, not worried me.'

Lahi arrived, in her usual form. She was taller than either of the others, her figure more mature, her eyes far more knowing. She leaned against the wall. 'Not interrupting you two, am I?'

Ashri didn't bother to reply. Feshni threw a cushion at Lahi, which Lahi sent back, much harder, with a flick of her power. Feshni's shield was a heartbeat too late and he grunted as the cushion hit his head with the force of a hard punch. He seemed to swell as anger burst from him.

'Oh just go away,' said Lahi, her tone bored now. 'I want to talk to Ashri without you fussing about.'

From her position by the window, Ashri saw the strength of Lahi's command as her silver eyes stared Feshni down. With no further argument, Feshni vanished. Ashri willed herself to calm, smoothing her outer appearance to the usual bland and mild facade she always maintained. Lahi sat where Feshni had been sitting, smiling at Ashri.

'You didn't find us. Why did you give up so soon? Did something upset you?'

Ashri stretched her eyes wide in surprise. 'Upset me? What ever could do that? I'm sorry, I was distracted, watching the birds in the gardens. Did you know the blue tails have made nests in the arches under the outer halls?' She kept herself calm, relaxed, even as she felt Lahi's mind scratch at hers. She gave no sign that she was aware of that, just waited for Lahi's next words.

'Oh well, if you're sure nothing bothered you.' Lahi rose, turning to go. 'There's been a lot of rumours, about things on the world. Those funny humans are going to fight again soon, I heard. That will be worth watching.'

'If they are "funny", why do most of us wear their shapes I wonder?' Ashri asked, unable to keep the question behind her lips.

Lahi paused than looked down at herself. 'It often feels clumsy but it does seem to have many potential uses.' Light from the window caught her eyes and silver flashed momentarily. 'I had hopes for you, Ashri. So many of the lesser ones among us are astonishingly stupid. I thought you were better than most.'

Ashri managed to look suitably chastened. Lahi shook her head and drifted away.

Ashri turned back to gaze from the window. There were no doors here. What use were doors when most of the occupants of this place could pass through solid stone if they so wished? She remained as she was until she sensed Feshni's presence again.

'She's got very close to Lord Hanlif and his followers. She wants us, well, *you* anyway, to join them too.' His words were inside her head. Aloud he offered a suggestion for another amusement. 'Why don't we go and see what the sun is really like?'

Gratefully, Ashri laughed. 'That's not safe, even for us. You know that as well as I do.'

He sighed. 'Did you know Lord Darallax has a new bird? He says her name is Anfled. She's enormous, and black feathered. He said Mother sent it to him, as a gift,'

Ashri sat on the bed beside Feshni. 'Did she send something to Lord Hanlif too?' she asked very softly.

'Not that I heard,' he grinned. 'Lady Lerran has less and less to do with Lord Hanlif of late.'

'She's very involved with those creatures she found, on

the world.'

'I know.' Feshni spoke even more quietly. 'Lord Hanlif jeers at her, all the time. Have you noticed that, Ashri?'

She nodded but she was scanning the area around although she thought this section was empty but for the two of them. 'Yes,' she replied at last. 'He tries to cause trouble for the one who Lady Lerran has chosen. I've seen him and his followers try to start fights with him.' She leaned closer to Feshni. 'He won't defeat them. Lady Lerran, Lord Darallax and the lesser god, Dabray will live far longer than Lord Hanlif,' she whispered.

Feshni looked at her. Ashri saw the question he wanted to ask hovering in his mind and hoped he wouldn't ask it. She was relieved when he just nodded. 'Many follow Lord Hanlif now though Ashri. Lahi shares his bed quite often.'

Ashri had guessed as much but she shivered slightly when Feshni put her suspicion into words. 'Just try to keep out of their way,' she murmured.

Feshni transformed into his favourite form, a ball of golden light, and began to bounce between the walls. Ashri watched him for a moment then rose and left her rooms. The ball floated rather than bounced, following her down the stairs. 'Go and find Dalmek or Korron. I'll see you later I expect,' she said when she reached ground level.

The ball of light sped away along the outer colonnade and Ashri stepped down into the garden. She had discovered a large section which had been left untended and thus remained empty of gods, and that was where she headed now. She passed a group sprawled on the grass beside a clump of tall purple flowers whose petals were twisted like wires, and moved on beneath trees laden with both blossom and fruit. A little further and Ashri slipped through a slight gap in a bedraggled kind of hedge. She squeezed along a narrow path formed by bare branches.

Ashri never transformed to reach her special place. Somehow it was important that she maintain her usual corporeal appearance when she chose to come here. Probably an example of her stupidity, if Lahi had heard of it. Emerging into an open space, she felt relief. She always felt freer here, unwatched by anyone. The grass was longer, rougher, small flowers scattered randomly among the tussocks. Ashri walked round the edge of the space until she reached a pool. It was scarcely big enough for her to fit her two feet in - she'd done that a few times. Its water was ice cold, fed from somewhere underground and the surface lay flat and unmoving. She sank down beside it and waited.

She could not have explained what alerted her but she looked across the pool just as a glitter of golden droplets solidified into Youki. Ashri smiled at her. 'You've been gone longer this time,' she said.

Youki knelt opposite her and Ashri wondered, for the hundredth time, who could have birthed her. Youki wore no clothing, covered in a silvery fur. Ashri thought she was beautiful with her eyes of no colour and all colours, but she knew others mocked her.

'Hanlif is planning more wickedness,' Youki murmured. 'The beautiful city my children have made. That is what he wants to destroy.'

'Can you not ask Lady Lerran to intercede?' Or Mother herself?'

Youki shook her head. 'I would not involve them, sweet Ashri. I have the charge of caring for them when first those creatures began to show awareness of more than their basic needs. It rests with me.'

'You will have helpers though, Youki. Through all of time, there *will* be those who care too.'

Youki glanced sharply across at Ashri. 'You have Seen this?'

Ashri shifted uneasily. 'I have *dreamed* this.'

Youki tilted her head to one side. 'How do you *dream*, Ashri, when we do not sleep?'

Ashri drew up her knees and rested her chin on them. 'I don't know if I sleep, as the creatures down on your world sleep, but pictures come into my head, and sometimes words, so I thought that must be dreaming, as you say they do?' She could feel Youki's doubt. 'I heard Hanlif today. I think he plans his attack soon but maybe not on your particular city, Youki. He is always consumed with jealousy of both Lerran and Darallax.'

Youki frowned. 'You think he will try to hurt those

beautiful creatures Lerran has been spending so much time with?'

'I don't know. Urtax was arguing with him. He sounded most reluctant to anger Lerran.'

'Angering Lerran would be very unwise.' Youki sounded thoughtful. 'I will try to prepare my children for possible trouble, but Lerran too should have some warning, Ashri.'

'I have little to do with the exalted ones, Youki.'

Youki scoffed. 'We are all the same, children of our Mother. Do Lerran or Darallax act as if they are "exalted"?'

'I will think on what you suggest,' Ashri conceded.

'Send me word, if you learn more, dear one.' Youki's figure faded into the golden droplets and Ashri was alone once more.

She considered the many here in the gods' space. There were but a handful newer made than her. Mother Dark had been angered by the constant fighting and needless hurt so many of her original offspring seemed to find such delight in, but there were still plenty left who would cause trouble given half a chance. Ashri thought of Youki's suggestion to speak to Lerran or Mother of her fears. She had never spoken to Lerran and had only heard Mother's voice when she'd first emerged and become a lesser god. She hugged her knees tighter. There was another of whom she'd heard spoken of, only once.

Another son, born with Lerran. Once only had she heard his name spoken and that had been by Hanlif. Hanlif had been in one of his towering rages, unfortunately a not uncommon occurrence. Many of the lesser gods had hidden away in terror as he'd screamed his fury at them all. 'You should all appreciate that you have *me* as your ruler and not Olekatah, foulest spawn of the Dark. rightly cast out by Mother herself for his vileness."

Ashri had never heard mention of the name since that day and never dared ask anyone about him. She didn't allow herself to even *think* the name, just imagined a blank space when her thoughts turned in his direction. All the stories she'd ever heard about the origins of the gods was of Mother Dark creating the Three. *Three*, not Four. She began to get to her feet, her gaze caught as light suddenly flashed across the flat surface of the pool.

She stood, half upright, and stared at the face she saw as clearly as if it was her own reflection. Dark, dark skin. Eyes dark with a gold edge around the pupils. Straight thin nose, high cheekbones. Hair blowing across the face, dark as the eyes which bored into hers. Then, it was gone, even as Ashri took a clumsy step back and nearly fell. She stood unmoving for several moments then turned away, making her way back, out through the hedge and into the perfectly sculpted gardens. Ashri emptied her mind of all her thoughts as she walked towards the great edifice where all the gods lived.

A few voices called to her, inviting her to join a game or a group of chatterers. Ashri merely smiled and walked on, climbing the stairs back to her room. She paused at the entrance then moved round the bed and found Feshni sitting on the floor beside the table. 'What's wrong?' she asked him.

'Dalmek is going into the Dark, to ask Mother to fix him forever as a human child.'

Ashri frowned. She lay on the bed, staring at the ceiling which today showed racing clouds in a green sky. 'He wants a mortal life?'

'No.' Feshni half rose to his knees, his arms folded on the edge of the bed and his chin resting on them. 'You know he's always liked playing games? More than anything else, more than anyone else ever does? Well, he wants to play forever, be able to visit the human children on the world below. *But,* he wants to keep his powers so he can visit here when he wants.'

'His powers could hurt human children too easily. Surely Mother won't permit it?'

Feshni shrugged. 'I don't know. Perhaps she can put limitations on his powers? Do you know?'

Ashri reached to ruffle Feshni's light brown hair. 'No, I don't. Dalmek just wants to play? Forever?'

'We've gone down lots of times, Ashri. Me and Korron and Dalmek. Some of the human children don't live very well you know. The adults hurt them. Now, I don't think

34

that's good or right, and nor does Korron, but Dalmek gets angry and sad.'

They were silent for a time then Feshni spoke again. 'I think Dalmek plans his own war. Against certain grown humans who hurt the children. Mother might think that's a good plan?'

'She might,' Ashri agreed. 'Will you not join him?'

'We'll visit him sometimes, but I wouldn't like to be there for long. Nor would Korron.' Feshni stared into Ashri's clear blue eyes. 'How long have we been here Ash?' He lowered his voice. 'Hanlif was shouting about time when we were by the Triple Lakes. I don't understand time.'

'Time is not something we need to bother with.' She propped herself up on one elbow. 'What was he saying?'

'He said it was all being wasted. We didn't *have* to stay, shut up here. We could have all the world below to do with as we want.'

'We're *not* shut away here. We have infinity to explore if we want,' Ashri objected.

'That's what Urtax said.'

'What was Hanlif's reply?'

Feshni hid his face in his arms. 'I think he killed him.'

'*What!?*' Ashri sat upright.

'I didn't see. I was hiding with all the others, but the palace trembled. Didn't you feel it?'

'I've been in the gardens.' She looked down at the back of Feshni's head. 'Keep away from Hanlif. I've told you that before.'

'I know, and I do try to. When he's here, he seems everywhere. How long *have* we been here Ash?"

'I don't know. I can see time passes when I watch the world. The land turns brown for some of the time then green then white, then green again. I know it takes a while for plants to grown, for all the animals to change from such helpless things to their adult form. That's as much as I know.'

'I've heard the humans talk of mornings, and afternoons, night and day. Are they all just bits of time?' Feshni raised his head to stare at her again.

'I think they must be. Feshni, are you *sure* Hanlif killed

35

Urtax?'

'I didn't see. I told you. But Meru did and she said Hanlif put his sword through Urtax's body and then smothered him with his gold light. Then the palace shivered.'

'Where is Korron?'

'He went with Dalmek. He said he would watch and wait until he came back from the Dark.'

'Don't you want to be with them?'

'It feels safer with you. Some of them seem to think nothing special happened, but quite a few have disappeared. Shall we go and explore somewhere?'

'I have things I want to think of, Feshni. Won't Ekari or Meru go with you?'

Feshni rose. 'They might. Why do you think so much, Ash? I don't.'

She laughed. 'Perhaps you'll start thinking more. Is Hanlif still in the palace?' Again, Feshni shrugged.

The golden sphere dipped across the room and whisked out of the door space. Ashri lay back, staring up at the ceiling. A simple thought and the white clouds became grey and the sky crimson. She felt a sudden alarm and another thought turned the ceiling a uniform milky purple. Ashri knew what had sparked her alarm. The crimson sky suggested the worst of Hanlif's rage. Only once had she seen that red fury. He had destroyed half the gardens before Lerran stopped him, muffling him in the black of Darkness. That was the first time Ashri had truly comprehended the concept of fear.

The immensity of the power Hanlif had summoned and unleashed was terrifying. Then Lerran's use of Darkness to utterly quash Hanlif's fire had shaken Ashri to the core. Judging by the hushed atmosphere through the palace, she hadn't been the only one utterly stunned by the show of such power by two of Mother's children. She had never wondered about actual power. Everyone here was of Mother Dark. All could change to any physical form they chose, as far as she knew. They could alter their surroundings as the mood took them, conjure birds or flowers at a whim. The power both Hanlif and Lerran had revealed was an entirely different matter.

Ashri understood both could wreak utter destruction. Hanlif had encouraged battles among the various groups of developing humans. He had destroyed their earliest towns and cities, crumbled mountains to rubble heaps. Mother had stopped a great deal of that. Hanlif and his followers, and he had many, had ruined so many small achievements the humans made. Ashri knew that Youki only encouraged those humans, she didn't teach them how to build or how to farm.

Hanlif had given many groups the gift of metallurgy, shown them how to make tools and weapons. Since she had become aware of herself, Ashri had spoken most often with Youki. She felt a connection with her strangeness, her difference. There were others, like Feshni, with whom she'd played and laughed and talked, but only Youki's talk fascinated and intrigued her. She recalled Youki saying Lerran should be warned, but Ashri wasn't even sure where Lerran might be.

She concentrated then faded into invisibility. In some trepidation, Ashri began to search through the enormous number of rooms in the palace. She stayed clear of one wing, near the Triple Lakes, which throbbed with a smouldering heat. Clearly Hanlif was still here and still angry. Ashri skirted a much smaller building, unattached to the main palace. Darallax lived there and mist wreathed around the dwelling obscuring any windows or entrances. She could sense nothing there and understood Darallax had full wardings in place. It was well known he avoided contact with his brother as much as he could.

Ashri halted, hovering close to one of the many spires adorning the roof of the palace. Surely she had searched everywhere? Perhaps Lady Lerran was on the world, with her chosen lord, Dabray? About to abandon her search, a faint darkness drew her attention. Another building, half hidden under huge trees, just beyond the end of the palace furthest from Hanlif's quarters. Was it possible Lady Lerran lived there?

Ashri had never made a point of knowing where the Three spent their time. If she'd been forced to offer any reason for avoiding them, she would have said she was far too unimportant to push her presence onto their awareness. For the briefest moment she hesitated, then scolding herself for her cowardice, she moved to the building beneath the trees. Settling on the ground a little distance from a door, a real door she noted, she transformed to her usual body. Now she was here, what should she do? Still dithering, she saw a figure solidifying in front of the door.

Tall, very tall. Female. Long dark hair loose over her shoulders. Narrow face, straight nose, high cheekbones. Ashri stood frozen, her gaze fixed on the golden eyes staring straight into hers. 'You wish to speak with me, Ashri?'

How did she know her name? Ashri had sensed no touch on her thoughts. Power, she thought. Truly, they had *such* power. 'I spoke with Youki. She said I must tell you.'

'Tell me what?' Lerran moved a little closer, her tone warm, friendly, making Ashri relax a little more.

'Well, I think I had a dream. I often seem to. I know we don't sleep but that's what it feels like.' Ashri stopped speaking abruptly, aware she was babbling.

Lady Lerran smiled. 'Sit with me.'

A simple bench appeared beside her and she sat gracefully, indicating Ashri should join her. 'Tell me your dream.'

Ashri did so, thankful she was now quite calm and in control of her words. When she fell silent, Lerran nodded. 'I don't often see Youki but I have enormous interest in her. She has a truly heavy burden on her shoulders.' She paused, her brilliant gold eyes fixed on Ashri's face. 'Mother is much concerned over Hanlif.'

Before she could stop the words, they spilled from Ashri's lips. 'Who is Olekatah? Can he not help?' She stopped.

Lerran stared at her in shock. After a pause, Lerran replied. 'Olekatah is my brother too. Birthed in the same instant that I was. He cannot help us.'

Ashri was aware of a huge wave of grief, sorrow, that infused the First Daughter of Mother Dark, but could only sit helplessly silent.

'I thank you for your warning, Ashri. I believe Mother will summon you soon.' She read the sudden panic that filled Ashri and reached a hand to stroke her face. 'Do not worry. She will do you no harm but she will need to speak with you.'

Chapter Four

Endis chose the time when he first joined the Augur each day to ask her things that particularly puzzled him. He always made her a pot of tea and she seemed content to answer him before plunging into ever more complicated lessons. Today, he asked what happened to the souls, or spirits, of the lesser gods who died or were killed.

'I thought I spoke of that, child. They are reabsorbed by Mother Dark, except for a few.'

'That's what I meant; what happens to them?'

The Augur pursed her lips. 'They are sent to the Vortex,' she said, her tone flat.

'Are they then reborn, somewhere else?'

'I know nothing of the ways of the Vortex, Endis. It was there, at the beginning of everything. I imagine it will remain long after our existences are forgotten.'

'Does infinity have any borders?'

The Augur stared at him. 'I expected you to have questions, child, but my word, you have so many!'

Endis gave her an apologetic smile. 'You have so much knowledge, Ancient One.'

Her gaze sharpened on him. 'I do, and you must learn it all.'

Endis grew still as the kettle began to steam and bubble. She truly meant that, he realised, but how could he possible learn all she knew? Was he to remain here forever, just learning? Why would that be necessary? He'd surely be far too old to do anything with the information by the time she finished. She waved a hand. 'Make the tea, Endis. I have decided certain parts of the history you must know will be more easily understood if I show you pictures in your mind.'

Pouring the tea, Endis nodded. 'Tika did that, showed pictures in my mind. So did Fenj.' He put a bowl beside the Augur's chair.

'Indeed. Dragons are able to do this and a very few mages through all the years.'

'Why can Dragons do it?' Endis sat in his usual chair and sipped his tea.

'I think that was because they were so beloved of Lady Lerran, but we will come to that later.'

Understanding question time was over for now, Endis focussed all his attention on the Augur.

'Back when Mother Dark first chose this world to be hers, it was still not much more than a ball of rock. It was cloaked in raging clouds of gases which, after a great deal of time, became the air you can breathe today. When life began, the creatures breathed an air which would have killed you.'

Endis listened but he struggled to understand the idea of air being different, poisonous to him.

'Close your eyes and I will show you that first world.'

He found himself drifting, perhaps three man heights above a grey surface. Looking over an empty landscape, he saw a heat shimmer in the distance. So it must be summer?

'No, child. The world was hot. Too hot in many places for a human of today to set foot. Look closer.'

The picture in his head went lower, closer to a sluggishly moving stream from which steam arose. Then the water must be hot, he thought, like in Fenj's caves.

'Very like,' the Augur agreed with his thought.

He saw smears of colour on some of the rocks along the edge of this stream, orange, blue, green. 'That is life Endis. The beginning of life on your world, from which all else has sprung.'

'Everything?' he asked in disbelief.

'Everything, child.'

'How long must it have taken to grow from that smudge to all the life today?'

'Longer than you can comprehend as yet. Don't worry, you will. Over such spans of time, creatures grew, Mother Dark brought her children into existence and then some of the lesser gods. They caused some strange animals to appear, changed them, as they wished, until Mother ordered them to stop.'

The picture in Endis's mind blurred then cleared. He saw an endless grass land, stretching in all directions, and a

41

large herd of animals grazing. He held his breath, staring at the creatures. They had six legs. Those legs looked "wrong" to his eyes. He looked more closely and saw they had two joints in each leg, not the one "knee" he would have expected. One of the animals raised its head. Two large eyes stared round but Endis saw no spark of curiosity such as he might have noticed even in a cow in his world. 'Is there no intelligence yet?' he asked.

'Very little. All life concentrated on feeding, growing, living for one more day, and producing offspring.'

'Where did awareness begin?' he asked.

Again the picture blurred and grew clear once more. Endis caught his breath. Trees of a kind he didn't recognise, soared high above, their fronded branches locking and loosening as a breeze riffled through them. Movement caught his eye and a creature the size of Liekke, the orange cat he'd befriended, scuttled from a hole among the roots of one of the trees. It had a pointed snout, whiskers, large dark eyes and ears set high on the sides of its head. It scrabbled with its front paws in the earth, drawing out a long worm, whose many legs waved helplessly as the animal ate it. The creature constantly watched all around as it fed, clearly alert to every sound.

This time when Endis looked at the dark eyes, he saw the glimmer of some sort of awareness. He almost jumped at a sudden deafening roar coming from somewhere among the trees. His gaze lifted at the sound but when he looked back, the small furred creature was gone. 'What was that noise?'

'One of the giants that ruled the world for a time.' The Augur didn't add details although Endis would have very much liked to have seen giants.

'Where is this forest?' he asked.

'It is long gone, Endis. I will take you high above the world, in pictures remember. There is no need to worry.'

Endis felt no sensation of movement even though the pictures in his mind were so real he could almost believe he was experiencing this flight above the land. He stared down with no recognition. There were clumps of land scattered in a band across the middle of the world, a foaming, angry ocean surrounding them all. 'But this can't be the world,' he burst out. 'I've seen maps and Navan showed me where Iskallia is and where the Asataria was.'

'And they will be in those positions eventually Endis. What you see now is how it was when those forests grew on some of the islands.'

The view point moved slowly across the world. Then there was an interruption to the pictures which Endis had begun to realise meant time was passing. But how *much* time, he wondered? Marvelling now that most of the island shapes had merged into one enormous land mass, he watched in silence. The images in his head twitched, warning him a great amount of time was passing. Now he saw the huge land mass was splitting apart but, his breath caught. In places where those splits were just beginning, the earth was bleeding!

'No Endis. That is melted rock, magma. The world is full of such material and when land moves at a deep enough level, so that red hot rock spills out.'

He opened his eyes to stare at her. 'Could that still happen?'

'It does, in certain places.'

'There were no signs of red rock on Navan's maps, and I'm sure he would have spoken of it had he known about it.'

'Endis, the hot rock cools quickly once it emerges.' The Augur paused. 'Do you know of the stone called obsidian?'

'Oh yes. Teyo said that's what these were made of.' He dug in his shirt pocket and held out several tiny arrowheads to the Augur. She leaned forward to inspect them, nodding.

'They are indeed. This stone came from a volcano. It will always stay sharp.'

'Volcano? Like Vagrantia?'

'Let me think,' the Augur said. 'Ah yes. This was another time. Close your eyes.'

Endis did so and saw another empty plain but this was of sand or rock. In the distance five hills rose. Endis floated higher within the pictures then he flinched. One of the hills exploded. Its top blew off and flames and rocks gouted out and up, climbing ever higher in the sky. Then another hill followed suit. The red poured down the

43

hillsides, as though the land was bleeding, mortally wounded.

The Augur watched the expressions change on the boy's face as she let the pictures flow from a part of her mind to his. After a while she withdrew from his mind and waited for his comments. It was some time before he spoke. 'This world is mostly quiet now, but it contains such power. Such violence, right under our very feet.' He fell silent again then looked across at her. 'It could all start again though you said? Is that what I must understand?'

The Augur smiled. 'It *will* all start again one day perhaps, but for now, it is as you say, quiet enough. If it chooses to reform itself, then it can all begin again.'

'What was that animal, the one in the forest eating the worm?'

The Augur shrugged. 'I have no idea if it had a name, but it was one of your ancestors.' She smiled at his look of disbelief. 'Everything changes, Endis. It grows, or it dies. If it remains always the same, it stagnates and fades. This is the way of all things.' The Augur spoke softly then climbed to her feet. She limped the few steps to the hearth to set the kettle over the heat again.

'Why must I learn all these things?' Endis asked, his voice as quiet as hers had been.

She met his gaze. 'Because I ask it of you, child. Is that reason enough?'

He pondered that question then managed a faint smile. 'It probably is. For now.'

She laughed, moving back to her chair.

'All that earth splitting, the volcanos. Were there humans at that time?'

'There were those who had nearly become human, yes. But it happened again, later, when true humans began to build cities.' She leaned her head back as she thought. 'Lord Hanlif thought it good sport to open the earth beneath those cities on several occasions. When Mother Dark discovered what he'd done, she cast him from the gods' space and made him physically mortal but still eternal. He kept his powers except for being able to transform himself, or vanish, or fly. He was very angry with her, and he told his human followers they must always shun the Dark. He called himself the Lord of Light from that time on.'

'He must have looked like an ordinary man yet he was still capable of such great powers? For how long?'

'A very long time, child. Until he was killed in the Last Battle.'

Endis shook his head, trying to grasp what the Augur implied. 'Did he not grow old? He had many followers you said. Did they not wonder, that he continued to live even as they aged and died?'

'No. They called him a god from the very beginning, Endis.' The Augur raised a hand and let it fall. 'There were several lesser gods who had followed him to the world, and they too lived long lives and were treated with great respect by the human followers.'

'I have never heard of any Lord of Light.'

'Shut away in that Asataria, I'm not surprised.' The Augur retorted. 'That's why it is both easy and difficult to teach you now. Your mind is not filled with a confusion of tales, but on the other hand, as all is so new to you, I have to furnish far more details than I would wish.'

'Were the lesser gods who followed Hanlif all destroyed too?'

'No. Well, most were, yes,' she corrected herself. 'But some had already crept away, concerned that Hanlif's temper had grown ever more volatile and dangerous.'

'What happened to them?'

'Some hid within small clans of people, helping them to grow rather than hurting them as Hanlif had always encouraged. A very few asked to return to Mother Dark.' The Augur's lips thinned into a tight line. Endis decided against questioning her further and made more tea in silence. He put her tea bowl close to her chair and sat down again. 'Have you found the library yet?' she asked.

'No. I work in the garden when I leave you then I make a meal.'

'And write in your notebooks?' An eyebrow arched at him. 'You will need many more writing implements and paper, child. You will find plenty in the library, just take what you want.'

'I understand that I may have some small talent, or affinity, with the earth, and, since the mage fevers, I can See things, but how do I *use* such talent? I've seen Tika do things, where she directs her abilities to actually *change* something. Will I be able to choose who I See, or travel where I wish?'

The Augur remained silent so long Endis wondered if he'd offended her, or asked too much. 'You will be able to choose who you See, where you travel. And so much more. But not yet.' She shook her head when Endis drew breath to speak again. 'Leave me now, child. Showing you so much of this world's past has tired me. And yes, you will be able to make pictures in the minds of others. But not yet,' she repeated with a faint smile. 'Find my library, child. I will see you tomorrow.'

Still uncertain as to whether he'd misspoken, Endis rose and bowed before quietly leaving the Augur's rooms. He stood for a moment outside the door, then began walking along the passage to his left. He reached the recessed white door to her infinity room. Tempted as he was to see if he could make all those spheres whirl into motion, he looked to the opposite wall, seeing another door set back in the wall.

He lifted the latch and stepped inside. From darkness a gentle glow began to spread out before him. Endis could only stare. Books and scrolls lined a multitude of shelves which stretched ahead of him. He closed the door behind him and continued to stare. He had seen the library in the Asatarian Academy but this room made that library seem insignificant. Small tables were dotted about, each with a single chair. Clearly a person could take books from adjacent shelves and study them in comfort at a table.

Immediately to his right was a large open cupboard filled with jars of inks, notebooks of various sizes, stacks of parchment and trays of both pencils and pens. Endis gazed around. Where could he even begin? He started to walk along the right hand wall slowly, peering at the books to read the words on their spines. Some were in words he understood; many had symbols or scripts he couldn't fathom. The first book he decided to actually examine had a five petalled flower on its spine, the reason he'd chosen it.

He was delighted to find it was full of detailed illustrations of hundred of plants.

Replacing it, he checked along the shelf and discovered every book dealt with plants, flowers, vegetables and fruit trees. Endis stepped back to look along the many rows. Is that how they were organised? By subject alone? He let out a breath. This was as wonderful in its way as the infinity room he thought. His stomach growled, suggesting it was later than he realised. Turning back to the door, he took several notebooks and pens before letting himself out into the passage again. Making his way back and walking through the garden, he wondered how long that library had been there. Where had all the books come from?

That was his first question next morning but the Augur's reply was vague. 'They've been collected through the years,' was all she would say.

'How close are we in the "history lessons" to this time in the world?' was his next question.

'Quite close now, about twenty thousand years, perhaps a little more.'

Endis nearly poured boiling water over himself. 'Twenty thousand years was "quite close"?' He concentrated on filling the two tea bowls without further mishap. When he sat down he met the Augur's blue stare. 'How do *you* know all this? Who taught *you?'*

'Such questions are irrelevant right now. All your questions will be answered, Endis, in the fullness of time.'

He kept his expression calm accepting, although inside he felt a sudden spike of irritation. He truly wasn't at all sure how all this history, from so very long ago, had any bearing or use to his life as a Seer now. Admittedly he found it fascinating, but did he really need to know all this? He caught the slight amusement on the Augur's face and let go of his annoyance with a sigh.

'Hanlif built a city of his own, in the middle of what is now a desert in the lands across the sea from Drogoya. He lived there for a while then he grew bored, razed the city to the ground and somehow reached Drogoya.' The Augur stared at the fire for a moment. 'There is no record of any humans building ships capable of such a journey at that time, so it is not known how, or when exactly Hanlif reached what is now Drogoya and Kelshan.' She was fully aware of Endis's worries although she had refrained from reading his thoughts. His face was an open book to her; she had no need to delve further.

'Is your Mother Dark so all powerful?' he asked. 'If she is, surely she can see all that happens, could surely make everywhere safe?'

'Whether you have heard of her or not, Endis, she *is* the Mother of all on this world. Without her watchfulness, life would still be smears on a stream. She doesn't require worshippers, as Hanlif and some of the other lesser gods demanded. Very, very rarely has she intervened here. She moved against Hanlif because he was her own creation and he was mocking the mortal life she had nurtured and encouraged for so long. It causes her great grief when there is destruction, either of a natural kind or caused by humans, but she does not interfere. The number of you who have what you call mage talents is decreasing, and only Tika has a power that could have matched, or overcome Hanlif's. And Tika will bear no children who could inherit her blood.'

Again the Augur showed Endis pictures, but now human life was more obvious across the world, more organised. He was amazed at the beauty and complexity of certain towns, their soaring towers and clean streets. The pictures were close enough for him to see people generally but too distant to make out faces or expressions. At one point, he opened his eyes. 'Why are there no ruins, to tell us of these people?' he asked.

'You've seen how the world tears itself apart, Endis, and, if it has the help of a being such as Hanlif to aggravate and aid the destruction it causes, how might anything remain?'

'You haven't shown me Hanlif in these pictures,' he pointed out.

'Very well. This is the city he built in the lower lands of Sapphrea.'

Closing his eyes again, Endis gasped. Slender spires rose up so high above the buildings. They appeared to be sheathed in gold and silver, glittering under a blazing sun.

48

At first glance, it seemed breathtaking, beautiful beyond anything he could imagine, but slowly his opinion changed. The spires and pinnacles were indeed graceful, magnificent in their delicacy and height, but the buildings from which they rose, jarred the eye. Endis had the sense the buildings were too square, too rigid; they marred the slender beauty of the spires.

The view moved closer to the largest building. A man stood on a balcony, staring out over the city. He was of moderate height from what Endis could estimate. His hair blew around his shoulders, as golden as some of the spires. His skin seemed to glow, a lesser gold than his hair but noticeable as unhuman. The man raised his head, seeming to stare directly at Endis. His handsome face twisted into a snarl and his blue eyes filled with a mixture of hatred, anger and madness. The pictures stopped and Endis looked at the Augur.

'That was the Lord Hanlif,' she said, her voice calm, almost disinterested. 'In his city of Behuba.'

'He destroyed all those buildings?'

The Augur's eyes sparked with something - pain, anger, hurt? Endis couldn't tell.

'He destroyed the city, and most of the poor fools who had flocked to join the great Lord of Light,' she agreed. She raised her hand. 'Enough, child. I find these times of showing you so many things far more tiring than I had hoped. Leave me now. Let me rest.'

Endis rose, bowed and left her. He stayed in his garden for the rest of the day, writing a great deal after tending the seedlings. Then he made a meal and went to bed. He expected to sleep as he had done each night he'd been here - deeply and without dreams. After a time, pictures began to stream through his mind. He saw blinding flashes of light, cool impenetrable blackness. Stars spun and fell all around inside the blackness and Endis twisted and turned, tangled in his blankets. He thought he saw the vaguest outline of a large figure, an even darker silhouette against the black.

He felt an intense, unbearable longing to reach out to that figure from which he could sense such pain. As with many dreams, Endis found himself unable to move, his limbs refusing to respond. Through pain, Endis felt a curiosity, surprise. And then he woke with a sensation of falling onto his bed from a great height. He lay for a few moments then rolled into a sitting position and rubbed his face. A glance at the window when a large bee flew drunkenly against the glass, suggested it was around the usual time he woke.

After washing and dressing he went to the table. He wrote every detail he could remember of the dream while it was still so vivid, so real, in his mind. Feeling the tug in his thoughts which warned he was expected to attend the Augur, he made his way through the garden and across the passage. As usual Endis went to heat water to make her tea. Waiting for the water to heat, he turned to her.

'Ancient One, I dreamed last night.'

The Augur frowned. 'That is not possible, child. Your rooms are warded for now, so you are not disturbed while you are learning from me.'

'If I didn't dream, was it a Seeing, a vision?'

As the Augur shook her head, still frowning, Endis went on: 'Then can you tell me who Olekatah might be? It was him I saw. I knew his name, but I have no idea who he is?'

Chapter Five

Ashri fled back to her rooms, noting the wing Hanlif occupied still glimmered but its golden light was streaked with an ugly red.

'Where have you been?' Feshni asked.

'Just drifting. Couldn't you find Korron or Dalmek?'

'I found Korron. Dalmek is lost in the Dark he thinks.'

'Lost? Why did he go into the Dark anyway? Did Mother call him?'

Feshni closed his eyes, burrowing into the pillows. 'He said he wanted to ask her something but he never said what it was.'

Ashri felt alarm. It seemed Dalmek had been gone far too long. Lady Lerran had said she, Ashri, must visit Mother Dark. The idea made Ashri nervous. Nervousness made her restless and she wandered into the room, opening one of the cupboards and staring at various dresses hanging within. None of them pleased her. She dismissed them, closed the door and went to the window. The night was dark; a softer dark than the utter black of infinity.

A few stars showed but Ashri had yet to decide if they were real or illusion as so much else was here. A few faint lights flickered in the grounds and the sound of soft singing reached up to her window. She turned away. 'Feshni, what do you intend to do?'

He opened his eyes wide and glared at her. 'I want to play. Play games with the children on the world. They play better than anyone here.'

'Is that really all you want?' She was curious rather than scornful as Lahi would have been.

'Yes.' Feshni sat up. 'Have you ever heard them laugh, Ash? It is the most beautiful sound, and it makes *me* laugh too. Although, it makes me sad at the same time.'

'Will you go to the world soon?'

Feshni moved to sit cross legged as usual in the centre of the bed. 'I've been looking at some of their towns.' His

51

voice sank to the barest breath. 'I don't want to be near Lord Hanlif. Can he tell where we are *all* the time do you think?'

'Well, *we* can tell where we all are if we want,' Ashri replied. 'I'm sure the greatest of us must be able to, even more easily. Will your powers not be restricted, down in the world?' she asked when he didn't reply at once.

'Not much. I've never tried to do a lot. I've never wanted to make things like some of the animals Bresha was so fond of creating.' He shuddered at the memory.

'Bresha is gone,' Ashri reminded him. She sat down facing him. 'Will you come back here often? Won't you miss your friends?'

'I will have *new* friends Ash! I'll come here sometimes I expect, to see you. I think I want to make a proper place to be down there.'

'Will you tell them you are from the gods' space?'

'I don't think so, not unless I *really* like them.'

Ashri smiled. 'I'll miss you.'

'You'll be gone soon though, Ash. I'm sure there'll be something you want to do.' He reached for her hands. 'You'll keep yourself safe, won't you? I'd come if you need me you know?'

'I know. You only have to call me too, Feshni.'

'If Dalmek isn't back soon, I'm going to the world, Ash. I don't like it here now. Too many follow Lord Hanlif. It makes it all so - itchy. A lot of them seem so cruel, so nasty, Ash. I hope Mother tells them off very soon.' He flung himself back onto the pillows, an arm across his face.

Ashri watched him then rose. 'I'm going to drift again. I feel too restless to stay in.'

Feshni didn't reply so Ashri let herself fade to nothing but thought and moved through the labyrinth of the palace, eventually emerging on the roof again. Partially manifesting as a wispy shadow of her usual form, she sat down, her back to the base of a pencil thin structure. It was surely too thin to deserve the name of spire. Ashri always thought of these narrow things as needles, trying to reach up to stitch something across the sky overhead.

Very few lights showed anywhere in the buildings or gardens, except for Hanlif's quarters. She wondered why all of them, the gods, copied the humans so closely. Gods needed no sleep, no food really, although they sometimes ate, as a novelty. Here, in the gods' space, they adhered to a day and night pattern of life, resting at night as humans slept, and more active in the day time when most humans toiled. So many of them, the gods, were contemptuous of all life they saw below. Ashri stared up the sleek smooth black stone of the needle. Why would they mimic something they regarded as so ridiculous?

Like most of the gods, Ashri too had spent quite a lot of time observing humans. Unlike most, she had never revealed herself, in any form. She had taken note that several of the lesser gods had set themselves up as *real* gods, pretending they would help certain groups of humans who worshipped them. A very few had genuinely wanted to help but most were only out to cause mischief. Once, Ashri had watched Simert, whom Mother Dark had instructed to collect the souls of humans. He had known she was there of course, but to begin with he had ignored her.

She had returned, day after day, intrigued by his dealings with the people, and by his appearance. He had taken the form of a really insignificant man, a moderately successful farmer, or merchant perhaps. He had an air of solidity, of a slight absent mindedness, but Ashri had seen him comfort a mother as the last of her five children died. She'd been aware of his silent plea to Mother Dark for mercy, and of his humble acceptance when no such mercy was forthcoming. It seemed very clear to Ashri that Simert took his role with complete seriousness.

She found herself increasingly impressed and interested in him. After she'd watched him for several days, and he was alone in his small dwelling, he looked directly at her. 'What is it you find so fascinating about me, child?' he asked aloud in a mild voice.

Ashri manifested in the form she always wore in the gods' space, a spindly girl dressed in a simple pale blue shift, and bare footed. They stared at each other, Simert sitting on a stool by the fire as he sewed a button onto a shirt, and Ashri standing across from him.

'Ashri.' He said her name softly, nodding as he spoke,

53

as if she was well known to him.

'That is my name,' she agreed after a while.

Simert smiled. 'You are welcome here child. Whenever you choose or need a refuge.'

What had he meant by that? His words confused her. She'd turned her attention to the shirt on his lap, and the button was restored to its place.

'I do everything as a mortal must, child, but I thank you. I do detest sewing.'

'You like living here, as one of them?' Ashri asked.

'It was difficult at first, but now I know I shall be here as long as I have an existence and I am content.'

'You like humans?'

'Again, at first, I thought them quite simple creatures but Mother was quite correct of course. She told me they have potential to be so much more. They think of so many things Ashri. Not all of them of course, but more than you might expect. And unless I collect their spirits, they wander, lost and confused.'

Ashri had settled herself cross legged by the hearth. 'I have never seen such spirits,' she said.

'You will, I'm quite sure.'

Ashri thought of that first conversation she'd had with Simert while she sat on the roof of the palace.

If she was summoned by Mother Dark, could she be strong enough to accept whatever command she might be given? Not for the first time, Ashri wondered how long she had been here, in the gods' space, one among so many lesser gods. She knew Feshni had been here when she - what? Did she just become aware? Just wake up, and find herself as she was now?

She had a body when that occurred, the one she had kept for - however long she'd been here. Becoming irritated that her thoughts seemed to be going in pointless circles and knowing it was partly due to her possible summons by Mother Dark, Ashri faded again. She shot skywards, bracing herself for the change in pressure as she breached the boundary of the gods' space. Then, once through, she paused, the sensation of freedom almost overwhelming. Stars, worlds, busy meteorites, larger comets, moving in ordered or random beauty, and the infinity filling every space.

The sun that owned this world blazed; she could hear the crackle and hiss as it consumed its own gases and matter. Turning her back to the sun, the gods' space and the world spinning slowly just beneath, Ashri headed for the dark space beyond the outer worlds. She had no way of knowing how long she wandered through the infinity. She paused to study some of the many worlds, amazed at the extreme diversity of their life forms, She saw the glint of a few other lesser gods close to some of the distant worlds but they were all bound by Mother's command not to interfere as they had on the world she had chosen.

Ashri moved on, sometimes drifting round a small cratered moon that hurried restlessly around the world that had captured it. At other times, she sped through the infinity, chasing particles of rock, or of light, revelling in her solitude. When she at last decided she had gone far enough, she let only a thought quest on ahead. She realised she was further than she'd ever been. The Vortex was beyond her full awareness but its presence swelled out towards her. Ashri stayed exactly where she was for a moment then the sense of power rippled in her direction. Filled with sudden terror, she willed herself back, as fast as she had ever moved herself through this immense playground they were so privileged to enjoy.

When she reformed her body in the room she called hers, there was no sign of Feshni. She felt a twinge of guilt. There were groups of the lesser gods wandering the gardens but Ashri had no way of knowing how long she'd been gone. She would look for Feshni later, she decided, but for now she still wanted to keep to herself. Sitting on the window seat, Ashri sensed someone approaching. Lahi. She took her usual pose, leaning against the wall, her silver dress clinging to her figure. Ashri turned her head to study her visitor. Was it her imagination, or had Lahi's hair more of a golden tinge to it? She waited for Lahi to speak, although she suspected she knew what might be coming.

'Lord Hanlif said he heard you'd visited his sister. Why ever would such a weakling as *you* dare to approach *her?*'

'You are such a friend of the Lord's now, that you run messages for him? Have you become such a favourite, Lahi? I hear he keeps females a very brief time before he - disposes of them.' Ashri saw a flare of anger in Lahi's eyes and felt pleased she'd at least stung her a little.

'Lord Hanlif will rule the world below, and once he's done away with his pathetic brother, his sister who is besotted with the lesser creature, Dabray, *and* Mother Dark, he will give us the freedom to rule *all* the worlds beyond. As we should, and however we choose to.'

Ashri kept her expression impassive, her thoughts tightly shielded, although she was deeply shocked by Lahi's words. Hanlif planned on destroying Mother Dark?

'Surely he will need someone far grander, more powerful, more beautiful to stand at his side, Lahi?' Then Ashri smiled.

Coldness suddenly filled the room. Lahi spun to the corridor just past the door space and then took a step back. The figure there, dressed in black shirt and trousers, stared down at her with eyes like molten gold. Ashri slipped from the window seat and bowed. Lady Lerran's tall slender form blocked the door space and Ashri realised her power had completely snuffed out Lahi's attempts to dematerialise and thus escape.

'If my brother continues to trust such simple minded creatures as you seem to be, I think there will be nothing to fear from him.'

Straightening, Ashri gave Lahi grudging admiration that she had recovered enough to stand facing Lady Lerran. She was trembling, true, but her back had stiffened and her chin was jutting in defiance. 'You're never here, Lady Lerran.' Lahi's voice was a little higher than usual but it was steady.

'Maybe not here but I am frequently below. I will not allow Mother's orders to be questioned, let alone transgressed. Perhaps you should relay that to my brother, little spy.' Lady Lerran stepped aside. clearly dismissing Lahi.

With a quick glance back at Ashri, Lahi went past, perhaps a little faster than politeness expected. Ashri shivered at the hatred she'd seen and felt when Lahi looked at her. Lady Lerran moved into the room and sat on the bed. Ashri waited. 'I will keep watch over you, little Ashri. Mother has been much occupied but she *has* heard of you.'

Ashri gaped. 'Why would Mother know of *me*?'

Lerran smiled, her thin stern expression softening into beauty. 'Youki has told her of you, I understand.'

'Youki?' Ashri realised she must sound utterly foolish. 'I like Youki,' she hurried on. 'I've never understood who or what she is, but I do like her.'

'Mother Dark found Youki soon after she discovered this world.'

Ashri frowned. 'So Youki is of this world? Yet she can travel here, to our gods' space?'

Lerran nodded. 'I know only that Mother has a great interest in her. She was here, on this world from the earliest time of its formation. She told Mother she is there to protect it.' Lerran smiled again. 'I don't think even Mother knows what Youki means by that, or exactly what power she might possess. While I accept Mother's strength and wisdom, I reserve judgement until I have far more information, Ashri. I *serve* Mother. If my continuing existence is a price I am asked to pay, I will pay it gladly. While Youki professes her love for Mother, I do not believe she *serves* her except where their hopes or wishes coincide. Thus I am cautious. I would suggest you are, as well.' Lady Lerran rose, moving towards the door space. 'We will speak again, Ashri. You have my word neither my brother, nor any of his followers will harm you, but even so, be cautious, little one.'

Unable to think of any kind of reply, Ashri took refuge in another bow. When she rose, she was alone. She suddenly wished Feshni was around. She sent a part of her mind on a quick search through the palace but found no trace of him. Changing her focus, she sought out Korron. Hurrying down the stairs and through the halls, she found Korron half buried in a large bush which was covered with particularly garish orange flowers. No one else was anywhere near this section of the garden and, after a quick scan, Ashri wriggled into the bush to sit next to Korron. 'What's wrong?' she whispered.

'Dalmek is gone.' His voice hitched. 'Feshni's gone. I don't want to go down to the world but I miss them both. I don't know what to do, Ash.'

'What do you mean, Dalmek's *"gone"*?'

'Gone,' he repeated angrily. 'Whatever stupid thing he wanted to ask Mother, he's never come back. I can't sense him anymore. He must have annoyed her. Feshni, well, *he's* gone to play with human children. Forever, he said.'

'There are many others here, Korron. Ekani used to always be with you three?'

Korron frowned. 'Dalmek argued with him. He stopped being with us.'

'Well go find Ekani. See if he still wants to play games.' Ashri saw by Korron's face he was searching the palace for Ekani's mind signature.

'He's by the Ice Pool. On his own.'

'Then go and talk to him.'

Korron vanished, but Ashri remained in the bush. So Feshni was gone, down to the world, to an eternal childhood. She stayed where she was until the light beyond the leaves and flowers began to fade. She considered moving back to her room in an unbodied state but chided herself for cowardice. She was confident in Lady Lerran's assertion that she would protect her, so she emerged from the bush and began the walk back up to her room.

There were many questions in Ashri's mind but she had no idea who she might ask. Since she became aware, she hadn't drawn close to any of the other gods. Feshni and his friends seemed always like young children, looking to her for suggestions for new games and never willing to talk seriously about anything. Lady Lerran, as Mother's first creation, must surely be knowledgeable above all others but Ashri doubted she would dare go and ask her. The thought that somehow Youki had been present on the world below so long ago was circling round and round in Ashri's mind. Had the world looked like so many of those barren, or pitted, or volcanic and gaseous worlds she'd seen scattered throughout the infinity? Had it been Youki that set all life in motion?

There was no way she knew of to contact Youki. She

only ever encountered her in the hidden, forgotten corner of the garden, and that only occasionally. Ashri considered those meetings. She was aware of Youki's imminent appearance only by the slightest change in pressure, a sort of shiver in the air. She had never *sensed* her, as she could sense other gods. Lying on her bed, she reviewed all Youki had ever said to her, little although that was. She set wards around the section of the palace in which her room was situated and allowed herself to sink into the resting condition which passed for sleep among her kind.

When she roused as light began to creep across the window, she continued to lie still. Had she *dreamed? Again?* Faces had filled her mind. Not human, or gods as far as she could tell, or perhaps both? She had recognised none of the faces. They had been young and old, dark and fair. Some had been males, some female, and some she couldn't be sure were either. Ashri rose, the feeling of restlessness still with her, and she just could not understand why. She had always been wary of Lahi, never talking to her of any real subject. And with Feshni, Dalmek and Korron - they wanted only to be treated as children.

Staring from her window, the thought occurred to her that she should question what was a *real* subject? Was *she* even real? Growing increasingly exasperated with herself, she left her room, intent on talking to some of the lesser gods who might be willing to talk to her. Ashri did indeed find many who were happy to speak to her, but their conversation she found, as she'd half expected, wasn't helpful. They talked of things they *might* do on the world below. Ashri realised all of them had visited the world on brief occasions, had some amusement toying with various humans. None of them seemed to have any strong desire to spend any length of time there, preferring their life here in the gods' space. She had four more nights when faces streamed across her inner vision. So many, and all different.

Although she had little hope of discovering anything about either the world below, its history and its present condition regarding clans or tribes at war, or about the faces she saw, she joined a group she'd spoken with yesterday.

She casually mentioned dreams to them. There was much argument and disbelief in such conversation. Ashri discovered most of the lesser gods thought humans imagined their dreams. The general consensus was that human sleep was a strange, boring state so they invented ever wilder stories of pictures in their heads during such a period of wasted like.

Ashri realised her fellow gods made no real effort to try to understand anything about humans, not their physical limitations or their mental capacities. They saw humans as simply another form of the animal life that Mother allowed them to amuse themselves with. Ashri was surprised that many of these lesser gods with whom she mingled, appeared to like her, calling out to her to join them when she walked through the halls or the vast chambers intended for gatherings.

She was startled into saying as much when one of them, a female as small and finely formed as she herself was, remarked on her beauty. Ashri stared at her. 'Neefah, that's an unkind jest,' she said.

Several who had heard Neefah's comment turned to Ashri. 'She isn't teasing you,' said another woman, tall and fair haired.

Ashri's face showed her confusion. 'I'm not beautiful,' she answered. 'Not like you, Meru, or Lady Lerran, or so many of you. This is the first form I wore when I became aware, and I've kept it. It is how Mother chose to make me.'

'But you *are* very lovely!' That was Yejo, a handsome young man. He smiled and reached to stroke her white braid. 'No one else has your colouring. White hair so *very* white and such clear blue eyes. None of us can copy it and we've all tried.' He laughed, not unkindly, and Ashri saw heads nodding in the group around them.

'Well. Thank you,' she managed to stutter. 'You're very kind to say so, although I'm sure you're mistaken.'

She stayed with that group for the rest of the day, listening but saying very little unless asked something directly. Later, she returned to her room, the earlier conversation still in her thoughts. It was only after Yejo had pointed it out that she realised no other among the lesser gods *did* have white hair and blue eyes. Why would Mother have made her so different? All of the others had hair shading from a pale honey gold to black as the infinity. There were blue eyes among them but most were of a pale colour that was closer to grey.

When light faded so did Ashri, going up to sit on the rook close to one of the needles. Her thoughts were more unsettled than they'd ever been and so many things had begun to concern her. She had noticed that she was the only one who seemed to sit up here, alone in the dark, and wondered why she alone was so drawn to this high perch. Had Mother marked her out as a mistake, to be cast into the infinity, or worse, into that Vortex? Staring down, Ashri saw even Lord Hanlif's part of the palace was less brightly lit than it normally was of late.

She returned to her room, no calmer than she'd been before, and lay on her bed. Closing her eyes, yet again the procession of faces began to move through her mind, vivid as though she saw them in reality. Then her eyes flew open. The whole room was a silent inferno of flames, reaching from the walls towards her bed. Hands of scarlet and gold stretched through those flames, grasping blindly to engulf and destroy her.

Chapter Six

The Ancient Augur stared at Endis. To her he seemed such a child. And yet. How could he have dreamed? How could he possibly have heard the name of Olekatah? Endis saw he had truly surprised her but whether it was because he'd dreamed or because he knew the name of that being, he wasn't sure. Turning back to his tea making, he missed her changing expression. When he put the tea beside her, she was calm, her face impassive.

'I will have to check the wardings, child. Perhaps I was careless and somehow dreams reached you,' she said. She continued speaking, explaining he had to know more of the three creations of Mother Dark.

Endis listened but he was fully aware she had avoided commenting on the creature he had sensed. He wondered if he might find out something from the library, then the thought of hunting through that vast quantity of books made him quail. He forced his attention back to the Augur who had stopped speaking, obviously aware of his wandering thoughts.

'I have heard of Lady Lerran,' he offered. 'Tika said it was she who gave her the land of Iskallia.' He frowned, considering. 'If Lady Lerran was a god, she must have lived *so* long?' He stared at the Augur as he realised the enormous amount of time, of history, the Lady Lerran must have witnessed.

'Gods, by their very nature, are eternal, child. I had hoped you'd realised that by now.'

'You said they could be killed, or die. How could a god die, *other* than being killed?'

The Augur sipped her tea. 'They can choose non existence.' She spoke slowly, quietly. 'They can fade, but whether into the infinity or back into Mother, is not clear.'

'I had never heard of the others - Darallax and Hanlif.'

'Few have heard of Darallax, for many generations of human life. He has recently re-emerged from hiding now, to a certain extent. Neither he nor Lerran yearned to be worshipped or wanted to rule the world. That was only Hanlif's desire and his most devoted followers among the lesser ones. Darallax,' The Augur paused. 'He is the Lord of Shadow. He and the people he befriended and lived among in the land now called Drogoya, suffered even more severely than Lady Lerran's people. Darallax chose seclusion for the many years of their recovery, as did Lady Lerran.'

'Couldn't they have taken their human followers to wherever the gods live, to keep them safe?'

'All three of them chose to relinquish their link to the gods' space. They could still speak with Mother Dark by *entering* the Dark, but they were all bound, physically, to this world. Now, I must speak of the First Skirmish,' she ended firmly.

'Lord Hanlif breached all the protocols of behaviour in the gods' space. He attacked one of the lesser ones and that was when Mother banished him forever.'

'A First Skirmish suggests there were many afterwards?' Endis suggested. 'When did this happen?'

'I do wish you weren't so devoted to time, Endis. It is one of the strangest peculiarities humans have invented.' The Augur sounded almost snappish. 'It was about twenty thousand of your years ago, I think. I'm sorry I can't be more precise.'

Endis squirmed under a truly icy glare. After a short pause as she made sure his questions were suitably quelled, for now at least, she went on with the lesson.

'The First Skirmish was with Lady Lerran. She had established a small community in north-west Sapphrea, on the coast. Lord Hanlif had built a city much further south, towards where Harbour City eventually developed. Remember, he was one of the first of Mother's creations, more powerful than the lesser gods who came after them. The three retained many abilities even while being in the world deprived them of a few others. Hanlif and his two favourites, Eoki and Natavi, spied on Lady Lerran where she lived between the mountains and a swathe of fertile coastland. Many lesser gods had joined Lady Lerran and they worked easily with the still simple humans who dwelt in those lands. They encouraged the humans, helping in only small ways, so they did not infringe Mother's command not to interfere.'

The Augur paused, leaning her head back for a moment before continuing. 'This was the time when Lady Lerran and Lord Dabray studied the Great Dragons of Sapphrea. They gained the trust of the Dragons, who taught them many skills.'

'The Dragons taught Lady Lerran?' Endis interrupted.

'Indeed they did. There was another creature involved. You seemed not to recognise the name when I mentioned it before - Youki?'

Endis shook his head.

'She is a god, of sorts. She has always been here. The Dragons knew of her, and revered her. The gods of Mother's making also knew of her, but they mostly mocked her as a primitive spirit. I don't believe there's any record of Youki interacting with Lord Darallax. Definitely not with Lord Hanlif., although she has spent time with Lord Dabray.'

'Wait.' Endis sat forward. 'Does she look different? I think I saw her, in a dream, or a vision, weeping over the death of an enormous man.'

The Augur was silent.

'She was fur covered, small, not like humans at all really,' Endis went on. 'Are there others like her?'

'There are a few, very like her, who I believe serve her. She has also had help from humans throughout their existence.' The Augur hesitated. 'Youki cares for this world, for the life upon it. But she cares for particular kinds over others. At least, that is my belief. She would not hesitate to remove one kind of creature if it proved to be too great a threat to those she favours.'

'How could Lord Hanlif *spy* on Lady Lerran? As gods, are they not aware of everything around them?'

'Gods can scan an area around them. Tika is also able to do something similar, and a few other humans who have mage talents. They do not do it constantly. Lady Lerran and her followers were deeply involved with both the humans who lived in that area and with the Great Dragons. With hindsight, she should have kept a far more regular watch for Lord Hanlif. He kept his distance though when his closest follower, Eoki, began the attack on the small town the humans had built. As always, fire was the weapon used and most of the town was destroyed, along with a large number of the humans. Lady Lerran was in the distant mountains where the Dragons preferred to live. When she had word of the attack, she and Lord Dabray took Dragon form and attacked Lord Hanlif's men.'

'I thought they had to stay in human form?' Endis interrupted.

'Hanlif yes, his followers no. The ones who attacked that first town took the shape of winged cats, huge creatures with wings and claws of flame. Many of them were destroyed by Lady Lerran's forces. Hanlif accused his sister of attacking his followers with no cause and swore his revenge. From then on, for countless human generations, Hanlif caused whatever damage he could to any humans offering homage to Lady Lerran. During those times, there were humans who built great cities and warred with each other, unaware of Lerran and Hanlif's presence on the world. Some of the humans announced *they* were gods, to make their followers trust them and obey all the many rules humans seem so fond of. It is enough to say that for several thousands of your years, there was a constant rise and fall in different places, always accompanied by much bloodshed and pain.'

When the Augur grew silent, Endis rose to make the tea that, as far as he knew, was all she consumed. The silence extended and he glanced across at her, wondering if perhaps she'd fallen asleep. He was disconcerted to see her clear blue eyes fixed on him, her expression unreadable. He bit his lip then decided to ask a question that had bothered him since these "history lessons" had begun.

'Why?' he asked. 'Why must I know all this of the so distant past of this world? Is it really relevant, necessary, to what the world is like now?' He waited but the Augur didn't speak. Endis turned back to his tea making. When he'd sat down again, unsure if he was meant to remain here, the

Augur chose to reply.

'I know it seems confusing, pointless even, child, but I am afraid it *is* necessary for you to know all that I know. No.' She raised a hand to stop him speaking. 'There *is* a reason that you must learn all this, but I am not ready to give you that reason. I ask that you be as patient as you can and attend to my words as closely as possible.'

There was no reproach in her tone and Endis felt abashed that he had questioned her. There was no doubt she was an incredibly aged lady, spending so much of each day talking to him, showing him mind pictures which must surely take strength. Especially since, from all he'd observed, she lived such a solitary life in this place. 'I'm sorry. I do find all you say of great interest, really I do. I was only asking because I cannot see how such long ago events have bearing on life today. Forgive me.'

The Augur's expression softened. 'You have my word you *will* understand, child, why you must know these things. Now, you may ask one question and then leave me to rest.'

Endis thought hard, reluctant to irritate the Augur as he feared he had already done. 'You said some humans set themselves up as gods. Are they still worshipped even though they surely could do nothing to truly help their believers?'

'Indeed, there are still many, scattered across the world. They are mostly harmless, although occasionally one will still grow beyond a little local cult, and then become a danger to themselves and others. Humans seem to like having a magical being to offer their life and loyalty, sometimes even at the cost of their own lives.' She saw Endis draw breath. 'No. That was your one question for now, child. I will see you tomorrow. Leave me now.'

Endis slept that night with no dreams, or visions or whatever they might be, and answered the Augur's summons next day determined not to ask her too many questions.

'I have decided to show you some things from a different perspective, child. It may help you understand the reality better.'

With no further explanation she closed her eyes and Endis simply followed suit. He felt a tug, much stronger than what he felt when the Augur summoned him. Then a picture formed. Part of his mind registered shock. He was *in* a group of people who were clearly agitated. But he realised he was actually seeing them from *within* one of them. Glancing down at himself, he saw he wore loose woven trousers and a faded and patched shirt. The others around him were similarly dressed, men and women both. At first he struggled to understand their speech then it became clear.

'I saw it, I tell you,' an older woman was insisting. 'A great cat, big as big. Yellow fur.'

'There are so such cats here, Ressa. The only large cats are far in the mountains. It must have been a wolf,' said a man, trying to calm the woman.

'You really think I don't know the difference between a great cat and a wolf? At my age, Mecki? It was a *cat*, I tell you.'

'We should fetch the animals into the barns, in case.' Another, younger woman spoke. 'Ressa isn't stupid. If she saw a cat, I'll believe her. We should get the children back from the fields, too.'

Endis listened and was aware of the rising concern in the man whose body he seemed to be sharing. The group of people scattered, Endis carried along as his host ran for the open fields. Together with two other men, they chivvied a large herd of goats back towards the buildings at the edge of the small town. In the distance, Endis saw other adults calling children to come indoors. A wind gusted and Endis smelled the tang of an ocean. Beyond the town, mountains rose, peaks marching away, their summits white capped.

Endis sensed the man's panic rising when they'd shut the goats into a well built barn and he shared his thought of a young woman holding a baby. It only now dawned on Endis that somehow he was experiencing what the Augur had called the First Skirmish, and he began to share this unknown man's fear. Then he, *they*, were running, shouts of alarm coming from behind, from the pastures they'd just left. Down a side street, past small shops where people emerged in consternation as the alarm spread. Bursting through the door of a small house, the man shouted a name. 'Malli! Malli!'

A woman appeared, frowning, from a back room. 'Oh hush Tomma! I've just managed to get her to sleep.'

'Get anything you need. Quickly! Something bad's coming.' As he spoke the man was grabbing a shawl draped over a chair, pushing it into a bag. 'Hurry please! I want you to run north. Find the Lady Lerran. You'll be safe with her!'

The woman finally seemed to see his urgency and vanished, reappearing with a baby clutched in her arms. 'Is it sea raiders again Tomma?' she asked, her face white now.

'I don't know. It's bad though. I can feel it. Run, my love. Make sure you and our daughter get to safety.' He slipped the bag over her shoulder. 'Please, Run!'

'Aren't you coming with us? Tomma? We need you!'

'I'll come when the trouble's dealt with here. Now go, run, as fast as you can.'

He pulled the woman to the door. He hugged her tight enough to wake the baby into an indignant squall. Gazing down, he kissed the crumpled face, then Malli's forehead. 'Run, my love. Be safe.'

He waited for a moment as his wife carried his daughter at a run along the lane leading north. The cries were growing louder from the town behind him. He returned to the house and grabbed up a long sturdy pole which had a metal point at one end. Then he left the house for the last time, jogging back to the heart of the town.

Women young and old began to appear, running in the direction Tomma had sent Malli: north. Some were carrying small children, pulling along others, and trying to help some of the oldest women at the same time. Now Endis smelt burning, or at least, Tomma did. Ahead now he saw men converging from different directions as smoke billowed from blazing barns. Animals screamed in terror: too late Tomma realised they would have been safer in their fields. He could see no attackers though and as he reached the main group of men, he asked what was actually happening.

Before anyone could answer, a sense of dread, like an almost visible cloud, descended on them. Several men groaned, holding their heads and dropping whatever weapons they'd brought. Tomma gritted his teeth against the sudden feeling of loss, of desolation, that threatened to overcome him, and stepped forward. 'Who are they?' he demanded. '*Where* are they?'

Mecki turned to him, his face as white as Malli's had been. 'Cats. Great cats,' he said. 'Made out of fire.'

Tomma stared at the man while Endis, hidden somewhere in Tomma's head, shivered, remembering the Augur's description of these "cats". 'Where did you see them?' Tomma asked.

'By the barns.' Mecki shook his head. 'Huge beasts. Not sure our arrows will be much good against such as they.'

'We'll do our best surely? Come on, Mecki. If we can fight off sea raiders, we can scare off a couple of cats.'

A man further along spoke up. 'A couple of cats Tomma? Look.'

Tomma, and Endis, looked where the man indicated. He could only stare. Seven gigantic creatures were rising from beyond the burning buildings. They were cat shaped but far more lithe, with enormous front paws extended before them as though they were in mid pounce. Flame flickered all over them, glowing angry red at their claws and teeth. What petrified Tomma, and Endis, were their eyes. They seemed *almost* human eyes, gleeful at the terror they were unleashing on these pitiful farmers.

One of the seven opened its mouth wide and roared, a sound which reverberated through people's very bones, apparent even to Endis who sincerely hoped only a part of his mind was actually present in Tomma's body. The creature in the lead who had roared, rose higher, its claws suddenly spouting fire at a building beyond the barns, closer to the town. The walls burst apart, sending chunks of stone in all directions, the wooden roof flashing into nothing in an instant. A man beside Tomma dropped to one knee and loosed an arrow towards the cat. The arrow disintegrated before it was anywhere near its target. The man notched another arrow immediately, muttering to himself. Endis couldn't tell it the words were prayers or curses.

'Mecki!' A new voice called. 'We must do something or run!'

Already several in their group were backing away, some running back into the town. Three of the cats rose higher, splitting away from the others and increasing their speed. Tomma turned his head to follow their flight above his town. He could feel the air getting warmer and told himself it was because of the burning buildings. Deep inside the man, Endis knew the growing heat was from the proximity of these - *things*. He found he was quite incapable of influencing Tomma's thoughts or actions: he was simply an observer, somehow hidden within another body.

Noise began to crash over them: roars from the advancing cats, the crackle and crash of more buildings being destroyed, and beneath those sounds, screams and cries of dying people. Endis realised Tomma had braced himself, feet apart, metal tipped pole held across his body. He wanted to scream in the man's mind - 'No, no! Just run! You have a wife, a child! Run!' but Tomma, and perhaps thirty men, now stood firm as the four cats came ever closer. They didn't come in for the kill at once. Like the true cats they mimicked, they circled a few man heights above the group, toying with their victims.

The man beside Tomma fired the last of his arrows and a claw extended, almost delicately, to swipe down the man's body. He toppled sideways, his body jerking and twisting while it was consumed by fire. Tomma didn't look down, his gaze still fixed on the one who seemed to be the leader. Endis perforce stared up through Tomma's eyes. He saw a change in the creature's gaze. There had been amusement; now there was calculation.

Tomma's right arm drew back in a smooth practised swing and the pole left his hand, flying not to the cat Endis had stared at but at the one following. The ungainly spear wavered then held true and, with an audible thump, hit the cat in one eye. There was a blood chilling scream and the creature began to fall but the leading cat spun in mid air and blasted flame towards the injured one. The cat Tomma had struck simply vanished, even as the leader spun back, radiating anger.

A new sound reached them from the north, a different roar, but just as full of anger as the cats'. Tomma had time for one quick glance to see several huge white and gold Dragons speeding towards them. Tomma turned back to the immediate threat, smiling. Lady Lerran had come. Malli had managed to reach her. His wife and daughter were safe. Tomma had time for that thought before flame hit his chest. His heart burst even as his body still contorted as fire shrivelled his flesh and Endis was jerked away from Tomma's agony.

Endis found himself back in the Augur's room, gasping for breath as tears streamed down his face. He brushed them away and saw the Augur setting a bowl of tea on the table at his side. She limped back to her chair, sat down and just watched him. He didn't dare reach for the tea, he was trembling so badly, so he concentrated on calming his breathing and stemming his tears.

'How did you do that?' He finally managed to ask.

The Augur smiled vaguely. 'It is not difficult, child. You will also be able to do such a thing. In due course.'

'I can't imagine why I would want to,' he retorted, still so badly shaken by his experience. 'Who was that poor man you sent me to?'

'Tomma? An ancestor of yours, through your father's line. It is easier to move a mind if there is even the slightest blood link.'

Endis decided to risk lifting his tea bowl and was grateful his hand only trembled slightly. From the Augur's words and demeanour, she obviously didn't think it an unusual occurrence, to move into another person's body. Endis's breathing shuddered into steadiness and he thought back to what he'd seen. 'Tomma injured one of the lesser gods?'

'He did. He was able to do so partly because he carried the blood of a lesser god, and partly because he had black metal on his spear. I have never discovered why one particular kind of such metal can cause harm, even death, to the gods. It was that type of metal that killed Hanlif in the end, wielded by a human with no god's blood in his veins.'

Endis drank his tea. It had a slightly sweeter taste than usual but it was good. He felt exhausted, as though he had physically experienced what that poor man had. 'Were the Kelatis here, at that time?' he asked suddenly.

'They were newly arrived, in the far northern snow lands. The gods knew they were there although the Kelatis never had knowledge of them or Mother Dark. Not for many, many years.' She studied the young man for a moment. 'Go and rest, child. I do know how that visit has shaken you. Understand that at such times you *are* safe. You can return here whenever you wish. I'll explain all that another time.'

Endis got to his feet, stumbling slightly.

'I thought I might show you more of this place,' said the Augur. 'When we've both rested, tomorrow I'll take you on a tour.'

Endis looked down into the wrinkled face and saw only kindness in the clear blue eyes. He managed a smile in return, bowed, and left her presence.

The Augur remained as she was, staring unseeing at the fire flickering in the hearth. He had so very much to learn, so much to accept. The more she taught him and the more she gave him, the less time she had herself. She had always understood this was how it must be, but it was only now, when it was actually happening, that she realised how very many memories she had to give him. Many were painful. She drew her hood over her head. She hadn't known that *remembering* so many things was more painful than the giving of her very self.

Chapter Seven

Ashri saw flames everywhere, from the walls, the floor, the ceiling. Before she could even grasp an intelligent thought, the flames just vanished, but she was now aware of turmoil elsewhere in the great palace. She stayed exactly where she was, bolt upright on her bed, and also remained in her bodily shape although part of her mind urged her to become invisible spirit. Slowly, as though she was a human, recovering from a long illness, she slid off the bed and went to the window. Flames, some in the most grotesque of shapes, some formed as humans, flared across the gardens followed by darkness. Where the darkness touched the fire, they guttered out completely.

Ashri watched, her thoughts frozen. Why would the great Lord Hanlif bother with the least of the lesser gods, as she truly believed herself to be? Would he really risk the wrath of Lady Lerran, just to punish Ashri? So Ashri passed the rest of that night, her mind numb, while she watched the fires extinguished, even those which always pulsed around Lord Hanlif's section of the palace. As the indeterminate light that served as sunrise began to brighten across the sky. Ashri remained where she was.

A few hesitant figures ventured outside. Ashri saw them walk to places where a fire figure had stood in the night, and stare at the ground. As far as she was able to see or sense, there was no sign of burning left on the grass. She felt an air of disturbance permeating the palace, a general nervous apprehension. She wished Feshni might suddenly appear but he was gone to the world below. Ashri saw some of those she'd spent the day with yesterday, walking much closer to each other than usual, and she knew everyone here felt the discomfort of whatever had occurred last night.

Very carefully, her mind quested out, towards the house beneath the trees beyond the palace. It was empty. She sensed not a single mind inside or anywhere close by. Ashri simply watched from her window for half of the day then made up her mind to go outside and find Neefah and Meru. She located them sitting in the exact same place as yesterday then realised they always sat there, whenever she'd noticed them before. They welcomed her among them and she sat between Meru and Yejo, listening to their talk of last night's fires.

'Did you see what happened?' asked Neefah. 'I saw fire shapes out here.'

Ashri shook her head.

'I thought there was fire on the side of the palace.' That was another female, Tellika. 'The side where you live,' she added. The smile she offered Ashri as she spoke was curious rather than accusatory.

'I just watched from my window,' Ashri replied, relieved when others began to repeat what they'd seen.

So the days passed, and gradually the uneasiness dissipated and the lesser gods continued in their usual ways. Ashri noted no one mentioned the glow that always seemed to surround Hanlif's quarters slowly dimmed, or the fact that neither he nor his followers were seen strutting through the halls or gardens. She wondered if anyone else *had* noticed, or were they all deliberately avoiding any mention of it. It was as if the night of fire creatures had never happened with the gods walking, talking, playing, just as they always had. Ashri had stayed in her room, or joined Meru's group since that night, but finally decided to risk going to her favourite rooftop perch.

She leaned her back against the slender needle spire and stared out over the immense expanse of roofs with their multitude of decorative pinnacles and transparent domes. She stayed there through most of the period of darkness, trying not to let her thoughts dwell on Lord Hanlif, or Lady Lerran. Eventually, she rose to return inside. A glimmer to her right made her pause. Lord Hanlif's wing of the palace was shimmering with light. It was nowhere near as bright as usual, but it was there. Ashri looked at it for a while. So, wherever he'd vanished to, he was now back here, in the gods' space.

Next day Ashri wandered through the gardens with

Meru and the others, following the same route they always took and then settling on the grass near the fruit trees. The air felt noticeably warmer to Ashri, which was making her nervous, but no one else remarked on it. For the first time in many days, she excused herself, saying she wanted to just walk, and she left them to stroll under the trees. Reaching the gap in the overgrown hedge, she slipped through, emerging into the small neglected meadow. Sitting by the pool, she somehow wasn't surprised when Youki appeared. Neither spoke for a while and then Youki sighed. Ashri had always found that odd. Why did Youki breathe when none of the gods needed to do so? She knew those, like Simert, who spent time on the world below, imitated human breathing, but Youki really did need to breathe.

Before Ashri could speak, Youki tensed and then was gone. Ashri looked back the way she'd come in sudden alarm, fading to nothing and flashing back to the orchard. Taking her usual form, she hurried back to Meru. All of them were staring at the palace, specifically Hanlif's wing. The glow was intensifying, the air definitely much warmer. High overhead, a cloud was forming, not the picturesque fluffy clouds that occasionally wafted across their sky. This was a great mass of black, churning cloud. A lance of blazing gold shot up from Hanlif's quarters, piercing the blackness as it drew ever closer. Black spears rained down. More gold roared up, noise growing as the black cloud halted directly above that section of the palace.

Lesser gods stood clustered in the gardens, hurrying out of the halls and colonnades. Tension mingled with rage and the atmosphere boiled with disturbed feelings. The rumbling crashes were familiar to the gods who had witnessed thunder storms on the human world but it never normally occurred here, in the gods' space. Why would it happen now? Then everything, the ground, the palace, the gods themselves, shuddered as Mother Dark spoke. Ashri found herself on her knees, the sheer power of the voice shocking in its immensity.

Mother called forth Hanlif, to stand before her. Most of the lesser gods watched, none moving any closer when Hanlif, accompanied by perhaps thirty others, strode out of his quarters. Ashri saw the building was shimmering dark red, like a dying ember might glow in a hearth fire. No glow surrounded Hanlif now and certainly none of his followers. She saw Lahi among those, standing a few paces behind Hanlif. The great cloud now stretched across the palace, light gleaming still all around its edges. Ashri could hear a voice, or a million voices, but could make out no words. She saw Hanlif raising an arm, waving furiously, obviously arguing, Pressure bore down on her head, her thoughts, and nothing was audible above the roar.

Ashri was aware all the other lesser gods were on their knees, some completely prostrate, and understood Mother's words were for her second creation alone. Her eyes hurt, staring at the group where Hanlif was the only one still upright, but Ashri was determined to see what would befall him. In fact, neither she nor anyone else saw his transference from the gods' space to the world, along with his group of followers. One moment they were there; the next they were gone.

The wing of the great palace that had been Hanlif's own was also gone, and pine trees stood there, darkest green, tall and straight. The roaring sound moderated.

'Hanlif is henceforth banished. His ability to reach here, or infinity, is removed from him. He is world bound, for eternity, and I will be displeased should any of you here offer him aid or assistance.'

The noise slowly faded as did the huge cloud which had remained directly overhead. Ashri looked across the short distance to Meru and those with whom she'd walked out here earlier. All of them appeared as shocked as she was. Even when Mother spoke those last words, her voice was impossible to define. One voice? Many? Who could guess?

Ashri got to her feet and moved closer to Meru and those others, expecting to hear comments about what had just taken place in front of them. Nothing. Their conversation resumed slowly, but it was a continuation of what they'd been speaking of before. Ashri listened as they spoke, watching their faces. They all seemed so young, as she knew she did. How old were they all, in truth? Why had Mother brought them all into existence? Again and again, in the chaos of her thoughts, Ashri wondered if *any* of them were tormented and confused by such questions as it seemed she must endure.

Tika was in her high room this afternoon, reading through reports that had arrived from Wendla and Harbour City. There was a loud thump on her door. 'Come in,' she called.

The door flew open and an elderly woman stumped in, breathless and glaring.

'Konya!' Tika was surprised to see her.

Konya slumped onto the nearest couch, puffing gently and still glaring. 'Those stars cursed stairs are a pain, Tika!' she managed.

Tika smiled. 'They're all right for now but I agree I might have to rethink my living arrangements when I'm old,' she agreed.

'For those of us no longer so young,' Konya began.

Tika snorted. 'You mean already old?'

Konya's glare intensified. 'Those of us past the first flush of youth,' she continued with dignity. 'We find it more than exhausting having to struggle up here to see you. Especially after fighting our way along from the medical school in the depths of winter with all this stars damned snow.'

Rising, Tika went to the hearth to make tea. Konya was genuinely upset it seemed. Looking over her shoulder, she saw Konya's eyes were closed and felt sorry she'd teased her. Shortly, she took a bowl of tea to her visitor and resumed her seat at her low table. 'I'm sorry Konya. You know you only needed to ask Kija or any other Dragon to call me downstairs?'

Konya sipped her tea. 'I wanted to speak to you more privately, Tika.'

'Is there something wrong at the school?'

'No, no, but Aifa spoke to me. She said there was something worrying her about Veka. You know Aifa's other senses are much more sensitive since her blindness. Veka very rarely says much about herself but back before the snow arrived, Aifa said she thought something was bothering the child. She asked Tokkar if Veka showed any sign of illness. Tokkar won't be returning to Deep Fold by the way. He's besotted with Aifa,' Konya added as an aside. 'Tokkar said Veka seemed a little paler than usual but nothing alarming. Anyway, the days passed but Aifa was aware that whatever was amiss, was still bothering Veka. She had only asked if she was well a few times, she didn't want to press her.'

Konya held out her empty tea bowl and Tika obediently went to refill it. 'It was Shea who mentioned it to me. You remember when Shea damaged her shoulder in training? She came to us for Aifa to treat her with massage.'

Tika nodded. 'I remember.'

'Shea casually mentioned that Veka had bad headaches, always at night, followed by vivid dreams. She said Veka was always fine in the mornings.'

'Is it still happening?' Tika asked.

'I think so. Obviously, I haven't questioned either Shea or Veka. I don't want to alarm either of them, but Aifa feels there is still *something* about the child. You know how reticent Veka's always been. She's still close to Sney I think, but I preferred to discuss it with you. Palos has made a point of calling in when Veka is working with Aifa. He agrees with Aifa. *Something* bothers the child.'

'Is there any sense of urgency?'

Konya frowned in thought. 'I don't believe so, no. Veka has always been such a shy quiet girl. I know she has a talent with languages; Mardis and Dog ask her about some of the stranger books they acquire, so Veka has told Aifa. She's reached a reasonable level of competence in the training sessions, which she only joined because Sney was so eager. The twins are fond of her, but she seems almost a shadow, lost in the crowd who live here.' Konya shook her head at Tika's expression. 'I don't think she is, or even *feels*, that she's neglected in anyway.'

'Are you concerned about her headaches or her dreams? Has she told Shea what the dreams are about?'

'I don't think so, no. I'm not happy when people report regular headaches, Tika. It seems odd that they only happen at night. It could be something as simple as a particular food or drink setting the headache off. Aifa is very fond of the girl. She works well with her, Aifa says, and her writing up of the notes about the plants we use, are clear and neat.' Konya rubbed her eyes. 'I wanted to tell you of this so you could perhaps check there's nothing serious going on with her. I hope I'm just being over cautious, and I suspect I am, but I'd rather you had a look at her. You can, without her knowing, can't you?'

'I can, yes, and I will when I see an opportunity. She's fourteen now, isn't she?'

'Fifteen. She still shares rooms with Shea, although I think Shea said she was moving soon.'

'Moving? Moving where?'

'Nearer Jarko's rooms, I think.'

Tika grinned. 'I hear you and Palos are very friendly too.' She was delighted to see Konya's cheeks turn pink, and laughed aloud. 'You deserve some happiness, Konya, and if Palos makes you happy, I'm glad for you.'

'Well, we spend a lot of time together of course, being so involved with the school,' Konya muttered. She got up, trying to ignore Tika's smirk. 'Have you heard from that boy, Endis?'

Tika's amusement faded. 'No, and I don't expect to. He said the Augur, whoever she might be, told him time was - changeable, or different. I didn't know what he meant when he told me and I don't think he did either. I *think* he means he could be gone a short time for him but a lot of time might pass here. Or the other way round. I just hope he's all right. He's a pleasant lad.'

Making her way to the door, Konya stopped. 'What actually happened to the Asataria? Tokala, she came with Endis didn't she? She never mentions it at all.'

'I don't believe either of them had a pleasant life there, Konya. Endis at least had a mother who cared for him, but he rarely spoke of his life at the Academy. The Asataria itself? As I've told you all, it's probable the founders of the place used an old magic, a magic I couldn't recognise, nor could the Dragons. When the very buildings, or the watch wards embedded in those walls, decided the people living there had deviated far enough from the accepted beliefs and behaviours of the founders, it would dissolve into the earth.'

'Cold hearted bunch,' said Konya. 'Did Rhaki not know?'

'No. He said he wasn't surprised but he is a different man from the one who was raised in the Asataria. He seemed little affected by the news of its disappearance.'

Konya nodded and opened the door.

'I will check Veka and let you know. If you want to speak to me privately again, send one of your students with a message, and I'll come to the school.' She smiled at Konya's suspicious look. 'I'm not mocking or teasing you,' she said, unmistakeable affection in her tone. 'I agree the stairs are a nuisance to many.'

Konya humphed and set off on the long journey down. When she had disappeared round the first curve of the stairs, Tika closed the door and returned to sit by the fire. Green gold eyes stared at her.

'I like Konya.'

Tika stroked the black cat, Cerys, who stretched out in appreciation. 'I do too. She's a very good healer for someone with no mage gift. I'll check Veka later.'

Tika gazed into the fire, trying to remember every incident when she'd had any immediate contact with the girl. There weren't many, she realised, and even less with Sney. Veka and Sney were close friends when they came here but they were very different characters. Sney was determined from the first to join the Guards while Veka was more interested in the library. Her hand paused on Cerys' back. She remembered they'd visited Lord Mim in the Northern Stronghold. Veka had surprised Tika during a quiet moment there by asking if Mim had been very hurt. She agreed that he had, but he was recovering.

Now she frowned, trying to recall the girl's exact words. Veka had suggested that maybe everyone had to be hurt and sad, otherwise how could they know when they were safe and happy? Tika swore to herself. At the time, she'd thought she should keep a close eye on the child, but of course, she hadn't. Her Captain, Sket, had become progressively erratic in his behaviour, and then the beloved orange cat, Khosa, had died, and any thoughts of Veka had simply been forgotten. Cerys sat up, staring at Tika reproachfully.

'Sorry,' Tika said aloud, resuming her stroking.

'You can't remember everything or worry about everything. How many times must we tell you that?'

'Cerys, it's *my* land here. I'm supposed to be the Lady of Iskallia. It's my *job* to think of as many things as I can. Particularly when it concerns some of the youngest ones here.'

Cerys made no reply, just continued to stare at Tika.

'Do you know anything of Veka?' Tika asked.

'I've sat near her a few times. She's always very gentle if she strokes me but I've never spoken to her nor she to me.'

When Tika sighed, Cerys batted a paw at her hand, claws retracted. Tika stared at her in surprise. 'Kija and Pearl know much more of what goes on here than I do. Ask them. Really Tika, Khosa said you were too quick to blame yourself for anything that went wrong. She was so right.' The green gold eyes blinked slowly. 'I know it's a burden, Tika, but there are so many here who are willing to help you more than you let them.'

'Dog calls it delegating,' Tika smiled.

'Then start doing some of that, for stars' sake.'

After clearing the reports she'd been reading when Konya had arrived, it was time for the evening meal and Tika went down to the hall. Handing the papers to her advisor, Dromi, she glanced over the crowded tables, seeing Veka sitting with Ashoki, Sney and Shea. Tika sat at her window table, answering various questions from both Dog and Garrol. Food arrived and while the noise in the hall lessened as people began to eat, part of Tika's mage senses slid into Veka's mind. As always, although Veka had no idea what was happening, Tika was careful not to encroach on the girl's thoughts or memories. She was simply checking the physical condition of Veka's brain, and to her relief, she found nothing wrong.

Tika blinked. The people round her table were staring at her in silence, obviously thinking she was mind speaking someone. She apologised. 'Sorry. Did one of you ask me something? I was just thinking.' She ignored the sceptical

81

looks and continued heaping food onto her plate.

'I asked if you had plans to travel anytime soon,' Essa told her. Sergeant Essa had some mage talent herself and Tika knew she would have sensed Tika was doing a little more than just thinking.

'There's no reason for us to go anywhere is there?' Tika asked Dromi.

He shook his head. 'Lady Ricca continues to suggest we visit her in Kelshan every other day.' He smiled. 'We send salve to Queen Tupalla every few days. There's been no news from Strale recently but I don't think there can be any need for concern. Bad news is the news that travels fastest.'

Tika looked across at the Dragons clustered by the huge hearth. Kija, Farn, Pearl and Genia were apparently asleep which was their way of avoiding the smell of cooked meat. Garrol saw her checking them.

'Brin and Storm are permanent residents of the forge these days,' he said, grinning at her. 'Skay is usually there but she said she was going to visit Fenj and Lorak this morning.'

Tika grimaced. 'With three in your forge, is there really room for you to work?'

Captain Fedran leaned towards her, his voice exaggeratedly quiet. 'When I was there yesterday, I noticed when Skay gets excited when all the sparks really fly, she forgets to keep her tail out of the way. Mekla was not pleased when she fell over, although I did think Garrol laughed too much.'

'Is that why she's gone to Dragons Rest?' asked Tika.

She saw Garrol's bright blue eyes twinkling and guessed she was probably correct.

'Mekla isn't speaking to Garrol today either,' Fedran added.

Glancing round the hall, Tika saw Mekla was at a table next to Ashoki, with Garrol's four new apprentices. 'Shame on you Garrol,' she said, although she was smiling too.

The noise level rose when dishes were cleared away and dice games and singing began around the hall. Tika noted that both Veka and Sney left when most of the other young ones did, none of them much interested in the various games being argued over by their elders. 'Is Rhaki well?' she asked Dromi suddenly. 'Why isn't he here tonight?'

'He went back to Port Maressa this morning. He really likes being there.' Dromi shuddered. 'All that sea would make me ill if I was there for too long. Volk took him down in that little cart he uses for supplies.'

When everyone had left at last, Tika went across to the Dragons. Farn and Pearl had been watching a group playing a board game and had to explain all its intricacies to Tika. She listened patiently, fully aware of Kija's utter contempt for such nonsense. Genia listened to the two younger ones before commenting that she had thought it remarkably silly. Her lilac eyes whirred briefly when Farn and Pearl regarded her, then, without another word, settled themselves for sleep.

Kija's mind tone was fond. 'I quite agree with you, Genia. Humans are amused by extremely strange occupations.'

Tika moved closer to lean on the massive gold scaled shoulder. 'Have you been aware of any dreams Veka may have had, mother of my heart?'

Kija tilted her head to peer down at Tika. 'I have not? Why do you ask?'

Tika explained the reasons for Konya's visit this afternoon. 'If Aifa and Palos are concerned, I think I must be too.'

'I will watch her sleep, daughter. I'm sure if it was anything bad, I would know. Many here have bad dreams, of their lives before they came here, but none have been bad enough to worry me.'

'They do?' Tika was shocked. She felt Kija's affection wash through her.

'Farn still dreams sometimes,' Kija murmured.

'So do I,' Tika whispered back.

'Me too,' Genia's mind tone was the quietest of all.

Chapter Eight

Endis sensed the Augur's summons and hurried out to the passageway. She was waiting for him, her hood pushed back a little, just clear of her face. 'Hold my hand, child, and close your eyes. I'm sorry but I'm too old now to walk all the way.'

A little puzzled, Endis took hold of the hand the Augur extended to him. He was shocked by its fragility and held it as gently as he could. He closed his eyes and felt absolutely nothing.

'You can look now, Endis. The way we just moved can be unsettling. That's why I said you should keep your eyes closed.'

Endis heard amusement and sadness in her voice. Opening his eyes, he saw they stood in a wide pillared walkway, a pale sky filling the open arches directly in front of them. The Augur tugged him forward then released his hand. A wall, waist high, of the same white stone as the rest of the building he'd seen so far, ran along between each arch. Reaching that wall, Endis stared out over - nothing. A mist wreathed around over any land that might have been visible below but poking up through that mist were exquisitely perfect, thin spires. He glanced down as the Augur moved to his side.

'Are those spires on other buildings here?' he asked.

'No. They are all part of this place,' she replied. 'I call the spires my needles.' She smiled up at him. 'I used these upper rooms when first I came here, but now I can only visit on occasion.'

Endis peered down. He felt no sense of being at any great height because the mist reached nearly up to the level on which he was standing. He watched as it swirled and billowed, reminding him of a clean sheet being shaken out over a bed. Endis remembered watching his mother doing just that, and laughing, saying she was making clouds. He had thought the mist a luminous pearly grey but as he stared, he saw faint threads of colour drifting through it. 'What is the land like around the building?' he asked, still gazing down. When there was no reply, he turned to the Augur. She too had been gazing over the mist, but she raised her face to meet his eyes. 'Nothing Endis. Nothing at all.'

He found her reply partly acceptable and partly deeply shocking. 'Nothing?' he echoed.

'This is a Place Between, Endis. Between different worlds, or realities, child. Nothing can enter here without my permission or command.'

Endis continued to stare at her. 'Come. Walk with me.' She tucked a hand under his arm and, leaning heavily on her stick, urged him on along the walkway.

Birds suddenly swooped beneath the arches, whistling and calling. 'If there is no land around, where can they live?' Endis asked. 'What can they feed on if there are no trees, fields?'

The small figure at his side laughed. 'They have food here. Look.'

They'd reached the end of the walkway and Endis saw an expanse of small trees, shrubs, plants, growing wildly as far along as he could see.

'They seem quite happy here,' the Augur told him as they stood together.

He could hear the faint sound of water and the Augur laughed again. 'Yes. They have all they need right here, Endis.'

'There are no birds in the garden - downstairs, or wherever I'm staying.' His eye was caught by an enormously fat bee diving into a flowering bush.

'They visit that garden sometimes. I can ask them to again if you wish?'

Endis shook his head, not in denial of her words or suggestion, but because he was picturing birds finding their way down how many flight of stairs to reach his courtyard.

'Come.' The Augur turned away from this scene, so bizarre to Endis, positioned as it seemed to be at the top of a vast building. She turned through a gap in the wall and Endis saw an airy room. The walls seemed of glass on two sides, one revealing the trees and birds, the other looking out over the mist and three of the spires the Augur called needles. There were no individual chairs, just five long couches set around the space so a visitor could choose which view to look at. Shelves on one wall held various bowls and jars. The Augur sank onto the nearest couch and saw Endis looking at the shelves.

'I once collected tea bowls,' she said. 'I had no real reason for doing such a thing. Foolishness. It was long ago.'

Endis went closer. 'Some of them are so simple,' he said. 'Were some of them made by a child you knew?'

'In a way.' She sat with her hands resting on top of her walking stick, watching Endis make his way slowly along the length of the shelves. Reaching the end, he returned to sit on another couch close to the augur. 'You used to live up here?'

'I did. I loved high places and I always loved those needles.' She nodded to the three spires rising through gently twisting cloud or mist.

'Why did you call them needles?' Endis watched the Augur's face. Her expression seemed more relaxed than he'd yet seen her.

She smiled. 'A silly whim of mine, child. I imagined they could rise even higher and stitch patterns in the night sky.'

Endis had a momentary image of a young girl, staring out in the dark, and wishing the spires might shoot upwards into that dark. 'You lived in these rooms for a long time?'

She turned her head, the so clear blue eyes meeting his. 'Oh yes, child. An extremely long time. Go and look.' She nodded at another narrow open arch beyond the shelves.

Endis rose and walked through into another room with one wall clear and showing the spires beyond. The other walls were shelved and books filled most of them. A table and a solitary chair stood close to the glass wall. He didn't touch any of the books but he saw they were all notebooks, hundreds upon hundreds of notebooks. There was another archway which he only looked into. He found a large bed and another long couch, no cupboards or chests, and the now familiar clear wall with its view of the spires.

Returning to the first room, he saw the Augur still gazed out, her face peaceful. Sitting down again, he asked about the room with the notebooks.

'My diaries, records of my days here,' she said.

'Have you lived alone all this time?'

'Oh yes.' Her gaze remained fixed on the spires rising from the undulating mist. 'This part of the place is a quite narrow tower. I didn't want to *live* inside a needle, I wanted to be able to *see* them.'

Endis wondered how the expanse of trees he'd just seen might fit in or on a "narrow tower", but he didn't ask.

'It is quite a while since I last ventured up here,' the Augur continued. 'I considered returning to these rooms but I have the library, the infinity room, the spiderweb room, and so many others on the lower level. I made them there because there was more space for them you see.'

'Can you not come up the way you brought us just now?'

'I could, but if I use my own strength it drains me too much now, child, and I don't like to impose my will on others for a frivolous reason.'

Endis tried to sort through these comments. After a pause in which he watched the Augur gazing at the needles, he asked the question uppermost in his mind. 'Did *you* move us here today?'

'No, I did not.'

The quiet resumed. Endis thought the Augur seemed mesmerised by the gently undulating mist which broke like waves against the three spires in front of them. He admitted it was a very calm place here, the sound of birds calling in the distance the only interruption. He was content to sit as long as the Augur chose. It was a welcome change from the history lessons. When the Augur at last turned to look at him he was struck by the faraway, almost dreamy expression on her face. 'Did you have a name, before you were the Augur?' he asked softly,

'My name is Ashri, but it hasn't been used for long and long.' She stood, wobbling briefly until her stick and Endis's grip on her arm steadied her. 'The stairs to this tower are on the right, past the library, if you feel energetic enough to climb up.'

'But these are *your* rooms. It's clear to me how much pleasure you find in being here, looking out at your needles,' he replied with a gentle smile.

She began to move to the door space and then out, onto the walkway. 'It is not mine for much longer, child, but I would like to hope the next Augur leaves my needles alone! Now, close your eyes again, child.'

He did as she said and again had no sensation of movement.

'We are back now, you can open your eyes.'

Sure enough, they stood in the passage, the door to the Augur's rooms a few steps away. 'Do as you wish for now, Endis. We were longer up there than you might suppose. I will tell you more tomorrow of what lies ahead on your path.'

Next day when Endis went to her room, he had the feeling she had somehow diminished. He couldn't have explained what he meant exactly but he felt *something* had changed. He found she had already made a pot of tea and he poured it for them both. He sat, waiting for her to speak.

'There is less time than I had believed, Endis, and so much for you to know. Not just to know, you must also understand.' She began to speak of Places Between and Endis listened closely. She rose, moving to the hearth.

'I can make the tea,' Endis objected.

'You sit down.' She laughed. 'No, you are truly a good boy. Your mother raised you to an excellent standard. I will make the tea though.'

After he'd finished the bowl she gave him, he waited for further lessons. When she spoke, the Augur's voice was very soft. 'Sleep, Endis. It is simpler but cruder to give you the lessons directly, and time is so short. Sleep, child.'

Endis's chin sank to his chest, his eyes closed. The Augur looked at her hand in some exasperation. The dark blood oozing from the cut across the base of her thumb dried as she stared, the cut sealing to a pale line. Then she leaned her head back and began to empty part of her mind into the boy's. Opening her eyes again, she felt exhausted. She spoke aloud.

'Endis, go to your rooms now. Do not wake. In the morning, your mind will feel different. Do not worry. Go, child, and know Mother Dark is satisfied with your progress thus far.'

Endis got to his feet, walking slowly to the door. The Augur watched him through her senses until he settled onto his bed, and then she drew her hood down, hiding her face as she allowed herself to mourn.

A few days after Konya had spoken to Tika of her concern for Veka, Tika was in the library with Dog. Dog had been collecting every small scrap of any mention of Seers with the help of Mardis Fayle, and occasional pieces of information sent from the Dark Realm. 'There really is very little here, Tika.' Dog indicated the small pile of notes she'd made.

Tika pulled a chair over to Dog's work table. 'I think we'll just have to wait, and hope Endis isn't mad. Menan Kelati told me all Seers end up mad.'

'Do you trust her?'

'Stars above, no! Although *Pakan* Kelati has great powers, I don't think he'd ever bother to use them, except to cause storms to make sure people stay well away from wherever he lives. Menan, on the other hand, well. As a Seer, I presume she's been watching people here, but I'm not sure that's a good thing.'

Dog put her feet up on the corner of the table. 'I've been thinking of those Weights of Balance. Do you suppose Pakan might have Made them?'

Tika stared at her in surprise then considered the idea. 'Do you know, you might well be right,' she said slowly.

'I live to serve.' Dog smirked then grew serious again. 'Are you sure you know how many of the stars damned things there actually are or were?'

'One set secured in the Northern Stronghold. Another secured in the Menedula in Drogoya. I suppose the Weights in the Asataria complex must have vanished when the Asataria did.'

'So there is only the one, in Vagrantia?' Dog frowned. 'Do you think it's safe there? Why did Pakan Make them, if he really did?'

'They had something to do with changing time.' Tika shivered, remembering Bark's death when he removed one of those Weights that seemed to hang impossibly suspended by nothing but air.

'Ren aged too when he moved the one in the Menedula,' Dog added quietly.

'The Kelatis are not of this world, Dog. Who knows how they think? Pakan seemed reasonable enough when I spoke with him but he had no understanding or knowledge of the people who live here. He still has no real interest in us either, although he said he had at last spoken to Issi, the Wise Mother of the Zeminat.'

Dog nodded. 'I liked her. You should get a fur cloak like she wore. Very impressive I thought.'

Tika snorted. 'Issi is much taller than I am! She could look imposing. I have always accepted that imposing is not a look I'll ever achieve!'

Dog regarded her thoughtfully. 'Perhaps not,' she agreed.

After a moment. Tika glanced round the library, empty except for the two of them. 'Where is everyone?'

'The children? They're all with Telk and Jarko, exercising.' Dog rolled her eyes. 'I'm astonished how many people seem to enjoy it. There are fewer in the better weather but crowds trot along there in the winter mornings. Mardis is in the archives.'

'Veka helps here sometimes?'

Dog gave her a searching look. 'Yes. Mardis has her helping with some books he wants to translate. He said she's very good at puzzling out various languages. Why?'

'No reason. Does Shea still help?'

'Not so much. She works in the archives most afternoons and is one of the exercising fools in the mornings.' She grinned. 'That's because of Jarko.'

Tika smiled back. 'I'd heard about that.'

'What's your interest in Veka?' Dog asked abruptly.

'Nothing in particular. I haven't really spoken to her or

Sney since they came here. I only realised that the other day.'

'You really are a terrible liar, Tika. Perhaps you can fool some people but you never fool me. Or Essa.'

Tika scowled. 'Konya said Aifa thought Veka was worrying about something, that's all.'

Dog thought for a moment. 'You want me to ask her to bring some books up to your rooms? You could talk to her then?'

'That's a good thought. Yes. Do that please. There's no rush though.'

'Mardis is still hunting for clues about old empires he's convinced must once have ruled here and in Sapphrea. It's driving him mad that he can find nothing at all about the domes, too. He's been looking for information about them since he found those on his estate, years ago. His beard is a knotted mess when he thinks about them.'

'There seem to be many more books in here, Dog.' Tika sounded suspicious.

'Most are copies our printers have made. It's very unfair of you to keep accusing us of stealing books, Tika. Very hurtful.'

'Where are you getting most books from now?'

'We've had quite a lot from Salo Manis. That reminds me. Jarko told Shea there is a group of islands ruled by some Phoenix Emperor. They're called the Isles of Vremilia. Navan put that name on his maps. Jarko said the Emperor decided to have nothing to do with the people on the mainland so there's no trade or contact between them and Salo Manis. 'The islands are also known as the Phoenix Empire, and Jarko said they were reputed to be clever, skilful people.'

'When did they cut themselves off from contact with the mainland?'

'Oh long ago, but as Mardis pointed out, if you have ships, there's always the chance of a bit of smuggling.'

'You will *not* get involved in smuggling, Dog. You can trade with whoever you like but smuggling or theft will *never* be acceptable.'

Dog nodded. 'As you say, Lady Tika,' she agreed very

seriously.

Perhaps it was fortunate that the bell warned them of lunch being served. Tika contented herself with a glare at Dog's innocent face. 'I notice you don't go to the exercise sessions,' she said, standing up.

'No, I don't. *I* notice *you* don't, either.' Dog rose, hooking an arm through Tika's and heading for the hall. 'You still don't seem to have handed on some of your worries. We notice these things, Tika. The villages have been given much more control over themselves but there is still a lot of stuff you do here that other people would be happy to take on.'

'Stuff? *Stuff?* It's work I would have you know! Stuff, indeed!'

Reaching her usual table, Tika saw only Pearl reclining by the hearth. The day had begun bright although very cold so Tika guessed the other Dragons had gone to hunt. The sky was rapidly clouding now and she hoped they'd be back before the inevitable snow chose to arrive.

When the hall started to empty again, Tika asked those of her advisors who were present to wait. Dog sent her a wicked wink as she left with Ashoki and Shea. Tika had been pleased to see Werlan come into the hall with Dromi. The Dark Lord, being in the half death, often didn't join them for meals having no need for food any longer. He had a good mind, able to look at a variety of problems from many different angles no one else had considered. Navan, Dromi and Essa also remained at the table. Her Captain of Guards, Fedran, was visiting Port Maressa to confer with Port Master Vallek.

Once they were alone, Tika raised Dog's suggestion. 'It has been pointed out that I haven't handed on more sections of work here,' she began.

Essa and Navan spoke one word together. 'Dog?'

Tika gave a rueful nod. 'She's right unfortunately. Have you any thoughts on what we could change?'

Werlan was the first to reply. 'You split the housekeeping duties and that seems to be working satisfactorily. I have wondered about setting up a school, a proper school for the children?'

No one was surprised when Tika's expression darkened. She had an extremely strong dislike of the mere mention of schools and none of her friends were quite sure why. Tika had never attended a school or formal lessons in her life. She had heard stories though, many from Shivan, Lord of the Dark Realm, who had detested his school days, his sister Jian loathing them equally.

'Did you go to school Essa?' Tika demanded.

'No.'

'Navan?'

'You know full well I didn't,' he smiled at her.

'Dromi?'

'Not really. Not until I chose to go to the Brotherhood when I was fifteen or so.'

'Werlan?'

The Dark Lord gave her one of his rare smiles. 'Yes. And I disliked it as much as Lord Shivan I believe.'

Tika sat back, folding her arms. 'Well then. As most of us haven't been schooled, why do we need to make the children here attend such a place?'

'Tika, it needn't be as bad as you might have heard. I was thinking perhaps, each morning like they do now, but with others teaching them different things.' Werlan spoke gently. 'Mardis and Dog have been doing a great job teaching them to read, write, and do simple numbers. There are other things though. Mardis has told me two boys pester him for information about caring for animals. Surely Volk knows most about that? Navan knows about the world. He could show them maps so they would learn where different lands are?'

Still suspicious, Tika listened. 'You don't want a separate building then, or rooms where they'd all have to sit in lines and be polite?'

Werlan's gold eyes sparkled although his expression remained grave. 'No. I am certainly not suggesting that. Perhaps one or two rooms could be used for them to keep books and so on if they wanted. I did wonder if we could consult Lady Elora?'

Dromi nodded. 'Lady Ricca's new tutor seemed a most accomplished lady.'

Tika rose, wandering across to the hearth and back. Her advisors sat patiently, accustomed to their Lady's restlessness when deep in thought. She returned to her seat. 'Very well. Send a message to General Falkir explaining why you want to talk to Elora. Make sure he knows you're not trying to steal her away from Kelshan,' she added.

'She may well know of another, like her, who might be willing to come here for a brief time at least, to help us organise some kind of system,' Werlan suggested.

Essa was looking more interested. 'That could be the best idea,' she said. 'I agree that Navan and Volk could teach some things, as Dog and Mardis do now. But they all have their own work to do as well. Perhaps a tutor, like Elora, could be relied on to always be there, in a room the children know is for learning, to help with any questions?'

'I don't have anything to do with what the children learn, so how does that hand on responsibilities?'

Dromi steepled his long fingers. 'Tika, unlike other lands, we have no shops, or markets, no coins change hands here. We have no taxes, no real roads. Think of which tasks you most prefer in the ruling of Iskallia and concentrate on those. Anything you find really annoying or boring, ask us.'

'The main thing for you is diplomacy, speaking with other rulers. That is something you *have* to do,' Werlan added.

'Lists,' said Essa, knowing how Dromi loved lists. 'Think about it all, and then decide how *you* want to live.'

'I don't want shops or roads or taxes.' Tika sounded alarmed. 'Have people been suggesting such things?'

'No of course they haven't.' Dromi was quick to assure her.

'A market might be a good idea though.' Navan frowned in thought. 'We could choose a place, in the valley, somewhere central. People could meet for say three or four days, bringing animals, things they've made, to trade with each other? They could make camp and village could get to know village?'

Tika considered the idea, a vague memory of such things when she and Navan were slave brats in Return.

There had been an air of excitement among the women particularly, at the chance to escape their restricted lives for a while. No one in Iskallia was as secluded as those women had been but she could see a change of scenery and new people to talk to could be a good thing.

'Would they need coins?' she asked. 'You sent coins to each village didn't you, Dromi?'

'I did. Perhaps we can work on that idea for next summer.'

'No,' said Navan. 'Why not have two markets? One in spring and one in autumn?'

Essa nodded. 'It would give folk something to look forward to during winter and then to remember when the cold comes again.'

'Let's all give it thought.' Werlan watched the uncertainties play across Tika's face.

She nodded gratefully. 'We'll talk again in two days,' she agreed.

Chapter Nine

Endis woke, aware at once that something had changed in his mind but unsure what it was. He also realised he was fully clothed and his stomach was growling with hunger. Sitting on the edge of the bed, he wondered why he might miss a meal and then go to bed still dressed. He made a large breakfast for himself then felt the Augur's summons.

When he entered her room, she was putting tea beside his chair before she limped slowly back to her own. Endis sat waiting for her to speak but she sat with her eyes closed. He noticed she had not put any tea on the table beside her. He broke the silence. 'Shall I fetch you some tea, Ancient One?'

Her eyes opened, still so very clear and bright. 'No thank you, child. I need nothing. Let me show you pictures that I have shown you before. Only briefly, but I need your comment this time.'

Obediently, Endis shut his eyes and pictures of the earth splitting filled his mind. Magma poured like blood in a ragged line across a barren landscape, then was gone. 'Explain what you saw.' the Augur's voice was as quiet as usual but there was a note of command that Endis had not heard before.

He began to speak, not just repeating back the words he'd heard the Augur use when she'd shown him those pictures before. He talked for some time before it dawned on him that he was speaking knowledgeably, as though he had actually witnessed such an event. He stopped in mid sentence, staring at her.

The Augur smiled. Endis thought back over the seemingly endless days when she'd shown him pictures, explained the most mind boggling facts of the history of this world. Each lesson he considered, he could see as if he had been there to see it with his own eyes. He drew a long breath. 'What have you done?' There was no panic or fear in his words. Already he accepted an inevitability in his situation.

'I give you a choice, child. We can continue on this path, or we can stop. You can return to the world below, and live out your life, knowing it will end in madness.'

Endis didn't need to think. 'I will continue this path, but what *have* you done?'

'I have begun to give you my memories, child. You must take them all.'

'Does that mean that you will still have *some* memory or - stars above! Will *you* become crazed?'

The Augur laughed. 'I will be gone. Finished with this task that I was asked to undertake.

'That will make me a Seer? I'll be back living with Fenj and Lorak and I will know all these things you've shown me? How will I know who to seek out, to watch over?'

'All that will become clear, Endis. It will be a little longer until that clarity is vouchsafed to you.'

'You showed me your rooms yesterday. The ones high above here.

The Augur simply looked at him, waiting for him to continue.

'You said your name was Ashri. Who was Ashri, before she became the Augur?'

'Ashri has always been Ashri, child, as you will always be Endis.'

He sat in silent thought. Obviously there were to be no lessons today but perhaps answers of a sort. 'You said you didn't use your power to move us up to those other rooms?'

'I did not.'

'Then how did we move?'

The Augur laced her fingers in her lap. 'I was given some - helpers. Have you heard of Shadows?'

His blank expression told her he had not. 'I spoke to you of the three creations of Mother Dark, did I not? Of Lerran, Hanlif and of Darallax?' Endis nodded. 'Lerran returned to Mother Dark quite recently. Hanlif was killed. Darallax still lives on the world below. He is the Lord of Shadow.'

Endis could follow her words so far, and waited for more.

'Mother Dark gave Shadows to Darallax. Creatures she fashioned out herself and the infinity. 'They guarded him. She feared he was the weakest of the three, too easily overpowered by both Hanlif's love of Light and Lerran's love of Dark. She need not have worried that Lerran would hurt her youngest brother. She was most fond of him and grieved greatly when she thought he'd been lost after the Final Battle.'

The Augur smiled. 'Tika found him. He had cloaked himself and his followers in shadows and hidden away, just as Lerran hid her followers in the land now known as the Dark Realm.'

'Can you see these shadows who help you? If they belong to Darallax, can you rely on them?'

'I can see them perfectly well, child. You will also see them, when the time is right.'

Endis was unable to stop a groan and the Augur laughed outright. 'I do understand how frustrating and annoying you must find all this, Endis.' Her laughter faded and her eyes portrayed sympathy. 'It will truly not be long now before you understand all.'

'You say these shadows are yours to command, even though Darallax is their Lord?'

'These are mine. Made to serve me, and through me, they serve Mother Dark.'

'Are all the Seers able to use their talents? Is it shadows that moved me to see Zhora, the captain on the other side of the world?'

After a long pause during which Endis wondered if the Augur might decide not to answer, she did finally speak. 'That was through *my* power, Endis.'

'How does Menan Kelati move?'

The Augur shook her head. 'That is not clear to me. She and her siblings, if they are truly siblings, are of another world, another reality. I do not think she is aware of where this place is. As I say, she is of another world but she will not survive much longer. Her brother, Pakan, bears watching. He has no interest in much except Making things. There is more than a touch of madness within him and he can call considerable power, as you saw at Gerras

Ridge.'

Endis stared at her. 'That great explosion was Pakan's doing?'

'Unfortunately yes. The other one, Shashina seems content to stay deep underwater. She rarely has contact with Pakan and never with Menan.'

There was another pause while Endis worked through some of the Augur's words. 'Who knows of these shadows of which you speak?'

'*You* now know of the shadows that *I* command but several others know of the shadows who owe allegiance to Lord Darallax. He gave some of his to Tika I understand, with instructions to protect and obey her.' For the first time the Augur seemed to hesitate. 'Lord Darallax never really understood the strength, the power, in the shadows Mother Dark gave him. He speaks with them, but leaves them to their own devices most of the time. His child, Subaken, has more awareness of them I believe.'

'When I dreamt of the huge man, dying such a terrible death, I saw a strange creature clinging to him. It seemed to be trying to help him. Was that a shadow? It was Youki who was there at the end. Did you send me that dream?'

Endis couldn't interpret the expression that crossed the Augur's face briefly. Was it alarm or annoyance? Her tone was flat when she replied. 'No, it was not a shadow. I have told you, Youki has always been on the world, since the beginning. There is much I still don't know about her. Even Mother Dark doesn't know all concerning that creature. What you saw clinging to the man, was a creation of Youki's. And I did not send you that dream.'

'So you have no control or effect on Youki, or those things she has serving her?'

Blue eyes stared at him, chilling him with a sudden coldness. 'It took me a very long time, Endis, but yes, I can have an effect on them if I must. I think Youki has only just realised my power. She is not pleased to learn of it.'

Not knowing how to respond to that remark, Endis kept quiet.

'There have been others who have reached this world as well as your mother's people, Endis. I must tell you of them.'

'Who trained you, Ancient One, who taught you all of this? Did you *choose* to become a Seer?'

The Augur studied him. 'No one taught me of the history of this world, child. And I am not a Seer. I am the Sentinel, the shepherd of this world.'

Tika was in her rooms, staring from the eastern windows. She'd seen the Dragons land a little earlier, just before the snow began to fall again, and mind spoke them to make sure all was well. Cerys snored softly, sprawled on her back close to the fire, and Tika was wondering what exactly she should or could change in the running of this land of hers. A faint knock at her door made her glance round. 'Come in,' she called. She smiled when she saw Veka enter, two folders in her arms. 'Come in,' she repeated, crossing to the hearth.

She sat on the cushions scattered there and patted one, inviting Veka to join her. The girl did so, far from at ease. She held out the folders. 'Dog said you needed these. She would have brought them but her leg hurts.'

'It does?' Tika kept a straight face.

'Yes. She said it was injured in an explosion, long ago.'

'Yes, it was. I think it bothers her occasionally still.'

Cerys climbed across Tika's knees and settled on Veka's lap, her purr a comforting rumble.

'I apologise, Veka. I have not spoken with you or Sney much since you joined us here. I usually try to get to know everyone but somehow I've not paid attention properly.'

Veka made no reply, stroking Cerys's luxurious black fur.

'So tell me, Veka. What do you like best here? Or perhaps there's something you really *don't* like?'

'Oh no. I'm so glad I'm here, truly I am.'

'Would you perhaps have preferred to return to Druke or Salo Manis. Did you have family there?'

For the first time, Veka glanced up meeting Tika's gaze. 'I don't remember having a father.' She smiled. 'That didn't seem strange, where my mother and I lived in the poorest part of Salo Manis. When I was about six, she didn't come back. She said she was going to work, after supper like usual, and she wasn't there in the morning as she normally was. I stayed in the room two days but there was no food and my mother still didn't come back so I went out.' She shrugged. 'A gang of children gave me food, looked after me for a while, then a trader caught me. I'd been shown how to steal but I wasn't much good at it.'

Tika let the pause stretch knowing Veka would continue now she'd begun to talk.

'The trader took me in. I learned much later that his two sons had died so he'd taken me for his wife to look after and she fussed over me. They were kind, then they found I could read and write. My mother had taught me. My mother's name was Leella. That's all I know of her.'

Cerys purred louder, kneading Veka's leg with her front paws.

'And so you worked for the trader?' Tika prompted quietly when Veka remained silent.

The girl gusted a sigh. 'Yes. I learned to do the bills and keep track of the cargoes and the dealers. Hava, the trader's wife, got sick and I started travelling with the merchant caravans. I'd been working on the trade routes for about four years when the sea raiders took our caravan. I saw the trader who'd taken me in, Sadik, killed, along with most of the guards, and then I woke up on the ship with Shea.'

The silence when Veka stopped speaking was a comfortable one, the girl finally seeming relaxed. Tika pulled more cushions behind her to prop herself more comfortably and stretched her toes to the fire. 'Tell me what you enjoy here, Veka.'

'I like walking round the lake. In the better weather.' She gave Tika a shy grin. 'With Pearl, sometimes with the twins and Rivan.'

Tika hid her surprise, only nodding. She had thought Veka wary of the Dragons. 'You like Pearl?' she asked casually

'Oh I do, very much. She wants to know as much as I do. She's wonderful to talk to. There's a crow too, who often joins us when it's just me and Pearl.'

'A crow?' Tika echoed.

'Yes. He's as interested in things as Pearl and I are.'

Tika made a mental note to ask Pearl for more details on this talkative and inquisitive bird. 'You work with Aifa and with Shea and Dromi mostly?'

'Yes. I have most afternoons to myself.'

'But you can't walk in this weather?'

'Sometimes I stay at the school with Aifa. I can't go out much with Pearl in the winter.' Veka looked up suddenly. 'It's all right to go with Pearl? Should I have asked you?'

'Of course not. I'm glad you spend time with her.' A thought struck Tika. 'Have you flown on Pearl's back?'

Veka flushed scarlet. She just nodded. Tika laughed. 'But that's good, Veka! You were terrified on Dragon back when you first came here! Where has she taken you?'

'Along the river, further than we usually walk with the twins, but not as far as Oak Wood or Romaby. On the other side from here,' she added. 'There are lots of narrow canyons Pearl always wants to look at. She wants to know how they were made.'

'How they were made?'

'Yes. Pearl says mountains don't grow the way they look now. I asked Mardis and he said she's right.' Veka gave a slight smile. 'He read a book to her, about how wind and water and cold can wear away rocks. That's how she knew.'

'You thought she'd discovered that for herself?'

Veka nodded.

'My advisors say I should delegate more. I have no clue what they expect me to do. As I pointed out, there are no shops, villages build their own houses. Navan suggested a market twice a year. Somewhere in the middle of the valley, lasting three days or so. What do you think?' From the corner of her eye, she saw Veka pull more cushions behind her too, more relaxed than she'd yet been.

'Markets would be fun,' the girl agreed.

'What about coins? Wouldn't people have to *buy* things?' Tika asked.

'Not necessarily.' Veka frowned down at the cat on her lap. 'When I worked the caravan routes, a few traders took coin for their goods. Sadik took coin occasionally. He said it was wise to have enough in case times grew difficult. Mostly he and the traders he travelled with exchanged cargoes.'

'Exchanged?'

'Yes. Sadik specialised in cloth made by people north west of Salo Manis, beautiful cloth. He took other things too, but cloth was his main trade. When we reached Druke, or went to Gulat or Spurtok, he would exchange his goods for things he knew there were buyers for in Salo Manis. He said it was a waste to come home with a bag of coins and empty wagons.'

Tika sat up straighter. 'You think the villages would have enough different things to - exchange between them?'

'None of them are close to each other.'

'What do you mean?'

'Well, Rivan said it takes Kastin and Sarila over a day to walk to Romaby. He said he and Volk built a little cabin halfway for anyone to rest overnight. They've done the same along the tracks to all the villages now I think.'

Tika stared at her. 'You think a market would be a good plan?' she asked.

Veka blinked, looking over at her. 'Oh yes. It would be fun,' she repeated.

Making an instant decision, Tika beamed. 'Then as of now, you can organise it with Navan. Drag in anyone else you might need. Find a suitable place along the valley for people to make camp - when the weather improves.' Tika grinned. 'I'm sure Pearl will help with that.'

Veka stared in shock. 'Me?'

'Yes, you. You know more about trading than most of us here - who could be better?'

As Veka seemed stunned, Tika asked a blunt question. 'Have you had bad dreams or anything, since you've been here? A lot of people report bad dreams. Most folk have had unpleasant experiences in their lives before and seem to suffer such dreams for a while.'

'I have had bad dreams, yes. Always of that woman, Captain Udanna.' Veka shuddered.

'Udanna is dead, Veka. You are safe. You have a home

here for as long as you wish to stay. Veka, if anything bothers you, confuses you, come and talk to me. I don't bite. I'm usually here, or somewhere around the House. Never think I'm too busy to talk to you or that you're too unimportant here. Understood?'

When Veka nodded, Tika rose, reaching a hand to pull the girl up. Cerys was tipped from Veka's lap and after a baleful glare, set about washing herself.

'Go find Navan and tell him you and he are to organise the markets. Wait! I'll write a note so he knows it's an order!'

Tika scribbled quickly, handing the unfolded paper to Veka. 'Come and visit again when you've time.' Tika smiled.

Veka nodded, took the paper and left but Tika was aware of the girl's interest in the market idea. There was a nervous excitement in her now, but also a determination to do the best she could.

'I notice you haven't mentioned the dreams *you've* been having.' Cerys was working busily on cleaning between her toes, her eyes closed in concentration.

Tika regarded her. 'What do you mean?'

Cerys continued her washing. 'You are such a kitten sometimes Tika,' she grumbled. 'Your dreams *leak*. Not always, but these have done.' She lowered her hind foot and green gold eyes met Tika's. 'Dreams of those children.' Her mind voice was flat, giving no hint whether she thought the dreams were good or bad.

'They're just dreams.' Tika attempted to brush the subject aside.

'No.' Cerys sat up straight, tail across her front paws. 'They are *sent* dreams.'

'Sent? What are you talking about?'

'I've seen her, on the edges. I didn't think you did, but *I* saw her. The blind one who walks in dreams.'

'Zamina,' Tika whispered.

'She has been calling you,' Cerys agreed. 'I haven't spoken to Kija. She hasn't sensed these dreams. I think I do because I'm closer when you sleep.'

Tika sat by the fire again. 'I really do want to see how

those children are managing, Cerys, but I so fear anyone finding them yet. It is far too soon. They have to grow more. Gremara worries me too. That child, Kahn, I'm sure he means her harm. The children grow so very fast, he will surely soon have the power to hurt her.'

Cat and woman sat in silence before Cerys spoke again in Tika's mind. 'Veka will be fine,' she said.

'Yes. I think so. The dreams are memories of the time she was taken as a slave. I hope she deals with the market plan. Navan will be careful with her, I know.' Tika glanced behind her at the windows where yet again, snow was piling on the sills. 'I refuse to ask the Dragons to take us on long journeys yet. It's far too cold for them, no matter what they say.'

'I will travel with you when you visit the children.'

Tika stroked a finger between Cerys's ears. 'Even if it's still chilly?

Cerys ignored that and settled herself more comfortably. 'You rarely think of the boy,' she murmured, closing her eyes.

'No. I noticed that myself,' Tika replied aloud. 'It's almost as though those barely two years he was here ever happened. I feel guilty; he was only a child.'

Cerys heaved a sigh, her eyes firmly closed. 'I told you, he was older than he appeared. Volk and Onion both sensed it, and so did Kija after a while.'

'He should not have died as he did.'

Cerys chose not to answer that remark.

'The dreams from Zamina, I feel no great urgency to them.' Tika returned to the earlier subject.

'No more do I, but she is asking you to visit.'

'Perhaps I should start thinking what to take to them. Syamak will want books for sure.'

'Do you think Youki knows of them?' Cerys's question sounded too casual.

'I don't know. She must know of Gremara don't you think?'

'You said you would serve Youki. I have been surprised by this. Khosa spoke of it once.'

'What do you mean?' Tika stared at the cat in some

confusion.

'Khosa said she was surprised that you didn't serve Mother Dark. It was she after all, who rescued Farn, through Lerran. So Khosa said.' Cerys was now curled in a tight ball, eyes still shut and Tika realised the cat was tense. Her words held more importance than Tika had assumed.

'Cerys, I'm not sure I follow what you're trying to tell me. Of course I hold Mother Dark in enormous respect.'

'But Youki *asked* you to serve her, and Mother Dark didn't.'

Tika shook her head, still unclear what Cerys really implied. Was the cat worried about Youki? Cerys chose to say no more and Tika was left to wonder what had brought these thoughts to her mind. She stroked the cat gently, aware that tension remained in the cat. They stayed thus as the day darkened until the bell warned that the evening meal was about to be served. Tika rose and was turning to the door when Cerys finally spoke again.

'That thing that killed Tarel? It was a creature of Youki's wasn't it? Do you think Mother Dark would have hurt him as thoroughly as that thing did?'

Tika froze, her hand on the door latch. Without replying, she went on, out to the head of the stairs. Such a long flight of stone stairs, but if she fell, she might get some scrapes, bruises, bumps. There was no way every bone in her body would be broken, as had happened to the boy. Tika began to walk down, her thoughts badly troubled by Cerys's suggestion.

It was almost a relief to emerge into the noisy chatter in the hall and have to speak to various people as she passed them. Forcing thoughts of Tarel, Youki and Mother Dark from her mind, she reached her table. She smiled when she saw Navan had seated Veka next to him and the two were deep in conversation. Dishes arrived laden with roasted meat and vegetables and everyone helped themselves.

'I've appointed Veka in charge of organising two markets a year in the centre of the valley,' Tika announced in the relative quiet. 'Navan will be assisting her but Veka has my permission to ask anyone else to help get this idea working. Hopefully, the first market will take place once the weather begins to warm when this stars cursed snow disappears.'

Tika sat down again as chatter increased. She began to eat, half listening to generally enthusiastic comments about her news. She saw Veka staring at her and smiled. 'If you want someone to help, you heard me give the order.'

Veka nodded.

Tika saw how the girl sat straighter. Maybe that's all she'd needed, just a small nudge. By showing *she* had faith in Veka's abilities, already she saw a burgeoning confidence. Tika listened to the talk, joining in occasionally, while at the back of her mind, Cerys' words echoed and re-echoed.

Chapter Ten

The Augur was increasingly weary each time she dismissed Endis after a day of teaching him. There was much she could simply transfer, from her memories to his, but she felt he needed context, he needed to really understand so many feelings involved in this history. Although she knew Endis was becoming aware of his new memories, he was still calm and accepting of the situation in which he found himself.

The Augur knew the day would come, all too soon, when he would truly understand it all. She also knew she must be prepared for the panic or rejection it was quite possible he might display at that point. It had been so very long that she had endured in this body, years beyond counting, and now, at last it was failing her.

Mother Dark had extended the life of this body beyond any other except for Lerran and Darallax. Simert, Ferag, and a few others of the lesser gods who used the human form, at least had the opportunity to return to the gods' space for occasional respite. The Augur, Ashri, had never yet returned there. Not since the day Mother had drawn her deep into the Dark and explained what she was asking of her.

This afternoon, she was weary beyond belief. The final stages of preparing Endis drained her mentally as well as physically. The Augur sat, perfectly still in her chair, but she found herself smiling at a wayward thought. Even her eyelashes hurt right now! *Could* eyelashes *really* hurt?

'Of course they can, beloved child!'

Ashri closed her eyes and sank into the comforting embrace of the Dark. Mother's many voices were muted today, one female voice slightly more distinct than the usual chorus.

'There is still so much to do, so much to teach this boy,' Ashri whispered.

'Hush. Trust me a little longer, sweet Ashri. You have done so well. I know you are tired. I can give you some strength, enough that your aches diminish, beloved child, even from your eyelashes.'

The voice surrounding Ashri in the deep Dark was lovingly amused. 'There will be one more choice for you to make.'

Ashri seemed to float, weightless and pain free in the endlessness of Mother Dark.

'When your long service is ended here, I offer you a choice I have offered no other. You can return to me, to oblivion within my love. Or you can return to the gods' space and live with the few who still dwell there.'

Ashri floated, listening to Mother's voice. She knew she would feel refreshed, a renewed sense of vigour filling this ancient body she wore, when she was returned to her rooms.

'The boy must come to me soon, little Ashri and I will tell him many things. That is when he will decide whether to take the last step.'

'I have no idea if he will accept or deny you, Mother.'

'That is not your worry, my child. We are so close now, to securing a successor to your long service. The shadows I gave you as helpers are once more gathered, re sworn to the service of my Sentinel. Rest, little Ashri. You have done more than even I dared to hope, even knowing how strong you were.'

The Augur opened her eyes again, aware of the gift of some restored energy in her weak form. She was grateful. She knew the final days would be hard, as Endis began to understand where she had been leading him.

When Endis joined the Augur the next day, he noticed she seemed a little less bowed than previously, her limp less pronounced. Again, she had made tea for him and waited as he drank. 'I must speak of Namolos, child. Have you heard this name?'

'I think I may have read it. Tika gave me some of Dromi's reports, of their various travels. He was one from the star fields?'

'He was. He had two daughters on whom he inflicted many experiments and abuses. One still lives. A sad, sad creature now, but she is near the end of her long existence and will soon find peace.'

The Augur spoke for a long while before rising to make more tea, waving away Endis's offer to do so.

'You said you were not a Seer. I was thinking of your words last night.' Endis sounded thoughtful. 'How then can you train me?'

'I told you I was the Sentinel, appointed by Mother Dark, to guard the life on this world.' The Augur paused, aware of how close she was coming to revealing too much too soon. 'There are no Seers, child. There are some who can foretell some events. They have untrained mage talents usually, the result of the blood they inherited from ancestors who were lesser gods. Untrained, unhelped, they become confused to the point of madness.'

'How then did I See the captain, Zhora? I had never heard of him and I'm sure I somehow travelled to his house.'

'You travelled by your own unconscious thought. You dreamed of Zhora and thus *believed* you had a link to him. That's my belief anyway.'

'But what of the crystal Pakan Kelati gave me? I See things in that - faces, people.'

The Augur's eyes widened. 'You have a crystal? Like the one Menan Kelati bears?'

Endis raised his hand to his chest, nodding, slightly alarmed by the Augur's reaction to this news. She was silent but her thoughts raced. She knew beyond doubt that the crystal was wrong. It was not made for a human. What might it do to this boy?. She hadn't sensed it within him, as Menan's crystal always jarred her awareness.

'I am most interested in all you've told me, truly I am, but why would you want to teach me? I can see how tired it makes you.'

'Mother Dark asked that I bring you here and show you these things of the history of your world. You will meet her soon and you will be able to ask her more yourself.'

'I will?' Endis glanced nervously round the room as if expecting some figure to manifest in front of him.

'You will,' the Augur replied cheerfully. 'I can assure you, Endis, she will not harm you.'

'How do I meet her?'

'She will draw you into her Dark. Don't worry child. You will be quite safe.' The Augur waited but Endis asked no more. She had half expected him to question just what he was being trained for but he didn't. So far that hadn't been an urgent thought. She wondered if he was deliberately shying from that, beginning to suspect what her answer might be. When he remained silent, she asked if he had gone up to her old rooms again.

Endis gave her a rueful smile. 'I have. Did you know there are seven floors to walk right up?'

She returned his smile. 'That's why I moved down here long ago,' she agreed. 'I have another room or two to show you here but that can wait a little longer.'

Understanding he was dismissed for the day, Endis bowed and left her. The Augur glanced down at her hand. The cut across her palm was healing but more slowly than it should. Even with the infusion of strength from Mother. Another indication of her condition weakening far more rapidly than she had expected. She leaned her head back. Mother had offered her a choice. Ashri was well aware of what an honour that was but she was uncertain which one she would take.

To return to Mother Dark was such a temptation. To become part of the mystery that was Mother Dark. After the aeons of time here, oblivion would surely be balm. But then of course, she would be unaware of that balm, scattered into thousands of fragments within the Dark. If she returned, to her original form in the palace in the gods' space, would she not want to know what was happening on the world still?

Pulling her hood over her head she considered her choices, aware of the advantages and disadvantages of both. Who still lived within the gods' space? Would she not grow bored there after this existence here in human disguise? But oblivion. Ashri knew Mother allowed some souls to be reborn but she, Ashri, was both more and less than a human soul. Would that course even be possible for one such as she? It was a dilemma Ashri had not contemplated until now, and time was growing short. She sent her senses

111

across to Endis's rooms and saw him busy in the garden, seeming unconcerned.

The thought of the crystal in the boy's chest made the Augur shiver for a moment. Why had Pakan Kelati made such a thing for a human boy when he had no knowledge or interest in the humans of this world? Because she had always felt an aversion to the shard of crystal within Menan, she had never tried to investigate it further. Now that she'd learned Endis too bore such a thing, she decided she should do so while she still had extra strength from Mother.

As usual it took the Augur a while to locate Menan Kelati. Pakan and Menan seemed to spend most of their time disembodied. The other one, Shashina, was very different to those two. Now, after at last sensing Menan's mind, the Augur summoned her. It took longer than she liked but finally there came a knock at her door. 'Come,' she called quietly.

Menan entered, fumbling the latch as she closed the door behind her. 'It is unusual that you ask for my presence,' were Menan's first words. 'Has there been a problem with the boy? It wouldn't surprise me. I found him weak, as are most humans.'

'There is no problem with Endis. He is far more intelligent than I had dared hope,' the Augur replied.

Surprise showed on Menan's face then her usual blank expression returned. 'You are the Ancient Augur, of course, but you too are human. We find humans far beneath our intellectual powers.'

Ashri was startled into a burst of laughter which she saw offended Menan Kelati. So the creature had no idea who the Augur really was, hidden inside this weak body? 'I apologise for my amusement, Menan, but I fear you and your brother Pakan, if brother he truly is, are sadly blinded by your arrogance.' Not pausing to allow any response, the Augur continued. 'I summoned you to ask of the crystal you bear. Why do you find such a physical object a necessity?' Now the Augur sensed a growing confusion and anger from Menan.

'My kind always use crystals for Seeing. They have to be formed by a Maker and are presented when a future Seer becomes accomplished enough to use it properly.'

The Augur shook her head. 'An amplifying device? You actually need such assistance? Alas, I had not realised your powers were so paltry. May I ask, can it be removed safely? I mean permanently? Perhaps it is the presence of the crystal which encourages the madness to grow within you?'

'Of course it isn't. It couldn't be,' Menan snapped back but the Augur heard doubt in her tone.

'Surely it must be a constant drain on you though?' The Augur stared into Menan's face, her own expression guileless. 'To keep such a solid object hidden within your being. You are usually an unbodied form, are you not?'

'Being a Seer is considered of great importance and power among my kind.'

'But you are not *among* your kind now, are you? So who must you impress? You rarely if ever see Shashina, and Pakan only infrequently. I have been aware that most of your Seeings are of events on other worlds rather than this world. How can you possibly affect anything across the vast distances of the infinity?'

'What can you know of such things as worlds beyond this one?'

The Augur grew cautious now, aware that Menan's descent into aggressive bluster could herald the use of powers she was yet unsure of. 'I know far more than you might imagine, Menan, and far more in *fact*.'

'You are world bound,' Menan scoffed. 'My kind travel where we wish.'

'Am I *truly* world bound?' The Augur's clear blue eyes impaled the creature seated opposite her. 'And why do you travel? Were you outcast from your world? It might be amusing to some, to have your powers and cause mischief on world after world?' Her last words were a complete guess but Ashri saw the effect they had on Menan Kelati, and knew she was correct.

'We are superior in every way to all life forms we have encountered,' Menan declared. Her body was wavering, the outline blurring as though her anger was affecting the concentration needed to hold to her human form.

Ashri braced herself; she still had the powers she'd been granted when she was first brought into existence and could use them, even in her present body.

Menan remained silent, clearly fighting for control.

'Tell me what happens to one who is unfortunate enough to have a crystal put inside of them.'

'His powers are enhanced, obviously,' Menan managed to say.

'And if it is removed from him?'

'There is no reason for him to wish that to happen. It enhances him, I told you. Makes him more intelligent.'

'I really disagree with that assumption, Menan, but tell me what happens if it is removed.'

'He will revert to his previous dullness of mind.'

The Augur sat in silent thought. 'It is also a device for you to know where he is, is it not? And yet you still couldn't trace his route here.'

The wavering of Menan's outline was more pronounced but the Augur was at last able to see some of what Menan was actually composed of. Perhaps Pakan was different, stronger; perhaps every one of these beings were unlike each other. The Augur saw the crystal embedded in what would have been a chest had Menan's body been a reality. As she had suggested moments before, she saw how much of the energy which composed the being called Menan Kelati, was being used to conceal that crystal. Ashri was almost disappointed to realise Menan had such very limited powers. Enough certainly to astonish any ordinary person with her tricks and conjurings but there was no real power at all. She relaxed, smiling at Menan.

'You are trying to mock us,' Menan said, even her voice now distorting slightly as her anger controlled her rather than the other way about. 'You will regret it, no matter how ancient or wise you think yourself, little human.'

The Augur laughed again. 'I do not think of myself as at all wise, Menan, but yes, I am ancient indeed, in this form I wear.'

'Pakan's anger will make you realise our strength,' Menan spat back then the Augur's words seemed to register. She drew back. 'The form you wear?' she repeated, frowning suddenly.

'Leave me now. Know that you are a useless presence on the world below and be gone with you.'

The Augur's words rang through the room and Menan Kelati simply vanished. Ashri sat forward, concentrating on following the speck of energy moving towards the boundary of this place. She intensified her focus at the point where Menan would breach that shield to return to the world below. A coruscating flash of light, and the Augur sat back. She had rarely disposed of any creatures she reflected, but now two in a short span of time. Feeling a small glow of satisfaction, she thought that perhaps it was time she left this existence after all.

Dismissing all other thoughts, the Augur watched Endis settle to sleep. For the first time, she really studied him, his physical body, not just his mind. there were no changes or distortions so far at least, to her sight, for which she was thankful. The crystal was a smudge to her senses but she focussed intently and at last was able to see exactly what it was. Unsurprised, she saw it was not a true crystal. Tighter and tighter she focussed, seeing minute mechanisms buried in its very centre. With painstaking care, the Augur began taking the miniscule pieces apart.

It took far longer than she wished and drained the reserve of strength Mother had granted her. By the time the mechanisms were removed, speck by speck, the Augur was trembling with fatigue. She considered leaving the crystal itself for another day then decided to go on. Her hands gripped the arms of her chair as, very carefully, she transformed the crystal to mist and watched as it seeped from the young man's sleeping body. Ashri let herself relax against the pillows at her back and closed her eyes. She had not been able to tell if Pakan Kelati would sense the destruction of something he had Made, but she forced the very last of her energy to strengthening the boundaries surrounding this place. Her work finished, she considered what power Pakan Kelati actually had. If Menan was an example of their beings, then the Augur had no worries. She suspected Pakan was stronger although she couldn't have explained why, but even ten times stronger than

Menan, he would prove no problem to her, weak as this body now was.

Although her mind was alert when she summoned Endis in the morning, her body ached. She had prepared the tea before she called him and managed to return to her chair by the time he arrived. She had time to wrap a piece of rag around her left palm and hide the hand beneath her cloak just as he entered the room. 'Is there something wrong, child?' the Augur asked, seeing his frown.

'I'm not sure,' he replied, reaching for the tea she'd prepared for him. He rubbed his chest. 'There was a sort of odd ache, here, when I woke this morning. I thought it was a call of some kind, that I had to witness something. I tried to summon the crystal but nothing happened.'

'I told you, child, Seers are not what you have presumed them to be. As for the crystal, I removed it.'

He stared at her in utter confusion.

'Endis, *think!* Pakan Kelati *Made* that object. He is a being from another world who knows nothing of humans and cares even less. There were certain things within the crystal which could have caused you great harm. There were also things which allowed Pakan, and quite possibly Menan too, to be aware of where you were at any time.'

Endis nodded slowly. 'That wouldn't be a good thing,' he agreed. 'Why would they want to know that though?'

'I don't pretend to understand them, child. Perhaps it was a strange form of curiosity on Pakan's part. He was all too aware that you are of a completely different form of being to him, so he could have been interested in what the crystal might do to you. That is simply a guess, Endis,' she added, seeing the young man looking annoyed. 'Tika visited Pakan, did she not?'

'She did.'

'It's possible Pakan was aware of the power within her. She was concerned for you so that may well have aroused his interest at last in the humans on this world.'

'Is he powerful enough to hurt her?' Endis sounded anxious.

'I think not, child, but he gave her a gift also I believe?

That gift had enormous destructive power at the place called Gerras Ridge?'

'It did. So many died. It looked as if the hillsides were bleeding.'

The Augur pondered for a while. 'I believe trees then grew on this Ridge?'

'They did indeed. All in one night, thousands of trees. Was that Pakan's doing, or Tika's?'

'Neither. Pakan clearly intended only destruction. Tika might well be able to call trees forth but I suspect it was Youki.'

'Tika spoke of Youki a couple of times,' Endis said.

'Hmmm. I think you should return to Iskallia, child, for a brief visit before I inflict more lessons upon you.' She smiled as she spoke.

Endis leaned forward. 'I had dreams of Youki. Well, of a giant man who seemed to die a terrible death. A small creature clung to him, trying to take his pain, then Youki arrived and wept over their bodies. They crumbled into the earth by her knees.'

'That was long ago, Endis. I think you must convince Tika she must give you the pendant Pakan Kelati Made for her. Such things do not belong in the world below. I would ask that she relinquish it and let you bring it to me. I will not return it to her but nor will I keep it. I will try to see its makings, its exact purpose, and then I will destroy it.'

Endis nodded. 'She may be unwilling to give it to me.' He looked at the Augur. How had he thought she looked so much better yesterday? Now, she was *so* old, *so* weary. He glanced down at her lap and saw her left hand, just slightly revealed as her cloak slipped aside. He saw a bandage roughly tied but she pulled her cloak back over it when she realised where he was staring. 'What should I tell her? She really might not give it to me.'

'Tell her the truth, child. That's usually the best course. If she is reluctant to give it to you, bring her here.'

Endis stood. 'How do I travel there? Suppose she's not there?'

The Augur closed her eyes, white lashes trembling slightly. 'She is in the place called The House. You can move yourself there, but I will do so this time.' Blue eyes met his stare. 'You have more in you now than when you arrived here. You must begin to understand and use what I give you.'

Endis sighed. 'I am trying,' he said. 'One thing: you said you were putting your memories into my mind. Will that leave you - *empty?*'

Such a tired smile greeted that remark. 'No, sweet boy! I should perhaps have said I was *sharing* my memories rather than *giving* them to you. Go. Try to persuade Tika to give you the pendant. If she refuses *I* will bring you both here. There is no real hurry. I will rest while you are gone.'

Before Endis could say any more, he saw lights blazing in dizzying patterns all around him and squeezed his eyes tight shut. Then his feet hit stone and he staggered slightly. Opening his eyes, he found a huge gold Dragon pushed up onto her haunches, eyes whirring in consternation. Slowly Kija relaxed again. Endis saw three other, smaller, Dragons close to her, all registering alarm: Farn, Pearl and Genia.

'I'm sorry,' he managed to stutter. A glance round the hall showed no people present for which he was grateful. Kija lowered her head to study the young man.

'Tika is on her way. She was at the forge,' she told him. 'Why don't you sit down, before you fall down?' she added.

To be honest, Endis wasn't sure he could actually move anywhere at that particular moment. The door opened and Tika came hurrying in.

'Endis!' she exclaimed.

'I believe he is as surprised as we were, daughter of my heart,' Kija said, her mind voice sympathetic.

Tika peered more closely at Endis and sent a pulse of calmness to him. He drew in a breath as his stomach settled and she took hold of his arm.

'Come and sit down Endis.' Tika dropped her fur cloak over the back of a chair and urged him to sit beside her. 'Now, tell me how you are.'

Chapter Eleven

After the first moments, Endis found he could speak freely and he explained how the Augur had removed the crystal from him. Tika had seen the crystal once, when Endis had told her of it. Before he could continue, the hall began to fill with people hungry for the evening meal. Conversation at Tika's table became general and when it became clear Endis was uncomfortable with questions, no one pressed him. Tika joined in the talk although the little Endis had told her caused her some concern. She noticed he ate normally so it would seem he was being properly fed while with this Ancient Augur at least.

'You can use the room along from my quarters tonight, the one you used before. Why don't we go up now and you can explain more about that object you spoke of.' She rose and Endis followed her across the hall, up the long stretch of stairs and into her rooms.

Cerys yawned and rolled onto her stomach. 'Greetings, Endis.' Her mind voice was soft, warm but the green gold eyes watched him carefully.

He stooped to stroke her back and Tika waved him to a cushion as she sat the other side of the cat. 'Can you tell me anything of your training, Endis? I'm very interested but I don't wish to pry.'

Endis sat down across from her. 'The Augur has told me so much, about the history of this world. Pictures in my head of volcanoes, the earth splitting, strange animals long vanished, towns, cities, all gone.'

'So you have to know of the past to be able to See the future?'

Endis looked up at her and sighed. 'The Augur says there are no Seers.'

Tika stared at him. In the light from the fire and the several small lamps around the room, his eyes seemed different but she concentrated on his words for now.

'She told me she is known as the Ancient Augur but in

fact, Mother Dark appointed her as the Sentinel of this world. She watches all that happens here.'

'That must keep her very busy.' Tika managed a casual reply.

'She has helpers who I have yet to meet. They are shadows.'

Tika grew still, her left thumb suddenly cold as ice. She cleared her throat. 'She has shadows at her command?' she asked.

'Yes. Mother Dark gave them to her. She gave shadows to Darallax, but he has never really-,' he paused, trying to remember the Augur's exact words. 'Darallax has never really *used* his shadows. I'm sorry, a lot I don't really understand yet.'

'Mother Dark appointed her?'

'Yes. She has spoken a great deal of how Mother Dark found this world and created the gods and the lesser gods.' Warming to the subject, Endis spoke more confidently. 'First she created Lerran, then Hanlif and then Darallax. After those she created lesser gods. Oh, she spoke of Ferag and another - erm, Simert? They have been collecting the spirits of the dead since humans first grew into existence. I told her I'd met Ferag.' He smiled at Tika who was simply staring at him.

'Why does Mother Dark want the spirits of the dead?' she asked.

'She felt sorry for them. They wandered lost and unhappy so she has them collected and brought to her. The Augur said some of the lesser gods followed Hanlif here when Mother Dark cast him out. She ordered that none of them must ever interfere in any life here. She watches, through the Augur. Oh, the Augur's name is Ashri. She told me that.' Realising he was just rambling now, Endis paused. 'The reason she sent me to you now is that she's worried about the pendant Pakan Kelati gave you. She thinks it might have wrong things inside it, like the crystal he Made for me.'

'What was wrong with the crystal?'

'I don't know, Tika. the Augur said there were small things inside it that she thought would help Pakan or Menan trace where I was. Also things to harm me.'

Tika pulled the pendant free over the neck of the sweater she wore. 'Surely it's too small to hide anything inside this?' It was barely as big as Tika's little finger nail.

Endis shrugged. 'The Augur asked to see it,' he said.

'How do I reach her?'

'She will move us, if you agree to come with me. I think it's very unusual for her to invite anyone there.'

'Where is "there"?'

'Aaah.'

Tika smiled and waited.

'The Augur said it is a place Beyond.' Endis smiled back, pleased he'd remembered.

Tika's smile slid off her face.

'Have you heard of such places? In the Asataria we were told that when people die they go Beyond but I never thought Beyond was a particular place.'

'Places Beyond are where I understand the gods live. I have been to wherever Ferag lives but only when she moved me there.'

'Oh.' Endis frowned, trying to recall what the Augur had said. 'She said there was a gods' space, where the lesser gods lived. They could come and go between there and this world. That's all, I think. Will you come with me, and meet her? She is genuinely concerned about that pendant.'

Tika was silent. Although Endis was quite unaware of the fact, she had kept a mind link open with Kija throughout this conversation. Now she waited for Kija's opinion.

'I would advise you to go with the boy, daughter. The Augur clearly reveres Mother Dark and is esteemed in return. I believe no harm will befall you.'

Endis continued stroking Cerys, allowing Tika time to consider the request.

'Very well,' Tika said at last. 'It's late now and I'm tired even if you're not. I'll come with you tomorrow. You remember where your room was?'

Moving Cerys with great care to another cushion, Endis smiled at Tika. 'Thank you.' He stood and was turning to leave her room when he looked back. 'The Augur is so frail, Tika. I don't think there can be any other person as old

121

as she is.'

Tika heard the affection in his words. 'Have you been looking after her then?' she asked. 'Cooking and so on?'

'I've never seen her eat anything,' he confessed. 'She drinks a lot of tea though. Good night Tika. Thank you.'

A thought from Tika set two lamps alight in the room further along the passage and she stared into the fire, her mind whirling.

At breakfast in the hall, Tika told those round her table that she intended to visit the Ancient Augur with Endis. She assured them there was no need for alarm. She was unsure how long she might be gone but the Augur had expressed concern about the tiny pendant Pakan Kelati had given her. Several people nodded, reminding Tika that not one of them had actually touched the pendant. They had looked at it as she held it up for inspection but no one had touched it, not even Garrol. He was one who nodded when Tika spoke of the reason for the Augur's invitation.

'When I looked at it Tika, it seemed to blur as though it was hoping to stop me looking too closely. I for one am glad that you might learn more about it.'

'Gave me the shivers,' Dog admitted.

Tika was surprised. No one had spoken of this before, but by the expressions on faces round the table, it was clear it was a general feeling. She rose, crossing to the hearth to hug the Dragons. 'Don't be afraid if you can't feel my mind for a while, Farn. I will be quite safe,' she told her soul bond. She hoped she was correct but she really didn't want Farn to panic if he couldn't sense her. Returning to her table, she stood, giving Endis a quizzical look.

'You're in charge of this journey. What do we do?'

Endis rose and stepped towards her, a hand extended. 'I think,' he said as she clasped his hand, then he said no more.

Eyes clamped tight shut against the dazzling brilliance she'd been plunged into, Tika wondered how long this trip would take. She'd barely finished the thought when her feet touched solid ground. Opening her eyes cautiously, she discovered she was in a garden, a riot of colourful blooms on bushes and climbers everywhere. It reminded her at once of the gardens in Darallax's palace on Skaratay, except the colours here were bright and his had been all of muted shades. She glanced at Endis.

'I should have warned you to close your eyes,' he began.

'I did, believe me,' she smiled. 'This is the Augur's home?'

'Yes, but this is where I've been staying.' He indicated a door nearly obscured by huge flowers nodding up the sides and across its lintel. 'There are rooms back there where I write my notes, cook my food and sleep,' he explained. 'The Augur is ready to see you now. I'll take you to her room and I'll wait for you here. I think she wishes to talk to you privately. This way.'

Tika glanced up as she followed him through the garden. She saw no sky, just a diffuse mistiness. Endis took her through an archway into a wide white stone passageway and, looking in each direction, Tika could see only white walls and a vague fogginess in the distance. Endis led her directly across to a door set back some way from the passage and entered the Augur's room. Tika noted Endis's smile as he bowed to the small cloaked figure in the chair. 'Lady Tika of Iskallia,' he said.

Tika moved closer, looking at the Augur. Her hood was pushed back off her face and her great age was all too apparent. Except for her eyes. The Augur smiled. 'Make some tea please, then leave us, child. Please sit down, Tika. Thank you for agreeing to visit me.'

Tika sat down in the chair Endis usually occupied and openly studied the ancient woman across from her. White hair, purest white, as were the eyebrows and lashes; the deeply wrinkled skin. The blue eyes drew Tika most; such a very clear blue they were. The Augur stared straight back, into Tika's own strange eyes. Green eyes, a brilliant green, surrounded by tiny silver scales instead of the usual white. Endis placed a bowl of tea beside Tika's chair then took another to the Augur. To his own surprise, he bent and kissed her forehead. 'I'll be in the garden if you need me,' he said.

The door closed behind him. 'He is a sweet boy,' the Augur murmured. 'He has a hard path to follow.'

Tika merely waited, offering no reply. 'I asked you here because the pendant Pakan Kelati gave you worries me,' said the Augur.

Without hesitation, Tika undid the clasp and leaned towards the Augur, offering it to her freely. The Augur took it in her right hand, staring at the delicate thing. 'It is very beautiful,' she said. 'There are mechanisms inside it, nonetheless.'

Tika frowned. 'I could see nothing, no matter how tightly I focussed. Surely it is too small to hold anything effective?'

'It caused rather a large explosion at Gerras Ridge, did it not?'

'It did,' Tika agreed. 'Then it caused trees to flourish there.'

'No, child, it did not. It enjoyed the destruction, the deaths. I felt it. Pakan too felt it and rejoiced.'

Tika stared at the ancient woman.

'Youki's old magic, which is riddled throughout Gerras Ridge, made the trees grow.' The Augur sat back in her chair, the pendant loose on her palm. 'You serve Youki, so I heard.'

Their gazes locked. Tika nodded silently.

'I would ask that you consider that, child. Youki visits here, very occasionally, but she hasn't been since I destroyed her creature. The one who killed a child so viciously. The same creature who was tasked with guarding you from your birth, and who failed so conspicuously.' She spoke softly, calmly, but Tika heard the truth in each word.

'What would you have me consider?' she whispered, aware not only of the Augur's great age, but also the immensity of her knowledge and power.

'I would remind you of Lerran's sacrifice in restoring Farn to you, whole in body and mind. Lerran, Mother Dark's most beloved child. Did either Lerran, or Mother Dark herself, demand a price from you? But how many have paid, in your service to Youki?'

Tika's eyes burned with tears. A dozen names reeled through her mind without any conscious thought.

'Again I ask you, child, did Mother Dark exact such a

price from you?

Tika shook her head, speechless with sudden grief. The silence lengthened and Tika fought down her tears. 'I understood Youki protects the world,' she said finally.

'She protects what *she* chooses, Tika, who or what *she* deems worthwhile. She made those creatures like the one you saw, Pesh, but they are very few and less with each year, and I believe she is now unable to create more. She was here when Mother Dark found this world and chose to remain here. Youki is old. Even older than I.' The Augur gave Tika a faint sad smile. 'Mother Dark gave two commands to all her creations, gods and lesser gods. That they must wear human forms on this world, and they must not interfere in the natural growth of life here.'

'Youki interferes,' Tika said softly.

'She does.'

'I gave my word. I swore I would serve her, no matter the cost.'

'And there is always such a cost.' The Augur watched as Tika rose and began to prowl round the room while her thoughts raced. She drank her tea and waited.

Tika returned to her chair, sinking into it with a sigh. 'I have so many doubts about my ability to rule Iskallia,' she said. 'I feel I am too stupid to do so most of the time. I miss things or put them aside to deal with something more obvious. Like Tarel.' Her voice dropped. 'My friends noticed things about that boy which I ignored or made excuses for, and you are correct. I didn't consider the cost to Lerran or Mother Dark when they gave Farn back to me. Oh I saw the physical cost to Lerran but I truly thought she would recover.'

The Augur made no comment, simply waiting for Tika to continue. 'If I give my word, I keep it as best I can. How can I take back an oath to serve Youki, as it seems clear that I should?' Then words came faster. 'She always seems so sad, so alone whenever I've seen her. She weeps and it hurts my heart,' she burst out. 'It is a struggle for her to protect her world. Is she one of the Ancient Ones I've heard tell of?'

'No, she is not. Even Mother Dark has no definite idea

of what Youki really is. The Ancient Ones have developed into a different guise since Mother Dark set them here.' The Augur raised her hand, the pendant's silver chain sliding through her fingers, to halt Tika's questions. 'Think, child. Youki is a creature of the very earth that your world is made of. Have you seen creatures who live within the earth, when they emerge into the light of day? Their eyes often water, sensitive to the sudden brightness, not because they grieve. So it is with Youki. As for breaking an oath, was it a blood oath?'

Tika looked blank and the Augur hid her relief. 'A blood oath has serious consequences should it be broken or betrayed. Show me your hands.'

Bemused, Tika held her hands out towards the Augur, turning them to show the palms. There was scarring on her left fingers from burns when she had clasped her egg pendant during the battle when Seela died, but none on her palm. Looking at the scars, Tika added the Gijan children to the tally of what her promise to Youki had cost. 'Thinking of it now, I would have thought Mother Dark would have been greatly angered at the loss of First Daughter Lerran,' Tika said. 'Yet she has saved me twice since then.'

The Augur nodded. 'You have been into the Dark several times but it is not yet your place.'

'Is it yours?' Tika asked bluntly.

'Well, that is an interesting question. Mother Dark has offered me a choice when my service here is ended.'

'What choice?'

'To return to the Dark, to oblivion. No memories. Perhaps to be reborn in some form or another.'

'What is the other alternative?' Tika queried when the Augur stopped speaking.

'To go to the gods' space.'

Tika considered what the Augur had said then she gave a slow nod. 'You mean, to *return* to the gods' space? You *are* one of Mother Dark's creations, aren't you?' She sent a tendril of her mage sense towards the Augur and shocked to realise the woman was physically human.

'That was my choice so many, many years ago, child. I

126

accepted Mother's request to be her Sentinel and remain in human form throughout my service.'

'Endis told me your name. Ashri? Well, there is only one choice to make isn't there?'

The Augur waited with interest. 'You've been here so long, you must *surely* want to watch what happens next, so you have to choose the gods' space.'

The Auger's laugh was bright and young. 'I believe that is the choice I must take,' she agreed. 'Even if I am not permitted to visit this world, I will hear from others what takes place.'

'Others? Like Simert and Ferag?'

'Serida, and others too, return to the gods' space occasionally so yes, I would hear.'

'Serida.' Tika frowned. 'I'm sure I've heard of him.

'He helped you in your fight with the creature Yartay.'

'Oh yes. A hunter god?'

The ensuing silence was comfortable, then Tika spoke. 'What are your plans for Endis?'

The Augur met her gaze. 'You know what I will ask of him, child, except *I* will not do the asking. Mother Dark will do that. She forces none to serve her; She *asks*.'

'He will live here, alone, for as long as he lives?'

'He will have a long life, child. Perhaps not so long as mine but close enough.'

'He is human. At least, his father was human. Humans don't live that long.'

'The lesser gods bred children among the humans. Males gave children to women and female gods bore children from human men.'

Tika tilted her head as she thought over that. 'Is that where mage talents come from?' she suddenly asked.

'It is. I will tell you this, child. The Dragons know of it, the mating of gods and humans, and the gifting of powers. I believe they had forgotten much of what they once knew. The Final Battle was cruel to so many races.'

'Did you ask me here really to tell me these things?'

'I am worried about this trinket. Rightly so I believe. It is a pretty thing. I will remove the mechanisms inside and cleanse it, and you can have it back if you wish.'

'No.' Tika shook her head. 'I don't think so. Will I be able to visit again? Or Endis, later?'

'You are welcome here, child. You carry Mother's pendant. That will bring you here with but a thought.'

The door opened and Endis appeared. 'Tika will return to Iskallia now, child. Why don't you stay there for a day or two before returning to toil at your lessons? You could visit Lorak and Fenj, could you not?'

'Could I? I would like to see them.'

'Then do so, child.' The Augur looked up as Tika approached her. 'As I said, you are welcome here.'

Tika leaned down, kissing the withered cheek. 'I would like to ask more, about who and how to serve,' she said softly.

Endis reached for her hand, and then they were standing in the hall in Iskallia. Dog sat at Tika's table with Veka, piles of papers in front of them. Veka looked startled, Dog clutched her chest.

'I do wish you wouldn't do that,' Dog grumbled. 'Can't you warn people you're just about to pop in? Ring a bell, or shout, or something.'

Tika laughed. 'I don't think that's possible.' She turned to hug the Dragons. 'How long were we gone?' she asked.

'You just missed lunch,' Dog replied with some satisfaction. 'What did the Augur say about that pendant thing?'

'It had things inside it so I left it with her to do as she wishes with it.'

'Good.' Dog turned her attention back to Veka and whatever they were working on.

'Are you hungry, Endis?' Tika asked. 'Come with me.' She took him through to the kitchens. 'It seems we missed lunch,' she told Kastin. 'Can you feed Endis, please? I'm not hungry.'

Leaving Endis to be fussed over, Tika went back to the Dragons. Farn bumped his chin against her head. 'Although we couldn't see what you saw, or hear anything, you were still *there* somehow, my Tika. You felt safe.'

'I was quite safe, dear one. I will tell you of it later. Endis would like to visit Fenj and Lorak for a day or two

128

before he goes back to the Augur.'

'I will take him, daughter,' Kija said before Farn could offer.

'He will go back himself I presume, the same way as he took me. The Augur said I could visit her again.'

'How?' Farn demanded.

'I just have to hold the egg.' Tika patted the front of her sweater beneath which lay the egg pendant she'd found in Fenj's treasure cave on the other side of the world.

'We still don't know what that really is,' Kija's mind tone was thoughtful. 'Iska didn't know did she, but she saw it properly. Most people still don't.'

'I'm beginning to wonder if it's connected to Lerran, or even Mother Dark,' Tika replied. She was aware of Kija's instant attention but changed the subject to warn her to ask no more for now. 'Are you sure it's not too cold for you to take Endis to Dragons Rest?'

'It is midday and not snowing. It will be quite all right. I will leave him there and come back directly,' Kija said firmly.

'What was the place like, Tika? asked Pearl.

'Endis has a garden full of flowers and rooms there too. That's where we arrived. Then he took me across a wide passageway into the Augur's room. That's all I saw. I'll show you pictures later, my dears,' Tika added as Endis emerged from the kitchens.

He had a large covered basket. 'Kastin sent a cake, for Lorak,' he explained.

'You'll need a cloak or you'll freeze on Kija's back. Let's find one in the cupboard.'

They went out of the great hall and Tika found a cloak for Endis as Kija paced after them. Tika pulled open the huge outer doors, shuddering as cold air swirled in. 'I hope to see you again soon, Endis,' Tika called as the young man scrambled up between Kija's wings. He gave her a wave but Kija was already lifting into the sky, flying fast towards the east, to Dragons Rest. Tika watched for a moment then hauled the doors almost closed again and hurried back to the fire in the hall.

Chapter Twelve

Tika spent the afternoon in her rooms, writing her private journal and thinking of her visit to the Augur. When she went down to the hall for the evening meal, her expression was preoccupied and people left her to her thoughts. She stayed in the hall, half listening to the chatter and teasing until everyone wandered off to their beds. Kastin came from the kitchens with Bird, her newest helper, and they extinguished all the lamps, leaving Tika and the Dragons with just the firelight.

Tika moved across to sit on the floor, her back against Farn's chest, and showed them all she'd seen. Apart from Farn's comment that the Augur seemed a very nice old lady, there was silence from the other three Dragons. Tika waited patiently, half dozing, while Kija contemplated what she'd seen.

At last Kija sighed. 'It was interesting that the Augur admitted so openly that she had destroyed the creature which killed the boy. I wonder how she did it?'

'She is a god, even though she wears human form, mother of my heart. I didn't try to touch her power but I would guess it is immense.'

Pearl shifted from one front foot to the other, eyes whirring to show she was nervous of joining this conversation, but Kija lowered her head to watch her, tacitly permitting the young Dragon to speak.

'The most interesting part I thought was about mage powers coming to people who had gods as their ancestors.'

Silence greeted her comment at first.

'I also found that of interest,' agreed Kija. 'It surprised me that she said we Dragons knew of this, the matings between gods and humans. I can find nothing of it in my memories just as I could find nothing about the Elder Races, the Gijan and so on.'

'She did look so very old,' Genia murmured. 'Her hair was the whitest I've seen.'

'No,' Tika said, thinking back. 'I believe she must always have had white hair.'

'Like Mardis's granddaughter,' Farn put in helpfully.

'Yes, exactly.' Tika reached up to stroke his face as he peered down at her. She felt his surge of pride at having suggested something useful.

'She knew of Namolos, of Gremara and the Asatarians,' Kija went on. 'What she said of Youki is of concern. We have *known* of Youki and of Mother Dark, but neither of them have spoken with us much at all. Apart from Lerran long ago. I have memories of Lerran.' She paused, her great golden eyes looking at Tika. 'I fear she was correct when she said Youki always exacts a price, daughter.' She rattled her wings against her back, a sure sign of some agitation. 'I will speak with Fenj when Endis leaves again. I will not interrupt them now.'

Tika got to her feet and yawned. She hugged each Dragon, pulsing affection through the mind links, and made her way up to bed.

In the morning, Volk the Steward arrived in the hall. 'Snow's melting in places,' he announced.

There were cheers of approval around the tables. Even the most ardent snow enthusiasts were heartily sick of the stuff by now.

'Is Onion still living in that ice house he made?' Tika asked.

Volk shook his head, dark eyes twinkling. 'It's melting fastest,' he told her.

'Where *is* Onion at the moment?'

'He said he was going to the library. He's been staying with me the last few days,' Volk replied.

'I'll go and see him now, before he vanishes again.' Tika slid out from behind the table and hurried out.

In the library she found Onion at a table with a large book open before him. As she reached him she saw it was a book of plants. Sitting down, she smiled. 'I thought you knew all about plants,' she said.

'I know a lot but not *all*.' He returned her smile.

'Onion.' Tika put a hand over his. 'I need to know who you serve.'

131

His one brown eye stared down at her. 'I serve *you*, Tika. You are first in that matter.'

Tika's heart thudded, a slow single judder. 'Who is second?'

Onion grinned suddenly, shaking his head. 'No second. Two firsts. You and Mother.

Tika let out a breath she hadn't realised she'd held. 'I thought you served Youki,' she said softly.

Onion studied her, his affection for her clear. 'I knew nothing of Youki until we'd been here a while. I've always loved Mother, then you.' His smile faded and he bent his head closer to hers. 'The flowers don't like her,' he confided.

'Do they not?'

'No. She's not bothered about flowers, only the animals she specially likes.'

'She brought those plants to grow by Akomi and Khosa's graves?' Tika pointed out.

Onion nodded. 'She knew it would please you. She fears you.'

Tika gaped at him. 'Fears *me?* But she is some sort of god. How could she possibly fear me?'

'Well she does,' Onion said without answering her question further. 'She didn't order that thing, Pesh, to kill the boy but she didn't stop her either. She thought you would be pleased and grateful and even more willing to serve her. And she's not a god, not like Ferag.'

Tika knew Onion was enormously fond of Ferag but trying to get clear, concise information from the once engineer was difficult in the extreme. On this occasion he was a little more forthcoming.

'She was confused when you dismissed Pesh. She really thought you would be glad.' He bent even closer. 'She's still looking for that Pesh.' He chuckled and sat back looking happy.

'Is it likely she will visit me, do you think, ask me about Pesh? Does she know Endis is with the Augur, or that I have met the Augur?'

Onion was surprised by the question. 'She doesn't know of Endis or that you even know of the Augur. Youki has

132

visited there too. Not very often, but she knew her when the Augur was just a god, before Mother asked her to be the Sentinel.'

Tika sat quietly. She'd found it was often just comforting being near Onion, even if he so rarely made any sense when he decided to talk. 'Do you talk to Mother Dark?

'She talks to me sometimes. Mostly through the flowers. *She* likes flowers.' He looked back down at his book and Tika knew she'd get no more from him now.

She rose, and watched him reading for a moment, then left him, returning to the hall.

Dromi, Navan, Werlan and Fedran were still at her table and she saw scroll cases in front of Dromi. She sat down. 'What news,' she asked.

'A report from Chaban. They are pleased to tell us there has been no trouble along their western border for some time now. It sounds as though the Kelshan arms men have either wandered back to the city or settled down on farms somewhere. King Troman also sent word. The Meness clan chief, Taysuku, reported his warriors found the Black Clans and attacked them. Reading between the lines, it sounds like another slaughter.' Dromi passed the relevant pages to Tika who read through them quickly.

'A report came from Harbour City too,' Dromi continued then just handed her several sheets of paper.

Tika read, with increasing worry, of new trouble in the far north of Malesh, close to the great Desert. when she looked up, Navan and Werlan were spreading a map across her table. Thankfully, she at least recognised the expanse of the desert so was able to follow the talk.

'All along here.' Navan's finger traced a line along the southern edge of the desert towards the sea to the east. 'There must be hundreds of little villages, like the one we stayed at,' he said. 'The trouble started in the western region. Tiny farming communities burnt down, folk killed and brutalised.'

Tika studied the map, trying to understand distances involved when maps were truly things she found impossible to grasp. She glanced back over Chevra's message and sighed. 'He says Emperor Kasheen has ordered a force of Blossoms to that area. If they're marching from the coast, it's going to take them a while to get there.'

'As he admits, he has very few arms men left himself, and he needs them in Harbour City to continue the rebuilding.'

Tika looked at the map. 'Even if he sent the few he has, they'd take even longer to get there than the Wendlans,' she said. She studied the message again. 'He doesn't say if he's warned the people in the City of Domes?'

'They have no warriors though do they?' Werlan asked. He had read all Dromi's archived records of the journeys with Tika and had an amazing memory for the smallest details.

'I don't think so. They were kept in subjugation by the Qwah. I imagine the Qwah are attacking the villages but I wonder why they haven't tried to retake the City of Domes?'

'They were a very superstitious lot.' Navan frowned. 'Could they believe it is too dangerous to try to return there?'

'Why would they think that?' asked Dromi.

'Perhaps they feared the Dragons?' suggested Fedran.

'They knew we'd left, gone south to Harbour City,' objected Tika.

'Well, what do you want to do?' Dromi sat back, watching her.

'It's obvious from this message that Chevra is indirectly asking for help again.' Tika shrugged. 'I'm sure he hates *needing* help but he's in a bad position. To be honest, I'm not sure how long Harbour City will be able to claim it controls all of Malesh. It's six years since the devastation. None of Chevra's government staff have travelled far beyond the City. There's still so much to do there. But those tiny farming villages have no defence and the Qwah are a ruthless people.'

The four men waited while Tika sorted through the options then she shook her head. 'We have an agreement with Chevra. We have no choice but to at least go and see what's happening and if there is any way we might help.' She looked at Dromi who smiled.

'You are correct,' he said. 'Chevra has not asked explicitly for your help but it's very clear he would appreciate your offer. In this instance, it could not be construed as interference.'

'Then send word to Chevra please, that we will go directly to the north of Malesh and see if we can find out what's going on.'

Dromi nodded, he and Werlan moving to another table to write the necessary message.

'If you let me know which Dragons might take us, I'll choose which Guards will come,' Fedran said.

'They're all hunting now but I'll tell you as soon as I've spoken with Kija,' Tika confirmed.

Fedran left to go to his office, leaving Navan rolling up his map. 'Is all well, Tika?' he asked softly.

'I have things to decide, Navan. It's been pointed out to me that maybe I should have said I would serve Mother Dark after she saved Farn. I didn't even *think* of it, Navan.'

'There has been talk,' he said.

'*What?* What do you mean?' Tika was alarmed.

'Only among us in the archives,' he clarified. 'Rhaki mentioned it once, long ago, and then when you said you would serve Youki there was more discussion.' He hesitated. 'We know Jian too said she would serve Youki but Werlan told us Corman is deeply worried. Jian is, after all, Shivan's sister, Granddaughter of Mother Dark.'

Tika clenched her fists in frustration. 'Things seem so simple, straightforward, then all sorts of complications arise. Is Rhaki here at the moment?'

Navan shook his head. 'He's still at Port Maressa. When do you plan that we go to Malesh?'

'As soon as the Dragons are willing. It sounds fairly urgent from Chevra's message.'

Navan sat back as Dromi came to show Tika the letter he'd written to Chevra. He offered her a pen, wax and the Iskallian seal, and she signed as soon as she'd read it. Dromi sealed it in a scroll case and went out to the great mosaic circle in front of the House to send it on its way.

'Tika would you consider letting Veka come on this journey? She is really doing well with the maps and seems so much more confident. She told me she'd flown with Pearl and isn't afraid of that any more.' He grinned.

'She told me that too! Ask her if she would like to come, Navan, but please don't make her feel she *has* to.'

'Of course I won't.'

It was after midday when the Dragons returned. There was the pleasant sound of water dripping as the snow finally melted from the front of the House. Glad to lose the snow as they were, Sarila and Kastin despaired at the wet slush everyone brought in as they tramped through. They demanded that all boots were to be removed at the outer doors but then stared helplessly when five Dragons paced in.

Tika immediately went to speak with Kija, glad to see Brin had chosen to come here rather than go to Garrol's forge. She explained Chevra's message and Kija instantly agreed to take them to Malesh. 'I will summon Flyn and Twist back from the Port,' she told Tika. 'They can remain here to protect Iskallia with Skay.'

'Where is Storm?' Tika asked.

'In the forge with Skay,' Brin told her.

'May I come?' Genia's mind voice was hesitant.

Tika stroked the dark purple scaled cheek. 'If you are sure you want to, you would be most welcome, my dear,' she replied.

'There will be six of us,' Kija agreed. 'Brin and I will carry four, the younger ones two.'

'Thank you, mother of my heart. I'll go and tell Fedran. When shall we go?'

'Tomorrow, early. We fed well today and can rest until tomorrow.'

In Fedran's office, Tika told him which Dragons would be carrying them and that Kija had suggested they leave tomorrow.

'Onion came in just now.' Fedran spoke cautiously. 'He said he will be coming.' Tika grinned. 'He said he will travel with Genia and Geffal.'

'Well, there you are. That's two Guards you have for your list.'

Fedran scowled.

'Oh, Navan is going to ask Veka if she'd like to come too.' She laughed as Fedran rolled his eyes.

'Am I allowed to choose the rest?' he asked her.

'I'll go and see Telk to tell him he'll be in charge in your place while we're away.' Still laughing at Fedran's outraged expression, Tika headed for the smaller hall where Guards' training took place in winter.

In the morning, sixteen people waited in the hall, all in the blue Iskallian uniform except for Dromi, who wore his usual brown. He climbed onto Pearl's back then reached a hand down to help Veka up to sit in front of him. Tika had already asked Pearl to warn her if she had any concerns for Veka. Onion and Geffal strode over to Genia. and Storm carried Navan as always, with Ketro behind him. The other Guards divided between Brin and Kija and when all were settled, Brin rose, flying to the east through still icy air, before plunging into a gateway.

It was a long gateway taking them north-east to the edge of the Desert which formed a natural barrier to the land of Malesh. They emerged into a clear sky, warm air, and Tika estimated it was near to mid afternoon as the Dragons circled above a long coastline. Brin spiralled down, landing some distance back from the shore, on rough grass somewhat sheltered from the blustery breeze from the sea. Sliding from Farn's back, Tika went straight to Brin whose eyes were already closing.

'Thank you Brin. Rest now for as long as you need. We're in no hurry to travel on.'

He settled himself and was asleep even as Tika turned to Kija.

'It is more tiring the more Dragons and people you have to move through a gateway,' Kija murmured. 'I will seek meat for him in a while.'

Tika hugged her then moved on to speak to each of the younger Dragons. Essa and Dog already had a small fire going and Geffal had found a stream a short distance away. As Tika joined them, she spoke to Veka who was laying out her bed roll beside Ashoki's. 'Was the journey all right?' she asked the girl.

'Yes. I don't know why it frightened me so much

before.'

'Veka, you had seen your friends killed, been taken as a slave, sold to Bodaket, then suddenly come face to face with Dragons. It's not a surprise that everything worried you then, but now you've been safe with us for a couple of years, you can accept things much better.'

Veka smiled. 'I feel quite safe on Pearl and with all of you,' she admitted.

Tika walked towards the fire, noticing that Onion seemed to have vanished. Fedran joined her. 'He went in that direction,' he said, watching as she checked over the Guards.

'He'll be back.' She smiled up at her Captain. 'He always is.'

Fedran muttered something that sounded suspiciously like an oath which Tika chose to ignore. She sat by the fire waiting for the inevitable tea to be made.

'I didn't see any signs of farms or towns as we came out of the gateway,' Essa remarked.

Everyone agreed they had seen only grassland, with the starkness of the desert beginning just ahead of them.

'I could go and see what I can find.' Farn joined the conversation, eager to be helpful.

Tika paused but Kija made no comment. She looked across to where Farn reclined with Pearl. 'You can go and look if you wish, but you *must* remain shielded, Farn. You must only *look*.'

'I'll go with him,' Storm announced.

'Be careful, both of you.' Tika watched both rise into the air, rising high and fast before vanishing from view as their shielding hid them.

Sarila had given them plentiful supplies, fresh baked pies, bread and cold roast meat for their first meal, which they ate as the sun set. Tika was beginning to wonder just how far Farn and Storm could have gone when they returned, drifting down to settle close to the Guards. They clearly had news, their eyes sparkling with delight.

'There are several farms not a long way away but they are all burnt down. No people anywhere near them. We saw another one further along, which looked unhurt then we flew over the desert.'

Tika frowned and Farn added quickly: 'We didn't go over *much* desert, my Tika.'

'There was a group of funny buildings,' Storm put in helpfully.

Tika's gaze turned to him. 'Funny buildings? Show us what you mean, please.'

Storm sent pictures to their minds and they realised they were looking at roughly built huts made of some sort of large bricks or just cloth hangings for walls.

'Qwah,' said Navan.

Tika nodded. Under one large striped awning she'd glimpsed the horses the Qwah treated far better than they ever treated most people. 'Did you go as far as the farm you thought was still untouched?'

'No,' Storm replied. 'We were flying high, that's how we saw it, but we didn't go there.'

Onion, who had returned with no comments in time for food, was lying on his back on his bed roll. 'We could look at that farm tomorrow,' he suggested. 'Surprise the Qwah if they turned up?'

'I wonder if there are other groups of Qwah all along the edge of the desert, preying on the farms?' Fedran mused.

'I can't see how they're surviving,' said Dog.

Navan agreed. 'There were the original people of the desert - the Vintavoy people? They were the ones who grew all the crops weren't they? It looks as though the Qwah fled the City of Domes and probably killed those Vintavoy, taking what they wanted but then having no idea how to replace their supplies.'

Geffal nodded. 'Sounds about right to me. People can be surprisingly stupid. I saw enough of that when I was a child.'

Tika realised she had no idea what Geffal's early life had been like and scolded herself yet again for her ignorance of such things. 'Then we will do that tomorrow but we will only watch. If nothing happens, we could see if there are other groups of Qwah along the desert. Only if the Dragons are agreeable and Brin is recovered.' She looked across to where Brin was snoring softly.

'He will be quite recovered in the morning,' Kija assured her.

'There were cattle wandering on the grass lands, my Tika. We thought they might have escaped the Qwah attacks on those burnt out farms. There were no villages to the south as far as we could see,'

Although she was glad there was a possible supply of food for the Dragons, Tika was still impelled to give them her usual caution. 'Make as sure as you can they don't belong to anyone when you hunt, my dears.'

Kija gave a slightly derisive snort but made no comment. Farn settled by Tika and Storm moved closer to Navan; the other Dragons spaced around the small camp, and silence fell. Tika lay along Farn's side, staring up at the stars. These were the stars more familiar to her from her childhood. The stars in the far south were still a slight surprise to Tika when she stared up from her garden in the summer. She watched them for a long while, even as everyone else slept. Fedran hadn't set any watch, as Sket would have insisted on.

The Dragons would alert them long before anyone could get near to them but Sket had never been satisfied unless he set sentries. At last Tika turned over, closed her eyes, banished the maelstrom of thoughts in her mind, and slept like her friends.

As Kija had told her, Tika was glad to see Brin was his usual self in the morning and quite ready to travel on. The company ate breakfast, packed up their camp and climbed onto the Dragons, Kija leading the way. Tika insisted they flew shielded and at an easy pace. They had covered several miles, over flying three blackened communities where nothing whatsoever seemed to have survived. Kija sent a thought to Tika and Farn flew closer to his mother, so that Tika finally saw the disturbance which had alerted the gold Dragon. Tika focussed her mage sight and she and Fedran stared down as they neared a group of riders. Tika counted twenty seven horsemen and a glance ahead made their objective clear: the cluster of buildings indicating a larger community than the previous places had been. Tika thought perhaps five or six families might well live there.

They all peered down as Kija took them a little higher and began to circle above the buildings. All the company were surprised to see little or no defences, and no sign that the occupants were prepared for any kind of attack. Yet they must surely have been aware of their neighbours' fates, if only by the smoke that would have risen from the burning buildings. Tika mind spoke the Dragons. 'I wonder why no one seems to be watching for danger. They must know what happened to those other farms.'

To her surprise it was Pearl who offered a reply first. 'It doesn't *look* right. They aren't very good farmers, not like in Iskallia. Perhaps they're lazy, or they don't care?'

Tika frowned, looking at people working around the buildings then she felt a spike of alarm. She realised she saw no adults, only children, younger than Veka's fifteen years.

Chapter Thirteen

For the two days of Endis's absence, Ashri simply rested. Her affection and admiration for humans increased daily. Although the life span of this poor body she wore had been vastly extended, its ageing process slowed to its lowest possible level, she ached everywhere now. Her feet, her knees, her hips, her back, her arms. She smiled to herself. She had watched humans, a trifling sixty or seventy years old as this world measured time, struggling on with their gardens, their weaving, forging, day after day, with aches just like she was experiencing now.

The Augur had noticed some humans made a point of complaining endlessly and bitterly about the woes of increasing age while others kept their pain to themselves. Now, she was able to sympathise even more fully with their problems. Suddenly she was glad it would soon end. She had felt ambivalence: Tika had guessed correctly. Yes, she wanted to still watch, see what happened next to the world below, and even more to see how Endis coped with his life. He still had a choice of course, but she thought Mother had chosen well to follow the bloodline of one of the lesser gods which culminated in Endis.

She had chosen even better with Tika, too. The Augur was pulled from her thoughts by a breach in the boundary and she braced herself for her visitor. A sparkle of golden flecks and then Youki stood before her. Her expression was grave although Ashri had never been able to read Youki's moods or her intentions. She smiled in greeting and waited for her visitor to open the conversation. Youki's head tilted to one side, her eyes fixed on the figure in the chair. 'How did you do it?' Youki asked, her tone merely curious.

'Do what, my dear?'

'My creature, Pesh. She served me well, for many cycles of years.'

'Pesh.' The Augur frowned. 'Is she the one who failed to protect the child Tika, and a couple of other children as I seem to recall?'

Youki's lips thinned momentarily. 'You are the Augur, the Seer, the One who Sees all, appointed by Mother Dark. Did you not See what happened to her? I can find not a trace.'

'I do not See all,' Ashri corrected her gently. Inwardly, she was astonished that Youki seemed to *believe* she really *was* an augur, a seer. 'And you, my dear, are not human nor yet are you of Mother Dark, so it is not likely that I can See you or your creatures.'

Youki sank to her knees, tears trickling through her furred cheeks. 'I knew you could not trace us,' she murmured.

Interesting word, Ashri thought; trace rather than just find.

'I was sure it must be you who had caused my dear Pesh's disappearance but now I see you could not have done so.'

'Your creatures flicker sometimes, in my Sight, but that is all.' Ashri spoke the lie quite calmly. She chose to probe a little further. 'The one you speak of, Pesh, she *is* the one who left the child now called Tika to danger and harm, is she not?'

'She was needed elsewhere.' Youki's reply held an edge to it.

'Hmmm. Then she left *that* child I think?' Ashri felt a guilty twinge of shame, but she was rather enjoying herself.

'Another was sent in her place but unfortunately arrived too late.'

'Quite so.'

After a brief pause again, Youki continued. 'Most of the lesser gods who dared to come to my world are gone now.'

Ashri's brows rose. '*All* of them? I thought you told me you'd met Ferag and rather liked her?'

Youki shrugged. 'She confines herself to the Dark Realm and her own Realm She's a silly female but harmless.'

'I also heard you healed a young human of whom Ferag had become fond?'

143

Youki's head tilted again. 'She had a chenzaldi stone. I did little. She was healing when I went to answer Ferag's appeal.'

'So she would have recovered anyway?'

Youki smiled and Ashri felt a faint chill at how feral Youki suddenly appeared. 'It impressed Ferag greatly,' she said. Then, in an eye blink, Youki was on her feet again, standing close to the Augur's chair. A speculative expression crossed her face. 'You have been too long in this form Ashri. Mother Dark is cruel indeed to force you to endure it.'

'It is *my* choice, Youki, always, my choice. Mother suggested, and I accepted.'

Youki patted the Augur's arm. 'You cannot last much longer in this pitiful state. Will you stay in this body, and die as *it* dies?'

'Perhaps. I have yet to decide.'

'Your Mother Dark permits you to choose?' Youki clearly found that surprising.

'Of course she does.' The Augur hesitated. 'Mother Dark extorts no price from anyone.'

The fur on Youki's face and arms seemed to bristle as the Augur's words sank in. 'Nothing is truly worthwhile without a cost,' she retorted.

The Augur smiled. 'On that we will always disagree, my dear.'

Youki still lingered. 'I *will* find out where Pesh is, or what has been done to her,' she said softly. 'If I find someone has hurt her, no matter who, they *will* pay my price.'

The Augur inclined her head very slightly as the shiver of gold hid Youki from sight. She felt the slight echo as Youki breached the outer boundaries of this place. Leaning her head back, the Augur considered what she'd learnt. Obviously, Youki had been unable to sense anything of Pesh. What intrigued the Augur most right now, was that Youki believed the Augur was only a Seer. She had no idea that in fact she was the Sentinel, no Seer at all. Or else, Ashri corrected herself, Youki was playing games: telling her she believed Ashri was but a Seer with no powers to take any action, only sent to witness events when really she knew Ashri had destroyed Pesh?

Ashri *did* know more of Youki than she had revealed to either Endis or Tika. Now, she had to decide if she should take action herself to protect Endis. He was so painfully young, with so little experience of life or of people. Even with her memories he would struggle. She glanced down at her left palm. The scar had healed but it had taken longer than it should. She would just have to put up with it: blood was the only way the boy would reach full understanding.

Behind Tika on Farn's back, Fedran leaned closer to her. 'Look! There!'

She looked where he pointed and saw fresh turned earth. 'Graves. Maybe there's been some illness here, or a previous attack,' Fedran went on.

Tika stared back, towards the desert to the west, and from this height she glimpsed riders. She made a swift decision, mind speaking Guards and Dragons. 'Everyone down except Pearl. You will stay high, Pearl, keep Dromi and Veka safe. Once all Guards are down, all Dragons stay in the air and shielded. Quickly now.'

She saw several children near where the Dragons landed look around in some alarm at the sound of wings but her company remained shielded even as the Dragons rose again. She saw Onion looking at her and nodded, releasing the shielding around both him and Dog. 'Get the children inside somewhere, Dog. Fast.'

Children yelped as two blue uniformed people appeared in front of them but Tika sent pulses of compulsion and calmness over them. They listened as Dog spoke quickly then began running to a stone built barn, calling others to join them. Kija sent images to Tika, of the approaching riders who would be visible to those on the ground in heartbeats. Fedran had signalled to the Guards even as Dog and Onion herded the children inside the barn and Garrol sheltered by a fence with Kazmat who had already strung his bow and nocked an arrow.

Across from them, Ashoki had scrambled onto a water butt at the corner of a smaller building, climbed onto the roof and crouched against the chimney, her bow also at the ready. Ketro was similarly perched on another roof. 'When will you release the shielding?' Fedran asked, watching Geffal standing at an open upper window of another small house just beyond Garrol.

'When the Qwah arrive.' Tika shrugged. 'It's not the same group we saw earlier, unless others have joined them.'

Fedran looked down at her. 'How many?'

'Over forty.'

'Not so bad,' he said.

Tika smiled and loosened her sword in its scabbard. Fedran's sword was already drawn and Navan, at her other side, drew his. 'Do you really need to stand here in the open like this?' Navan asked conversationally.

'I will release the shielding when I'm sure of their intent. They may not be coming to attack.'

'Oh, of course not.' Navan nodded. 'Silly me to think it's blindingly obvious that's their plan.'

Now they could hear hoof beats and Tika moved forward a few paces into the centre of the space between the cluster of buildings. Then they heard shouts, fierce war cries and Tika drew her own sword. She sent rapid orders to Kija and Brin and released the shielding which had hidden her and her Guards from sight. The first riders thundered into view. Standing quite at ease, Tika hardened the air around herself and the two men with her. The leading riders charged between the houses, two swinging either side of the leader, and bending low, with drawn swords. One fell, an arrow in his throat. The other hit the hardened air, his sword flying from his hand. He screamed as the collision snapped his arm but he didn't suffer long as he was felled by another arrow.

Horses slid into each other, whinnying and fighting their bridles, and the Qwah raiders stared wildly in all directions. Tika released the air and stepped close to the leading horse, her sword sliding up under the man's ribs. Then Fedran's sword took another warrior to Tika's left even as Navan engaged another on her right. She saw Guards moving in, pulling men from their saddles, and the air filled with the clash of metal and the smell of death. Tika fought whoever appeared in front of her, pausing when one voice suddenly screamed her name among a stream of words she didn't understand. She stared, then smiled. She couldn't think of his name but he was one of those ordered to take her and her company away from the City of Domes and to kill them in the desert. He pushed one of his fellows aside. The man stumbled as Garrol's axe sliced through his neck and shoulder.

Tika was vaguely aware of that but was watching the Qwah who she recognised rush towards her. He continued shouting but she understood not a word so she just waited, her sword hanging loose at her side. He struck downwards, a double handed slice, and then nearly fell. Finally he stopped shouting, spinning to find she'd moved two steps to her left. He snarled, lifting his sword for another blow. As his sword came down, Tika's sword, barely half the length of his blade, blocked his stroke and again, she moved back. His expression grew serious, wary, at last.

He could never have imagined a woman, as small as she was, with a sword he would have considered a mere toy, could block any attack he could make and suddenly he was more cautious. He stared into the strange, brilliant green eyes and saw her begin to smile. He gave an enormous bellow of rage and swung his sword in a side cut, and then froze, staring at the small black blade buried in his chest. He had time to look again into the woman's face. The smile remained but the green eyes glittered like splintered ice. He shivered but whether that was fear or approaching death, who could tell?

Tika withdrew the sword then looked around. She was impressed how quickly her Guards were dealing with the Qwah. A good half were dead and of the remainder, several had thrown down their weapons and surrendered. Shea and Jarko stood over six such men who knelt on the ground, hands on their heads. She watched as Essa sliced a man's throat and tossed him aside. Garrol was cleaning his axe on the robes of a fallen Qwah, watching as Navan and Fedran dealt with the last three attackers. Tika stepped over several bodies to join Garrol. He grinned up at her. 'Not as invincible as they thought they were, eh?' he said.

147

Tika glanced up, sensing the Dragons had dropped their shielding. She watched Brin and Storm flying north, presumably checking the Qwah's route to this small settlement. The other Dragons followed Kija as she circled lower, finally settling a short distance away. Essa and Navan were checking the bodies and piling them together. They turned to look at Tika, having removed various weapons and trinkets from the corpses and thrown them to one side.

Tika raised her hand. Cold blue fire flashed from her fingers, blanketing the heap of bodies. When the fire winked out, the bodies were gone. Turning back to the houses, Tika saw the six prisoners looked utterly terrified now, seeing four Dragons reclining in their line of sight and having witnessed the incineration of their comrades. She checked the Guards but there were no serious injuries; a few cuts, a fair number of bruises but nothing that needed her healing powers. Looking at the six Qwah prisoners, Tika saw two were young, the others in their thirties and older.

'Which of you speaks the common tongue?' she asked.

One of the younger ones ducked his head. 'I speak small,' he said.

An older man next to him snarled something and Jarko knocked him onto his face.

'Come here,' Tika ordered the boy.

Shea hauled him to his feet and shoved him towards Tika, who moved a short distance away from the group. 'How many of you are in the desert?' she asked.

The boy frowned then nodded. 'Many.' He waved a hand.

Tika sighed audibly and waited. Finally the boy held up both hands, the fingers spread. 'This many hundred maybe are.'

'I'm guessing you killed all the Vintavoy farmers and now have no idea how to feed yourselves?'

The boy scowled in concentration then he smiled. 'Vintavoy,' he agreed and drew a finger across his throat.

'Food,' Tika repeated.

'No food much.'

She nodded at Ketro who stood nearby. 'Put him back

with the others for now and move them further away.'

Ketro pulled the boy back to the other prisoners. 'What do we do with them?' asked Fedran.

'We'll discuss that later. Are the children still in that barn? I hope Dog or Onion have found out why they're on their own.'

'What about these horses?' called Essa.

Tika glanced over. Most of the horses seemed to have scattered, stars knew where, but perhaps a dozen remained, grazing quietly quite close to the Dragons. Tika realised Kija had calmed them. She saw Veka had joined Essa and Dromi was beside Navan. 'Leave them for now,' she replied to Essa., 'Perhaps they'll be of use to the farmers.' She called Jarko and Shea away from the prisoners and walked towards the barn. The man who had snarled at the boy immediately made to rise then he gasped. Tika had set a tight restraining ward around each of them. She glanced back, met his shocked gaze and grinned at him.

The barn door opened, Dog came out to meet them. 'Most of the children watched from up there,' she said, jerking her thumb up at the windows in the upper storey.

'Why are they here alone?' Tika asked.

'They're not.' Dog grimaced. 'Wounded adults in the loft up there. This place was raided a while ago and most of the adults were killed or injured. The children were told to grow more crops and the Qwah would be back to collect it.'

'How many injured?'

'Twenty three. Some pretty bad Tika. Onion's up there with them.'

'I'll go up now.' Tika followed Dog through a crowd of children, up a wide ladder at the back of the barn. Before they reached the top, Tika was swamped with the pain and fevers of the people lying in what was usually their hay loft. A quick check with her mage senses and she knew which were in most urgent need. 'I'll need water to drink and then they'll need water to get cleaned up,' she said, walking round and between the prostrate figures, some of whom were silent, some who moaned softly.

Tika settled on the floor beside a woman whose hair was wet with fever sweat, sent a thought to Kija, and sank into her healing power. She worked through the rest of that day and long into the night, Onion and Navan close beside her. Navan gave her water at frequent intervals, Onion kept his hand on her back, sharing his strength along with that of the Dragons. When at last she'd dealt with them all, Tika stretched, groaning as her back clicked.

'Food and sleep.' Onion smiled at her.

Looking around the hay loft, she was surprised to see Veka with Ketro still cleaning away bloodstained clothes and bedding. Navan followed her gaze. 'Veka's doing well. She offered to help,' he murmured.

The lower floor was empty but Navan and Onion took her back to the Dragons. She saw the prisoners, presumably asleep but she checked her wards anyway. Essa had made camp away from the buildings and Tika saw children huddled among her Guards, all sound asleep. Kija had shared Tika's healings, showing the images to the Guards who were all still awake, waiting for her return. Dog brought her a large bowl of stew and half a loaf which Tika wolfed down. 'Some of them will be up and about tomorrow, more of them will need more time to fully recover,' she told them.

'Some were very badly hurt, my Tika.' Farn as always was much troubled at the sight of serious wounds.

Tika leaned back against his chest, reaching up to stroke his face. 'They were, dear one, but they will learn to cope.' She gave a jaw cracking yawn and blinked at the chuckles around her.

'Sleep, Tika,' Navan told her. 'Tomorrow is another day, and you can sort out what to do then.'

With no arguments, Tika lay down, snuggled against Farn and slept instantly.

Everyone else soon followed Tika's example, only Brin staying half alert through what was left of the night.

The sun was well clear of the horizon when the camp stirred. Dog put more kindling on the fire and staggered off to fetch water from a well they'd found yesterday. When Tika roused, she found the children had gone searching for their healed relatives. The Guards were gathered round the fire except for Onion and Veka who had gone to check the

150

wounded.

'What will we do with those prisoners?' Dromi repeated Fedran's question of yesterday.

'Let them draw straws,' Tika replied steadily. 'The two who draw the shortest can take word back to the Qwah to leave these farms alone.' Her words were received in silence.

'And the others,' Dromi pressed.

'They will die.'

It was Kazmat who spoke into the ensuing silence. 'That is fitting punishment,' he said, satisfaction in his words.

'All of you understand how fragile some are when I have recently healed them.' Tika waited for nods from her audience. 'Spend today talking to them, try to explain what's happened. Except for you Geffal, and Seko.'

When just the three remained, Tika smiled at them. 'I would ask you to fly east,' she began.

'I'll take them!' Pearl interrupted, then paused, her eyes whirring anxiously.

Tika hid a smile. 'That is kind of you, Pearl. I am grateful for your offer.' She twisted back to the men before her. 'Chevra said Emperor Kasheen ordered a force of Imperial Blossoms to work their way along the desert edge, clearing out the nests of Qwah wherever they found them.' Tika looked over her shoulder at Pearl. 'Do *not* fly too far for your strength, dear one. That is not what I want you to do. I'm hoping you might glimpse the Blossoms advancing although I have no idea when they began their march from the east coast. Chevra didn't make that clear.'

'And if we do see them?' asked Geffal.

'I'll write a message. They should recognise your uniforms and I don't think many others travel with Dragons.' She gave a wry smile. 'Tell them what we've found so far and ask for news of their successes. I don't imagine the Qwah would have much fun against Blossoms.'

Tika reached for her pack and rummaged under a stack of clothes to find paper, ink and pen. She could have asked Dromi but he had discovered the headman of this place and was busy talking with him. Consequently, the writing of the message left a certain amount to be desired in the matter of neatness and an unfortunate number of blots, but Tika signed it anyway, sealed it and held it out to Geffal. 'Take supplies for the day but I expect you back within the day.'

'Tomorrow morning?' Pearl asked, to be absolutely sure.

Tika stared at the young Sea Dragon, saw both Geffal and Seko grinning, and sighed. 'No later than midday tomorrow then, Pearl. I won't be pleased if we have to come looking for you. And *be careful!*' She rose, hugged Pearl and watched Geffal and Seko fetch their packs and climb onto her back.

Farn ducked his head down to Tika's level. 'We thought we might hunt, my Tika. Perhaps these people might like a feast?'

'That would be kind of you, dear one. Where are Brin and Storm now?' Tika asked Kija.

'They went to search along the desert for any Qwah.' The gold Dragon's mind tone was calm.

'What will they do if they find any?'

Kija turned to meet Tika's gaze. 'They will fire any camps they find, daughter. They recognise Qwah from Vintavoy, but so far they have found none of those farming people.'

Tika nodded. Such an action would have shocked her a short while ago; perhaps she should still be shocked. Knowing how brutal the Qwah usually were, and having spent the better part of yesterday healing the terrible wounds they'd inflicted on this small community, she offered no objection. She moved to Genia. 'Is all well, Genia? Do you regret asking to come with us?'

Pale lilac eyes regarded Tika. 'I am glad I came. I do not understand many of your human ways but this I *do*.'

Tika showed her confusion at the remark.

'Bad humans hurting far more helpless humans and their children,' Genia went on to explain. Her mind voice was barely a whisper in Tika's head. 'So it was becoming, in the Sun Mountain Treasury. It is the reason I sought out Kija.'

Tika was appalled. 'Seela's Treasury? Dragon attacking Dragon?' she asked.

Genia gusted a sigh. 'Dragon was *killing* Dragon,' she corrected.

Tika had no reply to that and then Genia and Farn rose into the air, heading south. Tika hugged Kija in silence then made her way to the western side of the houses, to where Fedran had pointed out fresh dug graves as they arrived yesterday. She noted several of the mounds were small. Not just adults had died here then. She sat beside the graves and stared west and south. The land was very flat, but it became rocky, hilly, perhaps a mile to the north.

These farmers must have thought the desert hills offered both building material and shelter. Her fingers dug idly into the soil and then she paused. She could always sense the circles, and water courses, through the ground. What else might she feel? Tika closed her eyes and let her mind sink down, into warm welcoming earth.

Chapter Fourteen

Most of those whom Tika had healed joined her camp that evening. Three had to be carried, having lost at least part of a leg or foot. Tika had spent time with these three, two men and one woman, explaining that she could heal but she could not replace missing limbs. Garrol had measured them and he and Ketro had already made crutches for these three. Tika was aware the number of women was greater than that of the men and guessed the new graves held the answer to that. Several of the older children had talked to various Guards, explaining how they'd tried to help their injured elders and had buried the dead.

Tika was aware her Guards had been gentle, praising those children who had desperately *tried* to help, had done what they could to comfort younger ones. They told the Guards that it had been eight days since the attack but the Qwah had come from the east, not the west. As the sun sank, some of the women more fully recovered, helped Tika's Guards hand round a good meal, and, to Tika's relief, Brin and Storm reappeared.

A sudden silence fell over the farming people as they watched the enormous crimson Dragon settle, light as a breath, and pace towards them. The far smaller, more slightly built grey green Storm landed and settled beside Farn, his eyes flashing. Onion had sat down next to Tika to eat and now he leaned towards her. 'Ask Brin to tell everyone what he's seen. It will cheer them, and stars know they need some cheer,' he murmured.

Tika glanced across the fire to where Brin reclined behind Fedran and Essa. She spoke aloud. 'Brin, tell us all what you and Storm discovered.' She paused, then added: 'Show us pictures, too.' She looked at the farm people. 'Brin will speak in your minds. He and Storm have been searching for Qwah camps today.' She watched people's faces. Most showed astonishment as the deep male voice began to talk inside their heads, but none showed any fear.

Brin showed pictures of his flight over the start of the desert land then they saw a camp, similar to the one Tika had seen previously. She held her breath as fire poured from Brin and a similar stream of flame came from Storm, just visible beyond Brin's left wing. The Dragons had circled and returned to deliver another blast of fire. Yet again they turned, and those watching the pictures saw only blackened ruins, figures lying unmoving, horses running in all directions. Brin's mind voice resumed. 'We found four more such places, Tika, and we dealt with them in the same manner.'

Before Tika could comment, just as Onion had suggested, there was cheering from the farmers. Brin pushed half up on his haunches in alarm before he realised they were *pleased* with what he'd shown them. His eyes began to sparkle and Tika smiled. She would wager Brin would be occupied regaling these new admirers with some of his stories this evening. But she saw Onion had been right. She looked at the faces of those she'd healed and saw life, and hope, had been rekindled in them.

Later, in the star filled dark, Tika saw children sleeping cuddled close to a parent they thought they'd lose, and sent a thought to Brin. She reminded him that most of the adults were only recently healed, several from grievous wounds. He should let them rest soon and tell more stories tomorrow, she proposed. She waited as the present tale drew to a close and his audience sighed. She wasn't sure if the farmers believed the stories or were just grateful for some unusual entertainment, but they seemed content enough.

Essa had reported the houses had been ransacked, and none of the wounded had yet asked to return to their homes. She and the Guards had spent much of the day trying to clean and restore some order to the far from luxurious homes. Now Tika watched Dog, Onion and Shea, going among the people with whatever blankets, rugs and pillows they'd found, so everyone could sleep where they were. It was a warm night, it would do no harm to let them stay where they were.

'What did you do, my Tika?' Farn murmured sleepily,

as the camp grew quiet.

'Do? What do you mean?'

'When Genia and I went to find meat for this feast. You did something. I felt a sort of warm hug.'

'I just tried touching the earth. Go to sleep, dear one.

Farn curled tighter around her and slept almost at once. Kija spoke on a single mind thread.

'You went deep, daughter of my heart. I could not follow you. As Farn said, I felt only a warm embrace.'

'I'm still trying to understand it myself. Let me think more. There were no words, just feelings, and foggy pictures.'

'Foggy pictures?' Kija was puzzled by the words.

'Pictures that were half hidden, not clear. I don't know who the earth is, or what it is, or if there is some being within the earth who was trying to communicate with me.'

'I will leave you to think, daughter, but I wonder. Could this be the one who made the circles?'

Tika stifled a groan. 'Kija, I don't know. It's just that after speaking to the Augur, I have wondered even more about what powers I might possess.'

'You use your true powers so rarely, my child. We know you could do far more than you have so far chosen to do.'

Tika absorbed that comment and could think of no adequate reply. 'Sleep well, mother of my heart.' She sent that thought and then tightened the usual protections around her own mind. There was too much going on right now for her to take the time to give serious thought to her own personal concerns. She resolved to retreat to her tiny cottage for a few days solitude as soon as the chance arose.

Next day, Dog and Essa moved to speak to Tika as soon as breakfast was done. They sat beside her, looking north towards the brown hills which rose at the beginning of the desert. 'What Brin showed us last night,' Essa began. 'Is there anyway of knowing if there are more camps, deeper in the desert?'

'Can't you far seek?' added Dog. 'We know you don't like the idea of letting the Dragons fly too far in. I remember that desert as well as you do, Tika. I'd hate to see them suffer like that again.'

Tika nodded. 'I'll far seek when Kija comes back. I suspect most of the Qwah will have moved closer to these lands.' She indicated the buildings in front of them. 'If all these settlements are as undefended and open as this one, they are easy picking for the Qwah.'

'I can't imagine the Qwah changing their ways, you know. I'd wager they'll always prefer to just take whatever they want rather than actually try their hands at farming for themselves.'

'That boy said there were thousands of Qwah. Do you think he was just trying to frighten you?'

'I don't think their numbers can ever have been very high, Essa.' Tika considered the idea. 'There weren't crowds of them in the City of Domes, were there?'

'They were more like a military group, who Kertiss had hired as his rule enforcers,' Dog agreed.

'Hmmm. You think they've always been just a small tribe, who survive on bullying other less violent tribes?'

'There were stories of similar tribes among my people, but long ago now.' Essa frowned in thought. 'That would make sense, Tika. Those camps we saw from Brin's mind were scrappy, not well made or organised.'

'As if they've never learnt to do anything except ride those horses and boss everyone else around,' Dog agreed.

'Whoever their leaders are, they can't be too clever,' Tika remarked. 'The farms we saw that they'd burned to the ground. How did they think more crops would grow, and who would harvest them?'

Essa drew in a thoughtful breath. 'Once they had no access to food here, they'd start moving south. There are no towns in such a vast area of Malesh yet all these farms were sending their excess to the enormous monster that was Harbour City.' She grinned at Tika. 'And since the devastation, I would guess they could probably overrun what's left of that place.'

'They don't know of Chevra's treaty with Iskallia and Wendla though,' Dog pointed out.

'I wonder if all these are separate groups, or if they do answer to a single leader?' Essa's eyebrows formed a single

157

line as she thought more. 'How long do you intend to keep the prisoners alive?'

'I will kill them as they sleep,' Tika replied calmly. 'They deserve death but I do not believe it should be made a public spectacle.'

'Will you send one back to their camp, with news of their defeat here?'

'I don't think so, Dog. From Brin's pictures there is no camp to the west left with anyone living, so unless they know of another Qwah group there's no point in warning them now. Did you feed them yesterday?'

'Fedran said to give them travel bread and water,' Essa told her.

'Let's go and see if they have a leader they're willing to talk about.' Tika stood and strolled across the short distance to where the six men still sat.

The man who had growled at the boy yesterday, burst into speech as Tika, Essa and Dog approached, then he glared at the boy. 'He say. where is food,' the boy reported, an insolent grin on his face. 'Qwah, we eat meat.'

'Dead men need no meat,' Tika replied.

The boy looked confused then spoke to the man, and shrugged as if he hadn't caught Tika's meaning. The man understood all too well. His eyes narrowed but Tika spoke before he could. 'Do you have a leader among the Qwah?' she asked. 'A chief?'

After a moment's thought while he processed her words, the boy shook his head. The man spoke again, his words sharp with anger. The boy listened, paling slightly.

'He say, who can us be killing? You women do killings?'

Tika quirked a brow. 'Well, I killed several of your friends without too much trouble. Does it matter who kills you? Dead is dead after all.'

The boy spoke to the man again but before he'd finished, the man burst out with another torrent of words. Tika suspected he could understand enough of the common tongue to get the gist of what she said at least. By making the boy translate, perhaps he thought he could learn more from anything she or her Guards said between them.

158

Another man reached over and tugged the speaker's arm and was angrily shaken off. Tika muffled his ranting with a scarf of air and asked the boy what had been said.

'He say, weak are you,' the boy said, now clearly confused and alarmed. 'Women can fight not.'

'Didn't he tell you that it was I and my company that cost you the City of Domes?' Tika replied.

The boy lapsed into silence, staring at the man who was obviously still shouting although his words were unheard. Tika shrugged, turning her back on the Qwah and retreating to their camp with Essa and Dog. 'Where's Fedran?' she asked, unable to see her Guard Captain anywhere near. 'What's everyone doing today?'

'Jarko and Ashoki are with some of the children and the headman, Metti. They're explaining some of the training exercises,' Essa said. 'There are plenty of weapons we took from the Qwah so they must learn to use them.'

Dog set the kettle over the fire again, glancing up at Tika. 'Apparently Metti told Fedran he had some military experience years ago. He said he couldn't possibly be useful now he's lost half his leg.' She grinned. 'Ashoki told him off. She pointed out he still had a voice so he could teach the children *some* sort of defences. Fedran stayed with them while Jarko and Ashoki started simple drills with the children. Many of the women joined in too. They're in that barn.'

'Remember that village we stayed at when we first got out of the desert? Zeminth was their leader?'

When Tika nodded, Essa continued. 'They had dug that large cellar, where they hid with their animals, when the Qwah raided. Perhaps something similar could be made here? And I really think you should speak to the adults about living in slightly larger groups. I doubt there'll be many Qwah left to bother them once Brin or the Blossoms have worked through the region, but things have changed since the devastation.'

Dog poured boiling water into a tea pot. 'One of the women told me no wagons had come to collect their surplus crops for three years, but they had heard nothing at all from Harbour City. Like it or not, I don't see how Chevra will be able to claim he rules this whole land now.'

'So there were plentiful supplies stored here for the Qwah to take? How will these farmers live now? I see no animals around. How far is it to the next settlement?'

'Metti said it was four or five days walk. Fedran asked him yesterday.'

'There are the Qwah horses, if anyone here can ride them,' Tika suggested. 'Perhaps they can get a few goats, hens, from another settlement?'

'Dromi was talking to some of the women today he said,' Essa told her. 'From what we heard among them last night, Metti might be the headman in name but the women make the decisions.' She grinned down at Tika. 'The bits I heard were interesting. One woman said they had wanted to take in several groups of people to enlarge this place, but the men refused. Those groups went on west.'

'So presumably they were killed in those places we passed?'

'That's what I'd guess,' Essa agreed.

'Hmmm.' Tika thought. She'd healed eight men and fifteen women of various ages between late teens and forties or more. She hoped Dromi would convince the women to form a council where their opinions held more importance than they seemed to now.

'They've been venturing into their houses today,' Dog said. 'I think they were afraid of what they might find which is why we decided to clean up what we could. Some of the children said they'd taken bodies out of them.'

'The children seem to have reacted well to a nasty situation. Sounds like they may have good future leaders among them, anyway.' Tika studied the sky to the east and Dog laughed.

'Pearl will be back. Don't fret so!'

'I know, but I just do,' Tika retorted. 'I should go and talk to some of them, shouldn't I?' she ended, rising to her feet.

The three walked across the grass towards the buildings. 'It looks like the fields have been planted,' Essa observed. 'The Qwah probably weren't aware of that. They really do seem a very arrogant lot, Tika.'

Tika had noticed there were no young babies, the children all looking to be four or older. She wasn't surprised to find Brin by the side of the big barn with the smaller children climbing all over him. Genia watched at a distance, clearly not entirely sure what was happening. Storm was asleep and Kija enjoying the sunshine. Suddenly there were shrieks from the children making Tika jump. Then she saw Farn had crept around the end of the barn and swooped on the children with his wings half spread. Tika relaxed, realising Farn was enjoying himself immensely and she followed Essa towards a group of women talking by the barn door.

Tika enjoyed the morning, listening as the women spoke of their determination to continue farming here and their hopes more folk might join them.

'One day this will be a proper village,' said one grey haired woman. She was the one who had had her right foot lopped off by a casual sword swing as she'd gone to the aid of her husband. 'A proper village, Lady Tika, and I say we will call it Tika's Grace.'

Tika was taken aback but all the women nodded their approval. Not having any idea how to respond, Tika was grateful to see Pearl circling overhead and she excused herself from the group to hurry back to greet Geffal and Seko. She was pleased to see both men made a fuss of Pearl when they'd slid from her back. Tika hugged her. 'I'm glad you're safely back, my dear,' she said before turning to hear the men's report.

Geffal held out a scroll, marked with the glyph of the Crystal Emperor.

'The Blossoms main force is some distance away,' he said. 'Over a hundred miles we reckon from the description. We met a smaller force, thirty Blossoms under the command of Officer Tenzee. He said it's taken them longer than they'd hoped to get as far as they have as there seemed far more Qwah camps to deal with, closer together than they'd expected. Officer Tenzee's force are perhaps twenty miles east of here, maybe a bit more. We told him what we'd seen and he said he'd try to be here within a day or two. We saw three untouched settlements before we found

161

the Wendlans but Pearl kept us shielded and we didn't try to contact them.' Tika read the message Officer Tenzee had sent and found it more or less repeated what Geffal had reported. The Blossom did mention that he had two mages in addition to his warriors. She went to sit beside Kija, thinking for some time. Later she discussed her thoughts with Dromi and reached a decision.

Once more her Guards made a good meal later then Tika stood to speak to them all. She told the farmers what had happened in Harbour City, the enormous earthquake, the extensive loss of life. Several of the adults nodded, saying they'd heard only bits of news from rare travellers. Then Tika showed them pictures from her mind of the far southern coast. The sprawling City had once stretched very nearly from east to west coast and her audience grew still as they saw the new pictures of a barren landscape, devoid of buildings.

Tika continued to speak, as she and Dromi had agreed, trying to simplify the ideas she wanted to help them understand. She told of the new town on the western coast, independent but allied to Harbour City. She spoke of the great size of Malesh and its relative emptiness. 'You've seen how huge the City once was, how it relied on the thousands of small farms just like yours, to feed its many people. Lord Chevra is very slowly rebuilding Harbour City but he told us he doesn't want it ever to be such a vast place again. He doesn't have arms men to spare to help others now. In my opinion, all of Malesh will have to decide how you want to live for yourselves.'

Tika paused, looking at the serious faces watching her. She drew breath and spoke of Wendla, its treaty with, and aid to, Lord Chevra, and the imminent arrival here of a force of Blossoms. Darkness fell as she spoke on. 'The Blossoms are clearing camps of any Qwah they find,' she finished. 'You should therefore have no more trouble with raiders, although I do advise you to train your people in basic arms skills and to accept newcomers to your community. It is very difficult for such a small group to survive any disasters, be they raiders or illnesses. I hope you'll consider my words and make decisions on your future.' She sat down again and Dromi leaned closer.

'You spoke well, Tika.' He smiled. 'Just as a ruling Lady should speak.'

Tika shook her head. 'I'm going to rest. I think we'll have to stay until the Blossoms arrive. Do you truly think this place will be able to cope?'

'They had some supplies hidden nearby, Metti told me, enough hopefully to sustain them until the next crops are ready, if they're careful.'

'Where's Onion gone?'

'I don't know. He told me he and Navan had things to do, and they left with Storm before we ate.'

Most of the farmers returned to their houses, only a few remaining near Tika's camp tonight. She waited until everyone slept then she rose, moving silently towards the Qwah prisoners. They too slept and with no hesitation, Tika's senses slid into one after another, stopping each heart. When five lay dead, she roused the sixth, the man who seemed their leader. He sat up, glanced at his companions then up at Tika who stood watching him.

'Poison them you?' he snarled.

She smiled. 'No. No poison. But know this. If you had spoken better, the two boys at least might now be still breathing.' She raised a hand as he made to speak again. 'No poison,' she repeated. 'My powers.'

He died more slowly, fighting for breath and clawing his throat briefly before the end came. Tika stared at the bodies for a while then raised her left hand. Blue fire sprang over the corpses then guttered out. She turned away and saw five pairs of Dragon eyes watching her calmly.

Kija mind spoke her. 'A just punishment, daughter of my heart.' There was affection and pride in Kija's tone.

Making no reply, Tika walked back to curl close to Farn, and fell asleep at once.

Next day, Storm returned flying slowly above Navan and Onion who were herding several goats towards the settlement. Tika laughed, remembering the cattle Onion had somehow collected for Captain Zhora in Sea town. That put an idea in her head which she promptly discussed with Dromi and Fedran.

163

The Wendlans arrived the following day, the farm folk staring in some astonishment at the tall figures in their black lacquered armour and with the purple plumes in their helmets. Tika and her companions spoke with Officer Tenzee and his two mages, one of whom was a healer of House Topaz, the other a far seeker from House Jasper. Tenzee and both mages spoke the common tongue well and told the Iskallians of the building of a town, close to the desert on the eastern coast.

'Our Glorious Emperor suggested the plan to Lord Chevra. Commander Anikra reported a huge area of coast both west and east of these lands. He suggested it would be ideal for small towns, fishing ports and so on. It seems to His Magnificence, Emperor Kasheen, that no one used Malesh properly, with everything being too concentrated on the city in the distant south.' Tenzee waved an arm.

'All this good land being used by small farmers only to supply that city. To survive, Lord Chevra will have to accept many changes.'

Tika nodded. 'The, erm, Breathtaking Emperor has no intentions of taking any of this land for Wendla?' she asked.

Officer Tenzee looked shocked. 'He has no desire to take lands. Ledgroda could have been ours but it remains free.' He thought for a moment then shrugged. 'Perhaps some might wish to come here but that is the same as people from all lands asking to join you in Iskallia, Lady Tika.'

Explaining that she would be moving on at dawn to visit Sapphrea, Tika and her companions left Tenzee to settle his men and speak with the farmers.

'Breathtaking was very good,' Dog grinned at her.

Tika scowled. 'Well we'd had Glorious and Magnificent. It was all I could think of.'

Later, they bade farewell to the community, saying they would leave before dawn, and retired to their camp. Tika lay waiting for sleep when it occurred to her that not one person had mentioned the disappearance of six Qwah prisoners.

Chapter Fifteen

In pre dawn darkness, six Dragons lifted into the sky. Kija opened a gateway to the north west. 'I wonder what might happen to the port of Eddaven?' Fedran asked Tika as they travelled through the ashy world of the gateway.

'I think it will stay an empty ruin for a long time,' Tika replied. 'Too much nastiness, unhappiness, for folk to feel at ease there, I'd guess. It must be filled with angry ghosts still.'

'I thought Ferag or Simert gathered up all the dead souls?'

'Many ask to stay as ghosts, Fedran. A few of them feel they need to fulfil some task they neglected. As ghosts, there's not a great deal they can do really, but still they linger and hope for revenge.'

'Commander Anikra's report of his stop there was hardly pleasant,' Fedran agreed. 'You don't think the Hallavens might move there?'

'I'm fairly sure they won't. Teyo said none of the Hallavens had much interest in the coast or ships or the grand houses the Eddavens had. No, Fedran. It will last until the houses crumble I believe, unoccupied, but for its ghosts.'

The gateway shrank back away from them as Kija brought them out into a mid morning sky. Ahead, they saw the fortified town of Far and Brin bugled his deep cry of greeting. Kija led them to circle above Seboth's large house, and then she slowly spiralled down to settle in the wide forecourt. Once Tika had slipped from Farn's back she went to Kija to be sure she was all right. 'Hush, child. It was but a short gateway. I am quite well.' Kija lowered her head so her brow touched Tika's. Tika hugged her and turned towards the flight of steps leading up to the main entrance of Seboth's house.

Lord Seboth was already walking down to meet her, his hands outstretched and a smile on his face. He hugged her, nodding greetings to her company.

'Where have you been and where are you going? Come inside and tell me all your news.'

'We need to send a message to Harbour City while we're here, Seboth.'

'You can write it in my library. Come on.'

His Steward, Meran, bowed and smiled as he held open the door for them. 'Refreshments to the library, my lord?' he murmured.

'Yes please, and tell my wife we have guests please.'

Glancing back Tika saw several of Seboth's people were already talking to the Dragons and smiled. She knew how the Dragons loved the attention they always received here. In the spacious and comfortable library, Dromi sat near one of the many small tables and began drafting a report to Lord Chevra while Tika told Seboth their news. There was a brief, noisy interruption when Seboth's brother, his Arms Chief, Olam, and arms man, Riff, arrived and had to hug everyone.

Tika had to back track on her news, then Meran arrived with food and drink. Seboth fetched the maps Navan had given him and Navan explained where the various settlements were that they had seen. Olam and Riff joined them and they all agreed Malesh was a huge empty land, nearly as free of people as the extensive grasslands south of Sapphrea.

Lady Lallia appeared and again, everyone had to be hugged. Tika was glad to see none of their children were with Lady Lallia, although she made no comment. Dog, being less tactful, asked where the children might be and Lallia smiled. 'Dear Ferag is reading them stories before they have their lunch,' she said.

Hearing the remark, Tika looked across. 'Ferag is here? I hoped I might see her. I'll wait until she's free though.'

'Are they in the nursery?' asked Shea.

'Yes they are. Go and find them if you wish,' Lallia suggested. She gave a rueful smile. 'I'm sure Ferag will join us in a while. She seems to think it necessary to scold me each visit because I am not so involved with the children as she believes I should be.'

The talk revolved around Officer Tenzee's comments about settling more villages along the coasts of Malesh. Seboth's map was spread on the floor. It was all too obvious to those staring at it, that the land was astonishingly empty of areas of habitation. Seboth fetched out another map which showed Malesh before the devastation. The great swathe of Harbour City lay across the southern coast, yet still the inner lands showed no sign of anything more than the scattered solitary farms. Garrol shook his head. 'I wonder how long that land has concentrated only on the south coast? If they were a sea going people, why did they have no fishing villages or bigger ports towards the north?'

No one had any information about that, not even Seboth. Tika knew Seboth had read every book in his large library. She knew he was an avid book collector as were Dog and Mardis. Yet in all these volumes, he'd found no mention of any great civilisations in Malesh. Tika began to understand Mardis Fayle's obsession with believing there must once have been other civilisations, but how to find out about them was the problem.

'I told you before, I knew a lot of farm children who think of the work, the coin, they longed for fun they dream they might have in cities,' said Dog, 'The bigger Harbour City got, the more ordinary people they would need. As labourers, builders, cleaners, cooks. Children running away from farms would find plenty of mundane work but not so much fun as they'd imagined.'

Lallia agreed. 'Small as Far is, we still have wide eyed young ones coming in from outlying farms. Many return home once they find there's only similar work to do here as they did before.'

Jarko was still staring at the maps. 'There are fish in the sea,' he said. 'Everywhere. Not just down in Harbour City, surely? I wonder why no one seems to have chosen to live along the coast?'

'The Dark Realm have no ships,' Ashoki pointed out. 'And they have a long coastline. It's only once you get down to the Free Lands where you find ports and ships.'

'Yet south of Harbour City there are many islands which all rely on trade, or piracy, using ships.' Navan frowned. He pointed to Gaharn and Vagrantia, far to the east. 'No towns all down that coast either.'

'I have no wish to see any lands crammed with people in the way Harbour City was, but it does seem strange. Malesh is so *very* empty,' Tika began, then struggled to her feet, peering out of the window behind Seboth.

'What's wrong?' he asked in some alarm.

After a moment, she sat down again. 'I don't know if anything is *wrong*. Kija and Genia just flew off, fast.' Tika's eyes unfocussed slightly as she mind spoke Brin and Farn. She shrugged. 'Brin isn't worried. He said they may be gone until tomorrow but that's all he knew.'

The library door opened again and Onion unfolded himself to stand beaming at the beautiful woman standing there. Dog winced and tried to make herself smaller behind Veka and Kazmat. Veka merely looked bemused. Even Tika flinched a little when Onion threw his arms around the woman and smacked kisses on each flawless cheek. Faint colour tinged the white skin and incredibly long lashes fluttered in the most disarmingly coy manner. Tika rose again, stepping over and around people to reach the new arrival. 'Ferag! How wonderful to see you,' she said as she hugged the woman, albeit a little more gently.

'Well I'm glad to see you too poppet, but I'm here because I really feel those children need their mother's attention.' Ferag's gaze was fixed on Lady Lallia.

Lallia gave Ferag the sweetest smile. 'Darling Ferag, you *know* I've spent years giving them my *constant* attention. They must learn to be without me on occasion now.'

Before Ferag could continue her scolding, Tika caught her cold fingers. 'May I speak with you Ferag, out on the walkway? Just for a moment?' she begged. Knowing Ferag was quite easily distracted, she wasn't surprised when Ferag's frown changed to a smile.

'Very well, poppet. Lead on.' She waggled her free fingers at Onion who waggled his fingers back, and followed Tika from the library.

A covered walkway ran around the inner part of the house, overlooking the central courtyard. That's where Tika went, a few steps from the library.

'What can I help you with?' Ferag asked when they stood by the railing.

Tika met her gaze. 'What can you tell me of Youki? *Really* tell me?' she asked.

Exquisitely arched brows rose but Tika was relieved to see Ferag's long, dark red hair lay unmoving on her shoulders. 'Youki? I know little of her; stories, rumours, you know.'

Tika drew a breath. 'I spoke with Ashri recently,' she said.

Now those brows drew down. 'Ashri?' Ferag echoed.

'Yes. Do you know her?'

'I met her, sometimes, long ago. How did *you* come to meet her?' Ferag's hair had began to curl and move. 'Ashri is beloved of Mother Dark.'

'As you are too, dear Ferag.'

'What did you speak of?' Ferag's voice was almost a whisper.

'Ashri spoke of Mother Dark, of you, of Simert, and of Youki. She also spoke of a place called the gods' space.' Tika saw Ferag's hair lay unmoving again and waited for her reply. Ferag was clearly shocked.

'She told you of the gods' space?' she repeated. Tika nodded. 'Why did she ask you of Youki?'

Tika gripped Ferag's cold fingers tighter. 'Ashri asked me why I did not serve Mother Dark when it was she who had returned Farn to me. She pointed out that serving Youki always entails a cost.'

A look of horror crossed Ferag's face. Tika felt her trembling though their linked hands. Ferag stooped, her cool cheek against Tika's. 'I will come to talk with you soon. There are things I must look into now.' She straightened, her gaze locked with Tika's. Then she took a step back, and vanished.

Tika stayed where she was for a moment, really hoping she hadn't caused any trouble. She had a genuine affection for Ferag, and she'd felt an instant trust when she met Ashri. She didn't mean to cause any difficulties.

Roused from her thoughts as Shea came along the

walkway, Tika smiled.

'The children are being fed,' Shea told her, then she lowered her voice. 'They really could do with some discipline. I'm not at all surprised Lallia has escaped.'

Tika went back to the library with Shea and Dromi held out his draft message for Chevra. She read it, suggested a couple of extra comments and nodded. Dromi settled back to copy the letter in his formal handwriting, and Tika went to sit near Seboth. She smiled at Riff when he hunkered down beside her. 'How is your arm?' she asked.

He stretched his right arm out in front of him and she saw it shook once it was fully extended. He drew it back and grinned. 'I can use it, more than I thought I ever would, but there's not much strength in it still. It took me a while but I realise I'm lucky to be alive, one way and another.'

'I wish there was something I could have done, but it had been too long damaged by the time I saw you.'

'I've worked hard with my left arm. Olam helped a lot. I reckon I can use a sword again nearly as well as I used to with my right. It seemed to take so long to work out the balance, and how my eyes judged distances from that side.'

'Bet you still couldn't beat Essa,' Dog put in.

Riff glared at her. 'I could flatten you, for sure. Want to try a practice round?'

'I'd really like to but my leg plays up too much for those games now.' Dog's expression was innocent but that just annoyed Riff more. Everyone knew Tika had healed Dog's badly smashed leg years ago, and what Tika healed, stayed fully healed.

As Riff and Dog sank into an insult match, Tika returned to Dromi. He'd just finished the message to Chevra and Tika sat down to sign and seal it. 'I'll ask Navan to take it, on Storm,' she said. 'It won't take them long but if Seboth sends one of his riders it will take an age to get to the circle.'

As usual, everyone ended up in the forecourt later, where Seboth's household staff brought out a huge dinner, then crept back out to listen to the general talk. Lady Lallia herself brought out a basket full of the honey cakes for which she was famous. She offered them first to the

Dragons. Honey cakes were one of the very few cooked human foods the Dragons really loved and their eyes flashed and whirred in delight at the treat. Storm arrived just as Lallia was handing out the cakes and Steward Meran brought Navan a heaped dinner they'd kept back just for him.

It didn't take much persuading from Olam for the crimson Dragon to start telling some of his stories and the evening passed in laughter and applause. When Seboth's household retired for the night, Tika and her companions stayed with the Dragons. Once all was quiet, Tika mind spoke Brin on a single thread to ask where Kija might be.

'She bespoke me a while ago,' Brin told her. 'She said she will meet us at the coast where we've been before.'

'She won't return here?'

'No.' Brin sounded mildly confused but not alarmed, so Tika took his word that Kija and Genia were at least safe.

'When are we to meet her?' she asked.

'She's already there.'

'Then we will leave here after breakfast tomorrow please Brin.' She felt affection through their mind link and then settled back against Farn's chest. He was already asleep, snoring gently and leaning against Pearl.

In the morning therefore, Tika simply told her company they would be leaving Far, without telling them they were only going the relatively short distance to the coast. They made their farewells and climbed on the Dragons. Brin carried six Guards, Farn carrying two more with Tika and Fedran. Storm and Pearl both carried one extra in the absence of Kija and Genia. Once they were aloft and heading north, Tika mind spoke Guards and Dragons.

'Kija and Genia are waiting for us at the coast. I hope nothing is wrong. I'm sure Kija had a reason for leaving us at Far, but I've no idea what that might be.'

Brin turned to the west and led the company over the barren wasteland that stretched along this area until the glitter on the horizon told them they were close to the sea. Their shadows preceding them over the rough dunes, they flew over the beach and saw Kija and Genia. There were two other Dragons beside them and Kija sent a thought to

171

Tika asking her to be careful with these two: they were young and had had no dealings with humans.

Tika relayed Kija's words among her company even as Brin brought them down to land a little distance from Kija. 'Will we be here overnight?' Essa asked quietly. 'We can use that old camping place if we are.'

'I think that we will be. You go on and I'll see if I can talk to these two.' Tika nodded as Onion joined her as the rest of the company headed back behind the low cliffs. Dog took Tika's pack and Fedran retrieved Onion's as they left.

Tika sat on the sand, Onion next to her. They both studied the two new Dragons while they waited for Kija to speak. Tika guessed they were around Genia's age, perhaps twenty years old, still mere babies by Dragon reckoning. The male was such a dark blue as to seem almost black and Tika thought he might rival Brin when he reached his full size. She realised he had an injury, a deep gash down the back of his left shoulder. She felt Farn shiver where her soul bond had reclined close to her back. The female crouched between the male and Kija. She was a pale green, with a hint of yellow to it, not the apple green of Ashta's scales.

Tika was quite aware that both Kija and Genia were pulsing calmness to the two newcomers and she continued to wait. Kija finally spoke, her words also heard by the company now beyond the cliffs Tika realised. 'Genia heard these children call her, daughter of my heart. They were of the Sun Mountain Treasury, and known to Genia. They were not aware that Genia had reached us in Iskallia. Believing that she might still be in this land, they called her for aid when they were cast out and attacked.'

Tika replied aloud. 'Seela of such beloved memory, once ruled the Sun Mountain Treasury. I know Genia has spoken of the new Elder, Nanu. Genia was unhappy with her leadership and now she is a welcome part of Kija's Treasury.'

The new female pushed up a little and her mind voice filled their heads. 'Nanu is bad! She hurts so many young ones! She treads on new hatched children!' She was trembling but Tika saw it was anger, not fear, that caused her to shudder.

Kija hushed her but Pearl, lying just beyond Farn, spoke softly. 'The adults of my Flight tried to tread on me,' she said. 'Because I asked questions. Iskallia is a good place to live and Kija is an Elder to serve.'

Kija glanced at Pearl, surprised by her words, and sent warm affection towards her. She looked down at the male. 'This is Minyth. His sister is Heligg. I accept them both into my Treasury, daughter of my heart. I hope that meets with your agreement.'

Tika was on her feet. 'Of course it does. You have no need to ask.' She looked to the male, Minyth.

'Your shoulder is hurt. Will you let me mend it for you?'

'My Tika can make it better,' Farn added. 'She is a healer.'

Tika watched Minyth stare at the long scar down Farn's neck, where no new scales would ever grow again. 'Three of Nanu's males attacked us.' Minyth's mind voice was lower, husky. 'I made Heligg fly and hide but they caught me.'

Beside her, Onion murmured quietly. Tika nodded. She stooped, tugging off her boots and leaving them on the sand. Onion did the same. 'Will you come closer to the water, my dear? I promise you are safe but the sea water will clean that wound before I mend it.'

Minyth's eyes whirred in momentary alarm but Farn paced to the sea, wading in belly deep. He looked back. 'It's quite safe. Truly it is.'

Then the massive figure of Brin also moved down the beach, wading further out than Farn, making a protected space where Minyth could stand. Slowly, the dark blue Dragon followed and Tika saw how much pain his injury caused him. She bit her lip then moved forward. 'Can you stand in the water so your hurt side is in further,' she asked him gently.

Brin was sending calmness she realised as Minyth cautiously set foot in the sea. He was startled into speech. 'It tickles!' With more confidence, he moved towards Brin, and Onion slipped between the two Dragons.

Onion began to scoop water up over the wound which both he and Tika could now see was deep and ragged edged. 'How long is it since you were hurt, my dear?' Tika asked.

'Three days,' Minyth replied.

Tika had already blocked some of the pain and the young Dragon was visibly relaxing. Both she and Onion were soaked by the time she was satisfied the wound was clean and she coaxed Minyth back onto the sand. 'Settle as comfortably as you can, Minyth, and I will do what I can.'

He reclined with most of his weight on his right side and Tika stood by his left shoulder, Onion's arm holding her steady. Slowly, painstakingly, she sent her senses into the gaping wound and began to work.

The afternoon was half gone by the time Tika withdrew her senses and leaned back against Onion. She found she had a blanket wrapped around her and Essa sat nearby holding a mug of tea ready for her. Tika blinked. All her company seemed to have returned to the beach, staying a little further away than they usually would. Heligg seemed much calmer and Minyth turned his head to stare at his shoulder. The wound was closed, the dark blue skin smooth, bare of scales, as Tika feared it might well remain.

Minyth's eyes whirred. 'The wound is gone.' He sounded astonished. Forgetting he was new and unused to humans, Tika smiled, caught his long face between her hands and dropped a kiss on his snout. 'It may still feel a little sore but yes, it's healed,' she agreed.

'I thank you,' he murmured.

'Shall I get fish for you all?' Storm had stayed quietly with Pearl while Tika healed Minyth.

Tika tripped on her blanket when she turned towards him. 'That would be very kind of you, Storm,' she said.

Storm lifted from the sand and shot out over the water. Minyth pushed himself up in alarm. 'Where is he going?' he asked.

Tika realised he and Heligg had probably not encountered Sea Dragons before. Storm plunged out of sight, into the waves, and Minyth hissed. Brin quickly calmed him, explaining that both Storm and Pearl were Dragons of the Sea and were quite safe. 'I thought they

174

looked a little different,' Heligg murmured, staring where Storm had vanished. Some distance from where he'd entered the water, Storm heaved himself back up into the air, flying back to the beach to drop a large fish at Navan's feet. Ketro gathered up two and Garrol picked up the next two, taking them round to their camp. Navan managed to persuade Storm that after another two, that really was enough.

'Come with us,' Tika suggested to Minyth. 'It isn't far to walk and I'd prefer you rested rather than flew right now.'

Minyth stood slowly, wary of pain but found he had none. Heligg paced to him, twining her neck round his. Kija led the way and single file, everyone, Dragons and Guards followed her behind the cliffs along to a sheltered patch of lusher grass. Essa and Jarko already had the first fish baking and Kija reclined just beyond the small spring that bubbled from the ground. Heligg lay close to her, watching the Guards with a mixture of nervousness and curiosity but far calmer than she had been this morning. Minyth lay near Brin and seemed to be in conversation with both Brin and Storm. Farn bumped his chin on the top of Tika's head, and she reached up to stroke his face.

'Minyth's shoulder will be well now, my Tika?' he asked.

'Yes, it will. He's very lucky it wasn't any lower or it would have damaged his wing.'

'Will we go home tomorrow?'

'I'll leave it for Kija to decide, dear one. Those two were very shocked and frightened still when we arrived.'

'Minyth was hurt but Heligg was very angry,' Farn observed.

'They both seem more comfortable now but let's leave it to Kija whether we go home tomorrow or not.'

Chapter Sixteen

Ashri continued working with Endis in a mixture of actually putting some of her memories into his mind, and talking to him. She had veiled many of those memories, deeming it too soon as yet for her to reveal the full extent of what she was doing. This day, Endis began by asking questions. 'What powers do the gods actually have on the world, Ancient One?'

'That rather depends on several things, child. Until relatively recently, many of the lesser gods involved themselves in certain areas of human life. In Harbour City and in Kelshan many of them chose to help, or sometimes hinder, certain events. In Harbour City ships were of great importance so there were gods who helped the fisher folk, or sped up the movement of trading ships. There was also in that place a long habit of worshipping the Elder Races - the Gijan, and the Dragons, although it had been millennia since any had been seen there.'

'Two you've spoken of - Ferag and Simert, they have nothing to do with the sea or ships, do they?'

'Ferag confines herself mostly to the Dark Realm, to those with Dark bloodlines from the time before the Last Battle. Simert travelled everywhere, collecting the spirits of the dead. Throughout Kelshan and Drogoya there were many lesser gods who helped with the care of animals, the growth of crops.' She paused in thought. 'Then a man in Drogoya, a human, decided *he* knew better, was far wiser than any small god, and he encouraged people to turn from the gods and worship him. Many of those gods simply returned to the gods' space when they found their help was spurned.'

Endis nodded. 'So most of the lesser gods tried to be helpful?'

'They did. Mother Dark had commanded that none should interfere but if they were *asked* by the humans to help, they could do so within limits. Once the people stopped asking there was no point to them staying.'

Endis thought. 'That must have saddened them,' he said, surprising himself with that idea.

'It did,' the Augur agreed. 'Many asked Mother to take them to her care, no longer wanting to just exist in the gods' space.'

'Is the gods' space a boring place to be, then?'

The Augur smiled. 'In some ways perhaps it is. The lesser gods study many things. They play games. They squabble and fight. I think those who returned after such a long time working with humans felt too lost.'

'So *they* asked Mother Dark if they can go into the infinity?'

'No, child. To return into *her* Darkness from whence they came.'

'I'm not sure I understand the difference,' Endis admitted.

'Mother Dark is a being, an entity, alive. The infinity is the vastness between and beyond the stars.'

'And the Vortex you spoke of, isn't anything to do with her?'

'No. That too has been there as long as the infinity, perhaps longer than even Mother Dark.'

'Where does that one live, the one I saw in a dream when first I came here? Olekatah?'

The Augur's blue eyes fixed on Endis and he felt as though they truly pierced his whole being. 'I will speak of him much later, child. For now, go and do as you please today. I believe I will have a visitor.'

'Not Menan Kelati?' Endis rose, alarmed although unsure why he should be.

'No, child. She will not visit again.'

Endis started towards the door, hesitated and turned back. 'When I first came, you said there were once many Seers. Then you told me there are *no* Seers. Am I a Seer or not?'

Without turning to look at him, the Augur lifted a hand. 'It will all become clear, I promise Endis. For many, the concept of a Seer is easier to understand than what you truly will be. Go, child.'

When Endis had left her, Ashri sat quite still. She'd found her aches lessened if she didn't actually move. Smiling at her silliness, she waited until she sensed an approach to the boundary of this place. With a thought, she allowed access and waited a little longer. Ferag appeared near the door, glancing around the room. Neither spoke then Ferag walked to the chair Endis had recently vacated and sank into it, a picture of elegant perfection. 'Ashri.'

'Ferag. What brings you here?'

'I saw Tika. She said she had been here, spoken with you, Why? Why would you bring her here?'

'You know as well as I that child's importance to Mother.'

'She said you spoke of Youki. What have you discovered, Ashri? Even Mother doesn't know who or what Youki is.'

'She impresses you?' Ashri asked.

'She does. Did. She seems so small, so caring. She healed the sweet girl Kara when I brought her back through time.'

'No, my dear Ferag. Kara had a chenzaldi stone. She was already healing anyway.' Ashri watched Ferag think back over that occasion. She saw those beautiful eyes close briefly as she followed Ashri's words. 'Tika said that you pointed out to her that Youki always demands a price for service to her.'

'Mother asks for nothing.'

Ferag paused at Ashri's comment. 'Youki is the guardian of the world,' she said eventually.

'Did she tell you that?' asked Ashri. Ferag just stared at her. 'Who does she guard, Ferag? She does not guard the humans as she once claimed to me. You know of the creatures she made, to carry out her commands?'

Ferag frowned. 'I believe I've seen one or two of them. Strange little things.'

'Indeed. Somehow, and no, I do not know how, Youki learned of Tika's importance to Mother. She chose to send one of her creatures to "guard" Tika from the moment of her birth. The creature decided to leave her in favour of watching another child. This happened when Tika was thus left unwatched.' A single thought transferred information from Ashri's mind to Ferag's.

Ferag looked aghast as she absorbed what Ashri sent her.

'She was nine years old, Ferag,' Ashri murmured. 'You met the child Tika declared her heir did you not?'

Ferag nodded.

'This is what Youki's same creature did to him.' Again the information moved from mind to mind.

Ferag could only stare at Ashri, horror in her eyes.

'You *know* those creatures act *only* on Youki's command, don't you?'

'That is what I've always understood, yes.'

'And I believe she tried to lure *you* into her service? I heard that she asked you to collect the spirits of a certain family in the Free Lands at one time? When you went there, you found those people all alive and well. It was a test, dear Ferag. If you had taken their spirits and thus left them empty corpses, Youki would have gained a hold over you. It has happened among others of the gods, Ferag.'

'Why does Mother not know more? I understood Youki was here when Mother chose this world to watch over, long before she made any of us. How can she *not* know, Ashri? And if she knows more, why hasn't she told us?'

Ashri leaned her head back and winced as her neck clicked. She could show weakness before Ferag with no fear of mockery. 'You know as well as I, my sweet Ferag, that is not how Mother works.' She smiled. 'Through your friendship with Lerran, you must surely understand that.'

'Ah! Mother allowed Lerran to lose her life for the sake of Tika and the young Dragon. *That* was a heavy price to pay?'

'Oh Ferag! How long had Lerran longed to be with her precious Dabray? It was not a price, it was a release, a reward.'

Ferag at last relaxed her stiff posture and settled back in her chair, studying Ashri. 'Why is it you never return to the gods' space and refresh yourself? You really do look desperately old, darling.'

Ashri gave an undignified snort of laughter. 'It was a

condition of my service to remain here in this form until my service ends. You are older than I am, Ferag; imagine how you would look without your visits home.'

They remained silent until Ferag spoke again. 'Youki comes here?'

'Very rarely, and, I suspect she will not again. The creature who neglected care of Tika and killed the boy in such a vicious manner, is no more.'

Ferag's eyes widened. 'You destroyed it?'

'I did. I do have such powers, Ferag. It's just that so far, there has been little call for their use.'

'Perhaps not. You have stayed here, watching, for so long Ashri. I never heard that you took any such actions.'

'Only on Mother's command.'

'If you learn more of Youki or her intentions towards the humans in our care, will you tell me?'

Ashri smiled with affection. 'I will my dear. My time is nearing its end here. The boy who will take up my role is still so young, but he will be strong. Mother chooses most wisely.

Ferag bowed her head. 'As she always does,' she agreed. She got to her feet and took the few steps to Ashri's chair. Stooping, she kissed her cheek gently. 'You have done well, Ashri, far better than any others among us could have.'

Ashri looked up into the beautiful face and brushed a strand of the dark red hair back over Ferag's shoulder. 'Visit me again, Ferag? I have missed you.'

She was surprised to see Ferag's eyes brim with tears then, with one step back, her guest was gone.

Sending her senses out, overlooking the world below, she noted the desert region in northern Malesh was quieter. There were still pockets of energy which jarred in her sight but the angry redness of the area had dissipated. Moving her vision across the ocean, she focussed on north east Kelshan and felt anger, violence and bitterness around the area where the pitiful creature, Gremara, had sought sanctuary. As ever, she sensed no awareness of Youki but Ferag's words lingered in her mind.

Might Mother have learnt more? Slowly Ashri allowed

180

herself to slip out and down, down into the dark, begging for an audience with Mother.

Kija had spoken to Tika of her intention to take the two new Dragons to Fenj and Lorak first. Kija explained that she thought a few days resting there would help the two. Tika agreed, only suggesting that Kija summon her if she felt any concern that they were finding it hard to adjust to the proximity of the villagers. Consequently, after Tika had checked Minyth's wound, eight Dragons lifted into the air above the beach and Brin opened a gateway. Kija and Genia sent calmness to Minyth and his sister but they settled to the strangeness of the gateway world far sooner than Kija had dared hope.

Brin led them faster than on their outward journey and brought them down on the slopes of the Barrier Mountains which guarded the Dark Realm. After a brief rest, Kija rose again, the two young ones following her closely, while Brin led the rest of the company home to the House in Iskallia. The four Guards Kija had carried had transferred to the other Dragons for the short distance that remained. When they popped clear of the gateway over Iskallia, Tika was pleased to see how much snow had melted. There were still large patches left in more sheltered parts of the valley but there was also a great deal of green land once more.

Brin called, as he circled above the great mosaic circle in front of the House and spiralled down to settle. Several people came out to greet them and a quick glance at their expressions assured Tika all was well. Even as Dragons and Guards entered the House, the bell chimed for the midday meal. Beside her, Dog grinned. 'At least we arrived at a sensible time,' she said.

Telk was busy giving Fedran his report and the noise level rose as more and more people arrived in the hall. When everyone's hunger had been satisfied, Tika told them all that they'd found in Malesh. Then she explained two new Dragons had joined Kija and they were now at Dragons Rest. They would stay there until Kija decided they were ready to come to the plateau. People nodded their understanding, having grown used to new arrivals, and their nervousness over the years. Tika also told them one of these new ones had been injured. She sent mind pictures of the two and gave their names.

The hall began to empty; those who'd travelled with her taking their packs up to their rooms. Tika called Veka back. The girl sat down again but she seemed much less nervous than she had been. 'What did you think of our travels?' Tika asked.

'I really enjoyed it. Navan had told me you could see how the maps are just like how it looks when you're high in the sky.'

'You know the maps were made by a ship that once travelled through the stars?'

Veka nodded. 'He told me about Star Flower. Fareena and Naladi had spoken of her too.'

'The trouble with the Qwah didn't frighten you?'

Veka frowned in thought. 'No it didn't. I thought it might, but I was more angry I think. All those folk hurt, killed. All they were doing was working hard to grow food and the Qwah were just bullies and thieves.'

'So you'd be happy enough to travel again?'

'Oh yes please!'

'Is there any particular thing that appeals to you here, Veka? You've spent time in the archives, the library and the medical school. Do you prefer one over the others?'

'I like them all. Aifa's plants are really interesting. Mardis's search for old kingdoms is fascinating. I like listening to Dromi and Werlan talk about how Iskallia deals with other lands. Perhaps Navan's maps are the most exciting so far.' She grinned. 'Navan said you don't like maps.'

'I don't,' Tika confessed. 'They somehow make no sense at all. I look at a map and it's just flat. I can sometimes work out where places are, if I'm given lots of hints. I *did* understand how empty Malesh seems to be, but I still can't see why there were absolutely no towns there.'

'I've been thinking about that.' Veka leaned her elbows on the table. 'From Navan's maps, Harbour City was so huge. It must have been awful, living there. It would have needed such enormous amounts of food being brought in.'

'It *was* awful.' Tika shivered, remembering her arrival there, on foot, with three Gijan children. The packed streets, the noise, the smells of cooking and perfumes and overcrowded humanity. 'I agree with what you're saying but surely it would have made more sense to have perhaps half a dozen towns where supplies could be collected and then sent on south? I wonder why they didn't have ports, on either coast, where they could take those supplies by sea even quicker down to the City?'

'I'll see if I can find anything at all in the library but there aren't many books from there.'

'Let me know if there's anything you want to try, Veka. Have you been to Port Maressa? Does anything interest you there?'

'I've been there with Ashoki and Dog. I'm used to ports like Salo Manis and Druke - very busy places. Ships coming and going all the time. Port Maressa doesn't get many ships yet so it's much quieter.'

'And you'd rather be busy?'

Veka nodded. Tika smiled. 'Then carry on doing whatever you're doing. You only have to come and tell me if you want to try anything else.'

Veka trotted off out of the hall and Tika went to the Dragons by the hearth. 'Thank you for taking us, my dears. Do you know where Twist and Flyn might be? Or Skay?'

'Skay is at the forge, my Tika. Twist and Flyn are visiting Fenj.' Tika hugged Farn as he went on. 'Brin told them not to bother coming to meet us.'

Tika looked at Brin. He was leaning against the wall to the side of the hearth, snoring. 'He's not over tired himself again, has he?' she asked anxiously.

'No.' Pearl's eyes flashed. 'Storm and I helped him hold the gateway.'

'Did you? Well thank you again my dear ones. And you, Genia. I know you helped Kija calm those two young ones.'

Genia lowered her head towards Tika. 'They were very agitated when we found them,' she said. 'Minyth's wound was giving him much pain. Kija blocked some of it so he could fly to the coast. She thought it best to get further away from the Sun Mountain Treasury's lands.'

Tika hugged each of them, retrieved her pack and went up to her quarters. She put clothes to be cleaned in the basket and then dressed again in an old pair of trousers and one of the many garish sweaters she owned. Tika was convinced Essa's mother and Ashoki had hatched some plan to see which of them could produce the most eye watering mix of colours possible. She suspected that any comment from her would merely result in them redoubling their efforts.

Cerys informed her that Pearl had described their recent travels while Tika glanced over the few reports that had been left on her table. There were two private messages from Lady Ricca of Kelshan, requesting a visit. The second sounded definitely more urgent that the first. Cerys watched her. 'When will you visit those children?' she asked.

'Hmm? Fairly soon I think. Why?'

'Don't forget I will be coming too.'

Tika put down Ricca's letter and looked at the cat beside her. 'It will be good to have you with us,' she said quietly. 'We had all grown used to having a cat in our company when we travelled.'

Green gold eyes blinked. 'I should have come more often, I know. I've been trying to sort out all the things Khosa and Kija told me. At the end, Khosa told me so very much, and a lot of it was confused, Tika. She knew she had little time left to teach me it all.'

Tika stroked the thick black fur along Cerys's back and sighed. 'Do you think you've understood most of it now?' she asked.

'A lot of it, yes, but I may still have to ask you, or Kija, about some things.'

After a pause, Tika looked back at Ricca's letter and reached for paper and pen. 'Ricca sounds worried about something. I'll send word that she can visit when she wants now that we're back.'

She had just finished the letter and put it in a scroll case marked with the privacy line when Farn mind spoke her. 'Flyn and Twist are here, my Tika. Flyn is upset. He thinks you might believe he had neglected his duty to protect this place. He's afraid you'll be angry with him.'

'I'll be right down,' Tika replied.

'Poor Flyn,' Cerys murmured in Tika's thoughts. 'He is so very easily worried.'

'He is, but I know he would do his very best to protect Iskallia if necessary,' Tika agreed, making for the door. She hurried down the stairs and into the hall where she found Flyn pacing restlessly back and forth, his eyes whirring in great agitation. Twist reclined by the hearth, seemingly unperturbed.

Tika went straight to hug Flyn. 'Everything seems perfectly well here, Flyn dear. You and Twist are excellent protectors.'

Brin's youngest son halted, staring down at her. 'We weren't here to welcome you home.' His mind voice was a nervous stutter.

Tika caressed the butter yellow scales of his face. 'You were visiting Fenj. It would have taken only heartbeats for you to return here if there was anything wrong. Skay would have called for you at once.'

Flyn's eyes slowed their wild flashing. 'Are you sure? I feared you might be cross.'

Tika hugged him again. 'Of course I'm not cross. I thank you for staying here to protect Iskallia. And Twist of course,' she added, stretching to stroke Twist.

'We met the new ones,' Twist informed her. 'They seemed happy to be here.'

'Did they? Good. I hope they'll be comfortable with all of us soon. Are you going back to Port Maressa now?'

Flyn's eyes flashed briefly. 'We do like it there, Tika. Do you mind that we stay there so much?'

'Certainly not. And I know everyone there loves having you with them.'

Twist rose, pacing closer to her and touching his brow to hers. Flyn followed Twist out, turning his head back to look at her as he reached the door. 'I am most grateful for your service, both of you,' she assured him. She waited until they were gone before she went out to send the scroll through the circle to Kelshan. Although the plateau was nearly free of snow, the air was still far from warm and Tika hurried back to the hall.

Brin still slept, Storm close to his back. 'Do you wish to go to the port, Storm?' she asked him.

'Not today,' he told her.

She smiled. 'Perhaps we'll have to make the hall bigger, if more Dragons are coming to join this Treasury,' she said. Four Dragons round the hearth took up quite a large space. 'Will Brin need food when he wakes?'

It was Genia who replied. 'There is meat still frozen down by that little house near the lake. We can get it if he's hungry.'

Tika looked over her shoulder, hearing footsteps beyond the hall then Dromi and Werlan entered.

She joined them at her table and told them of Ricca's two letters. Dromi frowned. 'There has been nothing untoward in anything I've seen from the General.' He looked at Werlan for confirmation.

Werlan shook his head. 'Nothing at all,' he agreed. 'There is one small matter though, to do with the Dark Realm. I have wondered if I should speak to you of it. Fenzir wrote to me while you were gone.'

Tika and Dromi waited.

'He said Corman is growing increasingly worried about Lady Jian. She had been more amenable to working with him, Lord Shivan and Lady Lorca, but now she almost shuns them again. He said Corman mentioned that it reminded him of how she behaved when she first came back through time.'

'I thought she was much changed, improved, or at least, back to her old self.' Tika frowned.

'What could have made her change again?' asked Dromi.

Werlan made as if to speak then remained silent.

'What is it?' asked Tika. 'Have you thought of something?'

Now Werlan looked distinctly uncomfortable. 'Fenzir told me, some time ago now that Corman had been angry and very upset. To begin with, Corman said nothing, then eventually he told Fenzir.' Werlan paused but Tika and

186

Dromi simply waited again. Although they were alone in the hall but for the Dragons, Werlan lowered his voice.

'He said Lady Jian had called a meeting. That is when she explained that Endis had seen Enki's death in a dream. She announced that she would henceforth serve Youki. Apparently Lord Shivan was annoyed but he didn't fully understand the implications of her words. Lady Lorca was alarmed, and Corman was enraged, although he concealed it completely from them. Only Fenzir realised how disturbed he was. It appears that somehow, Youki actually entered Lady Jian's rooms.'

'She did,' Tika agreed. 'I was present. Why would that upset Corman so much?'

'Youki had never before been able to penetrate the Dark Realm's protections,' was Werlan's blunt reply. 'Now she's managed it once, Corman fears she could again.'

Chapter Seventeen

Tika was greatly disturbed by Werlan's information but the hall was already filling with hungry people and chatter was loud and general, forestalling further discussion of the matter. Tika told those around her table that Lady Ricca had asked to visit and she had written back telling the child she was welcome whenever she chose.

'In some ways she reminds me of Ferag,' remarked Shea thoughtfully.

Dog clapped a hand over Shea's mouth and glared at her. 'Do *not* say her name! Never forget who she is.' Slowly, she removed her hand and Shea glared right back at her.

'What do you mean, Shea? I see no similarities,' said Tika.

'She's lonely. I mean Lady Ricca. Yes, she has those few around her who I think she likes, but she's always aware that basically they are all her servants. She must wonder if they can truly like her, truly be her friend, if you see what I mean. She likes you, Tika, because you *aren't* her servant. You are a ruling Lady.'

'I do see what you mean but I think Captain Shtok, the boy, Mekla, and General Falkir genuinely do like her,' Tika replied.

'Yes, but *she* isn't sure about that. She's been treated as different, special, all her life, and I haven't heard that she even knows any other children.'

Teyo nodded. 'The children they might let her meet would probably be from the high families. I would wager those children would be given very strict instructions to treat her very properly, hoping for positions within her household or in her government when they're older.'

'I can't see how they might let her live a "normal" life,' Essa put in. 'She's used to being treated as an important person. Can you imagine what could happen if another child knocked her over, or got into an argument with her?

There's always someone with her and I'm sure they'd intervene at once rather than let a fight or argument continue.'

Tika retired to bed later, wondering if there was any answer to providing Lady Ricca with anything like the life of an ordinary child, and decided probably not. She refused to let herself think of Werlan's report on Lady Jian, knowing she'd be awake all night if she did.

When she went down to the hall in the morning, she heard loud chatter well before she reached ground level. Opening the door, she walked through and stopped in her tracks. *Something* was different but she wasn't sure what at first. It was Teyo who hurried across to her. 'What did you do?' he demanded, waving his arms around.

'Me? I haven't done anything.'

'But it's bigger!' he almost shouted.

Tika stared, slowly realising Teyo was quite correct. The hall was very nearly double the size it had been when she'd gone up to bed. The carvings Teyo and Nia had done all remained intact, although there was rather more space between them. The carved Dragons above the hearth were the same although, staring more closely, Tika saw the hearth itself was wider than it had been. She continued on to her usual table by a window, noting that there were four more windows in the outer wall.

Dog was scowling at the enlarged hearth. 'I know it would need to be bigger if more Dragons decide to come here, but you could have given us some warning, Tika,' she grumbled.

'I did *not* do anything,' Tika repeated as she sat down, then she paused and Dog pounced.

'*What?* What happened? You *did* do something, didn't you?'

Faces turned to her and Tika spread her hands in a gesture of helplessness. 'I was talking to the Dragons yesterday, and I said we would need a bigger hall if many more come to join us.'

'*Hah!* So the Dragons did it?' Teyo asked.

Tika shook her head. 'No of course they didn't. It's just this House.' She saw everyone was waiting for rather more

189

explanation. 'You all know Dark mages did a lot of work here long ago and you also know how extra rooms somehow just appear? The House must have heard what I said yesterday.'

'So now you're telling us the House *listens* to whatever we talk about?' Dog's eyebrows rose nearly to her hairline.

'Is it only the hall?' Shea asked, then hurried across to check the rarely used council chamber. Trotting back she was grinning. 'That's a bit bigger too,' she told them.

'Where are the Dragons now?' asked Teyo.

'They left early, to hunt,' Fedran replied. 'I asked Brin if he was well rested when they passed my office. My office hasn't changed,' he added quickly.

'Who has rooms above the hall?' asked Teyo.

'I do,' Essa replied. She frowned. 'I think there may have been more doors further along than usual but I didn't really pay attention.'

Shea and Veka both headed out to the stairs. Teyo finally sat down. 'I'm sorry Tika. It was just a shock to see it changed,' he apologised, still regarding the walls with some suspicion.

'Who else lives above here?' Tika asked.

'Shea, Veka, Geffal and me,' said Ketro. 'I didn't notice anything though when I came down this morning.'

'I live on the other side of the staircase, over Fedran's office,' Dog remarked. 'Nothing odd there.'

'Well there's nothing odd here, is there? The hall is just a bit stretched,' Tika said.

Judging by the looks she received, "just a bit stretched", probably wasn't an adequate comment.

Kitchen staff began to bring out breakfasts and food distracted people, for which Tika was grateful. Until Sarila stood beside her, staring down at her. 'The kitchens are larger,' she said calmly.

'Aah. Is that an inconvenience?'

'No. An improvement actually.'

'Oh. Good.' Tika beamed at her and began to eat. Sarila watched her for a moment then shook her head and retreated.

Shea and Veka returned, squeezing into seats round

Tika's table. 'Five new rooms along that passage, and more on the next floor up,' Shea informed them. 'No furniture in them.'

'Well *obviously*. How could you expect a house to provide its own furniture,' was Dog's sarcastic reply.

Once people had left, leaving only Dromi and Navan with Tika, Dromi smiled at her. 'The archives are considerably larger,' he informed her. 'Pleasingly so.'

'And my map room,' Navan grinned. 'Seriously though, do you think the House really does listen to everything?'

'Not to everything, no. But remember how poor Lord Dabray was trapped, in Dragon form, in the very stones of the Karmazen Palace. *He* was aware of things throughout the building, was he not?'

Navan looked alarmed. 'You think someone could be trapped here?'

'No, of course not. I mean it's possible perhaps that the rock of this place is somehow more aware? We know Iskallia was always a most special place for Lerran and Dabray. And they were gods.' Tika spoke the last words softly and waited for the men's reaction.

Dromi gave a slow nod. 'I admit I had wondered that,' he said. 'I'm presuming the Augur told you that?'

'She did. There is more too, but I'll tell you another time if you don't mind.'

'I was thinking of Lady Ricca,' said Navan. 'Rulers don't have to be so isolated do they?'

'What do you mean? King Troman and Queen Tupalla have little contact with people beyond their councillors. Nor did Chevra, although things have changed a little in Harbour City now.'

'No, they don't,' Navan agreed. 'But what about Lord Darallax?'

Tika and Dromi stared at him and waited.

'Remember when we walked from Darallax's palace, out to the bridge when you called to free the Chyliax? People just wandered up to chat to him. I heard one person giving him a new recipe for fish soup. No one bowed or treated him as special. He had a handful of guards yes, but they didn't carry weapons.'

191

Dromi frowned. 'I take your point, Navan, but peaceful and friendly as Darallax might appear, surely all his people must be aware of who he is? A Son of Mother Dark. By any measure, he must possess mage powers of considerable strength? Would you risk attacking him?'

Tika and Navan remained silent.

'Lady Lerran,' Dromi continued. 'She was approachable to a very small group - Lord Corman, Garrol, a few of the Dark Lords. She seemed to have no close friends, male or female, so I would say she was isolated, wouldn't you agree?'

'So really you're saying that is the cost of being the ruler of a land?'

Dromi nodded. 'Yes, Tika. Even among the clans, the leader is apart from the rest.'

'I would argue otherwise with the clans, tribes, in the Dark Realm,' Tika objected. 'The Bear, and other chiefs I met, were all approachable, genuinely part of their clans. I didn't notice the Bear was treated differently. He was respected, his orders obeyed in the battle of Ghost Falls and his judgement is asked in matters of dispute.'

'Tika isn't treated too differently when she visits the villages here,' Navan observed. 'Everyone seems pleased to see her and chat about anything.'

He and Tika waited again for Dromi's opinion. 'I agree that the people here have an affection and admiration for Tika, but I believe there is also a barrier, thin though it might be, to them treating her *exactly* as they would treat each other.'

Tika straightened suddenly. 'Visitors,' she said, hurrying from the hall.

Four people stood on the circle when Tika and Fedran emerged from the House: Lady Ricca, Lady Elora, Captain Shtok and Mekla. Tika saw at once that Ricca looked anxious although Elora did not. She smiled in welcome. 'Come in,' she invited them.

As they walked inside, Elora held up a large folder. 'May I go and speak to Mardis and Dog? I have some papers for them.'

'You know where the library is,' Tika nodded.

Lady Elora made for the stairs and Tika led the remaining three Kelshans into the hall. Ricca looked up at her. 'Captain Shtok and Mekla might watch if your children are training please?' she asked. 'I would like to talk to you privately?'

Mystified, Tika nodded. Fedran took the two men off to the drill hall as Ricca added. 'Can we go to your rooms?'

'Certainly. Come on.' Tika saw Ricca had a satchel, like Dromi used for his papers, and wondered what was so clearly bothering the child. They climbed the stairs in silence and Tika was concerned by the very obvious feeling of relief she sensed as they sat on pillows before the fire. Cerys sat up, staring at the girl, then stepped daintily close to her knees where she settled and began to purr. Ricca pulled her satchel round from her back, hugging it close.

'What's wrong, Ricca? Is it anything I can help with?' Tika asked, her voice gentle.

Ricca bit her lip then looked up at Tika. 'I think there's more trouble, in the middle lands, but General Falkir hasn't said anything. Why would he not inform me if there is trouble in my lands?'

'Perhaps he is investigating whether there really is a problem?' Tika suggested. 'Have you asked him?'

Tears welled in the dark brown eyes but didn't spill. 'I heard General Falkir talking to one of his staff officers. The door was open a bit. I had thought of something to ask him, he wasn't expecting me. He said to the officer that he wouldn't worry me with it. I left them and went back to my apartments. I am Imperatrix in Waiting. I *should* know of any trouble any of my people face. I *trusted* him, Tika!' She unfastened her satchel and drew out some papers. Her chin jutted. 'I took some of these from the officer's desk,' she said.

Tika had to admire the child's determination. She glanced at a page. 'Mertasia. Where is that?'

Ricca dug out a map Tika recognised as one Navan had given to her. She spread it on the floor between them. 'Here.' Ricca pointed to a town towards the eastern borders of Kelshan.

'Did you find out what the trouble actually was?'

Ricca took a breath. 'I think there was another large band of soldiers who were just raiding farms but Mertasia is quite a big town. Many of the farms to the east send grain there and there are some different mines to the south east. They send stuff there too, and then it all comes on to Kelshan City.'

'So if the soldiers decided to take over the town, they could stop a lot of food crops reaching the City.' Tika thought aloud.

'It's not just that, Tika!' Ricca burst out. 'I would like to go there and try to *talk* to those soldiers. They are *my* soldiers and they've been wandering around without their officers. I will treat them properly if they come back.'

Tika refrained from mentioning that from all reports she had had, the men had rebelled and killed their officers. 'I admire your suggestion,' she said, choosing her words with care. 'I don't believe General Falkir meant to keep this hidden from you for any bad reasons, Ricca. I would guess he has learned the names of some of those soldiers, and perhaps he knows more of their characters than you can know. I really think you should speak to him, as soon as you go back. Tell him honestly that you have heard of this trouble and want to know exactly what's happening. Truly, Ricca, General Falkir is a most trustworthy and loyal servant to you. This I will swear to.'

Ricca considered Tika's comments. 'Have you seen him? I mean, you can look in people, can't you, and see if they are honest?'

Tika paused. 'Yes, Ricca. The first time I met him, I did indeed see what kind of man he is. He is a good man.'

'Did you look in me too?'

'I did not.' Tika met those dark eyes, her expression serious.

'Why not?'

'Because you are young. I might have sensed that you were furiously angry about something, but that wouldn't mean you would become an angry or impatient adult.'

Ricca thought for a while then heaved an enormous sigh. 'You think I'm stupid, to have doubted the General.'

'No. As I just said, you are very young. You take your

responsibilities very seriously, maybe too seriously at times. I do think you should have spoken to the General straight away, rather than hurrying off and worrying about it.' Tika watched Ricca mull over her words. 'You told me you saw some of the fighting around the Citadel?' she asked.

Ricca nodded.

'Then you must realise that some, if not all, of those soldiers were most certainly not likely to stop and listen to you talk to them then? These soldiers in Mertasia must surely have heard that their rebellion or whatever it was is over? They haven't returned to their City barracks though have they? So I would assume they choose not to.'

'And they would probably laugh at a child going to talk to them?' Ricca's voice was very small.

'It is quite likely they would, my dear, but *I* think your suggestion is extremely brave and shows you care for your people.'

A blush spread over Ricca's cheeks. 'Thank you,' she whispered. 'I really do want to be a good ruler, so people might forget how awful Jemin and Veranta were.'

'Perhaps they shouldn't forget them.' Tika was thoughtful. 'If they remember them, they might be more watchful and never let a leader bully them so badly again.'

Ricca frowned. 'I've allowed the temples to be reopened. You know Veranta closed them all? Jemin kept them closed but Mekla told me people still worship their gods in secret. He said it gives them great comfort. I don't understand it really. I've never heard of any gods, but I told my council to let the temples and shrines open again.' Ricca began to gather up the oddments of paper and stuff them back in her satchel.

'Did the officer get into any trouble, for losing those papers?' Tika asked.

'I don't think so. I didn't hear anything about it and he's still on duty each day when I've been near the offices.'

'You understand he could have been dismissed or worse for the loss of documents? It sounds as though he hasn't told the General that papers are missing.'

Ricca stared at her in shock. 'I didn't think of that,' she admitted.

'So you have been worrying about a group of soldiers in Mertasia who you don't know while an officer you *do* know could be at risk of reprimand because you took his papers?' Tika watched thoughts work through the child's mind.

'I will go to General Falkir as soon as we go back and I'll tell him what I did,' she said at last. 'It's just that I don't always know which people I can trust.'

Tika barely heard the last words. She reached for Ricca's hand. 'I found it hard to trust people,' she told her. 'I trusted Navan when we were children together. Then, I met Kija and Farn and I learned I could trust them. This was before any mage powers grew in me. Now, I *accept* most people but I still need to get to know them to understand I can trust them. All the people here I count as friends, as family. Who do *you* count as friends?'

In the silence Cerys's purr was a comforting buzz. 'You. Mekla. Uncle Shtok.' Ricca sighed. 'General Falkir. Lady Elora. Perhaps Lady Hinna.'

'There you are. They can be the start of *your* family.'

'Family? But we are not related.'

'Family isn't always blood, Ricca. I'm not related to anyone here, not to anyone in the world as far as I know, but they feel like family. I believe the people you named like you, not because of *who* you are but because you are *you*.'

'Your Guards argue with you. Sometimes they're quite rude to you.'

Tika laughed. 'They are. Just as though they were part of a family.' She gave the hand she held a squeeze. 'What about all your wounded soldiers? I'm sure they count you as their friend?'

'They tease me sometimes but they do seem glad to see me.'

'What about other children? Do you know any?'

Tika saw the instant wariness in Ricca's face. 'Jemin made me meet some in the Citadel. I didn't like any of them. They didn't really want to be *friends*. They just hoped I'd like them and favour them when we all grew up. Lara used to try to make me invite some of her nieces but I wouldn't.'

'You never call Jemin your father.'

'No. I only saw him a few times and I didn't like him.' Ricca's reply was flat.

'Unless there's anything else you need to ask me, shall we go and see if Sarila has any cakes or pies?'

Ricca smiled, fastening her satchel then she paused. 'That boy who was here? Tarel?'

Tika kept her expression calm, relaxed, although with an effort, and waited.

'He was not nice. He said nasty things when he took me along to the medical school.'

'Nasty things?'

'Yes. About you. About Iskallia and the people here. I didn't like him or trust him.' Ricca's chin came up again. 'I'm glad he's not here anymore. You wouldn't have been safe. I like those funny twins though,' she added.

'Even when they're covered in mud?' Tika asked, getting up and pulling Ricca to her feet.

'I told my hurt soldiers about that. They said I should try it.'

Tika laughed, opening the door and they descended the stairs with a much less worried Imperatrix in Waiting.

In the hall, they sat alone at Tika's table while Sarila served them with a large dish of pies and another of various cakes. 'Where are the Dragons?' Ricca asked, spraying crumbs across the table just as her tutor walked in with Dog. Lady Elora rolled her eyes but made no comment as she joined them.

'They've gone to hunt. They're always hungry after they've taken us travelling. Two new Dragons joined us but they are at Dragons Rest, along the valley. They are still shy,' Tika explained.

'What are their names? Are they young or old? Why are they along the valley?'

'The male is called Minyth and his sister is Heligg. They are young. They are staying with Fenj. He is one of the very oldest Dragons and is Brin's father.'

Ricca paused as she reached for another fruit pie. 'Can I meet him one day?'

'If you want to. I can take you, on Farn.' Tika laughed

197

at the child's expression. 'Not today though. Let the new ones stay quiet for a while,' she added.

'Lady Elora has been most helpful,' Dog said. 'She's written a great many suggestions to help us with the teaching.'

'I also have someone who could come here for a while to assist if you allowed,' Lady Elora said. 'He is young but a gifted teacher in my opinion. I have spoken with him and he would be very glad to offer his services.'

Dog nodded so Tika shrugged. 'Send him along whenever you choose then. I think Dog and Mardis would appreciate the help.'

'We would,' added Dog fervently.

'His name is Rumak. I think you'll find him useful. I can bring him in a day or two if that suits?'

'That would be good as I'm expecting to have to travel again soon,' Tika agreed.

'This room is bigger,' Ricca suddenly announced.

Tika's expression was bland as she saw Lady Elora look around with a frown. 'I happened to mention, that with two new Dragons who will, no doubt, want to sit close to the fire during the winter, we would need a bigger hall. It appears that the House heard me and erm stretched itself overnight.' She gave an innocent smile while Lady Elora's frown deepened.

'The House *listens* to you?' asked Ricca.

'It seems to.' To Tika's relief she saw Fedran arrive with Mekla and Captain Shtok.

Mekla started explaining some of the drills they'd been watching and Ricca pushed the plate of pies towards him. Shtok glanced at Tika with a shy smile. 'The children work really hard,' he said softly. 'Even the littlest ones.'

'Could I learn their drills?' Ricca asked. Shtok nodded. 'Then I'll start when we get back. After I've seen General Falkir that is,' Ricca added after a glance at Tika.

As they escorted the visitors out to the circle shortly afterwards, Lady Elora turned back to Tika. 'I'll send Rumak to you either later today or early tomorrow I think, rather than risk you being away,' she said.

Tika nodded and watched them as they moved to the

circle's centre. Lady Elora's lips moved as she silently said the words she'd been taught to activate the circle. There was a pop of air and the Kelshans were gone.

Walking back into the House, Dog's elbow jabbed into Tika's ribs. 'The House stretched itself!' she scoffed. 'Just as if that's perfectly normal!'

'Well it *is* normal for this House,' Tika pointed out.

Fedran laughed. 'Captain Shtok noticed right away,' he said. 'I told him the hall had extended itself and he just groaned.'

'I meant to ask earlier - where are Volk or Onion?'

Fedran shook his head. 'Volk went off to Romaby apparently, two days ago. I have no idea where Onion is.'

'Who does?' Dog retorted. 'That man can vanish even when you think he's right next to you.'

Chapter Eighteen

Ashri rose slowly, reluctantly, through Mother's Darkness. Some of her questions had been answered although not all. Unsure of how long she'd been absent, she checked on Endis. He was cooking something in his rooms, humming a melody Ashri thought she recognised. She returned to herself and summoned her shadows. She asked them specific questions and received more information than she'd expected. Then Ashri praised them for their diligence in provisioning Endis with the real foods he needed to sustain him now, and asked them to seek out answers to other puzzles.

It had been too long since she had employed them as she could, and should, have done. They had wandered, aimless and confused, but she sensed a renewed determination in them to return to their original duties. While Endis slept, Ashri's senses roamed across the world below, pausing occasionally where something snagged her attention. She thought briefly of Ferag and hoped she wasn't too distressed. She also hoped Ferag would not try to confront Youki. Ashri was still not at all sure of Youki's real powers and she had no wish to see Ferag hurt, or worse.

Ashri was fully aware of the power of the shadows but right now she could spare none to watch over Ferag. Endis slept now, and the Augur continued to watch the world but neither she nor her shadows could locate Youki. One place in particular, the shadows had been told to mark more closely, but with no results so far.

When Endis joined her in the morning, he found a steaming bowl of tea beside his chair and the Augur sipping from her own. 'Have you explored further along the passage yet, child?'

'I've been to the library several times,' he said.

The Augur smiled. 'There are three other libraries here, one each on the next floors up.'

Endis stared at her. 'Wherever did you get all the books

that you must have here?' he asked.

'Child! Child! I've shown you the pictures of the mighty cities that have arisen and fallen on the world! I rescued many books from many places.'

He gave her an admiring grin. 'In Iskallia they don't let Dog and Mardis go away where there might be a library. They have been known to help themselves to quite a lot I was told.'

The Augur laughed. 'There are books here they might find of interest I'm sure but that's for another day perhaps.'

'Many that I've glanced at are in languages I can't understand.'

'Don't worry so, child. You *will* be able to read them.'

'You spoke of shadows to me once,' Endis began.

The Augur was slightly startled. It seemed odd that he should mention shadows when she had been thinking of them so much recently. She waited.

'Tika has shadows,' he said. 'She said Lord Darallax gave them to her. Are they the same as the ones you spoke of?'

'Tika's are similar, but they can be - wilder. They have been abandoned, ignored. It isn't simple to explain, Endis. After the Last Battle, Darallax hid the remnant of his people, quite understandably. But he let his Shadows do as they wished. All he asked of them was that they continued to hide the island where he had found refuge.'

'What do you mean - wild?'

'They can kill.' The sharp blue eyes met Endis's stare steadily.

Endis paled. 'You can command them to kill?'

'I can, although I have rarely done so.'

'What are your duties, as the Sentinel?'

'I watch the world, child. I have followed certain bloodlines through countless millennia.' The Augur watched the boy turning over her words in his mind and waited for his next question.

'What is Mother Dark's plan for this world? She obviously has a great interest in it, so has she an end in view, of how she wants it to be?'

The Augur held out her empty tea bowl towards him.

He smiled and set about making fresh tea. 'When Mother Dark discovered this world, it was fresh born from the Vortex. It was a mass of rock and fire. Something about it appealed to her, so she settled down to watch how it might grow. That is when she made the gods' space, which remained just an empty place for a long while. Then, as tiny life forms grew on the world, Mother created the first of her children.'

Endis took tea across to her. 'Lerran, Hanlif and Darallax,' he smiled.

'And Olekatah,' The Augur added very softly.

Endis grew still, now listening closely. This was the first time she had spoken of the man, god, being, he had glimpsed in his dream.

'Olekatah was the very first. Mother made all of her children in the form you have now. She had seen another, much older world, where similar creatures lived and she found the form pleasing.' The Augur fell silent but Endis said nothing, watching her face as she reached so far back in her memory.

'Mother saw a life form begin to develop on this world and was pleased. But Olekatah. He was the first, and she made him strong. Far too strong. It meant he was too powerful and also too wild.'

'Like the shadows?' Endis whispered.

The Augur shook her head sadly. 'Far more than the shadows, child. Very few of the lesser gods who came later, knew anything of him. He had little patience. He had no wish to watch the slow growth of a new world so Mother sent him away. He is bound by her command not to come near this world, or to enter the gods' space. He rages through the infinity, alone. He was still in the gods' space when Mother made Lerran, Hanlif and Darallax, before she realised her errors with Olekatah.'

There was another long pause and Endis stayed silent.

'Olekatah loved Lerran and Darallax and was kind and gentle with them. Even then though, Hanlif was jealous, always claiming he should have been first made. When Olekatah was absent, Hanlif hurt Lerran and Darallax. When Olekatah returned, he was enraged. Mother concealed Hanlif while Olekatah ripped apart the gods' space until nothing was left, then Mother revealed her power and sent him away. That is when he was refused any contact with the gods. Mother brought many more lesser gods into being but I believe she grieves still for Olekatah. There were vague stories told of him, of his monstrous anger, but I really think Mother would reclaim him if she could.'

Silence fell again and the Augur drained her tea bowl.

Finally Endis smiled at her. 'You know all these things because you too are one of the gods, are you not?'

She returned his smile. 'I am, yes, child, but I am in this human body for the length of my service here.' Her smile became a grin. 'This body is extremely tired now. It aches constantly, just to remind me.'

'What will happen when your poor body fails?'

'I will return to the form Mother first gave me.'

'Who will live here? Who will be the Sentinel?'

'Oh Endis.' The ancient being and the young man stared at each other until the young man closed his eyes.

'I am half Asatarian, half of this world. My Asatarian blood might let me live longer than many natives here but even so, I would not survive even a fraction of the length of your life.'

'Mother Dark has her reasons for choosing you, child. Ask her when you meet her. As for longevity.' She smiled again. 'That obstacle has been addressed.' She sensed sudden exhaustion in Endis and knew it was the last of his humanity trying to protect his full awareness from what was unfolding in his shocked mind. 'Rest, Endis. Mother will summon you soon and you will understand. Do not forget, you will have a choice, child. Should you refuse her request, you will return to Iskallia.'

Endis got to his feet slowly. 'If I return to Iskallia, I will end in madness, will I not?'

'You will, but it will be your decision, your choice, dear child. The Augur watched through her mind, as Endis trudged so wearily across the wide passageway. She saw him walk straight through the garden, barely noticing anything as he passed. He entered his small rooms and lay on his bed, staring unseeing at the ceiling.

Closing her own eyes, she sent a murmured thought to Mother Dark. 'The child is ready, Mother. He was more surprised than I had expected him to be. I imagined he had reached some conclusions by now but it seems he has not.'

Deep in the immensity that was Mother Dark, part of her awareness stirred, responding to Ashri's words. 'You have done well. I am grateful for your long service, little one. I ask your patience for just a little longer.'

Ashri felt a warmth as a small amount of renewed energy washed through this frail body, and she sank back into her pillows and relaxed.

Endis was awake, aware. He was quite sure of that as he could hear the rustle of leaves and the drone of insects through the open door to the garden. Then, he was engulfed in Darkness. For a brief moment, he panicked. It felt as though he'd been plunged into water of an unknown but terrifying depth. When he realised he was breathing, he abandoned the idea of water but let himself float. He could no longer hear the bees. He could hear nothing in a silence more profound than he'd ever before experienced. Slowly, he felt movement around him but in the complete blackness he couldn't begin to guess what or who moved near him.

After the first moments of fear, he calmed and realised he must somehow be near or even within whatever Mother Dark actually was. Gradually the sense of hearing returned. A multitude of voices; young, old, male, female, murmuring words he couldn't understand. Finally one voice came clearer, surrounding him. This voice was female, both young and old.

'You have learned much, child of Andis and Akiva. You believe your mother's blood precludes you from working as the representative, as the guardian, of the world below. It does not. Your mother's spirit was strong and true, focussed only on you and your survival. She knew you would be of importance to this world.'

'How?' Endis interrupted this quiet mix of voices, unaware of the tears on his face.

'I sent her dreams, little one. Dreams she understood were true foretelling.'

204

'What happened to her?' Endis managed to ask.

'She took her own life but I brought her to my Darkness. She did not sink into the earth with the rest of your people.'

There was a muted humming sound while Endis struggled to compose himself. At last he asked: 'What is it you want of me?' He felt a lightness around him, not of vision, which remained totally black, but of feeling, of emotion.

When the voice spoke again, it was still gentle but had a ring of seriousness. 'I ask now that you take my sweet Ashri's place, as the Sentinel of this world. I ask you to watch, to listen, to record and, in very few instance, to act.'

Endis found himself trembling as he floated in this strange, empty Darkness. 'You consider me worthy?' He wasn't sure if he spoke those words aloud or just thought them. He was enveloped in warmth, in affection.

'You are worthy, child.'

'Must Ashri leave me at once?' He sensed amusement from whatever power surrounded him.

'Not quite yet. She will help you a little longer. So do you consent, Endis of Iskallia?'

He let out a long, long breath. 'I do, but must I be always alone in whatever place Ashri dwells in?'

Again, affection and amusement washed over him. 'For a time, a considerable time by your way of reckoning, you will be free to return to the world on occasion.'

Once more Endis felt utterly exhausted but Mother's last words were clear, even as he fell into a natural sleep, back on his bed. 'I am grateful for your acceptance, Endis. Know that I will always keep you safe.'

When the Kelshans were gone, Tika went up to the archives, stopping at Navan's map room on the way. 'Have you a map of Kelshan with the towns marked on it?' she asked.

'Yes. Telk's been a great help with a lot of the names. Why?'

'Would you bring it up to the archives please? I'll tell you up there.

Navan took a rolled map from one of the wall of pigeon

holes and followed Tika out. In the archives, she spoke immediately. 'Ricca said she had heard there was trouble in a place called Mertasia, a large town in the far east of Kelshan. She said she overheard Falkir discussing it with one of his staff but he didn't tell her about it. That's what she was upset about.'

'Here.' Navan had spread his map over the table and now pointed to the name inscribed beside a large dot. 'Mertasia. It does look quite a bit bigger than most others there.'

Dromi frowned. 'I believe I've heard of it. It's a collecting point for grain crops I think, and for minerals.' He bent over the map, his finger tracing a route between Mertasia, north east, to pause at Braxton Mines.

Tika scowled. 'The mines were destroyed, weren't they?' she said.

Werlan shook his head. 'The offices and slave quarters were burned down, yes, but the mines are still there, below ground.'

'Ricca said Mertasia gathered foods then sent them on to Kelshan City. Another large band of soldiers are in the area now, threatening the town.'

'When did Lady Ricca hear of this? Did she ask General Falkir about it?' asked Werlan.

Tika sat down with a groan. 'I think it must have been when she sent the first private message to me, while we were away.'

'Five days ago,' Werlan told her.

'She was suddenly struck by doubts about trusting the General because he didn't speak of it. Ricca helped herself to some papers from the staff officer's desk. I'm guessing he hasn't reported them missing to Falkir yet as Falkir still hasn't spoken to Ricca.'

'So Ricca thinks he is deliberately withholding information from her.' Navan sounded sympathetic. 'Given her experiences, not really surprising.'

'She said she would go and talk to the soldiers and welcome them back.' Tika saw three faces showing sudden alarm. 'No. I hope I convinced her that wasn't likely to work in these circumstances. She said they had no officers to lead them. I don't think it has occurred to her that *they* had slaughtered their own officers by all reports.'

'It was a courageous idea,' said Werlan. 'If unwise.'

'She really does want to be a good ruler, but she is still so young. She can't see that some soldiers, those in open rebellion, would cheerfully kill her if they chose to.'

Dromi had been checking through his reports. 'There is nothing here from Falkir suggesting any problems.'

'Perhaps it isn't so large a group of rebels as Lady Ricca thought?'

Tika shrugged. 'Who knows, Werlan. She said she would speak to Falkir as soon as she got back to Kelshan and tell him she'd heard him speaking and that she took papers from his officer's desk.'

'She doesn't want for courage,' Navan said.

'I'm not sure if she truly understands that, as yet, she has no real power. She can *say* she'd like this or that done, but the power for now is in the hands of Falkir and the council.'

Navan was still studying the map. 'I could go and look, Tika. See what might really be happening at Mertasia?'

The three men waited while Tika considered the idea. 'Very well, but take Geffal or someone with you, and make sure Storm keeps you all shielded.'

Navan nodded. He rolled up the map and left the archives in search of Fedran. He'd prefer to ask the Guard Captain who he should take with him.

Tika followed Navan out and descended the stairs to the library. She found Mardis and Dog discussing the papers Lady Elora had brought for them.

'Elora said she'll send a young man maybe later today, to help out,' Tika told them.

Mardis shuffled the scattered papers then beamed at Tika. 'Some of these suggestions are so simple. I would never have thought of them, but I can see how clever they actually are.'

'We're not trying to wriggle out of teaching,' said Dog. 'But it does take up more and more of our time.' She glanced round at the shelves. 'We do have other things to do. It gets a bit easier when the weather changes but it still keeps us a bit busier than we need.'

Leaving the library, Tika went on down to the hall, then paused at the door when she saw the two sitting at her table. She continued in and sat down with them. 'Ama. Etto. How can I help?' she asked with a certain wariness.

'We didn't realise that girl was here,' Ama explained.

'Ricca,' added Etto.

'She came to, erm, ask me something.'

'Oh. Well, we would have asked her to join in, like you said, if we'd known.' Ama stared at Tika reproachfully.

'We told some of the others what you said,' said Etto.

'And Jarko and Seko,' added Ama.

'What I said?'

Ama rolled her eyes. 'Yes. When you said about not hitting her too hard?'

'Oh. Yes. I remember.'

'Jarko and Seko knew what you meant. They explained it better than we could, to the others.' Etto gave her a sweet smile. 'We practised fighting drills but without hurting anyone.'

'It's very hard,' said Ama, her brows forming one line, exactly like her mother's. 'But we're quite good at it now.'

'We do normal drills, then Seko suddenly calls out - *"ease!"* and we have to try to stop hurting whoever we're fighting.' Etto waved his hands wildly, indicating complicated manoeuvres.

'We would have asked her to join us if we'd known she was here,' Ama repeated.

Tika waited but apparently the twins felt they'd explained enough. She cleared her throat. 'I'm very impressed that you've given it so much thought. It is very kind of you and I'm sure Ricca will visit again soon. Perhaps I could suggest she joins you when I write to her next?'

Two pairs of the palest blue eyes stared at her then they glanced at each other and nodded. Ama slid off her chair and reached up to Tika for a hug. Etto repeated the gesture. 'You'll ask her soon, won't you?' Ama checked.

'I will,' Tika replied. She watched the two sturdy little figures trot out of the hall and then saw Pearl peer in. The Sea Dragon paced to the hearth followed by Farn.

'My Tika! We went to Dragons Rest. Minyth and Heligg have been meeting the people there. They are quite happy and mother said she will bring them here perhaps tomorrow.'

Tika hugged him. 'I'm glad they're content.'

Farn settled near Pearl as Genia came into the hall. 'Did you notice anything - odd - last night?' Tika asked.

'Oh there was a big tingly feeling but mother said it was just the House having a stretch.' Farn's mind voice was quite cheerful, matter of fact.

Tika looked to Pearl and Genia for confirmation. 'Tingly,' agreed Genia, amusement in her tone.

Tika had the sense that Pearl wasn't quite so comfortable with the change in the hall and reached to stroke her face. She thought it best not to question further, instead asking where they had gone to hunt. Farn launched into a description of the empty mountainsides beyond the Barrier Mountains north of Iskallia and Tika listened patiently. She stayed with the three most of the afternoon, greeting Brin when he paced in. 'Are you well Brin?'

'I am.' His mind tone held affection. 'Did you know the forge stretched too, last night.' From his tone now, Tika guessed he too felt a slight unease in the strange behaviour of this House.

'I hope it hasn't inconvenienced Garrol? I wondered why none of them have been here today. No one was hurt were they?'

'No. But they've been rearranging everything.' Brin reclined along the wall beside the hearth.

'The forge fire - that wasn't moved was it?'

Brin stared down at her. 'No. Garrol says there is room for another forge fire now and for more of us to watch them work. Skay told me it was a shivery feeling, similar to how the circles feel to us.'

'Tingly,' Farn agreed.

Brin's eyes whirred momentarily. 'Shivery, tingly, itchy,' he said. Even as he mind spoke, they all, Tika as well, turned to the door, aware that the great circle outside was active.

There was no doubting Brin and Pearl's alarm but Tika

soothed them quickly. 'Someone is coming from Kelshan.' She hurried out and reached the outer doors beside Fedran.

A young man stood on the coloured stones, a look of wonder on his face. He had a large pack on his back and an even larger one by his feet. A quick check told Tika he suffered no ill effects from his journey and she walked forward with a smile. 'You must be Rumak. Welcome to Iskallia. I am Tika and this is Fedran, Captain of Guards.'

Fedran stepped onto the circle and lifted the large pack. It was far heavier than he'd expected as Tika saw from his surprised expression.

'Oh thank you,' the young man said, as Fedran heaved the pack off the circle. 'I brought some books with me.' Following Fedran towards Tika, he halted, bowing. 'Lady Tika. It is an honour to offer what assistance I can.'

Tika studied him, sighed and slid an arm through his. 'First of all, Rumak, you have to understand how very informal we are here. You call me Tika, not Lady. Come inside. We'll find rooms for you later.'

Entering the hall and sitting at Tika's table, the young man at first didn't notice four Dragons regarding him with interest. He appeared to lose the ability to speak. Farn bustled over. 'I am Farn, soul bond to my Tika,' he announced in mind speech.

Rumak drew breath. 'I am glad to meet you Farn,' he managed to croak.

Tika laughed. 'The crimson Dragon is Brin and the purple is Genia.'

Pearl had followed Farn to the table and Tika stroked her cheek. 'This is Pearl.'

'Are you the teacher?' Pearl enquired. 'Like Dog and Mardis?'

'I am.' Rumak's voice was a little steadier.

'Mardis reads to me.' Pearl fixed her gaze on the new arrival.

'He does?' Rumak was clearly astonished.

'I want to know many things, but I don't understand the marks humans put on papers,' Pearl continued. 'Mardis reads the marks then explains things. Will you?'

Taking pity on the poor man who was quite out of his

depth right now, Tika replied. 'I'm sure he will help Mardis once he's had time to settle in here, and gets used to us all,' she said.

Pearl's eyes flashed, a silver glitter. 'Good,' she said and returned to the hearth, reclining against Genia.

'I do hope you haven't changed your mind?' Tika smiled sympathetically at Rumak.

'I have heard of the Dragons here but meeting them is a bit, erm, daunting,' Rumak answered, still gazing at them.

'Pearl's Flight cast her out because she asked too many questions,' Farn told him helpfully.

'Hush now Farn, let him be for a while. You know travelling a circle can be tiring.'

Farn pulsed friendliness and retreated to join the others.

'It will soon be supper time. You'll meet Dog and Mardis then.' Tika laughed softly. 'You *will* get used to us, I'm sure, Rumak.'

Chapter Nineteen

When Endis woke, he was disorientated. He swung his legs over the side of the bed and sat staring at the room with no recognition. Before panic could take hold, his mind settled and he knew where he was. Shaking his head at the oddness of that brief sensation of strangeness, he washed and dressed in clean clothes. Making tea, he leaned against the side of the door and looked at the garden. The seeds he'd planted were flourishing. He sipped his tea and watched the blooms swinging on the vines that climbed up beside the door. Then he froze, tea bowl halfway to his lips. He knew the name of the plant.

Endis looked at the other flowers and their names came clear to his mind. After a while, he turned back to his room, rinsed his bowl and sat at the table, quietly waiting for the Augur's summons. A smile touched his lips. Should he now call her the god Ashri, rather than the Ancient Augur, he wondered. He felt the light touch of her mind and he rose, walking through the garden, across the passage to her door. Entering, Endis saw she had made tea as she had done every day of late, and she was back in her chair.

He wished her good morning and sat down. Looking across at her, Endis straightened. He had grown used to her age, her frailty, but it seemed overnight she had aged even more. Still those clear blue eyes shone from the nest of wrinkles that was her face. 'Are you ill? What's happened?' It took Endis a moment to realise the rictus expression was an attempt at a smile.

'Drink your tea, child. I will make you no more I'm afraid.'

Endis moved to kneel beside her to hear the faint words.

'The end is here for this poor body which has served me so stoically for so very long.' Her right hand rose, trembling with the effort, and cupped his cheek. 'I will be able to help you a little longer at least, but not like this, not like this.'

Her fingers quivered on his skin and Endis lifted his

hand, laying it over hers and keeping it pressed to his face. 'I'm not ready for this, not on my own, not yet,' he whispered.

'Oh but you are, sweet boy, and you will not be alone. I will be near you and Mother is always close, as are your shadows.' Her breath stuttered and her hand tightened on his face. 'Serve well my dear Sentinel. Serve well.' Paper thin lids drooped, hiding her eyes and a soft breath sighed on to his face. The Augur's body seemed to shrink, become even smaller in the chair. Her cloak fell aside, revealing her left hand with its bandage through which blood seeped.

Endis bent forward, kissing the soft skin of the Augur's cheek, placing her right hand on her lap. Then he slowly rose, backing towards his chair, too stunned to begin to think. He drained the tea she'd made him, now cold, and saw a faint shimmer around the Augur's chair. The mist wavered then slowly took form. Endis stared at the slender young girl. She wore a simple shift and her feet were bare. Her hair flowed down over her shoulders, long and thick and the purest white. But the eyes were the same; crystal clear blue looking across at him.

Endis could only stare. Ashri looked down, holding out her arms and studying the firm, smooth flesh. Her laugh was that of a child as she raised her head, meeting his gaze. 'I promise you I will be close, Endis, for as long as Mother allows. All this is yours now, as are my memories. I am proud of you. I know you will serve well.' She glanced down at the body in the chair. 'Take that poor shell up to the top rooms, dear child. Let it lie at peace among the birds and give them whatever nourishment it might offer them.'

The look she gave him was of joy, and of love. Then, between one breath to the next, she was gone. The silence in the room was profound. Endis rose, returning to the body in the chair. Staring at the face, it seemed some of the wrinkles had smoothed out. With gentle hands, he drew the hood down, then gathered the fold of the cloak across the body. Endis lifted her with enormous care, saddened even more by her barely noticeable weight. Straightening, he turned towards the door, which opened even as he paused.

Out in the passage, he glanced down at his burden when the Augur's head settled against his shoulder. He pictured the airy upper rooms and, with no sense of motion, he was there. Endis carried his teacher to the wide arches, thinking to let her see her precious needles one last time. He sighed at his sentimentality and walked on to the impossible room at the furthest end of the walkway. At the entrance, he stared at an endless landscape, trees and grasses unmoving as he watched. He carried her to the small pool and knelt, finally setting her down on soft, lush grass. Endis folded her hood back a little and opened the front of her cloak.

'Thank you. I will do my best to fulfil your belief in me. And I will miss you.'

Bowing his head for a moment, he then rose, turning away, retracing his steps to the entrance. He glanced back when he heard the sound of wings and watched as several crows settled on a branch near the pool. 'Farewell,' he murmured, and strode back to where the stairs were, opposite the room with the spacious vista.

He descended, flight after flight, aware of so many things moving through his mind. He let his hand brush the stone wall beside him and he *knew* how they were made. On the ground floor, he walked steadily back along to the courtyard garden. He stopped briefly, looking towards the Augur's door but decided not yet. Entering the garden, he went on to his rooms and sat at his table. Today of all days, he understood he must begin to record far more than he had done before.

As the enlarged hall in Iskallia began to fill with people, Dog and Mardis arrived at Tika's table. She introduced Rumak, who apologised as Mardis fell over the large bag of books. At the mention of the word "books", Mardis and Dog beamed at the young man.

'Later!' Tika ordered. 'When you've eaten, you can take the books and Rumak, and get him settled in a room.'

Food was served and Rumak seemed surprised at the variety of dishes spread before him. Tika noticed, and wondered, not for the first time, just what most people ate in Kelshan. Dog watched Rumak eating, ready to pounce as soon as he finished. When they finally extricated him from behind the table and prepared to drag him and his bags to the library, Tika caught Dog's sleeve. '*Don't* keep the poor man up all night, Dog. Remember how angry you made me when the printers first came here.'

Dog paused, meeting Tika's eyes. She nodded. 'We'll treat him with great and tender care,' she promised, then spoiled the effect by winking.

'He seemed a bit shocked,' Shea observed, beside her.

Tika smiled. 'Well, he'll either get used to us or run gibbering back to Kelshan,' she said.

'He'll stay,' Essa put in.

'You think so?'

'Oh yes. He's quite like Dog and Mardis himself. Or Pearl,' she added after a moment's thought.

Tika quirked a brow.

'Endlessly curious,' Essa explained.

'You think Rumak is, too?' asked Shea.

Essa nodded.

'Pearl already warned him he would be reading to her at least.'

Those round the table listening to the conversation began to smile.

'She did?' asked Shea.

'Yes Shea. Almost as soon as he'd arrived.' Tika shook her head. 'Poor man.'

'Were you planning to travel soon, Tika?' asked Dromi.

'Not until Navan and Geffal are back. I suspect we might hear from Falkir fairly soon too. I hope he doesn't feel we should have reported what Ricca told me.'

'What about Gremara?' Dromi's voice was low. 'Will you visit her?'

'I really don't know,' Tika replied. 'I would quite like to, but I can't decide if it would cause her more trouble. That son, Kahn, he will have grown and I judge he could be vicious beyond all.'

'How many will travel?'

'I'm not sure, Fedran. Let's wait until we hear Navan's report.'

'How long would it take Falkir to get a force to Mertasia

from the Citadel?' asked Essa.

'Quite a while, unless he sends a mounted battalion,' Fedran replied.

'I'm going to bed.' Tika stood. 'Oh. Farn said Kija might bring the new Dragons here tomorrow. Let people know, would you?' She went across to say goodnight to the four Dragons at the hearth then went up to her rooms.

Cerys had left her usual position close to the fire and Tika was surprised to see the cat perched on a windowsill, staring out and up. Tika joined her. 'What are you looking at?' she asked.

'The frost. But I can't.'

Tika stroked the cat, wondering why she was making such an odd comment. It was more the sort of thing she'd expect Pearl to say. 'You can't see the frost?'

Green gold eyes squinted up at her for a moment. 'Well of *course* I can see it once it's *there,* but I can't see how it *gets* there.'

Tika decided silence was best and simply continued to stroke Cerys' back.

'There's still a lot of snow in the garden,' Cerys said after a while.

Feeling a little more confident, Tika nodded. 'It's mostly in shadow there still so it stays cold.'

'Well *obviously.*'

Realising that whatever she chose to say would clearly be the wrong thing, Tika went to sit at her table without further discussion.

Navan and Geffal arrived back as lunch was served next day, Storm following them into the hall.

'Storm can show you pictures, but there are a *lot* of men massing north and east of that town,' Navan said.

Storm sent mind pictures to all in the hall and Rumak, seated between Mardis and Dog, gave an audible gasp. Tika frowned. There were indeed a very large number of men in the area but she was alarmed to see just how close, how low, Storm had flown over them. Navan interpreted her scowl and grinned. 'Storm kept us shielded the whole time we were anywhere near people,' he said.

'So how many men would Falkir be likely to send to try to control that situation?' she asked.

'That would depend on how accurate the information has been that he has received,' Dromi said. 'It is a big town. I would have expected there to be some kind of military presence there. Not only is it a large town, it holds considerable wealth in the form of grains and ores.'

'Did all the various garrisons rise against their officers after I killed Jemin?'

'It appears so Tika. I've not heard of many big forces who returned to Kelshan City, only small bands or individual stragglers.'

'How confident would Falkir be about the loyalty of any men he might send to deal with this though?' Dog asked.

'If he has enough strong officers, officers who have the respect of their men, they should stay loyal,' said Fedran.

Telk nodded. He had been listening closely. Once a major in the Kelshan army himself, he had been all too well aware of many senior officers' bad handling of the men under their command.

'We saw no signs of any military group heading towards Mertasia from the City,' Geffal added. 'Storm flew high a little way west. We would have been able to see any relieving force if they were on their way.'

Now Tika was worried. 'I'm sure Falkir is determined to have a peaceful, prosperous Kelshan but it sounds odd if he hasn't ordered troops to that area.'

'Unless he has been receiving false information,' Dromi suggested with a frown.

All around the table sat in silent thought before the new arrival, Rumak, cleared his throat. 'There have been no large military departures from the City,' he said a little nervously. 'Most battalions leave from the Citadel when ordered away, and people along the streets wave them off.'

Now expressions showed more concern as faces turned to Tika for her opinion. She twisted one of the small gold hoops she wore in her ears, scowling in thought. 'I think we'll have to send word of what you've seen, Navan. I agree Falkir has probably been sent false reports from there.'

'If Mertasia is overrun by those rebel soldiers, it will

seriously affect food supplies to the City,' Dromi agreed.

'Navan, Geffal, go with Dromi and write to Falkir. Let me see your message but don't take too long. I want him to know quickly.'

The three men left in a hurry but Tika's scowl remained. She looked at Telk. 'Is it likely an officer could still remain, capable of controlling that many men? Like Major Jubar did, on Strale and Chaban's borders?'

Telk looked at Seko then both shook their heads. 'We'd heard of Jubar,' said Seko. 'But I don't know of any other.'

'Will you give it some thought please? It seems unlikely to me that such a large number of men would be gathered there. All our reports have spoken of groups of perhaps twenty or thirty, harassing smaller villages or farms. This seems far too organised to me.'

'It does.' Essa finally spoke. 'There has to be at least one man in charge of that many men.' She glanced at Dog. 'How many do you reckon were there?'

'Two thousand, probably more rather than less.

Essa nodded her agreement. 'Then I would guess there must be a *group* in charge, Tika, not one individual. Maybe a dozen? One man *may* be giving the orders but he would need several others at least to enforce those orders on a large group of unstable soldiers.'

'Unstable?' asked Shea.

'Unsettled, lacking their old disciplined routines, with a deep distrust of their officers,' Essa clarified.

Seko agreed with Essa. 'There were so many men, Tika, but they looked organised, not just a jumble of men. Their tents were in lines. There is *someone* in charge of them, that's for sure.'

'Could Kelshan split even further?' Mardis's beard was a tangle of knots as he thought. 'I mean Tarran, Jarred, Strale and Chaban have all reclaimed their independence. Are there other regions within Kelshan land that could decide to split away?'

Rumak realised all eyes were now focussed on him. 'There were many little city states and rural communities, long in the past. I mean *truly* long ago. I doubt many people even know they were once separate places. It's all just been Kelshan since before Imperator Jarvos, at least a hundred years. I know about them because I read books, scrolls, reports I found in the Citadel's archives. The archives are a polite name for a room where whatever previous clerks have considered to be rubbish is kept,' he added.

Mardis and Dog stared at him. 'If they are considered rubbish,' Dog said. 'Might it be possible for us to remove it for you?'

'Dog, stop it! You can talk about that later. Right now, I'm really worried about this situation at Mertasia. I think I'm going to ask you Fedran, and Essa, and Navan too, to take the letter when I've signed it, to explain exactly what we've discovered. I know it's already late but Falkir needs to know.'

Essa got to her feet, towering over the table. 'I'll get into uniform,' she said, striding from the hall. She hadn't been on duty today so was wearing the usual mixture of casual garments most people wore here.

'I can take them, Tika.' Brin's mind voice was a gentle rumble.

Tika looked across at him. 'I thank you my dear, but they will use the circle tonight.'

Most people in the hall had listened to the discussion at Tika's table but now they began to talk among themselves. Dromi, Navan and Geffal rejoined Tika, Dromi offering her the message he'd written. Tika read it through while Fedran told Navan of the plan to visit Falkir now, late though it was. Tika took the pen from Dromi, and the seal of Iskallia. Folding the message, she handed it to Fedran.

'I will await your return,' she told him.

Essa returned in uniform and then went out to the great circle with Navan and Fedran. Tika looked at Dog. 'I hope you've found a room for Rumak?'

'Of course. Just above the library.'

Tika shook her head. 'Rumak, do *not* let these two occupy all your time. Have a look around here. The snow is mostly gone so you can get outside now although it can be cold still. You do *not* have to work all the time.'

Not sure if she was teasing him, Rumak gave a slight

smile. Dog stood. 'We haven't even unpacked the books he brought,' she told Tika in a tone of offended innocence.

'Oh. I could do that now.' Rumak also rose.

Dog smiled. 'We'll help you of course.' She and Mardis Fayle escorted Rumak from the hall.

'Poor man has no idea what he's in for,' Shea murmured.

'Why don't you go and make sure they don't bore him to exhaustion?' Tika suggested.

'I'll go,' Veka said, already on her feet and heading out.

Shea laughed. 'You realise she's as eager to see what he's brought, don't you?'

'I do, but I suspect Veka will be more sympathetic.' Tika smiled although it was obvious to those still at her table that she was worrying about the report Navan had brought from Mertasia.

Much later, only Dromi and Dog sat with Tika, the hall dark but for the fire light. The House was silent around them as they waited for Fedran's return. Then the kitchen door opened and Sarila brought out tea and a loaf, slices of cheese, and cold meat. 'Just in case you're hungry,' she said. 'I'm off to bed but help yourselves if you need more when the others come back.'

'Thank you,' Tika smiled gratefully.

No sooner had Sarila vanished into the kitchens than Tika sat up. 'They're on their way,' she said.

Bare moments later and the three walked into the hall. Dog was pouring bowls of tea even as they sat down. Essa smiled. 'Strange isn't it? We were offered nothing in Kelshan, not even water. They are a strange people.'

'What did Falkir say?' Tika demanded.

'He was shocked,' Fedran replied. 'At first he doubted what we had to tell him but when Navan told him Storm could show him pictures of the men near Mertasia, he began to listen.' He drank some tea before continuing. 'We went to his office where he showed us the last few messages he'd got from his informant in Mertasia. Essa asked to see earlier ones. The writing was different. You had to study them side by side, but they were definitely different.'

Essa was cutting bread and piling cheese on a thick slice. 'It was clear his informant has been replaced by

220

someone more in favour of the rebel soldiers than of the authority of the Citadel,' she said, before taking a bite.

'I showed him on a map where the men were placed, north and east of the town. He'd called in General Parrak and several of his officers by then,' Navan told her.

Fedran pushed his tea bowl towards Dog for a refill. 'I'd guess they'll be up all night. They're moving four battalions out at dawn. All mounted.'

'Will that be enough?' Tika asked.

'Their numbers will be less then the rebels but Navan did not see any horses around Mertasia. Mounted soldiers would have an advantage over foot soldiers, Tika,' Fedran explained.

'Enough of an advantage?'

Fedran spread his hands.

'Geffal and I could stay over the mountains for a few days, keep an eye on any changes?' Navan proposed.

Essa nodded. 'Storm can mind speak back here to Brin or Kija, couldn't he?' she asked.

'He could,' said Tika slowly. 'You're suggesting we watch?' She glanced at Dromi. 'Suppose things go against Falkir's men? Will Falkir be there himself?'

'Oh yes,' Fedran replied. 'He was adamant that he would lead his men. General Parrak will have command in his absence from the Citadel.'

'It's late. Thank you for going to Kelshan. After breakfast I'd like a council meeting I think. I'd like to see what you all think we could, or should, do.'

'We do have a treaty with Kelshan,' Dromi pointed out. 'We are sworn to give them assistance, should they ask it of us.'

The following morning saw Tika and her advisors gathered in the council chamber near the great hall. She explained to those who'd gone to bed before Fedran returned what had occurred in Kelshan. 'I need to know what action you think we should take, if any. I think, with the distances involved between the Citadel and Mertasia, it's going to take several days for Falkir to reach the town, so if the rebels move in before he gets there, it will be harder to get them out.'

Fedran nodded. 'Fighting inside a town gets very messy and difficult, but if Falkir pushes too hard the horses and men will be exhausted by the time they get there.'

'I feel that we have a signed treaty with Kelshan.' Dromi steepled his long fingers on the table. 'We are bound by that agreement to offer aid.'

Tika looked to Werlan for his thoughts. He nodded. 'Dromi is correct regarding Iskallia's commitment to the treaty. Fedran is also correct. Unless Falkir is prudent and rests both horses and men, they will be seriously less able to fight. Your point, about the time it will take him to move his force that distance, is also valid.'

'Can we not do as Navan suggested last night? Go over the mountains and camp there, then keep watch over Mertasia?' asked Essa.

'And what do we do if we see the rebel forces begin to move in?' asked Tika.

'I'd like to know *why* they are holding back now,' said Werlan. 'They are only a few miles beyond the town. Why haven't they attacked already?'

'Is it possible there is still a loyal garrison within Mertasia?' Tika asked.

'Or are the rebels waiting for any particular shipment of minerals to brought in to the town?' Mardis put in.

'There is a garrison there. I asked Falkir last night. His informant was one of the soldiers there,' Fedran told them.

'Which means it could be possible the garrison is compromised,' said Dromi. 'If it is, then we have to wonder if it is only a handful of men who are disaffected, or the whole garrison.'

Tika paced restlessly round and round the chamber before sitting down again. 'I will ask the Dragons which of them would take us. Then, I think, Essa's plan is the one we'll follow.'

Chapter Twenty

Genia arrived in the hall soon after the council meeting ended and Tika went to greet her. 'Kija will be here later,' the purple Dragon told her.

'Are Fenj and Lorak well?' Tika asked.

'They are. I like Cadarn and Sisi. They do a lot for Lorak but he doesn't really notice.'

Tika smiled. The headman of Dragons Rest and his wife were truly kind hearted people. 'And Minyth and Heligg are content?'

'Yes, they are. They have met several villagers and didn't seem nervous.'

Tika hugged her, remembering how very nervous of people Genia herself had been. She left Genia to doze by the fire with Pearl and climbed to the library. A teetering pile of books on a table seemed far more numerous than could have possibly come from Rumak's pack but Tika thought it wiser not to ask. 'Where is the poor man?' she asked Dog instead.

'In that room that appeared behind the drill hall a while ago.' Dog sounded disapproving although whether of Rumak's absence or the appearance of a new room, Tika was unsure.

'What's he doing?'

'It's the room Mardis uses for teaching,' Dog replied patiently. 'He took Rumak there after breakfast.' She put down the book she'd been looking through. 'We'll be going to see what's what at this Mertasia place then?'

'We will. It's a confusing situation though. If there are so many rebel soldiers there, why haven't they already taken the town?'

At that moment Fedran came into the library. 'Telk has just told me he remembers a General, stationed at Mertasia. He thinks the name was Demisen, but he's not absolutely sure. He has heard him spoken of as a friend of General Parrak.'

'Presumably Falkir knows of him so that's not any help to us, although I am glad to know there is a garrison there. How loyal it might be is still questionable,' Tika replied. 'We will not get involved if it's at all avoidable, Fedran. I'm thinking we can over fly the town and observe. You sounded confident of Falkir's mounted soldiers being more than able to deal with the rebels, even if they're outnumbered?'

'Well, it would depend on how much they are outnumbered.'

'I could take a few poppers,' Dog suggested. 'Drop them among the rebel ranks, cause a bit of confusion?'

Not liking the look of approval Fedran gave Dog, Tika was far more cautious. 'I didn't think you had any left?'

Dog rolled her eyes. 'They're not difficult to make, Tika. I *am* an engineer, remember? I like to keep a supply handy.'

Not at all happy with that thought, Tika asked who Fedran would choose to come with them.

He shrugged. 'It depends on how many Dragons agree to take us and which ones. Pearl always says she can carry three but she's still so small. I don't like her taking more than two. Storm always takes Navan and usually Dromi. To be honest, I'm never sure if he'd be willing to take any one else unless Navan is with him.'

Tika had to agree. Of them all, Storm was still the one to show real anger in certain situations. 'Skay is still not happy travelling any distances so she will stay with Minyth and Heligg. It's much too soon for them to travel and witness what might occur.'

Fedran nodded his understanding.

'It is for Kija to decide who goes, Fedran. We'll just have to wait until she's back.'

'Should I leave Geffal in charge here? He doesn't mind once in a while, but I wondered if we should include Telk?'

'No.' Tika was firm. 'We're fairly sure Falkir recognised him as a Kelshan officer although he said nothing. Let's not upset things.'

'When do you want to go?' asked Dog.

'The day after tomorrow,' Tika told them.

After the midday meal, Kija returned, pacing into the hall with the two young Dragons at her tail. There were still a few people lingering after lunch and Tika was glad to see how they smiled and offered quiet greetings. Minyth and Heligg seemed at ease, eyes flashing but with excitement rather than apprehension, Tika sensed. They settled by the hearth, looking all around the hall with great interest. Tika strolled across to speak to them and was reassured that surprising as it had first seemed, these two had indeed accepted humans around them very quickly.

She told Kija they had news of trouble in the Kelshan lands and asked if she might carry them there to observe what unfolded. Kija lowered her head to press her cheek against Tika's. 'Of course, daughter of my heart.'

Brin had watched the new Dragons enter, his eyes bright. 'I shall show you the forge, children, and introduce you to my daughter, Skay. Come.'

Obediently the two rose again, pacing after Brin. 'Are they truly as calm as they seem?' Tika asked Kija.

'They are. They found Fenj very comforting and Lorak was most caring towards them.'

'I have been worried,' Tika confessed. 'They were so very frightened when we first met. Have they told you anything of the Sun Mountain Treasury? I can't believe it has fallen into such chaos so quickly after Seela was lost.'

'Indeed I have little memory of Nanu. I might have seen her once or twice but from what Genia told me, and what these two have added, she is similar in character to the one called Nula.'

Tika shivered. Kija crooned softly, understanding how just the mention of that name brought back memories of terror, of fire and death, at a time when Farn was new hatched and Tika still unaware of her powers. 'Hush child.' Kija's mind tone soothed her gently. 'Such things occasionally happen and the Treasury either resolves their trouble and goes forward, or breaks up with the members seeking other Treasuries to join. Fenj was distressed; he had a fondness for Seela.'

'And Minyth's shoulder gives him no trouble?'

'You healed him, silly child. Of course it doesn't.' Kija

stared down at her, affection washing through the mind link. Then the gold Dragon looked up quickly and Tika turned to see Minyth peering in the entrance.

'Come in, my dear.' Tika spoke aloud, holding a hand out towards him.

'I'm afraid I didn't much like that place.' His mind voice was very soft.

Pearl moved along a little, suggesting he should recline beside her. 'What was wrong with it?' she asked.

'The sparks were very pretty. I liked them but not the noise. The noise hurt my ears.'

Pearl leaned against him in a friendly manner. 'I don't go there either,' she agreed. 'I don't like the noise *or* the smell.'

Tika smiled.

'Heligg likes it though,' Minyth continued. 'She thought the sparks and the noise was very exciting.'

Tika stroked his face. 'Then you stay here Minyth. I'm sure there are many other places to see that might please you.'

'Oh there are.' His eyes whirred briefly. 'I saw two bears, with their new children, when we came here just now.'

Tika was surprised. She had been unaware bears lived in Iskallia. 'Two?' she repeated.

'Yes. With children. I like bears,' he added.

Kija gave a quiet sigh. Tika knew she was wondering if Minyth, like Farn had an inexplicable fascination for babies of all kinds. 'I'm going along to see Konya and Palos,' Tika told Kija, and left her to cope with any more talk of bears and their children.

Along the plateau path she hurried, having forgotten her jacket, and ran up the few steps to the medical school. She knocked on the door the staff used as their own quarters, and a voice called for her to enter. Konya sat at a table writing while Palos was stirring some concoction in a large jar. They smiled as they saw who their visitor was. 'Snow's nearly all gone,' Konya said with great satisfaction.

'It has,' Tika agreed. 'Soon you'll be able to moan about the heat again, won't you?'

Konya grinned. 'Probably. What can we do for you?'

'I was wondering if Palos had any information about the town and garrison of Mertasia?'

Palos looked up in surprise. 'It's one of the largest towns in Kelshan. I was there for a few days on my way to Braxton. Why?'

'Another large group of rebel soldiers are close to the town. Falkir was being sent information from someone in Mertasia but the more recent messages were lies. I don't really understand why he would need an informant there if he had a trustworthy officer in the garrison though. Is that normal?'

'There could well have been someone in the town, not necessarily military, but who had access to officers, who was reporting to Jemin, or even Veranta. Veranta in particular did love her spies. It could mean that those people who still exist, are continuing to send reports to the main military offices in the citadel.'

'Would Falkir read them and take them seriously?'

Palos set his jar aside and sat down, frowning as he thought. 'Falkir could be aware that many of these people like to earn the small amount they do, for their bits of news. I'd assume that their coin has still been paid to them throughout Jemin's time, and still now, with Ricca. If Falkir got round to checking the relevant accounts, he would know that, but perhaps he hasn't so far had time to do that?'

Konya had stopped writing as she listened. 'It was Imperator Jarvos who set up most of the web of informers, spies, whatever they are. It must be at least two years since an Imperator has really checked the accuracy of those reports I'd guess.'

Palos nodded. 'I doubt Falkir has,' he said. 'Or he's just taken them at face value. I would have expected General Demisen to report directly himself unless *he* has been given the wrong information too. He must send out patrols, or had scouts and sentries posted.'

Tika listened carefully. 'I know Falkir has had a lot to deal with within the Citadel itself. Reorganising the council, the household staff, getting to know an extremely young new future ruler. I'm surprised he hasn't checked more closely on some reports though. Mertasia must surely be an important place from all I've been told. If it still held true to the Citadel, he would have kept a closer watch on it, wouldn't he?'

'I knew Falkir when I was just another healer in the Citadel,' said Konya. 'Straight as an arrow was Falkir, an honest man, one who knew the men who served him. I don't believe he could change, but I do think he could have been misled, especially having so much else to worry about.'

Tika moved to the door. 'I just thought I'd ask you.'

'Wait.' Palos drummed his fingers on the table. 'I'm sure General Bafex visited Mertasia quite often, when he was in charge of Braxton. I couldn't say whether he and General Demisen were friends or if Bafex was simply visiting the town for the taverns or the gambling dens. Sorry I can't be more helpful, Tika.'

'At least we now know there is a garrison there, but whether they'll fight for Falkir when he arrives, or for the rebels is still a doubt.'

'I suppose you'll be going, to see what happens?' said Konya.

'Yes we have a treaty with Kelshan but I'm hoping we can just watch and we won't have to get involved. Oh, the new Dragons are here. Kija brought them along from Dragons Rest. They seem to have settled very well.'

'Then we will come and see them at dinner, later,' Konya told her.

Tika returned to the House, grateful not to meet the donkey, Chichi, who seemed to enjoy nothing more than braying at her. She wondered where Volk or Onion might be and realised Rivan had also been absent for a few days. She spoke to Fedran in his office and checked who he wanted to accompany them.

Tika told him which Dragons would take them and he began to make a list. 'Dog's suggestion,' he began. Tika frowned. 'Seriously Tika, it's not a bad idea. You could order her not to drop them *on* any soldiers, but a few poppers just in front of an advancing force might slow them down quite a bit?'

'Do you really think so? Jemin learnt how to make them when he was in the Dark Realm, remember? That's how Darrick died and Onion lost his eye.'

'I know, Tika, but Falkir will be facing rebels. You understand there will be lives lost one way or another? If Dog, and perhaps Kazmat dropped a few popper from high above, from shielded Dragons, it *might* offer a reason for at least some to surrender?'

'Why Kazmat?'

'Aah. Well, Dog says she shouldn't be the only one who knows how to make the things. Garrol can make them, I understand, but she's shown Kazmat, Geffal and Shea how to, too. It makes sense, Tika, it really does.'

Tika bit back the furious words she was tempted to say and considered. 'Where are they making and keeping the things?' she asked.

'You remember Sket insisted on a lock up, some way beyond the hall they use for drills now?'

Tika nodded.

'That's where they keep everything to do with explosives. And the door is locked,' he added quickly, watching her expression.

'Who has the key?'

'There are three. Essa has one, I have one and so does Dog.' Fedran continued when Tika remained silent: 'Jemin *did* learn how to make explosives but he didn't use them at Ferris Lake, did he? Dog wondered if he'd simply forgotten about them. Garrol always says he was never impressed with Jemin's intelligence.'

Tika frowned. 'Did they use explosives in Braxton Mines?'

Fedran leaned back in his chair. 'Aifa says not. Why would they need to, when they had a constant supply of slave labour?'

'You are the Captain of Guards, Fedran. Do as you think fit.' Tika turned away, missing the surprise on the Captain's face. 'We'll need supplies for several days, by the way. It's unlikely Falkir will have reached the town by the time we get there.'

Tika was relieved to see just how easily Minyth and

Heligg accepted the large number of people who arrived in the hall that evening. She also noted that neither of them appeared particularly disturbed by the smell of cooked food. They both showed great interest in some of the games people played that evening - singing games, nonsense riddles which had been invented to amuse Farn and Storm. Even Cerys had come down to the hall and spent the evening sympathising with Kija on the childishness of human amusements.

When Tika went to bed, she looked from the easternmost window, out over the starlit valley. Frost glittered but definitely less harshly than previously. She stared up at the sky and wondered where Onion might be. From Onion her thoughts went to Endis and the Ancient Augur. She had intended to speak to Ferag but decided that would have to wait until after they'd been to Kelshan now. Climbing into bed, she opened a book Dog had given her. It was called *"Tales of Old Kelshan"*. Dog told her it was one Rumak had brought and she might find it of interest. Settling back on her pillows, she began to read.

In the two days since the Augur's human body had failed, Endis had remained in his rooms, venturing only as far as the garden. He was aware of huge swathes of knowledge unfolding in his mind and he had also understood how the Augur had transferred much of that detailed information. This morning, as he drank his tea, he saw in his mind's eye, that thin left hand wrapped in a rough bandage. Ashri had given him her blood, in all those bowls of tea she'd made for him in the last days. Her blood had expanded his understanding; her very memories were his, he could see all she'd shown him in mind pictures, as though he had been there to witness those events himself.

Now, he walked across the passage and paused for a moment, staring at the Augur's door. Endis sighed softly, and lifted the latch. The room felt empty, utterly empty. He stood looking around. Scrolls and notebooks filled the shelves but Endis moved to the Augur's chair. He glanced down, feeling a pang of sorrow as he saw the pillows lining the chair still held the impression of that small body. Then he leaned across to the table beside the chair and lifted the notebook that lay there.

He had decided he would try to work backwards through Ashri's countless years of journals. Slipping the notebook into his pocket, he left the room, closing the door gently. Endis turned left, walking towards the room Ashri had called her infinity room. As he entered, he was aware of his pulse beating in his ears. Light slowly filtered into the empty space. Endis drew breath and called for the stars to appear. He sank onto the bench near the door and watched, mesmerised as before as worlds and their moons moved around their suns, spinning silently through the air. He lost track of how long he watched, identifying different sections as they drifted past, knowing their names.

Then he stood, the countless worlds vanishing at a thought. Endis emerged into the passageway and hesitated. There was a library opposite but he chose not to enter, instead walking on, again to his left. He stopped at the next door along and opened it. As light grew stronger, he could only stare. Threads beyond number stretched out and across, up and down, in places interwoven with each other. Looking more closely, Endis saw tiny glimmers of light along the threads and names came clear in his mind, even as he looked.

He focussed his vision more intently and understood what these were and he nodded. Leaving the room, he retraced his steps back to his garden. He made himself a small meal, bread and cheese was all he wanted for now, and sat down with Ashri's last notebook. He simply rested his hand on it for a while as he ate, then, pushing the plate aside, he opened the book and began to read. He read steadily, until he saw how dim the light had grown. Glancing across at the lamp, it sprang alight, and he understood without surprise, the powers Ashri, or Mother Dark or both, had somehow gifted him.

Endis read on, from the beginning of the book to the end, noting the handwriting grew ever more wayward, and shaky. He shed tears over the last three pages. They were quite clearly intended for him, a personal, final farewell from the Augur as he had come to know her. Closing the book, he continued to sit quietly. He knew he had only to call and Ashri would come to him, but he had recognised the sudden joy on her face when she was released at last from that poor body. He would not call her yet; let her enjoy her freedom for a while.

She had appeared so young, younger than he was, yet she had endured, in human flesh with all its aches and faltering systems, for longer than he could even imagine. He'd known she was in pain when she walked with him, yet she had complained only of tiredness, weariness. Then something seemed to move, a slight flicker seen from the corner of his eye. 'Shadows?' he asked, voice calm and steady.

'We hear you, Sentinel.' The words were faint but distinct.

'Did Ashri give you duties, that I should know about?'

There was an extended pause. Endis realised he could see shapes a little more clear. Not human, pale, etiolated figures wavering as though seen through a heat haze. 'We bring food for you. We watch. We serve.'

'Do you *choose* to serve, or are you *commanded* to serve?' Endis was unsure why that question should occur to him but it suddenly felt important. There was another wait before the quiet reply came.

'We always *chose* to serve but we forgot, for a long, long while. Ashri reminded us. We choose now to serve you, our new Sentinel.'

'I am Endis.'

'We know. You are Endis and you are the Sentinel. We serve you.'

'Thank you.' Endis felt those words were profoundly inadequate but he could think of nothing else at that moment. Then he thought of Tika. 'Are you the same as Tika's Shadows?' he asked. He found he was already growing used to the silence before these creatures, whatever they were, decided to reply.

'We were.'

That seemed a less than helpful reply. 'Can you explain that a little more? I am new at being the Sentinel. I feel I have still so very much to learn and understand.' Half closing his eyes, he realised there were several of these spindly figures wavering around him.

'You do. Mother made us all the same. She sent us to protect Darallax.'

Endis detected a definite warmth in the whispered words.

'We do protect him. We have hidden him and his people for long, but he rarely asks us any more.'

Another pause through which Endis just waited.

'Darallax gifted Tika with some of his Shadows, with the command to aid her, protect her and obey her. Mother asked some of *his* shadows to become helpers of the Sentinel. That was far in the past you understand.'

'I do understand,' Endis agreed.

'Ashri asked us only to watch the world below, to guard certain human bloodlines. She very rarely asked us to take action.

Endis felt a warning chill. 'May I ask what action you *can* take?'

All the vague outlines around him grew very still. 'We can kill. Ashri has asked that only a very few times. Many of us grew bored and wild. Mother called us back and reminded us of our duties.'

Movement returned to the strange beings. 'We had almost forgotten that she created us as Guardians. Now, we remember.' For the first time a shadow spoke without Endis prompting it with a question. 'The female Kelati is no more, or the creature made by Youki, who neglected Tika and killed the boy.'

Endis swallowed. 'You killed them?' Once more he felt that chill slide down his spine when the reply came.

'We did.' There was such a depth of satisfaction in those few words, Endis understood just how deadly these shadows could be.

'What do you do, in your role as Guardians, other than kill?' he asked cautiously.

'We remember now. We care for you. We watch the ones whose threads Ashri has spun. We protect.'

'Is Tika safe now? And Farn? And the others in Iskallia?'

233

'She is. He is. They are. We had forgotten we liked Dragons.' Sorrow filled the words now. 'When we grew wild, the Dragons knew we were disobeying Mother and they became wary of us. Now, we will be friends again, as we were before the Final Battle.'

For a moment, Endis's mind reeled at the vast amounts of time these creatures referred to as if it was mere days ago. 'How do you get food for me? And there are more clothes here than I brought.'

The voice sounded puzzled when it decided to reply. 'We find. We get. We bring.'

Endis though perhaps it would a wise idea if he simply tried to sleep, so he said a quiet good night to the shadows. Then he prepared for bed, his mind once again whirling with new notions.

Chapter Twenty One

Tika was touched when Minyth announced he would be proud to help Skay protect Iskallia in the absence of most of the other Dragons. Heligg agreed. She told Tika they would make sure everything remained safe while she was gone. As their company went out to the plateau to join the Dragons who would be carrying them, Cerys in her travel sack, Onion appeared. He gave her a smile but no explanation for his absence. She'd also noticed Rivan was in uniform and among those Fedran had selected to come on this journey. Rivan and Onion climbed onto Genia as Fedran swung up behind Tika on Farn.

Lifting into the early morning sky, Brin opened a gateway directly north. It was of short duration as Storm had shared his memory of the flights he'd taken with Navan to first look over the town. When the company emerged from the gateway, Storm led them east, where houses became few and far between. He took them down to a curving line of woodland on slightly higher ground. Ashoki and Jarko ventured among the trees and found a small water course as they searched for fallen deadwood, while Essa organised their camp.

Glancing around, Tika was slightly irritated to see that Onion and Rivan had already vanished again. Navan joined her. 'The town is directly west from here,' he said. 'About ten miles I'd guess. The rebels were perhaps two miles outside of the town.'

'Farn, will you take me to see this town before we settle here, please?' Tika asked.

Farn's eyes flashed and whirred. 'Of course, my Tika. Storm will show us where it is.'

Fedran called across to Essa that they'd not be gone long then remounted Farn behind Tika. Dromi stepped away as Navan climbed back onto Storm. 'Remember, shielded at all times,' Tika told both Dragons.

They lifted into the air and Storm flew a little ahead. In

a very short time the riders could see a long encampment ahead. As Navan had reported, it was neatly laid out; to tidy to be the sort of jumble it would be if these men were leaderless. Storm flew along the double line of tents even while Fedran tried to get a more accurate estimate of the number of men there. Flying north above the camp, Storm swung west again and they saw another encampment, slightly smaller than the first. Storm climbed higher until they were well above a walled town. Life seemed to be as normal, people in the streets, wagons moving in and out of the wide gates. Glancing back, Tika could see the smoke from the rebel fires and shook her head. What *was* going on here, she wondered.

The two Dragons circled slowly above the town. On higher ground in its centre was what looked like a building of importance, above which fluttered the grey Kelshan flag, bordered in green with the lighthouse clearly visible in its centre. Storm moved towards the west, flying high so the riders could see a further distance, but there was no sign of an advancing mounted force. 'Thank you, Storm, let's go back now.' Tika sent the thought and Storm made a sweeping turn south and east.

Once they'd landed at their camp, Tika hugged both Dragons. 'Rest, then you can look around or hunt if you need to. Just ...'

'Be careful!' Farn interrupted, his mind tone amused and affectionate. 'We know.' He bumped his Tika's head gently with his chin.

She laughed. 'Well make sure you are.' She watched them pace across to lie between Kija and Brin, shaking her head. She and Fedran walked to the fire Dog already had burning low.

'Smoke is blowing north east, into the trees,' Dog said as Tika sat beside her. She nodded in the direction Tika now knew Mertasia lay. 'We can see a bit of their smoke, maybe see more if the sky is clear tonight, but they can't see ours.'

'We couldn't see Falkir's force and we went several miles west. The townsfolk *have* to know the rebels are there. They've been there nearly a moon,' Fedran told the company.

Kazmat grunted. 'So obviously, whoever is in charge in Mertasia, is working with the rebels.'

Dog passed a bowl of tea to Tika. 'You reckon it's all to tempt Falkir out of the Citadel?' she asked with a frown. 'I thought he was getting reports saying everything was as usual there.'

'Yes, but *we* had to come and take a look, didn't we?' Tika pointed out. 'Is it possible someone in Falkir's office could have been involved? If there is such a one, they could have let Mertasia know Falkir is on his way?'

'How?' argued Veka. Then she blushed when all eyes turned to her. She swallowed but went on. 'If it's taken this long for Falkir to get here, how could a message get to Mertasia faster? They have no mages, do they?'

'Not as far as I know,' Tika agreed.

The company sat thinking over Veka's comment. Essa gave a rueful smile. 'She's quite right. I'd imagine whoever is in charge in that town was planning to perhaps set up as a separate little state. It is one of the wealthiest towns in Kelshan. It could probably rival the Citadel.'

'Could you far seek, Tika?' Navan asked slowly. 'Maybe if we knew what was going on in that building where the Kelshan flag was, we'd know a little more?'

Fedran quickly explained to the company what they'd seen as they flew over the town. Farn helpfully sent pictures to their minds. Tika saw heads nodding agreement as the Guards studied the pictures. 'That's where whoever is in charge is set up, for sure,' said Dromi. 'Could you see in there, Tika?'

Tika settled herself more comfortably and closed her eyes, a tiny part of her mind racing west. She ignored the encampment and paused near the walls of Mertasia. No soldiers patrolled the walls, she noted. The people crowding the narrow streets seemed to be going about the normal routines, no one appeared worried by the soldiers beyond their walls. Her mind moved on, past the houses and shops, seeing a long ramp ahead leading up to the building above which flew the Kelshan flag. The ramp led to wide double doors which stood open and Tika sent her mind speck drifting up and inside.

There were few people around. She paused, another part of her mind sensing for any group of people together. She found such a group, somewhere above her on the topmost floor. She simply rose and moved through the ceiling, then the next, gritting her teeth back in her body at the queasy feeling she had moving through solid things. Somewhat to her surprise, Tika found herself in a large office in which several men were seated. She moved back and up, hovering above their heads. A semicircle of chairs were arranged facing a large desk behind which sat a fairly nondescript man. The sort of man she would barely notice among a crowd. She was mind linked to both Kija and Farn who were showing her companions all she saw and heard.

'I'm still in favour of posting men on the main road west,' one man was saying. He was in his early middle years, well dressed in clothes of good quality and good taste.

'Why?' That was the man behind the desk. 'Vanji has been sending messages to Kelshan. There have been no queries. No one there is bothered with us.'

The well dressed man in the chair nearest the desk shook his head. 'A day will come Proctis, when someone at the Citadel will think to send an inspector out to us. Inspectors travel with an escort. I would rather be prepared for such a visit than be taken by surprise.'

Others in the semi circle nodded. The man behind the desk, Proctis, shrugged. 'If it makes you happy then you can arrange it with out dear Major Kaldor.'

'The fifth man in the semicircle, at the further end, spoke up. 'I heard he is styling himself Commander now.' He laughed. 'He missed out the rank of General and went straight to Commander.'

There was laughter from all except the well dressed man, Tika noted. 'As long as he can keep control of those soldiers, I don't care what he calls himself,' said Proctis. He glanced to his left, to the well dressed man. 'Remiad, this is all going just as I planned. The Citadel will have no hint of this until it's too late for them to do anything. There aren't enough soldiers left there to face the ones we have here.'

Remiad inclined his head but did not reply. Proctis

stood. 'If that's all for today, we'll meet again in five days.'

The five men facing him also rose and made their way out of the room, Remiad behind the man who had sat at the other end of their semicircle. The two of them dawdled along a corridor behind the other three whose laughter came back to them.

'I'm sure Falkir knows by now, Remiad.'

Remiad kept his gaze on the backs of the three in front. 'I believe you are correct, Urkin. I'm sure I wouldn't be convinced by Vanji's messages.'

They strolled in silence, Tika's mind speck floating above them. 'I'm going back to my family farm, the original one near the border with the Free lands,' Urkin's voice was a mere breath. 'I'd advise you to do the same, Remiad. I may not be the cleverest man alive, but with Proctis and Kaldor in charge, I fear the worst.' He nodded towards the three men retreating down the stairs. 'They're fools. Get out now, Remiad, before it's too late.'

Remiad smiled down at the smaller man. 'That was exactly what I intended to tell you, Urkin. I went along with these plans I confess out of laziness. I didn't think Proctis would go so far. When he killed Demisen, and his officers, I realised it had all gone too far. I will be leaving for my estates to the north this very evening.' He held out a hand.

The other man gripped it. 'May you stay safe Remiad, and may we meet in safer and happier times. Mother Dark watch your path.'

'And you, Urkin.'

They'd reached the outer doors and went separate ways.

Deciding there was little more to learn, Tika drew her mind speck back to the camp and her companions. Ashoki handed her a drink which she accepted gratefully. 'I didn't hear what their plans actually are but I think we can guess,' she said.

'I didn't see any signs of building of new barracks,' said Fedran. 'Not when we flew over the town or just now. Those soldiers won't be satisfied with just tents next winter. I would have expected signs of building somewhere.'

'I've met too many men like that Proctis,' Dog remarked.

When people turned to her, waiting for further comment, she shrugged. 'Small time street trickster. Always working out ways to get money without actually dirtying his own hands. Thinks he's much cleverer than he really is. I think now he's somehow got himself in charge of a place the size of Mertasia, he's not entirely sure how to proceed.'

Tika nodded. 'I'd agree with that. He didn't strike me as in anyway a man who should be in charge of anything. Those two I followed. They seem to have been dragged further along than they ever thought.'

'And now they're getting out, running for their homes as far from Mertasia as possible,' said Shea.

'At least now we know the General who was in charge is really dead, along with his officers,' Geffal put in.

'I wonder who this Major Kaldor might be? Or Commander as he now calls himself?' Garrol smiled. 'I've never heard the name. Telk, and some of the other Kelshans who are now in Iskallia, occasionally speak of officers they've known but I don't recall any Kaldor.'

'He must have some sort of strength of character or belief in himself if he controls all those rebels to the extent of them keeping such military discipline. He clearly does, as we can see from the neatness of their camps,' Essa pointed out. 'It's possible he could hold their respect, enough that they'll fight on his orders. I wonder if he has a good strategy for any confrontation with forces from the Citadel?'

'Somehow, I think the poppers you authorised me to bring could be of use,' Dog said with considerable satisfaction.

Unfortunately, Tika could see Dog's point but she chose not to admit that. 'I think some of us should look for Falkir and tell him what we've seen and the little we know. If Kija, Pearl and Farn take some of us west to find Falkir, some of you others could observe the town, the camps, the land around, in case it comes to a full battle here.'

'There was a big road, leading in to Mertasia from the west.' Jarko spoke with a little hesitation but Tika nodded to him to continue. 'I would guess it is the most direct route to the Citadel, the quickest way for goods to be transported.

Wouldn't General Falkir take the swiftest course to Mertasia if he thought there was trouble there?'

'So we should also watch for signs of traps along that road,' Fedran agreed. 'Jarko is quite correct, Tika. I think we should follow that road and I'm sure we'll find Falkir somewhere along it.'

'Then I'd like to make an early start tomorrow.' Tika glanced at the sun, already on its descent in the western sky. She looked at the Dragons. 'Will you need to hunt tonight?' she asked.

'No,' Brin replied. 'We didn't travel too far today and we fed well yesterday.'

'Then rest, my dears. Remember you must all fly shielded tomorrow please.'

Speculation continued for what remained of the day, as people tried to decide what Proctis's actual aim might be. Tika listened rather than taking part. Onion returned before too long but seemed to know all that had been spoken of in his absence. It was almost dark when Rivan slipped back into camp. He went straight to Tika. She could see the wolf in his pale eyes and thin face, and waited for him to speak.

'There is little to the east. Empty farmhouses. No indication of damage but they'd been empty for some time. The fields have been planted though, so people must have been there perhaps two turns of the moon back.'

Tika frowned. 'Why would farmers plant crops then just abandon them?'

Rivan shook his head. 'The soldiers have no sentries or lookouts. I got quite close to both their camps but no one saw me.'

'Did you hear anything?' Tika asked.

'Many grumbles and complaints about a Captain Mebbis and Major Kaldor, but nothing particularly helpful. The main complaint was that they are not allowed inside the town walls. Beer is brought out to them, with food, every few days but they wanted more beer '

'Rivan there's food here for you,' Essa called softly from across the low banked fire.

Rivan joined her and took the heaped plate gratefully.

'Sounds like an unhappy army,' Dog suggested.

'Indeed,' agreed Fedran.

Tika nodded slowly. 'Maybe, with the help of a few poppers, they'll be persuaded not to fight too much.'

Dog beamed at her and patted the old satchel she held lovingly against her chest. Tika tried to ignore that and thanked Rivan for his report. She glanced at Onion but he had Cerys on his chest and was leaning back against his pack, smiling up at the stars. Settling against Farn's comforting bulk, Tika too stared up at the stars. They were more familiar now but she still missed the ones she'd always known in northern Sapphrea.

In the greyness of pre dawn light, Tika saw all her Guards were checking their weapons. She made no comment. She'd ordered that they stay shielded so there should be no need for the use of any weapons. Tika had finally come to understand that it was a necessary routine for them though. Most of them had learnt this serving in other armies, and had the practise drummed into them constantly by Sket. Cerys picked her way through grass wet with dew, then shook each paw when she reached Tika. 'At least it's not cold, Cerys,' Tika murmured, holding open the sack the cat travelled in. She received a baleful look as her only answer and grinned, looping the strap over her head.

Kija rose into a slight mist, Pearl and Farn each side of her tail, and headed west. Below, Tika saw a broad paved road and Kija clearly intended to follow it as it wound across the country. It skirted a couple of lightly wooded hills then crossed a slow moving river bridged with stone. The sun was warm on their backs by the time they saw a dust cloud in the distance. Tika was perturbed by the fact they had passed over two much smaller towns but no one had stirred there. No people, no animals, no smoke from chimneys.

'How will we do this, Tika?' Fedran asked. 'Most of their horses will panic if we appear suddenly.'

'Kija will calm them, don't worry, Fedran. I'll mind speak Falkir to ask him to stop.'

Fedran was peering over her head, squinting to see into the swirling dust as they drew closer. Kija began to circle and Tika sought General Falkir's mind signature. She sent a thought, telling him they needed to speak to him.

'How far are they from Mertasia, do you think Fedran?'

'About fifty miles, perhaps a little less.'

'So they could be there, ready to attack tomorrow?' Tika felt him shrug.

'The horses will be tired but yes, it's possible.'

The cloud of dust was slowing and Tika asked the Dragons to settle on the road a little ahead of the many riders. She slid from Farn's back, her accompanying Guards moving to her side, still hidden by Kija's shielding. Dust slowly cleared and they saw Falkir with several officers, halted a short distance away. 'Release the shielding, Kija.' Tika sent the thought and watched the leading Kelshans react to their sudden appearance.

Falkir dismounted, calling a man forward to hold his horse, spoke to his officers, two of whom also dismounted, and began to walk forward. Tika and her Guards met them halfway, Tika apologising at once for their unexpected arrival. 'We have news of Mertasia for you, General,' she ended.

The two officers with Falkir, were staring at the Dragons but Falkir was focussed on Tika. 'Tell me,' he said.

Quickly, she explained all they'd learned so far, adding that the garrison officers, along with General Demisen, had been killed. 'I have no idea when that occurred, General, but I suspect some time ago now.'

Falkir was frowning as he took in her information but one of the officers spoke, if a little hesitantly. 'Sir? I knew Kaldor, or at least, I was at the military academy when he was there. He didn't pass his officer training.'

'He may not officially be an officer,' Tika replied. 'But he seems to have control of nearly two thousand men. Farn, show them the pictures of their camps outside the town walls, please.'

The officer who'd spoken paled as he saw the lines of tents and the number of men moving among them. There was a buzz of talk from the massed riders further along the road as they too saw what lay ahead for them.

'Mounted soldiers have the advantage,' Falkir said at

last, as Fedran had also pointed out a few days ago.

'They have the advantage of numbers,' said Fedran. 'Your horses and men are tired, another *dis* advantage for you.'

Tika sighed, inwardly. 'We will help as we can,' she said quietly. 'If you ask us for aid, we hold to our treaty.'

'How many are you?' Falkir asked.

'Sixteen of us and six Dragons,' she replied. She saw by Falkir's expression he wasn't sure that would be anywhere near enough.

'I think the idea is for you to advance along this road and arrive at the western gate, sir,' said Fedran. 'It is quite probable you wouldn't even see the encampment to the north; it's about two miles beyond the town.'

Falkir nodded. 'I believe you are correct Captain Fedran. You have another idea?'

'As far as we can see there is no urgency. They have posted no watchers along this road so they must feel completely sure no one will come from the Citadel. I would suggest you travel a little slower, so horses and men are less weary. We can look for another way so that some of your force can perhaps come on their northern camp with them unaware? That camp is smaller. It is the eastern camp which seems to hold most of the men.'

Falkir nodded. 'I see your point, Captain. You could contact us again, if you find another route?'

'Of course,' said Tika. 'It would mean splitting your force but you will have surprise on your side. Unless Proctis decides scouts should go out. That seems unlikely, given that they have taken no steps to post guards yet. You understand that the Dragons will be shielded? We could shield you too, to allow you to get much closer before anyone became aware of your advance? For now, I suggest you travel at an easier pace. The cloud of dust you're raising is visible for quite a distance. You need only think my name and I will hear you, General.' Tika turned away to rejoin Farn.

'Thank you,' General Falkir called. 'I do appreciate your information and your offer of assistance, my Lady.'

Tika swung onto Farn's back and looked at the General.

'We have a treaty General Falkir.'

Dragons and Iskallians vanished, the Kelshans aware of the sound of heavy wings and a sudden down draft of displaced air.

One of the officers walking beside General Falkir back to their horses, asked if Dragons truly used fire. Falkir grunted as he climbed into his saddle. 'So the stories tell us, Major. I've not witnessed it myself.' Falkir gave a few brief orders and the lines of horsemen, six abreast, split, moving onto the rough grass at each side of the road.

As they rode on, Falkir looked back, seeing the dust they raised was now much reduced. A stupid mistake, he scolded himself. Tika's words repeated in his thoughts as his troops travelled on. He, at least, had six scouts ranging ahead and so far, the only unusual thing they'd reported was a completely empty town a few miles ahead. He estimated they should reach that place by midday so perhaps then they might discover why it was deserted.

Falkir considered Tika's offer of help. He did not forget that she had killed Imperator Jemin, sword to sword, but even so, he had serious doubts about what real help sixteen Guards and six Dragons might actually achieve. He glanced up, scanning a pale blue sky dotted with occasional small clouds, and wondered if the Dragons were long gone or still close by. Then he shook his head and kept his gaze fixed ahead.

Chapter Twenty Two

Endis woke again, lying for a while as his thoughts adjusted. It seemed to him he knew more every time he slept and woke and he wondered if his head would burst with all the things that now filled it. He rose, washed and dressed and wondered whether he should investigate more of this place. He had yet to look in any of the rooms on the upper floors and he rather quailed at the very thought. There were just so many rooms or at least, doors. Endis paused as he poured hot water into his tea pot. But *were* there rooms behind all those doors he'd seen? He laughed. What a waste of Mother Dark and Ashri's time if he actually went mad now.

He sensed someone in his garden and went to the open door, looking out. He wasn't surprised to see Ashri wandering towards him, her fingers brushing the flowers that seemed to bend towards her touch. Looking up she smiled at him. 'Of course you won't go mad, dear child. It is a long time since I've been in here you know. It is lovelier than I remember.'

'Have you been in the gods' space since you left here?'

'I have indeed. There are fewer there than when I lived there before, which is a sadness, but it is a beautiful place, and restful.'

Endis smiled. 'Will you be busy there or might you get bored?'

Ashri laughed. Endis could only stare at her. She was so young, so beautiful, yet mere days ago she had been the Ancient Augur, wizened, frail and exhausted. Again he marvelled at her courage in enduring as long as she had, a time beyond my imagining.

'Bored? I don't think so. I am still permitted to watch over you, my dear. And there are many other things I want to discover.'

'You didn't tell me enough about Olekatah,' Endis said softly.

Her expression clouded. 'No, I didn't. I will tell you more, another time, not just yet.' She brightened again. and a wicked smile lit her face. 'I did forget to tell you, you can alter this place however you choose. Turn it into a castle, or a huge sailing ship, whatever you wish.' She paused. 'I'll be sad to see my needles go, but this is yours now. You can move the libraries all down to one floor if you like.' She smiled up at him. 'You've met your shadows?'

He nodded. 'I did. They are a little - strange, but they seem, erm, helpful.'

'They forgot who they were but that was partly my fault. I thought I had no use for them but I was wrong, and cruel.'

Ashri saw Endis's look of surprise. 'Yes, Endis, it was cruel. Mother made them to serve and I gave them no duties, no suggestions as to just how they should serve. I think you will use them far more wisely than I ever did.'

'Can I still visit the world?'

'Of course.'

'How?' Endis asked helplessly.

'You think of the place you want to be and step forward. To come back here, you think of here and step back.' Ashri seemed puzzled that she'd needed to explain that to him. 'Alternatively, you could ask the shadows to take you wherever you wish and keep you hidden until you choose to reveal yourself. I would advise you to close your eyes if they transport you. It can be unsettling.'

'Who could visit here?'

Ashri sat down on the doorstep. 'Any of the gods could, but none of them do, except perhaps Ferag.' The blue eyes stared up, piercing him as they so often had. 'Tika could, but she has yet to really understand that. She is still unsure of many of her gifts.' She patted the step, inviting him to sit beside her. 'You do realise Tika has immense powers?'

'I didn't *know* that, but I suspected it.'

'Fortunately she met one of the very best of your Asatarian people when she first found she had mage gifts. Iska.'

'Iska?' Endis asked in surprise. 'I've never heard her name but Tika's land is called Iskallia?'

'Iska taught Tika one of the most important lessons;

247

how to control her temper. Iska died, very soon after they met, and Tika reveres her memory. Thus she named her land, Iskallia.'

'Her temper? I've seen her grow angry once, at the new town along the coast from Harbour City. Two men angered her and they were nearly covered with ice. Is that what you mean?'

'It is. Iska taught her to pack her anger into a small box then freeze it even smaller and hide it deep in her mind.'

They sat quietly while Endis considered what he'd been told. Ashri chuckled. 'Occasionally it leaks,' she said. 'I admit to being amused when I've watched the child fight her temper. There was one particularly enjoyable time in Gulat, when ice formed all over a large hall. When Tika left, the councillors were paddling in icy slush. It was most enjoyable for me to watch. Probably not for those involved,' she added.

'That seems a lot of effort, just to keep your temper. I don't get very angry too often but I found if I just breathe deeply for a while it goes away.'

Ashri rose standing in front of him. She was not a great deal taller standing than he was sitting on the ground, he noticed. 'Have you not understood, child? Tika's power is such that she could destroy this world with the flick of a finger?'

Endis stared at her, horrified. 'Surely Mother Dark could stop her? Or you? Or the other gods?'

'I'm not entirely sure we could, Endis. Mother Dark could, but she vowed she will not interfere, never directly at least.' She rested a hand on Endis's shoulder, studying him with affection. 'Tika's power is still growing. Yet she does not fully understand it. She must learn to have complete control of both her temper and her powers, or she will destroy herself rather than destroy the world. Help her, Endis. Help her as best you can.'

'How can *I* help her? I have insignificant powers, touching the earth. No more.' He stood.

'Endis, you share my *powers* now.'

'I understand I have your memories but you are one of the gods. I am of the world below and of the world of the

Asatarians.'

Ashri stared at him. 'You have my *powers,* Endis. You have them through my blood. That is why that poor body died a little sooner than I'd expected. You share my powers as well as my memories.'

'Your blood? You were one of my ancestors?'

'No! Literally, child! In the tea I made you each day. My blood.'

Endis remembered thinking she was using a different tea, more pleasant, soothing. Blood? He'd been drinking her *blood?* He sat down on the step. He didn't think he could have stood up right then as her words sank into him. Ashri watched him. 'Search through the memories Endis, or the library. It isn't as terrible a thing as you might think.'

He leaned against the door jamb and closed his eyes. When he opened them, Ashri was gone, but he had seen the memories Ashri had suggested. He continued to sit on the step as he thought. If he had been told of people eating other people he would have been aghast, and, in certain circumstances it was an unpleasant habit some had fallen into. The memories he'd just looked at showed people grieving, mourning a beloved member of their family or clan. He saw them bringing tiny gifts, bright pebbles, a small flake of worked stone, beads made of what looked like shells. They wept as they set their gifts beside the dead man, then sat back as another man leaned forward and sliced some flesh from the corpse's thigh.

Endis understood, through Ashri's memories, those people hated to leave this dead man behind, all alone. So they ate parts of him, believing they could carry him on with them, still a part of their family. Endis at last got to his feet, going indoors to make more tea for himself. He felt an enormous compassion for the people Ashri must have witnessed actually doing this. An act of remembrance, he thought suddenly. A mark of respect, and of love, and of loss.

Endis wondered how Tika might view such a sight. Would she understand what they were trying to do, he pondered. He had much to consider. He chose to work among the plants here for the rest of that day, letting all these new thoughts settle into some kind of cohesion in his head.

Tika watched Falkir divide the great column of riders and saw how the amount of dust they raised diminished. 'One of us can keep watch over them, daughter.' Kija mind spoke Tika as they flew slowly back towards Mertasia.

'We could look for another path,' Farn suggested eagerly. 'We could take you back, then come and look.'

Tika felt Kija and Pearl's agreement with this idea. 'Very well then. If you're quite sure.'

Kija increased her speed and in a very short time the three Dragons landed by their camp. Kazmat immediately offered to stay with Kija to check the land while Fedran, Essa and Garrol remained in camp. Veka and Shea also asked to stay with Pearl. Tika sighed. 'Very well. But I don't want you flying until you're worn out,' she scolded Pearl and Farn.

Kija lowered her head to press her brow to Tika's. 'You really do worry far too much. I will not let them tire.'

Stepping back, Tika watched as they lifted into the air again, then vanished as Kija shielded them.

'What did you think?' Fedran asked Tika as they joined the other three near the remains of their fire.

'Falkir is far more worried and tired than he appears,' she said. She looked up and heartbeats later, Brin, Storm and Genia landed, their riders slipping down from their backs.

After exchanging what little news they had, Navan remarked that at least one of the two men Tika had overheard the previous day had left the town. He and Dromi had asked Storm to fly northwards and seen three wagons at some considerable distance from Mertasia, moving fast. Several men on horseback rode alongside the wagons and Navan recognised the man named Remiad as one of those horsemen.

'They must have left last night to get that far.' Dromi said. 'It would seem as if he at least expects trouble soon, one way or the other.'

'Do you think he suspects trouble from the soldiers here,

or from Proctis, or the Citadel?' asked Tika.

'Any of those,' Dromi replied. 'Perhaps he knows more of how the soldiers really feel, stuck here in tents and forbidden to enter the town. I'm not sure if he guesses troops are already on the way from the Citadel.'

Essa frowned. 'Would it be worth just asking him? It could help us if we knew more of how things truly are with that Proctis in charge. As Dog said, he seemed only a small time swindler, not in any big political game at all.'

Tika looked to Dromi for his opinion. 'It could be helpful,' he said at last. 'He was in that sort of council meeting when you watched him, Tika. He may know more of Proctis's plans.' He gave a nod. 'It would be worth a try.'

'Brin, would you take Essa, Fedran and Dromi? If I could come with you and Navan, would that be agreeable to you Storm?' She sensed embarrassment mixed with pleasure from the Sea Dragon at being asked so formally but his eyes flashed and he agreed at once.

'A gateway will be quickest,' Brin told them. 'Then we can be there and back in no time.'

Tika walked to Genia. 'Do you mind staying here alone, my dear? I don't believe we'll be too long, but I would be happier knowing one of you will look after the people who remain in camp?'

Genia's neck stretched a little higher and Tika was aware of how much more confident this Dragon was becoming. 'Of course I will watch over them,' she told Tika, a touch of pride in her mind tone.

Tika nodded at Essa. 'Keep a good lookout while we're gone,' she said moving towards Storm where Navan pulled her up behind him.

The two Dragons had barely risen from the ground when they entered a gateway. Four heartbeats and they re-emerged. Brin flew higher now, following Storm. Looking down, Tika saw they were following a road, but a much rougher road than the paved one leading west to the Citadel. There were wide fields to one side with flocks of sheep grazing, and a few small scattered huts, presumably used by those who looked after the animals. Then the land rose and became more thickly wooded.

'There,' Navan said, pointing ahead.

The trees had been cleared where the road curved around a hill and Tika saw three wagons escorted by riders. 'Can you get ahead of them, please Storm, and land on the road?' She felt the change in Storm's muscular back as he sped up, Brin close behind.

The road around the hill was almost bare of trees Tika saw with some relief. She knew how nervous the larger Dragons were of being trapped beneath trees. They settled on the far narrower road, an earthen track rather than a road now, and Essa, Dromi and Fedran went quickly to stand close to Tika and Navan in front of the Dragons.

'Release the shielding, please Brin, but stay watchful.'

The air shivered and the small group stood waiting. Two riders came round the curve of the hill, the horses suddenly cavorting and jinking. 'Calm them, Brin.' Tika sent the thought to the crimson Dragon and almost at once the horses settled, although their eyes still rolled in wild apprehension. Tika recognised one of the men as Remiad. The first wagon and two other horsemen came into view. Remiad and the man with him, moved at a slow walk towards the five people standing in the road ahead, in front of what were, quite unmistakeably, two Dragons.

Tika had to admit Remiad didn't lack for courage when he dismounted, handing his reins up to the man beside him. She took one step forward and Cerys helpfully stuck her head out of the top of her carry sack. Tika saw Remiad's frown deepen as he observed the cat, but she chose to smile at the man. 'Lord Remiad?' she asked. 'I am Tika of Iskallia. I understand you are leaving Mertasia to avoid the trouble which seems imminent there. I believe your friend, Lord Urkin, has also departed the town.'

She hoped her guess was in fact true. Dromi had come to stand beside her as she spoke. Remiad glanced at the Dragons who were watching him with interest, then he looked back at the small woman in front of him. 'I am Remiad, yes. I fear there will be trouble in Mertasia. How do you know of me, or the problems there?'

Dromi cleared his throat. 'My Lady of Iskallia is, of course, well known to be a mage of great powers,' he said in

252

a gentle tone.

Remiad's eyes widened while Tika bit back a surprised laugh at Dromi's words. She drew a breath. 'I heard you speaking with Lord Urkin yesterday,' she explained. 'I have also seen the large encampments north and east of the town. I do not know who Kaldor might be, but we believe, he commands those soldiers. The soldiers are in rebellion against the Imperatrix in Waiting, Lady Ricca. Iskallia has a treaty with Kelshan and that is why I am here.'

Remiad stood for a moment then he sighed, shaking his head. 'I have no idea how that petty criminal reached such a position,' he said. 'I have only been in the town for less than a full turn of the moon, and General Demisen and his officers had vanished by the time I arrived there. I have large farmlands two more days fast travel north. I come into the town at this time each year, to learn what is most needed in next year's markets.'

'You seemed to have some position of importance in Proctis's council,' Tika observed.

Remiad snorted. 'Only because I am one of the largest land owners. My family has always remained on our lands, coming to Mertasia only once each year, as I continue to do.'

After a pause which Tika allowed to stretch, he went on: 'Urkin has the same habit. His lands are extensive, and like mine, border the Free Lands. He was as shocked as I to find an armed camp at Mertasia.'

'Do you know what Proctis plans? Is there no sensible person who could govern there? The townsfolk seem unworried by the presence of soldiers. Are they aware they are rebels?'

'I heard there was much alarm at first but it was swiftly calmed when Proctis ordered that no soldiers were to enter the town.' He shrugged. 'People still need to work, Lady Tika, to earn coin to feed their families, pay for their rooms. Urkin said he believed the townsfolk were just keeping their heads down and carrying on, hoping for the best.' He indicated the wagons, all halted further along the road. Tika had seen men, women and small children climb out then stand huddled together when they saw what was causing the halt in their progress.

'I offered the staff who care for my town property the chance to leave with me now. I can house them, give them work, hopefully keep them safe.'

'General Falkir and two mounted battalions are approaching Mertasia as we speak,' said Tika.

Remiad closed his eyes. 'Proctis said he has spies within the Citadel. He had been sending false reports for sometime, I gathered. If he now knows of the General's advance, he has not spoken of it at any meetings I've attended.' He paused. 'If he *had* heard, he would be panicked,' he said. 'He is a typical criminal. If something goes awry with his plans, he would run for cover. I'm sure he cannot know.'

'Have you met Kaldor?' asked Dromi.

Remiad was dismissive. 'A similar type to Proctis.'

'How is it he commands all those rebels then, if he is of similar weak character?' That was Fedran's sharp question.

Remiad shook his head. 'Urkin thinks Proctis has agreed to the utter destruction of the town. Proctis has taken over a house about two miles south east. It did belong to the family of the head of the markets, Sekton. That family were known as honest, fair in all their dealings. They kept a small farm but worked in the town. Proctis now lives there. Urkin and I have to assume Sekton and his people are dead.'

'So Proctis would retreat there and let the soldiers loose in the town. Clearly he doesn't consider that they would probably come for him and whatever treasures he's hidden away there?'

'I wouldn't imagine he'd believe such a thing could happen, no.' Remiad agreed.

'From what one of my people heard among the soldiers, they have little respect for Kaldor. It sounds as though he's convinced them to wait a while before ravaging the town,' said Tika. 'Why might that be?'

'Gold comes in from south western mines in about half a turn of the moon. I'd guess that's what they're waiting for.'

Tika's senses told her the man was speaking the truth but there was one question she had to ask. 'If you discovered the state Mertasia had fallen into, may I ask why you didn't bother to alert the Citadel?'

Remiad met those strange eyes, brilliant green surrounded by tiny silver scales. 'We considered doing so but how to do it was the problem. Neither Urkin nor I have the sort of staff in town who could make such a journey.' He indicated the people standing by the wagons. 'None of them can ride. The men guarding them came from my estate two days ago. I had managed to get word home. I can ride but do you think I would get far? Proctis had servants watching most of us in his so called council.'

Again, Tika knew he spoke truly. Before she could ask more, he spoke again. 'The truth is, Lady Tika, I have no great feelings towards Mertasia. It is a place I have had to visit briefly, each year since I learnt the business of selling our crops from my father. There are other markets I could sell to, across the border in the Free Lands, or even to the Citadel, through the town of Ferris to the north. My only tie with Mertasia is business. Urkin is the only one I would call a friend and perhaps once a year we exchange visits to one or other's homes. Other than that, we meet in town at this time of year, for business, as I have said.'

'Are you married?' Essa spoke for the first time. 'Children?'

Remiad blinked as he really looked at her for the first time. He stared up at the tall powerful figure, into cold blue eyes, and swallowed audibly. 'I am. I have three children. My wife is from the Matay clan.'

Essa's stare warmed fractionally. 'You trade with the clans?'

'Whenever they need. We offer them shelter in bad times. There are some years when drought or floods makes their lives much harder. They know they can come to Tien Sah - my estates - at any time.'

'What of Urkin? Does he have strong links with Mertasia?'

Remiad shook his head 'His mother was a clan woman. He trades with two of the Free Cities. He would not lose sleep if he lost the market in Mertasia, I feel sure.'

Tika glanced at Dromi who gave the smallest shake of

his head. 'Very well, Lord Remiad. We must let you be on your way. One way or another, I suspect Mertasia will suffer in the next few days.'

Remiad offered her a graceful bow. 'If you are ever in the north, I would be glad to offer you hospitality,' he said.

The suggestion was genuine and Tika smiled suddenly, a wicked grin. 'I might take you up on that one day, Lord Remiad. I hope you don't mind my Dragon family visiting you, too?'

Remiad looked slightly bemused but he bowed again. 'You would all be made welcome. If perhaps a little cautiously.' His expression remained politely serious but there was amusement in his eyes.

Tika laughed. 'One day, perhaps, Lord Remiad. Safe journey.' She turned and walked to Storm. Navan boosted her up and climbed behind her as the three others clambered onto Brin.

The Dragons rose at once, circled above the group on the road, and vanished as Brin shielded them. Those on the Dragons watched as Remiad stared up to where he'd last seen them, then shook his head, and walked back to join his people.

'He seemed honest,' said Navan when they left the gateway and spiralled down at their camp.

'He was,' Tika agreed. Then she looked up and Kija, Farn and Pearl settled beside them.

'We found other paths,' Farn announced at once.

'Not much more than farm tracks,' Garrol told her. 'Odd thing was, the few farms were deserted, like those two towns along the main road.'

'I guess the farmers scent trouble coming. Their trail leads south, towards the Barrier Mountains,' Ashoki added.

'You told Falkir of these different approaches?'

Garrol nodded. 'He said he'll halt soon, let his men rest. They'll be here tomorrow.'

Chapter Twenty Three

Tika had a conversation with Cerys later, suggesting perhaps the cat needn't make her presence known quite as obviously as she had to Lord Remiad. Cerys refused to reply and made her way to Onion with whom she remained. In the morning, Tika woke first and climbed onto Farn's back, heading for the town. It was still dark enough that she needed to use her mage sight to check the lines of tents. No one stirred. There were still no soldiers posted on watch. Farn took her to the west, a bare five miles, and they saw Falkir's men, divided into three contingents, already up and tending their horses.

'Will there be a battle, my Tika?' Farn asked, his mind voice calm but sad.

'I think there will, dear one.'

'Why must humans fight so much?'

'I don't know, Farn. Take me back to camp now please.'

Dog was yawning when they returned, putting the old kettle over the embers of the fire. Tika sat next to her as others began to wake. 'Still no guards at the camps,' Tika said.

'That Remiad probably had the right of it, Tika. I'll wager they're waiting for the gold he said is due to arrive.' Dog grimaced. 'Too many people seem to lose their wits over gold. You can't *do* much with it, too soft. Only useful for making pretty trinkets, jewellery and such like. Never interested me, anyway.'

The company ate cold meat and travel bread for their breakfast and waited for Tika's orders. 'We watch, as long as Falkir seems to have control,' she said.

'Poppers?' asked Dog.

Tika bit her lip then nodded. 'I'm hoping you know where and when they'd be effective?'

Dog grinned. 'Of course I do, and so do the others too. We've gone over tactics many times.'

Tika felt slightly queasy at the thought but made no

further comment. She saw Onion's expression and impulsively suggested he stayed here, in their small camp. His one brown eye met her gaze. 'I'm coming,' he said softly.

Fedran saw the brief exchange. 'Onion, you and Rivan are with Genia. If she becomes upset or nervous, ask her to bring you back out of sight of any fighting please.'

Onion smiled and nodded. Tika turned to Fedran. 'Thank you, that was kind,' she murmured.

He shrugged. 'We all know Onion would fight anyone for you, but he doesn't like seeing battles,' he replied as quietly.

She nodded, looking up at the sky. Dawn was touching the east and she sighed. 'I suspect Falkir will strike early. Let's get into the sky and watch.'

Packs were moved deeper under the trees, weapons loosened in sheaths, and Tika saw Kazmat and Geffal had satchels similar to Dog's, strapped across their chests. She knew they carried the poppers she so hated but she simply went to Farn and settled herself on his back again, in front of Fedran. Brin rose first, the others following in single file. Onion had Cerys in her sack and Tika saw the green gold eyes watching with interest as they approached the town.

The Dragons flew a little higher, the riders looking down into the narrow streets where people were beginning to move around. Brin swung into a circling glide and Tika stared to the west. She saw blurred movement and knew it was one part of Falkir's force. It seemed they were making for the south side of the town, intending to come round to attack the encampment on the east. Twisting round to see more, she nodded. Another part of Falkir's battalions had emerged from the darkness, heading for the other camp. Now Tika's company could hear hoof beats, a faint drumming, increasing as the horses drew closer.

At last Tika heard shouts of alarm from both encampments. She saw men emerging from their tents, still pulling on shirts and boots. As the Dragons slowly wheeled above the town, Tika saw people running back inside buildings, doors and window shutters slamming shut. Soldiers at the eastern camp were suddenly aware of horsemen heading towards them, fast. Everyone of the soldiers turned away, rushing to the town gate. 'Stars help them!' said Tika, looking across to where Dog and Geffal rode on Kija's back. 'If those rebels get inside the walls, Falkir will have real trouble.'

Before Fedran could reply, explosions crashed below them. Debris sprayed out and up, riders peered down to see Dog's poppers had damaged the four large gateways allowing access to Mertasia. Now, cries of pain mingled with the shouts of alarm, and still the Dragons circled. The mounted troops led by Falkir closed on the western gate. Tika saw the General giving orders and several of his men rode in, through the rubble of the gate, clearly making for the large building that was on the raised area in the centre of the town.

Flames suddenly blossomed around the north gate and Tika blocked the sudden surge of pain she could feel through her mage senses. Fire splashed from one roof to another and in moments, many buildings on the north and eastern side of Mertasia were blazing. Tika hardened her heart. She was, finally, coming to understand that some things just happened, perhaps in some strange way, *had* to happen. She couldn't heal everyone, anymore than she could stop things like this coming to pass, no matter how she might wish that she could.

They heard further concussions of noise and Tika saw Kija had moved to fly in a tighter loop above the palace. A large section of its roof was a hole, flames licking from its edges. Smoke was beginning to thicken the air and Tika sent a thought, telling the Dragons to move away from the rising billows. Brin moved to fly above the northern gate where fierce fighting was continuing. Tika saw two of Falkir's men pulled from their mounts and disappear beneath wild sword blows. She urged Farn higher and wondered if Proctis was still in the town.

'Where did Remiad say Proctis had a house?' she asked over her shoulder.

'A farm, south east,' Fedran replied. 'No need to worry yet. The land all around here seems so empty. It would be easy to find a rat like him. I doubt he could survive in the countryside. He's a town rat, Tika, through and through.'

Tika saw that Falkir and his reduced number of troops had rounded the northern end of the town and were fighting the rebels who had begun to resist more strongly. From above, it was clear Falkir's group were seriously outnumbered but even as she thought that, Fedran grabbed her arm. 'He's down!'

'Set us down quickly, Farn!' Farn plummeted earthwards, Tika and Fedran off his back instantly. 'Go back to the sky, Farn. Shielded!' Tika spun away, her sword already drawn.

From the corner of his eye, Fedran saw the four Guards who had been on Brin's back, appear, quickly followed by Navan. The thought flew through Fedran's mind - how crazy were they to suppose seven of them could face down this many opponents? Then there was no more time for thought. The other Guards closed up, following Tika who was simply carving her way towards the place she'd seen Falkir fall. More explosions came from her right and ahead of her, but she ignored them, looking only for Falkir. It was no help relying on the uniforms to identify who was who; the rebels wore the same uniform of course.

At last, she saw a young major she remembered seeing in Falkir's entourage. She saw he was injured but he still stood, trying to protect the General's body at his feet. He saw Tika and recognition showed in his blood smeared face. She simply nodded, moving to stand, feet each side of Falkir, and raised her sword. Then Fedran was to her left, Navan to her right and rebel after rebel fell before them. Tika was only vaguely aware of the sky growing lighter, lost as she was battling for control of her raging sword. Such a small weapon! She had seen men stare at that sword with amusement that she carried a simple toy for a weapon. When she drew it in anger, whatever power resided within the blade roared through her body, forcing her arm into movement and imbuing strength into her muscles.

Time passed in a clamour of metal on metal, screams and moans of pain, curses and whinnies of injured, frightened horses. Tika grew peripherally aware that the Dragons were visible, still circling overhead, and there were continuing explosions somewhere south, inside the town. 'Tika!' Navan called her name and it was echoed from somewhere below her. Her breathing steadied, her sword arm dropped, trembling with sudden fatigue, and a hand grasped her ankle. She blinked sweat and blood from her eyes and looked around. Again she saw bodies, layered in a circle around her and her Guards, sprawled in the ungainly manner of death. She sucked in a long breath and stared down.

Falkir stared up at her, a massive bruise accompanying a lump on his forehead. There was a lot of blood on him but a quick scan assured Tika very little of it was his own. His left leg was badly broken and he had a few scrapes and cuts and an almighty headache but he would live. Someone pushed up beside her and Tika saw it was the major who had been protecting Falkir when she'd reached them. Her voice wouldn't work at first and she coughed and spat. 'Move him out of this mess,' she croaked. 'I'll see to his leg shortly. Don't worry, he'll be fine.'

Then Fedran was reaching for her as she swayed. Navan lifted her, Fedran took the sword from her hand, and they struggled clear of the carnage. Four of Falkir's troops lifted the General as carefully as they could, following the Iskallians out of the mass of bodies, emerging onto open ground at last. A flurry of heavy wings brought Farn and Genia. Tika saw Storm was still with Brin, Dromi watching from his back. Onion stared into Tika's face, gave a nod then he grabbed one of the Kelshan troops and hurried off with him, Rivan beside them. Navan knelt to put Tika on the ground but she struggled up. 'I'm fine now Navan, truly.' He studied her then released her. She moved forward on her knees beside Falkir. 'Someone cut his trousers?' she suggested, her mage touch making Falkir sleep instantly.

Her senses sank into his leg and she worked for some time, repairing his shattered knee. It went more quickly it seemed to her Guards, who watched her, and then she sat back on her heels, finding Farn's chest close to her back. She looked up at him and saw his eyes whirring anxiously.

'Are you hurt, my Tika?' he asked.

Tika put a hand to her face and felt the dried blood. She shook her head. 'No my dearest. I just need a wash.'

'The river goes under the town.' Farn still sounded worried. 'It doesn't come out again for a some distance away.'

'Hush. We'll manage, don't worry.' Tika's ears hurt from the sudden cessation of such uproar and she desperately wanted to get clean but, as ever, there were wounded to help. She looked at the major who still knelt by Falkir. 'I'm sorry,' she said. 'If I was told your name, I've forgotten it.'

He dragged his gaze from the General's healed leg and stared at her. 'Bars, Lady Tika. Major Bars.'

'Perhaps you could start seeing how many men you have who need help? The General will sleep for now but he's quite safe.' She smiled at Navan, then she checked her Guards. There were bruises and strained muscles, a few minor cuts, but nothing serious. Storm landed beside Farn and she saw the Sea Dragon was disturbed by the blood and the deaths. Brin landed, followed by Pearl. Veka and Shea slid from Pearl's back. Veka looked wide eyed at the bodies heaped around the town gate but she seemed calm. Squinting against the sun, Tika saw Kija was no longer in view but before she could worry, Brin assured her Kija and her riders were safe.

'They have the man called Proctis,' he told her.

Tika scratched at the blood coating her right hand and asked how far it was to the river. 'We have water, Lady Tika.' Major Bars offered her a leather flask.

She smiled. 'Thank you Major. I mean enough to wash in.'

The Major blushed. 'I've been to Mertasia a few times. They have bath houses here.'

'Do you think they're still standing?' Tika asked, watching as smoke continued to rise above the remaining walls.

'We could find out.' He grinned. 'I would recommend we check what's going on in there anyway.' He gestured at the gate. 'I've seen no townsfolk venture out.'

Tika nodded. 'Shea, Jarko, Ashoki. Stay here please.

262

The rest of you, with me. Let's see what's happened in there.'

'Can I come with you?' Veka asked.

'If you wish, just stay close.'

Major Bars spoke to some of his Kelshan troops who'd gathered near their sleeping General. Some remained there but the majority followed as he led the way towards the gate. Other troops were among the bodies, sorting out their men injured or dead, from the rebels as Tika followed Major Bars. They scrambled over blocks of stone tumbled from the gate and stopped for a moment, staring at rubble filled streets. Fires still burned but strangely, no one seemed to be rushing to extinguish them. Major Bars stared round. 'The fighting was all outside the town,' he said with a frown. 'Why is no one doing anything in here?' He gestured to some of his men who moved forward, banging on the closed doors of the buildings which were still mostly intact.

There was no reaction from any occupants and troops looked to Major Bars. He nodded. The men set about breaking the doors down as Tika watched. Wood splintered and from the house nearest to Tika, a man appeared, begging and pleading for mercy. Major Bars approached him and snapped questions at the man. His queries were greeted with tears and wails and hand wringing and excuses. Bars dismissed his words, a look of utter contempt on his face. He gave sharp orders, and very reluctantly the man left his house. The major beckoned Tika on. 'I'm not surprised the rebels could control this place,' he muttered when the Iskallians rejoined him. 'That man said he was afraid he'd get hurt. It's quite a wealthy place, easier living here than in many towns I've visited.' He shook his head, his disgust clear.

A little further in two houses were half demolished and water gushed from a broken clay pipe which protruded from a wall. Major Bars halted again. 'Well. I think this was where one of the bath houses was, Lady Tika. I'm sorry.'

Tika studied the water, looked down at herself and walked forward to stand under the broken pipe. She gasped as cold water pounded her head but stayed as she was, rubbing her face, hands and clothes. Her boots filled and felt distinctly uncomfortable but she also felt a little cleaner. She stepped away and saw Teyo follow her example. He spluttered and moved next to her, grinning. 'Can't you dry us, Tika? Surely your powers *must* be able to do something simple but really, really helpful?'

Guards and the Kelshans who'd heard Teyo's remark waited, some with interest, some confused. Tika concentrated and wisps of steam began to emerge from their clothes. Teyo laughed. 'That's better.'

Other Guards promptly soaked themselves then waited for Tika to at least dry the worst from them. The Kelshans stared wide eyed but chose not to follow suit. Walking on, Teyo leaned down to Tika. 'You missed the boots out,' he hissed.

She glared at him. 'Put up with it,' she hissed back.

Major Bars ordered his men to bang on every door and if it wasn't opened, he signalled them to break it down. 'It's a few years since I was here,' he said to Tika. 'It was a strange place then but now it's just a disgrace. The people here are nearly all reasonably well off. They are only interested in taverns, play houses, clothes and jewellery. They haul in workers from the farms for building work or anything that involves real work,' he explained.

Tika watched as men and women were pulled into the street and ordered to start clearing up and putting out the fires. She heard the Kelshans tell some of the men to go out of the town and start piling up the bodies. She touched Major Bars' arm. 'I will dispose of the dead,' she said quietly.

After a moment, he nodded.

Tika noticed the people who were reluctantly appearing were all well dressed, in good quality garments, and she understood Bars' previous remarks. Walking on she thought of his words: that labourers were brought into the town if any real work needed doing. It was a very fine distinction, she decided, closer to a form of slavery than people offering their services and getting paid for their toil. 'When they bring in farm folk to work, do they pay them?' she asked as the street grew steeper and they neared the ramp leading to the wide doorway she'd seen before.

'Of course not, Lady Tika! They send someone out to the farms and order in whoever they think looks fit and strong. They're fed while they work in town but no one here seems to realise it leaves the farms short handed.' Bars scoffed. 'Even years back, when I was last here, I thought the whole place was full of spoilt, too wealthy, selfish people. It looks like it's just got worse since then.'

Passing under the arch of the doors, they found Dog sitting on some stairs to the left. She rose when she saw them. 'We've got Proctis over there.' She nodded across the paved yard. 'He has very nice rooms. Lots of gold leaf all over the furniture.'

Tika saw Dog's cold eyes and guessed Proctis was an unhappy person. Dog led them to a half open door at the further end of the yard and waved them in. 'I'll wait out here,' she said. 'The smell of people like him makes me feel ill.'

Major Bars opened an inner door and looked in. Then he held the door wide for Tika and the others with them. For a moment they could only stare. Dog's description didn't come close to covering the reality. Nearly every surface was covered in gold and on several gold shelves were arrayed various, ugly, gold ornaments. Proctis sat in a throne like chair to the side of an ornate hearth. A large bruise decorated his left cheek and Essa leaned against the wall beside Proctis, her expression as cold as Dog's. Major Bars stood staring down at Proctis.

'I hope you'll arrest these people,' Proctis said as soon as he set eyes on Bars. He waved at the three blue uniformed Guards. 'They just burst in here, then one of them hit me!'

'Where is General Demisen?' Bars asked.

Tika *nearly* felt sorry for Proctis. He really had no idea how to deal with this situation.

'General Demisen? Why, he, he took a fever, yes, a fever, some time ago.'

'And his officers? His garrison? They *all* took a fever?'

'Yes. Oh yes. Exactly.'

'Why did no one notify the Citadel?'

'Well, General Demisen was the one who reported to

the Citadel of course. I had no contacts there, except when we sent shipments west.'

'Why have you allowed rebels to camp around this town?'

Proctis looked genuinely astonished. 'How would I stop them?' he asked.

Bars waved to two of his troops. 'Take him. General Falkir will deal with him.'

Protesting wildly, Proctis was dragged from his chair and pushed to the door. Major Bars stared around the room. 'You see what I mean?' he asked Tika. 'Many homes are just like this.' Tika sensed a slow anger stirring in the man. 'It's almost a pity the town wasn't razed to the ground.'

'I do see what you mean, Major, but surely the Citadel relies on a lot of food and minerals from this region?'

'It's not that much in actual fact, I don't think.' Bars frowned. 'I'd been checking the last few shipments on General Falkir's order, for a while now, and really, except for the gold I suppose, it isn't crucial to the Citadel or the City.'

Essa had listened and now she wandered across to join the Major and Tika. 'You think it might be worth searching for any documents, papers? Maybe find out who was sending false reports?' she asked Tika.

'It's worth a try,' Tika agreed. 'Are the administrative offices here, or somewhere else?'

'Just across the way,' said Bars. 'At least, they used to be.' He pointed from the door to upper windows along the side of the yard.

Garrol and Geffal joined them, looking up at the windows. 'We'll check.' Garrol nodded. 'That Proctis really isn't the brightest man I've ever met, so there may well be documents there.'

Major Bars watched the Iskallian Guards cross the yard then he looked down at Tika. 'I thank Mother Dark you were here.'

'We have a treaty with you, Major.'

They began walking back the way they'd come and passed a handful of town people moving fallen timbers and stone in a half hearted fashion. Major Bars paused, then he

266

explained, in very explicit detail, just why they should work better unless they *really* wanted to annoy him. Most of them began to move slightly faster but one man, in his early thirties Tika guessed, turned on the Major. He stood, hands on his hips, glaring at the officer.

'Why don't you get your men to do this work? Or let us send for the farm brutes? This is not work for us.'

Major Bars stepped closer and simply back handed the young man. From his position on the ground, the man stared up in disbelief which gave way to complete hatred. Bars turned on his heel and continued down the street.

'That is the attitude of most everyone in this place,' he told Tika.

She stopped suddenly, her Guards almost treading on her. 'I do understand your point Major, but this town is now under your control, or General Falkir's anyway. What are you saying you want to happen here?'

Grey eyes met hers. 'None of these people should be left here,' he said, his tone flat. 'Let them scatter, earn their living like most people must.'

'And what happens to Mertasia? It sits here, empty, crumbling into ruin, or providing a home for wandering trouble makers?'

'Turn it into a full garrison to care for the people in this region. An eastern Citadel if you like. It's just been proved it is too distant for the present Citadel to provide a quick response if something happens here - it took us six days of hard riding to get here.'

'You would perhaps set up a situation where this eastern Citadel would rival the western one and divide Kelshan completely?' Tika began walking again.

'General Demisen was a good man, Lady Tika. He would have remained loyal to Lady Ricca. There are other officers, and men, who would uphold her rule with honour.'

No more was said as they had reached the north gate again and they paused, staring in silence at the several heaps of countless bodies

Chapter Twenty Four

Endis was sure he had not slept but he had witnessed the fighting outside the town of Mertasia. He wasn't aware of how he was able to do that and he almost called Ashri to explain it to him. But he stopped himself from doing so. It was time he began to test the powers she had given him and started to live this strange new life which, according to her, stretched a very long way into the future. Endis watched, saddened by the slaughter, but he'd felt more distanced from it than he had when he'd seen such things before. He had seen Tika enter the fray, clearly fighting to reach Falkir. Endis saw the astonishing skill with which Tika fought. He saw the sword was ancient, forged of blood metal, a material only fashioned in the Dark Realm.

Although the sword had certain properties embedded within it during its making, it was in fact the power within Tika that gave her victory after victory. When Endis watched those events at Mertasia, he wasn't sure *how* he saw them. It was a totally different experience from the dreams, or visions, he had had before, nor was he a passive viewer: he could hear the noise, smell the stench of death, as if he was a participant.

He was interested in Major Bars and his suggestions for the future of the town. The battle over, Proctis a prisoner under guard, somehow Endis roamed the town, seeing the gaudy garishness of the interiors of so many of the houses, the way the inhabitants had changed their lives to live completely superficial existences. Endis heard snatches of conversation from the people ordered to clear their streets and all he heard was muted anger and outraged complaints. Their hands were dirty and blistered, their fine clothes torn, ruined!

Endis left his rooms and stood in the garden. He thought of the high airy room with its window walls, and stepping forward, he was there. Clouds undulated below the thin spires he would always think of as Ashri's needles.

Faint touches of colour tinged some of them, reminding him of dawn skies.

He sat in one of the armchairs considering what he'd seen and heard. Surely he had been drawn there for some purpose, but he was far from sure what that might be. Endis had realised Ashri had an intense interest in Tika. He too had been intrigued by her, fascinated even more when he read some of her Historian, Dromi's, reports of her travels. He rose and chose the stairs to return to the ground level without coming to any conclusions.

He had yet to revisit the impossible woodland room where he had laid the Augur's body. His thoughts shied away from what he might find there still. Entering the courtyard garden, he busied himself removing fallen flower heads and generally tidying over enthusiastic climbing plants. Endis let his thoughts wander where they chose, hoping for some sort of answer that he might understand or accept.

Later, when he'd cleared away the dishes he'd used for his supper, he wrote of what he'd seen then sat back in his chair. 'Shadows.' He spoke the word aloud although only softly.

There was the briefest wait before that strange murmur sounded in his head. 'Yes, Sentinel.'

'You saw what I saw?'

'Yes.'

This evening, Endis was aware only of the voice, he saw none of those vague strange figures around him. 'Is there something I should do? Would Ashri have done anything?'

There was a silence for some time before he received a reply. 'Ashri is not Sentinel now. You are.'

'Very well. Is there anything *I* should do?'

'No. We will.'

Endis felt a hint of alarm. 'What will you do?' he asked carefully.

'What should be done.' The shadows' words held a note of surprise that he needed to ask then there was an emptiness in his head and in the room.

With a decidedly uncomfortable sensation, Endis

thought he'd just go to bed and ignore the feeling. A stray idea suggested he could probably follow the shadows and see for himself what they might be up to. He pushed that idea away and closed his eyes.

When he woke, he waited a moment but there was no hint that shadows were around, or if they were, they didn't feel any need to speak to him. He made only tea for his breakfast then went out, turning right down the passage, to the library. He went in and walked to the centre of the huge room. Gazing around, he then stared up. Somehow he could locate the other libraries, one on each floor. He dragged a chair into the middle of the room, sat down, and concentrated.

After a while, he blinked and rubbed his face. There had been no sound, no tremor of any movement. Standing, he looked further into the library. And he smiled. A spiral staircase had sprouted a few paces from his chair. Endis approached it, staring up, then set a foot on the bottom step. Climbing up, he found the library on the second floor had moved from its previous position to here, directly above the other. Endis was delighted. It made far more sense to him to have each library directly over one another and he wondered why Ashri hadn't thought of it.

Still smiling, he concentrated again and moved the third floor library, and another spiral stair grew a short distance from the one he'd just climbed. He went back down, feeling rather pleased with himself when a thought brought him to an abrupt halt. Would this strange structure take the weight of seven enormous libraries, stacked one above the other? Was that why Ashri had arranged them in a scattered pattern?

He scanned the walls around, not even thinking what he was doing or how, then laughed at himself and returned to his rooms. Slightly carried away at his discovery of at least some of his new abilities, he spent the afternoon expanding his quarters. He was delighted to find he could also summon furniture, then, that he could dismiss much of it when the main room became too cluttered for him to actually move across it. Eventually, he pulled himself together and stopped acting so very ridiculously and began to cook a meal.

He had just finished eating when shadows spoke. 'Sentinel. Mertasia can be second Citadel.'

'It can? How do you know?'

'We make it so.'

'Is that what was needed?'

'Yes.'

'Thank you for telling me.'

'Enjoyed.'

There was smug satisfaction in that one word that somehow made Endis shiver. He chose to ask no more. He could also have overlooked Mertasia to see for himself, but he really didn't feel up to that right now.

Veka and Shea went with Pearl and Farn to retrieve the packs Tika's company had left in the woods, bringing them back to a new camp close to Mertasia's dismantled north gate. Tika found Cerys curled tight against General Falkir and sensed distress from the cat. Brin had settled close by and a soldier, his arm in a makeshift sling, also remained by the sleeping General. Tika saw wounded laid on the grass a little distance away, army surgeons with Falkir's battalions working along the line. She sighed and made her way to the injured, Fedran, Essa and Dog accompanying her. Once again, Tika surprised herself at the increase in the speed she could heal. She was becoming more used to the fact that she was no longer exhausted after a long session of using her mage powers to heal; tired, yes, but not on the edge of collapse.

Storm and Kija had continued to circle, watching for any signs of rebel soldiers either trying to get into the town or flee the area. Onion and Rivan were working with Falkir's men, catching the riderless or injured horses and gathering them into lines some way beyond the town. Genia had settled near the horses, calming them while Onion helped the Kelshans treat any injuries. By the time Tika finished healing the worst of the wounded, it was full dark and Essa urged her back to their small camp for food.

Major Bars was there, drinking tea which Ashoki and Jarko seemed to have constantly brewing. As Tika sat down, Bars asked if the still sleeping General would recover. 'Oh.' Tika had almost forgotten the poor man.

She roused him and, opening his eyes, Falkir stared up. Struggling into a sitting position, he pulled aside the blanket and looked at his leg. He studied the network of fine lines all around his knee and down his calf then looked up, finding Tika in the firelight. 'Thank you,' he said simply.

Major Bars watched while Falkir cautiously raised and lowered his knee, clearly with no pain. 'Lady Tika has healed many of our men, sir,' he said.

'Thank you,' Falkir repeated and accepted a bowl of tea from Kazmat.

'Rest the leg tonight, General, but it should be fine tomorrow,' Tika said through a mouthful of travel bread. 'There seemed to be very few survivors among the rebels,' she added. She gulped down her tea and got to her feet again, vanishing into the darkness beyond the fire.

Dog and Navan scrambled after her, standing to each side as she approached the first heap of the dead. A flicker of her fingers and cold blue flame blazed over the bodies. There were seven such piles that Tika disposed of in this manner before she turned back to their camp fire. She dismissed thoughts of the families, perhaps wives, or children, of those dead. If they had truly cared about any families, surely they would have found a way home to them, rather than continuing with their rebellion.

Tika sat down again and Farn moved closer to half curl round her and Navan stretched over to return her now clean sword in silence. Falkir still looked a little pale but Tika suddenly noticed Major Bars was quite white. She frowned, scanning him. Then she swore. 'For stars' sake! Why didn't you tell me that cut was so bad?' she snapped, moving to the Major's side. Everyone saw he was close to unconsciousness and Tika pushed him back without ceremony. 'Navan, get this boot off him please.'

Navan and Teyo both struggled to pull off the nearly knee high boot and tipped it, pouring blood onto the grass. Again, a trouser leg was cut away, Falkir watching in alarm. Tika was amazed that the man could have walked with her, through the town, up a hill and back, and yet given no indication, not even the slightest limp, of the deep gash she found in the back of his thigh. Bars groaned and Tika made him sleep as her senses probed the cut. The bone was chipped, nearly broken, and she wondered again how he'd managed to walk with her. She was aware Kija and Storm had returned, late as it was, and felt Kija's mind bolstering hers when she finally sealed Bars' wound and sat back. 'Why ever didn't he tell me earlier?' she asked Falkir, shaking her head. 'He's lost far too much blood, which I can't replace. He'll need longer to recover.'

The General managed a smile. 'Some men refuse to admit any weakness. Bars is obviously one to take it to extremes.'

Tika went to settle back by Farn's chest and her gaze fell on the young trooper on the other side of the General. His arm was in a rough sling and her gaze narrowed. 'I'm fine, Lady Tika,' he stammered. 'Just broke my wrist when I fell off my horse.'

'Show me.'

Ashoki was the nearest and she gently removed the sling, revealing a swollen and slightly twisted wrist. Tika sighed, sent the young man to sleep with a thought, and set about repairing the tangle of crushed bones. It was only when she'd finished that tiredness at last overcame her. She gave a jaw cracking yawn and snuggled down as Farn peered at her in concern. Kija let her mind voice be heard by all at the fire. 'Do not fuss, Farn. She is tired and needs sleep but she is not as worn out as she used to be. Let her sleep.'

Everyone else was suddenly aware of their own weariness and soon their camp, the Kelshan injured and uninjured, were all sleeping more soundly than might have been expected. It was Kija who roused them. She too had slept but when she'd woken, she instantly sensed something had changed. Tika came awake at the first touch of Kija's mind. Pushing her blankets away, she was on her feet, staring all around. Everything was calm. There seemed nothing to cause Kija's anxiety. Her Guards were less quick to wake, but Fedran and Dog got to their feet to join her at Kija's side.

'What is it, Tika?' asked Fedran.

Tika shook her head. 'I don't know, but something is different.'

Several groups of Kelshans were stirring and one young officer approached, with some hesitation. He saluted Tika, glancing at the still sleeping bodies of General Falkir, Major Bars and the trooper. 'I had a patrol check round the walls, Lady Tika. They report a sense of emptiness within although they didn't actually enter the town.'

Fedran called four other Iskallian Guards, knowing Tika would insist on investigating. Farn and Storm rose, flying low above then, Kija rising higher still, as Tika joined the captain and half a dozen troopers. They strode towards the gate, Tika mind linked to the Dragons. There were no people visible in the streets again, although it was long past sunrise and still much clearing up needing to be done. The captain gestured his men forward. They drew weapons and went into the first houses. They were not inside long, shaking their heads as they came out. They worked their way along four of the streets and found no one at all.

Tika stopped. 'Do you sense anyone, living or dead, mother of my heart?' She sent the thought to Kija.

'Nothing. Nothing at all,' was Kija's answer.

The captain gave her a questioning look. 'I'm sorry, captain. I have no idea what's happened here.' A thought occurred to her. 'Where is Proctis?'

'I checked on him straight after my patrols reported back to me. He is still under guard at the surgeons' camp.'

One of the troopers spoke up. 'There's no sign of trouble in these houses, Captain, Lady. No indication of any fights inside. Just - no people. Cook stoves were quite cold so they've been gone some time.'

Tika was as nonplussed as the captain. She looked up at the Dragons and let the Kelshans hear her mind speak them. 'Could you see if there are any people on any roads away from here, please, my dears?'

Storm wheeled away almost before she'd finished her request.

'I posted men to watch each gate, Lady Tika.'

'Everyone seemed to sleep very heavily last night,' said

Fedran, frowning. 'Could your men have fallen asleep?'

The captain took no offence at the question. 'I had six men at each gate, sir. I can't believe all of them would have fallen asleep at the same time. I agree that all the men were tired both from the ride here and the fighting, but they all swore they had taken turns sleeping. I believe them.'

Fedran nodded. 'You know your men of course. Yet they saw nothing?'

'Not a thing.'

Tika sensed an air of discomfort from Kija although the gold Dragon didn't offer any solution to this mystery. The captain stared around him in perplexity. 'How could so many people just disappear?'

Tika knew he was still wondering if she had something to do with this: many Kelshans had either seen or heard about her removal of all the dead. If she was capable of doing that, well, the captain understandably might suspect she had somehow emptied Mertasia of its many inhabitants. 'I don't know,' Tika repeated, meeting the captain's eyes steadily. 'Why would I want everyone gone?'

They walked slowly back to the gate. 'Will the General be fit to take command again soon?' asked the captain.

'Yes. He'll be up soon I'm quite sure.'

The two groups parted company, Tika and her Guards returning to Brin and Pearl. Farn settled beside Pearl and informed everyone that his mother was also searching for any signs of people on the roads from Mertasia. General Falkir was sitting up, looking rested and alert. He also wore a fresh pair of grey uniform trousers someone must have found for him. His smile faded when he saw Tika's expression. 'What's happened now?' he asked.

Tika sat down with a groan. 'Mertasia is empty. Apparently the entire population vanished during the night.'

Falkir looked blank. 'They all left? *All* of them?'

'That's not how it looks. Everything is still in place in their houses. It doesn't seem as though they took anything with them, if they really just walked out. And before you ask, I swear I had nothing whatsoever to do with this.' She saw Cerys had moved from Falkir to snuggle against Major Bars and wondered why those huge green gold eyes were suddenly so wide. The cat said nothing so Tika turned back to Falkir. 'I've just been in the town with one of your Captains. He can confirm what we found.'

'How could so many people get out without anyone seeing or hearing anything?' asked Veka. 'How many lived there?'

'About four thousand,' Falkir replied. He got to his feet with care but his leg was quite sound. Major Bars stirred and then hurriedly pulled himself up. The little colour in his cheeks disappeared and he closed his eyes.

'You should have told me you were hurt,' Tika told him. 'You let yourself bleed far too much. Now you'll have to rest for several days.'

'Has something happened sir?' Bars managed to ask.

Teyo, who was closest, gave him a swift account of the missing town's folk as Tika's attention moved to the other Kelshan soldier in their small camp. 'Your wrist is mended,' she told him. 'There are many little bones in the wrist so don't lift anything too heavy just yet.'

Falkir looked down at the lad. 'Stay with me today, in case I need a runner,' he said.

'Why don't you tell the General how you thought Mertasia might be used, Major? It looks like you'd have an ideal opportunity to change its functions now.' Tika grinned as Bars stared at her.

Falkir sat again. 'Well, Major?'

Slowly at first then with more enthusiasm, the major explained his idea. Tika had listened and when Bars stopped speaking, she added a thought. 'Many of those houses have everything covered in gold. Couldn't you use it to rebuild? Both here and in the Citadel? And many towns across Kelshan have suffered losses to rebellious soldiers. They must surely need help too?'

Falkir shook his head. 'We must see if we can solve this puzzle but first I must visit the injured.' He peered out over the scatter of cook fires. 'Were many men and horses lost?'

'Nearly a third of your men were killed.' Tika's voice was low. 'I'm sorry, General. There were fewer horses killed. When they lost their riders they simply ran clear.

There are some injuries among them but two of my Guards have helped some of your men collect up the horses. They have them safe perhaps a mile north.'

'More losses than I would ever want but still less than I feared,' Falkir replied. 'We owe you another debt, Lady Tika.'

'You owe us nothing,' Tika snapped. 'We have a treaty, remember? And don't stand on that leg for too long for a day or two. Give your knee a chance to recover completely.'

Major Bars moved as if he thought to rise and Falkir glared at him. 'Did you not hear the Lady Tika? You need several days rest, so you *will* rest. Is that clear, Major?'

'Yes sir.'

Tika smiled at Bars' dejected expression. 'Dromi, why don't you discuss Major Bars' idea, get something definite on paper that may perhaps be a workable plan.'

Dromi nodded. Veka and Shea both joined the two men and Tika left them to talk. She knew Shea was always interested in new ideas on how towns might be organised, and Veka seemed interested in everything. 'I'm going to see what's happening with the horses,' she announced.

'I can take you, my Tika,' Farn suggested at once.

She hugged him. 'It isn't far, my dear, and I hoped you might stay to watch over the major. Tell me if he feels faint and so on.'

'Oh.' Farn considered this then decided it was a useful task and settled back against Pearl. Brin lowered his head close to Tika. 'I will hunt in a while. There seems a lack of food here for all these people, unless there is food in the town?'

Tika stroked his long face. 'That sounds a good plan. I'm not sure anyone wants to get food from the town, at least, not yet.'

'It seems very strange to me.'

'It is, Brin.'

Tika found Garrol walking beside her as most of the Guards followed her in a generally north direction. 'I felt a familiarity,' Garrol said very softly.

'What?' Tika looked up at him. Other Guards were

catching up with them now. Garrol glanced back then turned to Tika again.

'Darallax,' he said, then moved aside as Fedran joined them.

Tika kept walking but her thoughts spun in shock. She suspected Garrol had said Darallax's name only to hint that he suspected Shadows could have been involved. She glanced down at her left hand. The line of black was tight beneath the silver ring on her thumb and seemed the same as usual, neither wider nor thinner. *Could* they have done that? How? Why? Kazmat had moved up beside Fedran and begun talking to him so Tika chose to mind speak the Shadows.

'Shadows?'

'Yes.'

'Did you do anything to the people of Mertasia?'

'No.'

'Do you have any idea what has happened to them?'

There was the pause she'd become accustomed to when trying to converse with these creatures before a reply came.

'Yes.'

Keeping her temper with an effort, Tika questioned them further. 'Can you tell me exactly what *did* happen to them?' Ahead she could see a large gathering of horses and Genia's purple form reclining near them.

'Tell exactly, no. Not sure. They are gone.'

'I *know* they are gone. Where? Who took them?'

'Brothers. No more people.'

'Brothers? You mean other Shadows like you?'

'Oldest of us. Lost they were. Now found. They took.'

Tika tried to make some sense of the Shadows' truncated speech. 'Oldest of you?' she asked warily.

'Yes. First made.'

There was definite respect, even affection in the tone.

'It is a good thing that they have, erm, somehow returned?'

'Yes. They remembered. So we remembered too.'

'Remembered what?'

'Why we were made.'

Feeling too confused to pursue that line of questioning,

Tika repeated her earlier one: 'Where are the people of Mertasia now?'

'Vortex.' The voice held immense satisfaction. 'People no more.'

Chapter Twenty Five

Tika spent the morning with Rivan and Onion, examining all the horses which had been hurt. There were some with wounds of varying severity but many had also damaged themselves when they'd fled in panic. Tika knew that Onion had somehow healed many of the animals although the extent of his powers was not something she wanted to look into. She knew if she questioned him he would either smile at her or start humming to himself. She had never tried to touch his mind and she had no intention of doing so now.

There were around forty Kelshan troopers who were helping, and they all seemed quite relaxed with Genia's presence. Tika spoke to the purple Dragon who admitted she'd been very interested in how all these men looked after the horses with such care, 'Thank you for keeping them so calm, dear one. Will you need to hunt soon?'

Genia's eyes flashed briefly. 'Pearl will be here soon. She will watch these poor frightened ones while I hunt.' Her chin bumped Tika's arm. 'What happened in that place last night?'

Her mind voice didn't suggest she was worried, more curious than alarmed. 'Did you sense something then?' Tika asked her.

'There was a shivery sort of feeling, that's all.'

'It is very strange. All the people in the town have disappeared.' Tika was reluctant to say anything about the possible participation of Shadows until she'd had more time to think it over herself.

When Tika and her Guards returned to the main Kelshan camp they could smell meat cooking as they approached. Clearly Brin had been successful in supplying fresh meat. They saw troopers still moving rubble from the gate and clearing the streets beyond. Falkir joined them as they arrived back. Major Bars had fallen asleep some time before, Dromi told them, but he roused even as Dromi spoke.

Kija and Storm also returned, having flown much further than any large number of people could possibly have managed to walk, but they had nothing to report. 'I should send messengers back to the Citadel,' Falkir said, sitting across from Tika. 'It will take eight days or more if they go at a more reasonable pace than we took getting here.'

Dromi began showing him the ideas he and Major Bars had been working on. 'It's just an empty shell now,' Dromi finished. 'And it is much nearer your border with both Strale and the Free Lands than it is to the Citadel. An administrative centre here would make a great deal of sense.'

'It does make sense,' Falkir agreed. 'The fact that all its previous occupants have disappeared into thin air is of some concern, to me at least. What if it happened again?'

'Aaah. I see your point.' Dromi frowned, looking at Tika.

'I've *told* you. It was nothing to do with me. It really wasn't.'

'We thought you should tell the local farmers Mertasia is - different,' Shea told Falkir. 'And find out what happened to those two empty towns. Why were they empty? Have the people been killed by rebels or did they just leave, hide among other settlements?'

Falkir gave a rueful smile. 'I think you are quite correct but there are many things I have to do, the first of which must be a report back to the Citadel.'

'Did your aides come through the fighting?' Dromi asked.

'Only one, unfortunately. And my horse was killed and I have no idea what happened to my saddlebags as yet. I'm wearing some other poor soul's clothes.' Falkir shook his head. 'Such is the aftermath of battle.'

'I have writing supplies,' Dromi offered.

'Thank you. I will make a report this evening, when I decide whether to send Proctis back to the Citadel or try him here, in military court.'

Tika walked along the line of wounded and found most recovering well enough. She used her healing power to

281

snuff out infections which had sprung up in a few cases, but otherwise the Kelshan military surgeons had things well in hand. Returning to the small Iskallian section of the camp, Tika saw Pearl settle beside Brin and that Kija and Storm were both asleep. She glanced over to the town and had the feeling the troopers working there were still nervous. She didn't want to discuss what the Shadows had told her as Bars and Falkir listened so she could do nothing to allay the troopers' worries.

The sun was nearly set when a trooper rushed up to Falkir, clearly agitated. Falkir was on his feet again at once. 'What is it, trooper?'

'Sir! Oh sir! We had worked clearing the streets up to that big place. We went inside because we'd seen the fire in one part of it yesterday and the big hole in the roof.' The man paused to gasp in more air before continuing. 'Sir, there's a bloody big circle in the floor! Beg pardon, my Lady. Like the one in the Citadel. It weren't there when I went with Major Bars to get that Proctis out. No sir, it definitely weren't.'

'What?!' Tika was on her feet. 'There was no circle there, General. I was with Major Bars too.'

'Looks like we'll have to go and see,' said Dog cheerfully.

'But it's dark,' the trooper stuttered.

Dog patted his cheek as she passed him. 'Never mind. We're not frightened of the dark.'

All of the Iskallians were up, clearly intending to go with Tika. General Falkir shook his head, the boy whose wrist had been broken, standing beside him. 'No, lad. You stay here, keep the major company. We won't be long.' He met Tika's eyes. 'I hope,' he added.

As they hurried towards the now cleared gateway, he glanced at her. 'I'm assuming you know nothing of this either?' he said.

'No, I don't,' she retorted. 'Believe me, I wish I *did* know what, by all the *hells*, is going on here.'

The streets seemed much darker, the houses crowding closer. Impatiently, Tika cast a mage globe just ahead of them to light their way. The trooper who had brought the news was with them, at Falkir's insistence. He paused halfway across the paved yard. 'In there,' he said, pointing to the door beyond which they'd found Proctis. Fedran didn't hesitate. Hand on the hilt of his sword, he strode forward and slammed the door open so hard it banged against the wall. Tika sent the light globe inside and stared as did everyone else, at the floor.

It was indeed a large circle. The blocks were of Kelshan green interspersed with grey, but the narrow outer border was Iskallian blue, as was the large central stone. 'Essa,' Tika murmured.

The huge sergeant joined Tika at the very edge of the circle the two sending their senses down. Tika sighed.

'Active,' said Essa softly.

Stepping away, Tika looked at General Falkir and shrugged. 'There you are. Your method for getting a message to the Citadel fast,' she said.

A noise made them look back into the yard and Jarko appeared with the boy Falkir had told to stay with Major Bars. He met the General's frown and his chin came up. 'You said I must stay with you sir, in case you needed a runner,' he said firmly.

Falkir looked at Tika. 'You say this works?' She nodded. 'Then I'll go myself now, and report what's happened. I'll come straight back.'

'Essa and Geffal will go with you, just to be sure this first time,' said Tika.

'It might not be safe?' Falkir queried.

Tika gave a snort of amusement. 'It will be quite safe but Essa is more used to moving people than you are yet General.'

Dromi scrabbled in his ever present satchel and produced the papers in which he and Major Bars had outlined the idea of a second, eastern, Citadel. 'Your clerks can perhaps find these helpful in any decisions on what might happen to this town,' he said.

Falkir took the papers then looked from Tika to the trooper who'd brought news of the circle. 'Major Bars has command in my absence. He is still not to try to move though. He needs to recover from his wound.' He reached over to grasp the shoulder of the boy who had followed him here. 'As you said, I might need a runner. Come, Mottis.' He drew him towards Essa, the lad's face paling.

When all four were close to the centre of the circle, there was a pop of air and they were gone. 'I hope those in the Citadel insist the General stays overnight at least,' Tika said. 'There should be Guards here to wait for them then Falkir or Major Bars will have to arrange a rota of their men to keep watch.'

'I'll stay tonight,' Shea offered.

'Me too,' said Veka.

Jarko and Kazmat nodded their agreement too. Tika moved to the door. 'Someone will bring your bed rolls up and some food. It doesn't really need guarding yet - we're the only ones who know it's here.'

The few remaining Iskallians headed out of the palace. 'There were very few papers up in those offices,' Dromi remarked. 'Difficult to tell if they just didn't bother with keeping any documents or if someone got rid of them.'

'Excuse me, my Lady. The General will be all right, will he?' asked the trooper who was still with them.

'Quite all right. Have you not seen the circle used in the Citadel?'

'Oh yes, I have, my Lady, but only when messages have come through or were sent. Never seen no people go like that.'

'It's quite painless,' Dog told him kindly.

The trooper gave her a very wary look but said no more. They told Major Bars of Falkir's departure to Kelshan and he began to smile. Garrol laughed. 'Looks like your idea could well be made a reality,' he said. 'It does seem very odd though, all the people gone and then a circle suddenly appearing.' He looked at Tika as he spoke and she scowled.

'Once and for all, I did *not* have anything to do with either event,' she said.

'Well how could you, my Tika?' Farn agreed. Tika smiled, reaching up to stroke his face. 'You've never made people vanish or made a circle, have you?'

Tika kept a firm block on her thoughts but she saw Teyo glance at her quickly then away. Teyo and a handful of his stone workers had witnessed her make a circle in Port Maressa but they had all sworn not to speak of it.

When the camp settled for sleep, Tika lay wide awake, her thoughts tightly shielded. She went over and over every word of the few the Shadows had spoken. They had told of "brothers" but in a tone implying a considerable difference, as though the ones of whom they spoke were far superior to them, revered and wiser older brothers. Tika made herself lie still, knowing Farn would start to fuss if he thought she was worrying. She had begun to wonder if the Shadows she spoke with were creations of Youki but had to conclude they couldn't be.

Mother Dark had created Shadows for her Second Son, Darallax. He, in turn, had given Tika some of his Shadows. Could there be others? She'd always been aware that Shadows had power but just how much would be needed to move four thousand people or more to - where? To the Vortex, so they'd told her. Where or what was that, she wondered. Was it a place, another being, like Ferag or the Ancient Augur? It was close to dawn when Tika finally fell asleep, her dreams a crazy muddle of too many things.

In the morning, Major Bars summoned the few surviving officers, mostly sergeants, and instructed them to arrange for shifts of four troopers to keep watch over the circle and explained that General Falkir would be back at some point today. He asked for reports on all the still recovering men and those back on duty. Then he gave further orders before dismissing them. The Iskallian Guards still by their fire, had listened while keeping any thoughts to themselves. When the various officers left, Major Bars leaned back against Brin without thought, his face white as snow. Tika sent a trickle of strength into him as Ashoki offered him a bowl of meaty broth. Bars opened his eyes and took the broth. 'How long will it take until I can do anything without feeling so dizzy or exhausted?' he asked Tika.

She smiled. 'At least another four or five days. Even then you'll have to rest a lot. It's your own fault for being so noble and brave. I knew you'd been injured but I didn't realise how badly. You do understand you would have died if I hadn't noticed when I did?'

Bars saw that she was completely serious and he looked apologetic. 'It didn't really hurt too much, after a while,' he said.

'Of course it didn't, you fool! The nerves were cut, your leg was numb. Don't be so heroic in another similar situation, please.'

'I'm sorry,' he said sounding genuinely abashed.

'So you should be. It took far longer to heal you then than if I'd been able to earlier.' Tika grinned at him, taking any sting from her words. 'Just keep drinking as much as you can and rest.'

Garrol and Ashoki wandered off towards the north gate. Navan went to sit with Major Bars, discussing the general layout of the town as Dromi scribbled notes. Tika would dearly liked to have had some time to herself, just to think, but she knew she couldn't just wander off. Kija and Pearl had gone to see Genia and Farn offered to prop up Major Bars so that Brin could fly. Bars apologised profusely as he realised he'd been using Brin for support. Finally Tika could sit still no longer but only Dog got to her feet to accompany her when she left the fireside.

Tika walked quickly to the south, the town walls towering to her left. Passing the west gate which troopers had cleared completely, she sensed there was a new air about the place. The troopers were no longer nervous of being within the town. Dog kept pace with her but said nothing. When Tika stopped at last, she stared round. 'Not a tree around. Nothing at all. Why is it so bare, Dog?'

Dog followed her gaze. 'Mertasia was a hub, Tika. Certain times of the year, folk brought goods in, whether it was grain or gold, I'd guess.' She scuffed at the bare ground with her boot. 'Looks like heavy wagons and carts stopped here regularly. Probably held auctions out here too. I can't imagine all those wealthy folk would want smelly horses and common folk messing up their precious streets, can you?'

'There's room for an awful lot of wagons, Dog.'

'It looks as if it was an awfully wealthy town,' Dog retorted. She watched Tika scowl. 'What's wrong Tika?

You have some idea about what happened?'

For a moment, Tika stood tense then she sighed, glancing at the engineer. 'An idea, yes, but not one I can discuss yet.'

'Endis would have been useful,' Dog remarked. 'His training must surely have let him *See* something like this. He could have warned us at least.' She smiled, suggesting it was just a teasing comment.

Tika returned a faint smile. 'I'm not sure he could, Dog. His training seems to have changed direction somewhat.'

It was Dog's turn to show some concern. 'Changed? What does *that* mean? Will he be a Seer or not?'

Tika began to walk again, but more slowly. 'I don't think he'll be a Seer, no, Dog. I'm afraid he might be much more.'

Endis had busied himself moving the libraries and he had also begun to try to understand how they were organised. He had no difficulty reading any book he picked up now, no matter how bizarre the writing appeared at first glance. The lowest library seemed the best arranged to Endis. All the books, scrolls, notebooks, dealt with the life of the world: plants, animals, fish, everything. History and geography were muddled together in the library above that one. The topmost one was a complete jumble of information and invented tales.

Endis decided Ashri must have begun with the top library first, when she gathered up any book she could get hold of, and gradually tried to be more systematic with the following libraries. There were also countless notebooks filled with Ashri's handwriting. Endis had not read more of these notebooks, which he knew contained Ashri's meticulous record of her numberless years as the Sentinel. The only one he had looked at was the one she had been using when her service was ended. He had read only the last few pages, discovering they were an affectionate, personal message to him, of confidence and belief in his ability to successfully continue in her place. Those pages were second only in importance to Endis to the letter from his mother, and he felt no overwhelming desire to read more yet.

Endis spent some time when he woke, and again in the later afternoons, overlooking the world. He had abandoned the idea of trying to understand just how this was possible and simply chose to accept that he could. He had seen the fighting and noted Tika's powers which she wrongly ascribed to the sword she carried. He had only briefly glimpsed Mertasia since then but was brought up short this afternoon. He quickly realised the inhabitants had gone and recalled his conversation with the shadows.

They said they had made Mertasia a suitable place for another Citadel, a stronghold for Kelshan government in the east. Had they taken all those people? Sitting bolt upright at his table, he called for the shadows.

'Sentinel.'

'Where are the inhabitants of Mertasia?' he asked, pleased that his voice remained steady.

'Gone.'

'Gone where exactly?'

'The Vortex.'

Endis closed his eyes. 'Did they deserve to go there? All of them?' He waited for the reply.

When it came, he heard confusion in the shadows' tone. 'Of course, Sentinel. People there love only wealth. Only gold. Fathers, grandfathers, long time.'

'Could they not have been persuaded to change their ways?'

'No.'

'Are you quite sure of that?'

For a moment, Endis saw two of the long, thin wavering figures briefly outlined against the wall. 'Quite sure not change. Men tried.'

'Tried?'

'Tried make those people think other. People killed. Not change.'

Deciding on a different approach, Endis asked another question. 'Do you often send people to the Vortex?'

'No.' Now there was definitely shocked surprise in the reply. 'Take to Mother. Only Mother approaches Vortex.'

'Thank you for explaining that to me. I have much to

learn and understand.'

'Yes, Sentinel.'

Voices and figures were gone, but Endis knew they were somehow still close, able to come to him whenever he called. He relaxed a little. If Mother Dark had truly sent the Mertasians to this Vortex, she must have felt it was the right, or perhaps the only, thing to do. Endis believed what Ashri had told him: that Mother Dark genuinely cared for life on this world without interfering. If she felt the Vortex was the only action she could take, then he bowed to her wisdom in the matter.

Endis did not believe Mother Dark was commanding the shadows. She had gifted them to Ashri, to her Sentinel, and now they were his. He had not commanded them to remove the Mertasians but it was possible he could have given the whole situation far more thought. He set about preparing a meal for later then went out to his garden. Working among the plants gave him comfort similar to the comfort Ashri must have felt gazing at her needles rising from those restless clouds. Endis found his thoughts could somehow rearrange themselves if he simply let them float in his head.

When he'd washed and taken his food from the oven by the hearth, he made a decision as he ate. Ashri had not shown him exactly how to access her sharp and vivid memories but he concentrated now on that walled town in eastern Kelshan, hoping she had surveyed it in some detail. It took longer than he'd hoped but then something seemed to click into place in his mind and Mertasia came into view. Endis saw straight away that the pictures he was watching must be much older: the people wore clothes of a very different style and the words they spoke had a slightly different inflection.

The images he saw offered no judgement. It was impossible to tell whether Ashri had viewed any of these things with sympathy, anger or amusement. So he now studied them with no prejudices one way or another. He sensed a vague mixture of sadness and anger in places but Ashri's memories showed she only watched; at no point did she interfere. Endis studied the pictures of Mertasia, listened to some of the conversations Ashri had heard. Restlessly he walked out into the passageway and strolled along to the infinity room. A soft amber glow lit the passage and Endis realised he had never come out of his rooms or garden at night before.

In the infinity room he sat on the bench and brought all the worlds and their stars into whirling movement. Where, precisely, did Mother Dark dwell he wondered, or was she just an unsubstantial cloud of power? Endis understood now, on a much deeper level, that Mother Dark truly did not interfere. Except for giving a very few commands to her own creations, even they could choose their own paths. Mother had made the shadows, both the Shadows who protected and cared for Darallax, Second Son of Dark, and the shadows she had given to her Sentinel. Ashri had admitted she had made little use of them and the shadows themselves had said they had "forgotten" the purpose for which they had been created.

Endis dismissed the multitude of worlds and returned to his rooms. Clearly Ashri's shadows had been called to provide him with food and clothes. He was still human, at least he thought he was, for now. He *needed* food which Ashri had not. Had those basic tasks been enough to remind the Sentinel's shadows of the reason for their existence? Endis understood they had been created to serve, while he had been *called* to serve. With Ashri's added wisdom, he fully appreciated now what service actually entailed. He would observe and watch the world and those particular people who Mother Dark had noticed from long in the past.

He concluded that the shadows' action in removing the occupants of the town of Mertasia was done without malice on their part. They had taken a decision, and implemented it. Mother Dark had seemingly offered no criticism of their behaviour so he had no grounds to either. Preparing for bed, he saw it was simply his remaining humanity, his emotions, that had been shocked by it, and resolved to practise distancing himself. Endis suspected there would be other instances in his future when the shadows, or perhaps he himself, would have to make similar choices.

Lying down, he allowed himself to overlook the cave in

the tiny village of Dragons Rest in eastern Iskallia, as he had started doing each night. The enormous black Dragon, Fenj, dozed beside the fire, old Lorak leaning against him with a bowl of some deadly beverage in his hand. A small black cat was curled against Fenj's chest but as Endis watched, her ears pricked. She raised her head, looking all around, then settled to sleep again. Endis too fell asleep, a smile on his face.

Chapter Twenty Six

It was the middle of the day when Tika felt the tingle of the circle being activated. She was surprised because she was a considerable distance from it, maybe half a mile or so. She warned Major Bars that the General had returned and continued to sit where she was. A sudden shouted order had Fedran on his feet in alarm and he saw troopers hurrying to form lines in front of the north gate. Tika joined him with the rest of the Guards.

'What's the matter?' asked Dog.

Fedran shook his head then Essa gave a short laugh. 'The Imperatrix in Waiting is with Falkir,' she told them, her height letting her see over the heads of the Kelshans blocking their view.

'We'll wait here,' Tika decided quickly. 'Let her speak to her troops and visit the injured.'

'I haven't got proper trousers on,' Major Bars exclaimed with some agitation.

Everyone laughed, but Veka took pity on him and hurried off to the surgeons' camp to see what she could find. 'You won't be standing up so what does it matter?' asked Dog.

'It matters,' growled Bars.

'Think he's feeling a bit better?' Dog asked Tika, who just laughed.

The Iskallians sat down again as Storm, Kija and Brin arrived to settle around them. Farn relinquished his position behind the major and moved closer to Tika. 'Why would Ricca come here?' Farn murmured through their mind link.

'I think she really has a concern for the men who serve her and Kelshan,' Tika replied.

Veka reappeared and dropped a pair of grey trousers beside Major Bars before sitting next to Shea. Tika had to smile as most of her Guards watched the major's contortions as he pulled on the trousers while lying under his blankets, with great interest. They all also noticed how exhausted he looked by the time his trousers were in place. Tika watched as Bars leaned back against Brin, perspiration on his brow. She checked the injury but sensed no sign of infection so she just sent a brief surge of strength into him.

Essa made more tea and Garrol smiled across at Tika. 'You know, it might be a good idea to bring some of Volk's beverage with us.'

Instead of snarling at the suggestion, Tika nodded. 'I did wonder about that,' she admitted.

'Volk's beverages are as good as dear Lorak's,' Farn agreed with enthusiasm. 'Well, perhaps not *quite* as good, but very nearly.'

Garrol chuckled. 'I believe Onion usually brings a flask with him,' he said.

'He does,' Farn agreed.

Tika's brows rose but she said nothing. They sat for a while then Bars realised he was wearing someone's blue Iskallian shirt. Dog stopped Veka from jumping to her feet again and glared at the major. 'You're *ashamed* one of us lent you a shirt?' she snarled.

Bars was aghast to think how his comment might have offended Lady Tika and could only splutter wordlessly. He was saved by the sudden arrival of General Falkir and Lady Ricca with her usual attendants, Mekla and Captain Shtok. Ricca looked a little pale but Tika held out a hand. The small Imperatrix in Waiting took it with obvious relief and Tika pulled her into a quick hug. Releasing her, she kept hold of her hand, urging her to sit next to her. Ricca looked across at Major Bars.

'I hope you are following Tika's, erm, *Lady* Tika's instructions, Major. You will be needed if the council agrees with your plans for this town.'

Bars nodded. 'I am, my Lady. I am not allowed to move and have to drink a great deal.'

Ricca looked a little confused by that answer but she smiled, turning to Tika again. 'Thank you for helping so many of my soldiers,' she said. 'Perhaps one day Kelshan will be able to help you and repay some of our debt.'

With no apology, Tika swore, making Ricca's eyes widen. 'There is *no* debt. We have a treaty. And we are friends as well as allies, are we not?' She paused then grinned at Ricca. 'Maybe you shouldn't repeat those first words. I shouldn't have cursed.'

Tika knew, by the glint in the child's dark brown eyes, that there was no chance Ricca would ignore those words. Falkir cleared his throat. 'We looked in some of the ordinary houses, Lady Tika. they are all decorated with gold.'

'Even the shops,' Ricca added, sounding disgusted. 'Shops which seem to be selling cakes and bread, or meat. They all had gold in them.'

'I would guess the Mertasian council, if there was one, was taking a good amount of all the gold brought in to be sent to the west,' Dromi commented.

'Where were the smiths then?' Captain Shtok asked, blushing as all faces turned to him. Despite his obvious embarrassment he went on. 'There must have been proper smiths, to make all those gold things.'

Falkir glanced across at one of his aides. 'Set men searching for any kind of forge or workshops,' he ordered.

Garrol rose. 'I'd like to join them,' he said. Kazmat moved to join him, and they left with two of Falkir's aides.

'We had a brief meeting with Lady Ricca's council. Their preliminary feelings were agreeable to this town becoming a garrison, possibly also a training place too. At the same time, the supplies from here, both grain and minerals, will still be needed in the west,' Falkir continued. 'In fact, Heskin Barl came with us.' He peered among his aides.

'He stayed in the town, sir,' a young captain told him.

'Lord Barl is in charge of everything to do with metals,' Ricca explained helpfully, when Tika looked blank.

Falkir got to his feet again. 'If you would excuse me, I will speak with some of the men.' He gave a slight bow when Ricca nodded, and left with his entourage of aides.

Ricca stared at Major Bars. 'Will he be all right,' she asked Tika.

Tika explained how Bars had bled so much, which was something his own body had to rectify.

'It was a good idea, Major,' Ricca told him. 'Do you

think there should be another garrison, right in the middle of Kelshan?'

Bars frowned as he thought. He looked for the map Navan had given him and found it under Brin's foot, then he nodded. 'Mertasia to Kelshan is along this line.' His finger traced across most of the map. 'This would be the centre, but that would still be five days or more from either place.'

Ricca went to squat down beside him, studying the map while the Iskallians watched and listened. Captain Shtok accepted a bowl of tea from Jarko and peered across at the map on the major's lap. 'Need post stops along the way then,' he said.

Ricca turned to him. 'Post stops?'

Major Bars nodded. 'A building to house perhaps a dozen troops and two or three dozen horses. So a messenger could take a fresh horse if his own was tired or injured,' he explained to Ricca.

'Perhaps you should decide where such a central place could be built?' Shtok suggested. 'Ask the folk round about if they'd mind such a place close by. Lot of people aren't keen on a bunch of soldiers in their midst.'

Ricca looked indignant. 'They should be proud to have them,' she said.

'Aaah. They might be, long as the men were disciplined, behaved their selves.'

Tika was fascinated to watch how closely Ricca listened to Captain Shtok. She knew the man was fond of the child, for her own sake, not because of who she was. Ricca looked over at Tika. 'How did a circle appear?' she asked.

Tika groaned in frustration. 'I have no idea at all. It was nothing to do with me. I really, truly don't know.'

Dog patted her shoulder. 'We believe you,' she said.

'Of course they do, my Tika,' Farn agreed at once.

'An awful lot of men died here.' Ricca sounded thoughtful. She turned to Major Bars. 'Why don't we have women soldiers? Lady Tika has women Guards and the girls train the same as the boys in Iskallia.'

'Very good question,' said Dog with approval. 'There are women in the army in the Dark Realm.' She gestured at Essa and Ashoki. 'The three of us were all in their army before we joined Tika.'

Major Bars was clearly flustered as attention focussed on him. 'I don't know, Lady Ricca, but I've never heard any young ladies say they wanted to become soldiers.'

Dog scoffed. 'Young *ladies*, you say? Probably from the wealthier families? Is that who you're thinking of? What about women and girls from ordinary families? I bet plenty of them would jump at the chance to be soldiers.'

'So many men have died lately, at Ferris Lake and now here. Perhaps women would join the army. We surely have plenty of room for them now,' Ricca suggested.

Dog grinned at her. 'Brilliant plan, Lady Ricca,' she said.

Ricca blushed at the praise. 'Where did all the people go? The ones in the town?' she asked.

Tika nearly swore again but bit back the words. 'Again, I have no idea. They were here, then, in the morning, they were all gone.' She spread her hands in a gesture of helplessness. 'I do not know,' she repeated slowly and clearly.

'It all needs a lot of thought and discussion, Lady Ricca, reorganising your army to encourage a few women to join.' Dromi attempted to distract attention from Tika. He knew she was irritated by the constant questioning of her involvement in both the people's disappearance and the circle's arrival.

'Then we will discuss it as soon as we get back to the Citadel,' Ricca said firmly. She looked more closely at Major Bars. 'Will you come back with us, help me explain about the other garrison and those post places?'

'Erm, of course, Lady Ricca. I am yours to command,' he managed.

Falkir returned at that point and told them Garrol and Kazmat had located extensive workshops, deep under the palace. 'There are venting tunnels, allowing smoke out towards the south of the hill the palace is on. The surgeons tell me none of the wounded are now serious, or need moving back to the Citadel. I believe most of the men can move into the town safely. That palace is bigger than it looks and there are all those empty houses they can use.'

'They won't vanish will they?' Ricca asked with a frown.

'No, I'm quite sure they won't, Lady Ricca.' Falkir assured her.

She stood. 'If we're going back now, I want Major Bars to come too,' she said.

Essa grinned and also stood. She went to the major and scooped him up in her arms. 'I'll take them back through,' she suggested.

Tika nodded. 'You still have to rest longer, Major,' she said. 'And keep drinking.'

Major Bars appeared to have lost the power of speech in his mortification at being carried like a baby by this huge woman but he nodded.

'We'll come and see you off,' Tika said, joining Ricca.

'Are you going home to Iskallia now?' Ricca asked.

'I think so, then I have to go to see someone else,' Tika told her. She noticed, as they walked through the Kelshan camp and into the town, how troopers paused to watch their small Imperatrix. Some smiled, some saluted, but Tika sensed respect for Ricca and appreciation that she'd come here and spoken to many of them.

Reaching the palace, Tika saw Proctis standing between two soldiers, his hands tied behind his back, his eyes wide with terror. At the door to the room where the circle had appeared, Tika bent to hug Lady Ricca. 'I'll see you soon,' she said, stepping away.

Two of Falkir's aides moved behind Ricca; Shtok and Mekla standing on each side of her. Proctis was pushed onto the circle by his two guards. Essa smiled at Tika, Bars still in her arms, then the air blurred, popped and they were gone. Falkir gave a noticeable sigh and caught Tika's questioning gaze. 'General Parrak will deal with Proctis perfectly well,' he said. 'I intend to try to sort out how we can change this place.'

Making their way back down the hill, Tika glanced up at the General. 'Ricca trusts Captain Shtok,' she said.

'She does. So do I. I would have said he was a very ordinary junior officer but he's much more than that. He will defend Ricca with his life; so will Mekla, and simply because they like her and care for her.'

Tika smiled. 'They do. She is fortunate to have them.'

Falkir had stopped, intending to take a different route to Tika. 'I believe she understands that, Tika. She cares about them. She hates it if anyone tries to brush them away as unimportant. Lara used to try that.'

'We'll be leaving when Essa returns,' Tika told him. 'You are quite confident about using the circle?'

He nodded. 'I am now.' He smiled. 'Thank you again, for your assistance.' He snapped a salute and strode in the direction of the surgeons' tents.

Tika saw a cloud of dust approaching the town. 'Onion's bringing the horses in. They'll be happier without the smell of death hanging over the place,' said Navan.

They saw Pearl and Genia flying slowly to each side of the herd. Tika wondered just how Onion had known she intended to leave now but she knew it would be quite pointless to ask him. Some of her Guards strolled across to watch as the horses were gathered in by a crowd of troopers. Falkir also stood watching. Tika and the rest of the company returned to the other Dragons and began to ready their packs for departure.

Arriving on the plateau, Tika stayed to thank the Dragons for carrying them. She paid special notice to Genia who had helped Onion with calming the horses. Onion also lingered, making a fuss of both Genia and Pearl, and he walked into the House beside Tika. 'What happened in Mertasia?' she asked casually.

'The people were not needed.'

'Who decided they were not needed?'

He looked down at her in surprise. 'Guardians of course.' Then he increased his speed and climbed the stairs to the upper floors. Tika turned left, into the hall, no wiser than before.

By the time those who'd been away had washed and changed their clothes, the bell summoned them for lunch. Tika had released Cerys from her carry sack up in her rooms. She didn't ask anything of the cat, who had been unusually silent for the last few days. Now, as she went to the door, Cerys mind spoke in a tone Tika couldn't interpret. 'It was shadows,' she said.

Tika paused, looking back. 'My Shadows?'

'No. Someone else's. The Dragons didn't notice, so I have said nothing.'

Tika watched Cerys begin a thorough washing session and shook her head. 'Will you talk to me later, please? They'll be expecting me downstairs now.'

'I will be here.'

Tika went out and down the long staircase, trying to think who else controlled Shadows. Putting aside such worries, she had to spend a while recounting what had occurred in Kelshan to the crowd in the hall. There followed a great deal of speculation over the disappearance of the Mertasian people. There was also great interest in the details of the gold covered items inside the houses. Tika noted none of those listening showed any approval of such ostentatious displays of wealth.

Rinda, the wife of Torgen the printer, was one of the most scornful. 'Why would you do that?' she asked generally. 'Think of all that cleaning!'

Sarila was sitting near Tika and she nodded at the laughter. 'Gold looks nice and shiny,' she agreed. 'But you can see every single finger mark.'

'How will they get it all off the furniture?' someone called out.

'Easy enough,' said Garrol. 'A lot will just peel off then you can heat it and use it for something else.'

'Like coins?' asked Veka with a frown.

'Probably,' Garrol agreed.

It seemed an endless time to Tika but she always told her people of any of her travels and let them question whatever they wanted. At last, they began to drift away, leaving only those who'd been with her, and Werlan and Volk. Dromi said he would get his report done for her by this evening and departed for the archives with Navan and Werlan, closely followed by Shea and Veka. Then Fedran asked the Guards to join him in his office with Telk. Onion had somehow disappeared as well at some point, leaving Volk and Rivan with Tika.

'Everything was well in our absence?' Tika asked her Steward.

He nodded. 'The two new Dragons came to look in my caves.' The treacle dark eyes gleamed. 'Not sure who was more surprised, Chichi and the goats or those two Dragons.'

Tika laughed. 'They seem to have fitted in here well anyway,' she said. Minyth had hurried to tell her how he and his sister and Skay had patrolled the valley each day she had been away.

'They have,' Volk agreed. 'Minyth is quiet but he is devoted to you already. Because you mended his shoulder. Heligg, well, I think she could be fierce, like Storm is sometimes.'

Tika frowned. 'Do you think so?'

'Oh yes. She listens very carefully to all that goes on, like Storm does. From what I've heard, he can show his temper quicker than the others. I reckon Heligg would be the same. She too is deeply grateful to you for healing Minyth. She greatly admires Kija and will always obey her, and *you,* but you should understand her anger. She was very afraid of the new Elder of her Treasury and terrified when Minyth was attacked. She was frightened and she *hated* being frightened.' Volk shrugged his broad shoulders. 'I believe she has sworn to herself that she will never show fear again. The best way to hide fear is show aggression first.'

Rivan also nodded. 'Storm still gets anxious,' he told Tika. 'He will never admit that.'

'He was terrified when we were trapped in the desert with the Qwah trying to kill us,' said Tika quietly. 'He told me later. He was so far from the sea, not even a river or a pond, just endless sand. That's why he was so quick to anger. He's better than he was but still I keep an eye on him at times. What happened when you went with Onion to find the horses?' she asked the young man.

Rivan smiled. 'Onion doesn't change his shape but he called them somehow. I was my wolf shape and herded them as Onion asked. Genia and Pearl calmed them. He healed several with bad cuts, mostly on their legs and flanks. From swords. Only a handful of those that we gathered up actually died.'

'Thank you Rivan. You did well to save so many.'

He grinned, his thin face lighting up. 'I'd better go and see what the twins have been doing,' he said, leaving the hall.

'Will you keep a couple of flasks of your beverage ready, please, Volk, for us to take when we have to travel?' Tika spoke softly.

A huge hand, the back of which sprouted hair as thick and dark as his beard, covered her small one. 'I know you have a dread of strong drink, child, but it does have its uses at times.' Volk's voice was a gentle growl. 'Lorak liked to tease you, I know, but he understood too. You must surely know neither he nor I would let harm touch you or the Dragons through anything we supplied you with?'

'I do, Volk. It's just taken me a long time to understand that. I saw how it calmed Farn when he became nervous but I didn't want to admit it.'

Volk patted her hand and got to his feet. 'Will you be off again soon?' he asked.

'In a few days I think, yes.'

'I'll have the flasks for you,' he said and strode off.

Tika was glad no Dragons were in the hall at present. Kija and Brin were taking advantage of warmer sunshine at last to bask on the rocks. She hurried back upstairs and found Cerys outside. The last snow had finally gone and Cerys crouched on the stone bench in the sun, close to the two small graves. Tika sat beside her and stroked the cat's back. Cerys sat up, turning to face Tika, wrapping her tail over her front paws. 'Can you tell me what you sensed?' Tika spoke aloud.

'It felt like when the Shadows speak with you. But different. Stronger.'

'Stronger?' Tika repeated, hoping her alarm wasn't obvious.

'Yes.' Cerys's eyes were wide, as they had been the morning they'd found the Mertasians missing.

'Can you explain any more clearly?'

Cerys glanced away, down at the grass beneath which Khosa lay, then back to Tika. 'I thought at first it was you. It *felt* like you, when you draw a great deal of power. Then I realised it was different. Not as strong as you, and with a focus I couldn't recognise. Those Shadows owe service to Mother Dark. I was nearly sure of that. They also serve another, but I couldn't understand more.'

Tika could feel how disturbed Cerys was and lifted her into her arms. 'Did they frighten you? Did they feel angry?'

The cat was tense against Tika's shoulder. 'No. They felt sad but determined. I couldn't feel their reason for doing what they did, but they felt it was necessary.'

Slowly Tika felt Cerys begin to relax. 'I can't think who might command Shadows, Cerys. The ones I have, have helped my Guards at times, but only when I asked them to. Lord Darallax of course, surely commands most, if not all. I know of no one else.'

They sat quietly, lost in thought. Then Cerys felt a change in Tika. She wriggled to stare into her face. 'What is it Tika?'

'I thought of someone else.' Tika shocked herself with her sudden fear. 'Jian. Lord Shivan's sister. She has Shadows to command.'

Chapter Twenty Seven

Tika was caught up in various reports from the small villages of Iskallia in the next few days. Fedran and Telk were also occupied with implementing the plan to send patrols through the valley. As they stressed to both Tika and to the Guards who volunteered for the work, the intention of patrolling was only to offer help if needed and to encourage easier communication along the length of Iskallia. Tika was adamant that the valley remain as it was as far as possible, even with people now living there and using the land. Volk and Onion were also involved in these plans and Tika knew they were both firmly against any large scale changes to the land.

Dromi had asked the people in the five villages to discuss what they needed or hoped for in their new settlements during the winter, and the replies had been arriving at the House in recent days. With Werlan and Mardis Fayle, Dromi had been studying the letters he'd received and also sent messages of his own back to clarify certain suggestions. He was relieved that none of the villages suggested anything of serious proportions: he had a feeling Tika would sooner close the villages and let the valley revert to its original emptiness than agree to extensive change.

Veka and Shea had been asked to do a thorough check on what was produced here, at the House. Beyond the kitchens, there were small areas of ground between the folds and pleats of the great mountains where Volk and Onion had successfully grown many of the vegetables used in the House. Grain came mostly from Deep Fold, with some from Oak Wood. Fruit came from Dragons Rest. As each report was written it was given to Tika to study.

Fedran had got his first patrol of ten guards and a junior sergeant, off along the valley, a mixture of Kelshan arms men and others. Tika had signed her approval to three of Dromi's reports and then she announced that they would be travelling the next day. She made it clear to Fedran that although five Dragons would travel with her, she would need very few Guards. Genia was content to stay in Iskallia this time although Cerys insisted on accompanying Tika. Heligg and Minyth both seemed to enjoy being with Skay, so Tika had no concerns for them.

Sarila brought packs out for the travellers after breakfast and ten people went out to the plateau. Tika had asked Brin to take them north, to Drogoya and the tower where she had hidden Gremara's three children, although she hadn't mentioned where she wanted to go to her companions. She had told Sarila, who had made up an extra pack full of special treats. There was a noticeable warmth in the air already, which was most welcome after the long winter, and five Dragons rose into a clear blue sky, before Brin opened a gateway north.

Tika was relieved when Brin brought them out again over a stretch of sand dunes. They had been in the grey murkiness of the gateway longer than she liked and she had made it clear she did not approve of Brin using so much of his strength without a pause. They were further north than she'd thought they would be. She had hoped they'd make their first stop near the site of the lost settlement of Hoffay, destroyed by rebel Kelshans after the battle of Ferris Lake. Now she realised they were several hundred miles beyond that.

She was aware that Kija was once again berating the large crimson Dragon for his stubbornness and decided not to add to his guilt. Storm was frolicking in the waves that rolled slowly onto the beach, and Farn and Pearl were paddling with caution. Navan joined Tika at the edge of the dunes, looking down at the beach. 'The waves are much bigger than they were when we were here before,' he said. 'Perhaps there's been a storm further out at sea.'

Tika shivered in spite of the warmth. Navan laughed. 'You can swim now, Tika. Why does it bother you?'

She turned away. 'There's just too much of it. It's too big,' she said.

'The water is quite warm here, my Tika' Farn's mind voice announced to everyone. 'Why isn't it cold, like at Port

Maressa?'

Tika groaned and suggested Dromi might have an explanation. She left the poor man to talk with the two younger Dragons and joined her companions just beyond the first dunes. 'I think we're further west than we were when we stopped here last time,' Essa remarked. 'Can you sense any tribes around, Tika?'

'No. I checked as soon as we came out of the gateway. Very little sign of any large animals or people.'

'Are we stopping here tonight or going on, Tika?' asked Fedran.

She glanced at the sky. Mid afternoon by her reckoning. 'Stay here I think. The Dragons could hunt tomorrow if the children need meat but let them rest tonight.'

Dog and Ketro went off to gather rough bushes and wind dried heathers for a fire. They all carried a small amount of kindling and a few of the black rocks Teyo called coal, but they were for times of emergency, used as rarely as possible. Where they settled to camp for the night, the sand was warm and it was easy to scoop out places to rest elbows and back quite comfortably, as Onion pointed out. The company had fish for their supper thanks to Storm, but he brought smaller fish, which pleased them all.

Settling down as the darkness deepened, Tika slammed a shield around them. She sat up, seeing Kija's great eyes glitter in the star light. 'What was that, daughter?'

'I'm afraid I suspect it was Zamina. She is a dream walker but she doesn't control where her mind seeks.'

'Can you teach her? It could put them all in great danger if anyone else sensed her touch.'

'I've been worrying about that a lot. I hope I can help her.'

Kija opened a short gateway in the morning to cross the wide sea channel separating Kelshan from Drogoya and then they flew, shielded, along the eastern Drogoyan coast. Dragons' memories always retained the various routes between places and after a while, Kija veered left, over a heavily forested landscape. Tika was aware that both adult Dragons were scanning the ground, just as she was, for any sign of humans. As far as Tika knew, this eastern part of Drogoya remained virtually empty of people, with perhaps a small population of Old Bloods much further to the north.

At last Kija moved into a circling flight high above a small clearing in which stood a stone tower. Looking over Farn's shoulder as he circled with the other Dragons, Tika saw a small figure emerge onto the roof of the tower, staring up. She smiled, releasing the shielding which hid them. The figure waved and dived back inside the tower as Kija and Brin floated carefully down between the trees. Once they were safely down, the younger, smaller, Dragons landed as well.

The tower door, a huge block of stone, rolled aside and Anshin stood beaming at them. His deep blue, green tipped wings half raised in his excitement at seeing them. 'Welcome!' he called. 'We have longed to see you, Tika! Come in, come in!' He went quickly to each Dragon, bowing low, wings flaring to each side and then hurried back to usher his guests up the stairs. By the time they'd reached the upper living area, Kyvar was waiting, smiling as broadly as Anshin.

Tika was glad to see Anshin's brother, Syamak, was smiling too. He and their sister, Zamina, were of Gremara's first brood, Anshin from the second. Syamak had been the most wary, most cautious, of the three siblings but his smile now was genuine. He bowed. He had grown, far more than Anshin, and was now nearly as tall as Onion. Finally Zamina stood. She was a little shorter than Syamak but her smile was joyous, her blind eyes turned in the directions of the visitors. She held out her hands. Tika grasped them and was drawn to sit next to Zamina. Freeing one hand, Tika released Cerys, explaining who Cerys was as she did so. After a moment, Cerys moved to Zamina's lap. Zamina gave soft trills of excitement, long fingers moving gently over the cat. Cerys settled to a steady purr and Zamina bent lower to listen.

Tika looked up to see Syamak watching. He nodded when he caught Tika's eye, his smile sad. Anshin had been chattering with Tika's Guards and when Dog, Dromi and Essa began revealing books from extra packs they'd brought, Syamak joined Anshin in excited investigation. Tika moved from Zamina's side to Kyvar, the last survivor of the settlement of Hoffay. 'Are things still safe here?' she asked quietly. She thought he looked well but he seemed to have aged more than she would have expected since she'd last seen him.

'There has been no hint of people anywhere near,' he told her. 'Anshin regularly flies over a wide area around here and he has never yet found any signs. He did see ships a while ago, sailing north, but they didn't put anyone ashore.'

Tika nodded. 'When did Yulla die?'

Kyvar sighed. 'Near the end of our first winter. She was old, Lady Tika. She loved these three but she grieved for all her friends in Hoffay. It was a peaceful end, although Zamina was much distressed.'

'Her sight is gone now?'

'Completely.' Kyvar's voice was low. 'She can no longer even tell dark from light. Is there nothing you can do for her?'

'I wish I could but it was a fault in her eyes from before her birth, or hatching. I did see if there was something I might do but there truly isn't. I'm sorry.'

Kyvar nodded, accepting Tika's word as the truth. 'Is this place still safe for them?'

Tika noted he spoke of the children's safety, not his own and was glad they had such a strong person with them. 'For now, yes. We sensed no one but Anshin or Syamak should continue to keep watch. It might be wise if they also search for another safe place, in case they need to leave here in a hurry.' Tika paused. 'I do wish there was more I could do for them, Kyvar. They may be safe here for a few years but the day will come when they must move on. There will be many different homes for them through their lives I'm afraid.'

'I know only Anshin looks a child still, but Syamak and Zamina are barely ten years yet. So young,' Kyvar sounded deeply worried.

Their conversation was interrupted by Syamak joining them. He held several blue covered books which Tika recognised as being Iskallian copies. 'We are most grateful for the books,' he told her. 'Anshin and Zamina have been making up stories themselves since last winter.'

'A lot of people do that in the hall in Iskallia when the winter keeps us all indoors. Some make songs too.'

'Zamina has always made songs. She sings up on the roof, and she and Anshin often dance there too.'

Kyvar watched Syamak put the new books with the few others they owned and smiled, his affection for them obvious. Dromi had opened the pack Sarila had prepared and there were renewed cries of delight as various pies and cakes appeared together with a veritable mountain of honey cakes. Tika watched Essa take some food to Zamina, kneeling beside the blind girl. Zamina's pale blue wings were half raised, sheltering Cerys as the girl stroked her and crooned gently. The hairless domed heads of the three reminded Tika of how her once trusted friend, Ren, had been changed before he died, to resemble these three. Lady Lerran too, had gone through several transformations before she returned to Mother Dark.

Anshin came to Tika, a honey cake in each hand, his leaf green eyes sparkling with happiness. 'May I go and speak with the Dragons?' he asked her.

'Of course you can.' She watched as he climbed the stairs to the tower roof, noting how small his high arched feet seemed, compared to Zamina's or Syamak's. She had a feeling Anshin would never grow anywhere near as tall as his siblings but she suspected his intelligence was the greatest of the three.

'Can you stay long?' Kyvar asked her.

'No. We will stay tonight, and perhaps tomorrow, but no longer,' she replied.

'Could they not find shelter with you, in Iskallia?' Kyvar asked tentatively.

'I'm sorry but they cannot. I would offer them sanctuary, believe me, but it's not how it must be.' Tika shook her head. 'It was like a foretelling, that's the only way I can describe it to you, Kyvar. There is a path they must travel, however long, hard or perilous. Yes, they would be safe in Iskallia but there is a part they must play. I do not know the details but I know they must wander. I'm sorry,' she repeated.

Kyvar nodded. 'I understand a little more. I will do my best to teach them to survive, come what may. They will have long lives though, and I will not.'

Tika drew a breath. 'I will watch them as best I can, and there will be others, like the people of your settlement, who will offer aid. That I saw, but only as flashes, hints, nothing clear.'

Dog strolled across to join them, looking at Essa, still kneeling by Zamina, the pair deep in conversation. 'Onion's gone to look at their plants,' she informed Tika.

'We've had good crops of vegetables,' Kyvar told them. 'We plant them in a different place each year. Onion told Anshin we should do that.'

'Does Syamak work as well?' Dog asked.

Kyvar nodded. 'He collects a lot of the wood, we always keep a good supply here, and he helps Anshin and me in the garden. He has trouble remembering which plants are which, but he doesn't resent Anshin for correcting him sometimes.'

Tika's company spent the rest of that day and the following day at the tower. Navan had brought more maps which thrilled Anshin. Zamina kept Cerys close to her, humming and singing strange wordless tunes. All three children went down to the clearing to spend time with the Dragons, Zamina pressing close to Kija who sang the lullaby song many times to the girl. Kija had brought back a large deer which Ketro butchered and showed Syamak and Anshin how to smoke some of the meat to preserve it.

The two nights Tika spent there she was very aware of how it had become a real home for the children. A safe place such as they had never experienced before. She desperately hoped it would serve them well for many years rather than a few. She had understood, from her foretelling, that these children would be very long lived, if they could only keep themselves hidden away. When they woke on the second morning and began to fold their bed rolls back into their packs, Anshin watched sadly. To Tika's surprise, he went to every member of her company, hugging each one briefly, his wings mantled around them.

Reaching Tika, he stared at her for a moment before repeating the gesture. 'Thank you,' he whispered. 'Will we see you again?'

Tears prickled Tika's eyes as she returned his hug. 'I hope so, Anshin, but not for a while.' She felt him nod then his wings folded back and he stepped away.

She moved to Zamina and Cerys slid from the girl's lap to be put into her carry sack. Zamina let her hands drop, empty, to her lap, suddenly bereft of the warm comfort of the cat's body. Tika wasn't surprised to see Essa hold Zamina gently before kissing her cheek, but it didn't help her to keep her own tears back. Anshin said they would watch their departure from the tower roof and Tika followed her companions down the stairs.

Kyvar went down with them. 'We keep the door closed when we're all inside,' he explained.

Tika nodded, glad Kyvar was so careful at all times. Being Old Blood himself, he understood all too well how it felt to live constantly expecting some sort of attack. He stood in the doorway watching the visitors climb onto the Dragons who rose, careful of the surrounding trees, and lifted into the sky. Tika looked down as the three children seemed to grow smaller and smaller when Farn carried her and Fedran ever higher. Then, they were flying above the trees, the tower lost to sight.

Brin opened the short gateway to take them across the sea separating Drogoya from Kelshan and the Dragons landed on the same stretch of beach they had before. The company was unusually quiet and the Dragons too seemed disinclined to talk. It was Onion who broke the silence as they all just sat on the sand dunes. 'They will be safe there for a few years,' he said, his voice deeper than usual.

'Has anyone heard any word of the settlement of the Oblaka?' asked Dog. 'They are still isolated in the north west aren't they?'

Everyone looked at Dromi. 'I've heard nothing,' he said. 'Not a whisper that anyone is still there. I don't know if the Wendlans have surveyed that coast. There has been nothing in any reports from Jakri.'

'Could small boats get across this water?' asked Shea.

'Probably, in good weather and with a strong crew.' Navan frowned as he considered the idea. 'There is a land bridge to the far west though. Drogoya and Kelshan are joined with solid land. It's wide.' He brought out one of his inevitable maps. 'Look, it's over fifty miles wide I would guess, all the way across.'

'Why has there never been contact between the two lands?' asked Veka.

Dromi shrugged. 'Long, long ago, Sedka came from Drogoya and tried to make the Kelshans follow him and his strange religion. He was thrown out of most towns and villages so he returned to Drogoya. At least, he was trying to when some mountain cats killed him.'

'Mountain cats?' asked Ketro. 'The real animals or the tribe?'

Dromi smiled. 'It was always held that it was the animals who killed him, Ketro, so it was told in the Brotherhood records, but I suspect he annoyed the tribes.'

'Good for them,' Dog put it.

Tika sat listening, letting the fine sand trickle through her fingers as she dug into it. She understood they were talking of such things to avoid speaking of the tower. All of them had been affected in some way by spending even such a short time with the children. At last the unsettled emotions among the company began to ease and Storm rose, flying out over the waves. Farn and Pearl followed him down to the water's edge and Tika realised the Dragons had remained silent since they'd left the tower in the forest.

Essa and Shea went to gather the makings for a fire and Ketro searched for the fresh water spring they'd found before. Tika got to her feet and went to Kija and Brin. She stroked their long faces quietly.

'Zamina is still a baby.' Kija's mind voice held great sadness.

'She is.' Cerys whispered the thought from her carry sack.

'I'm sorry, I should have let you out,' Tika apologised, loosening the ties around the top of the bag. 'I spoke to her only briefly, about her dream walking, but I'm not sure she understood. I don't know if she will be able to change it though. She seems to let her mind drift until she finds something that catches her interest.'

'She did not understand,' Brin agreed sadly. 'Kyvar will serve them well though.'

Tika hugged the crimson neck as far as she could reach, surprised by his comment. Brin rarely spoke in such a way. She felt embarrassment from him and let him go and turned to lean against Kija.

'Kyvar will serve them well, my daughter, Brin speaks truly. But he will not serve them as long as we might hope.'

'I sensed no illness in him.' Tika objected with some alarm.

'No. There is no sickness,' Kija replied gently. 'But he will not live long enough to be considered an old man by human measure.'

Brin moved away a little to stretch out on the warm sand and Kija did the same while Tika climbed back up the dunes to find Dog had started their fire. Cerys was just ahead of her and looked up as Tika drew level. 'This sand is horrible stuff,' she complained.

When Tika laughed, the cat's green gold eyes narrowed. She stalked on, climbing onto Navan's knees, her back to Tika, and shook each paw thoroughly. The company spent an unusually quiet lazy day, watching the long waves roll onto the beach until the sun set as they ate fish Storm had caught for them. Only then, as the stars began to flicker in the darkening sky, did they slowly begin to speak of how they felt about those three of Gremara's children.

'Could they not come to Iskallia, Tika?' asked Veka after a time. 'They'd be safe there and I'm sure they wouldn't hurt anyone.'

'They can't, Veka. For now, they must stay where they are. Later I believe they will find hiding places here in Kelshan. Anshin has a part to play in the future but I have no idea *when* in the future. They have to stay out in the world. I would give them sanctuary if I could, but that is not possible.'

'They will have sad lives, my Tika.' Farn's mind tone was full of sadness. 'I do like them, even though they are

312

wrong.'

Tika smiled as she leaned against his chest. 'They *are* wrong, Farn, but if these three are gentle, eager to learn, remember there are still all their siblings who are vicious and cruel.'

'Do you think Gremara knows of them? Knows that at least three are good, sweet creatures?' Pearl asked.

'No, Pearl. Gremara had no interest in any of them and I do not intend to mention them to her.'

'So are we going to see her next?' Dog asked softly.

Tika settled down on her bed roll. 'Yes. Tomorrow.'

Chapter Twenty Eight

The next day therefore, the company, led by Kija, flew at a steady pace southwards. They were shielded from any observers on the ground but the settlements were few, signs of permanent villages rare. Forested land appeared ahead and Kija spiralled down to land. Tika had called for a brief rest before the final part of the journey to the domes in which Gremara and her offspring sheltered. It was near midday when they reached the bare hilltop north of the domes and made their cautious way through the tangled undergrowth. The trail they'd followed before was clearly unused and in places the trees seemed to have extended branches above them.

Tika checked that the Dragons were not too disturbed by the constricting vegetation but they all assured her they had no fears. Well shielded, they emerged again onto the open ground facing the three conjoined domes. The Dragons settled close to the trees, Guards standing watchfully close by. Onion moved to Tika's side and calmly took her hand. Tika straightened her shoulders and began to walk out towards the dark opening of the central dome, her shield released.

She stopped some distance away and listened. She could hear no shrieks or snarls, as she had heard before. There was only a profound silence but before she could call, the son who had tried to refuse her on her previous visit, stood in the entrance. Stars above, but he had grown! Wide shoulders, muscled chest leading down to a narrow waist and slim hips. Eyes so dark a blue they were almost as black as his wings which were slightly raised, revealing the pale purple under feathers. He folded his arms, an insolent sneer on his face, and waited.

Tika offered a slight smile. 'Tell your mother I am here to visit her again, as I promised, child.'

The sneer changed to a snarl but before he could speak, he was knocked off his feet, crashing against the side of the entrance. Completely ignoring him, Gremara stepped out into the sunlight which glittered and shone on the silver scales that covered her. Her lips were curving in a smile of delight, her hands outstretched.

Onion released Tika so she could clasp both of Gremara's hands. He watched Gremara enfold Tika, her great silver feathered wings closing around them both. The gold tips on the feathers caught the sun as she closed them against her back and sat on the grass. Tika sank down beside her, Onion joining her. Gremara studied him then nodded. 'You came before,' she said.

'I did, my lady,' he agreed.

Tika studied her. She was still beautiful but there was a change. Her slenderness had a more haggard look and her eyes showed an agonising tiredness. Both Onion and Tika had noted the son, Kahn, slink back into the darkened entrance of the dome, his lip bleeding from the blow Gremara had dealt him. 'Are you well, Gremara?' Tika asked.

A shrug was her reply.

'Are the children annoying you?' Tika went on with care.

Gremara frowned. 'There are less here now. It's quieter.'

'Less? Have they left?' Tika's thoughts raced. She'd heard no rumours of the children attacking villages around here.

'No. He killed them.'

Tika moved slightly, her left hand unobtrusively seeking Onion's again. Onion delved in his shirt pocket and offered something to Gremara. Puzzled, she held out her hand and he dropped a smooth pale green stone into her palm. 'I found it and remembered you had many such stones. One of your sons collected them for you.'

She turned the stone over and over, smiling before looking up. 'Thank you,' she said. 'Mazanak brought me many but he's gone now.' A shadow crossed her face. 'I liked him a bit. He was quiet and polite and he brought the pretty stones just to please me, not so he could gain some favours. That one,' she jerked her head towards the entrance

315

without looking that way. 'He forbids any others to "bother" me, as he puts it.'

'Does no one talk to you now?' Tika had to clear her throat before she could get the words out.

'My sister talks to me. I think of her often and imagine all the conversations we could have had if I hadn't had to leave her.'

Tika's fingers trembled in Onion's grip. She stared at the huge smile and haunted eyes of the creature beside her. Before she could think of an answer the smile vanished. 'She is dead? Lamora? You said she was dead?'

'She is. She really is,' Tika said in a rush.

Gremara's head tilted and a look of suspicion grew. 'You said you knew her? How could you? Lamora must have died long ago, before you were born.'

'There were records, journals.' Tika explained. 'I read many of them. They were stored near the island where you lived. There was a great earthquake, floods. The records were destroyed some time after I read them.' Tika held her breath, hoping she'd convinced Gremara. 'I felt as though I had met her, reading those records.'

'She must have written them.' Gremara sounded thoughtful. 'I would have liked to read them. Are you sure you didn't keep any? Not even one?'

'I'm sorry. I thought I would have an opportunity to return there, study them again, but the devastation was terrible. Nothing remained.' Tika hated inventing this concoction of lies but Gremara had no idea their father had changed her precious little sister as he had changed her.

Gremara brushed Tika's cheek with her knuckles. 'Such a shame. It would have been wonderful to read Lamora's words. Did she have a long life as a human?'

Tika was beginning to struggle and Onion's hand tightened over hers. 'I believe so. It wasn't clear from the documents.' Desperate to change the subject, Tika spoke of the children here. 'Will your children live lives as long as yours, my dear?'

Grey eyes took on a stormy cast. 'A few might, if Kahn lets them live.'

'He still fears your strength though? You command

him?'

Gremara looked down at the stone in her hand. 'I don't command,' she said thoughtfully. 'I don't give orders. Isn't that what commanders do? I have only told them to stop killing people, to be quiet, to leave me alone. That's all I command.'

'And Kahn?'

Gremara gave them a sideways glance then stared back at the pebble in her hand. 'For now he still fears me, fears my strength,' she replied at last. 'He will kill me, or attempt to, fairly soon I believe.' She looked at Tika who saw such an eternity of pain in the grey eyes. 'I should have died long ago, with my sweet sister,' she added. 'I will be glad to end this.'

Tika was unable to reply but Onion smiled. 'You will have peace then, my lady,' he said, his voice deep, comforting.

Gremara returned his smile. 'I hope I might. One thing though.' She looked again at Tika. 'When you hear I am dead, will you destroy Kahn, please? I have done wrong things, bad things, but I recognise what I've done, and I have changed. Not just from woman to Dragon to this feathered form, but in some understanding.' She smiled. 'I am very far from a good person even now, but I am better. Kahn will never be better. He is his father through and through, superior, vicious, evil and wrong. While I live I can keep them here in some control. Kahn will let them loose.'

Onion stretched across Tika, patting Gremara's shoulder lightly. 'It will be as you say, my lady.'

Gremara seemed surprised he had answered her and looked back to Tika. Tika let out a long breath she hadn't realised she'd been holding, and nodded. Gremara's smile was suddenly radiant. 'Thank you Tika. If Mazanak still lived, I would have asked you to take him, shelter him somehow. If one of them could be kind, sweet even, why were no others?' She shook her head. 'I know. It's probably my fault and it's far too late to think these things, but such ideas come into my mind more often of late, and then I remember Lamora's gentleness. She would have

317

liked Mazanak.'

Tika had forced her own emotions down, enabling her to sound quite calm when she spoke again. 'Is there anything you would like, really like, Gremara? If I can, I would bring whatever you might wish for?'

Gremara smiled, such a beautiful smile. 'You cannot Tika. You cannot rewind time and take me all the way back to when I was but a stupid girl, willing to please her father if he promised to leave her little sister alone.'

'No. I can't do that. I wish I could. I'm sorry.'

There was the slightest sound from the entrance. Tika used her mage sense and recognised Kahn lurking in the shadowed archway. 'Kahn has returned to spy on us. He cannot understand what a friend is. I told him you were my friend and it made no sense to him. I think Mazanak understood the concept. He said once he was proud that I let him be my friend. I didn't really pay much attention at the time. I told you, I paid little attention to any of them. Only afterwards, when he disappeared, I remembered his words.'

Gremara rose in a smooth movement which made Tika feel clumsy as she too rose. Gremara stared down at her, so much taller than Tika as she was. Her wings flared open around both Tika and Onion for a heartbeat. 'I'm grateful that you've visited me, Tika. I wish we two might have been real friends in a different life.' The great wings snapped back to furl behind her and she turned away, striding to the dome.

Tika watched until she was completely gone from view then turned away with Onion. Distressed as she was, she kept the air hardened around their backs as they walked under the trees to join her company and the Dragons. She looked back one last time and saw Kahn standing outside the dome, staring malevolently after them. She was clinging to Onion's hand but her tears had retreated. She looked up into his one brown eye.

'We will destroy him.' Onion smiled at her. 'It can't be now. Things must take their course. He will kill poor Gremara very soon, Tika. Then, and only then, he too will die.'

'How?'

'That will be my task. Or Dog's.'

Utterly confused by his answer, Tika moved into the Dragons' shielding, vanishing from Kahn's sight. They watched in silence as he squinted, advancing a few steps to catch a glimpse of Tika and Onion. Then he scowled and strode back inside the dome. They waited for a short time then made their way back along the trail to the hilltop, still in silence. Once the riders were in place, Kija led them south again, until she saw open grassland ahead, with a river winding slowly across it. Landing, she waited for Essa and Onion to slide from her back before she paced to the river for a long drink.

Without asking, Dog dug out some turf and began a fire while Tika tried to sort out her feelings of the meeting with Gremara. She had been mind linked to the Dragons who had shared all they'd heard with the company, and now they just waited to see if Tika wanted to talk about it or not. Even the Dragons, although linked to her thoughts, had said nothing to her. She saw Onion sit beside Dog and murmur quietly. Then she joined them all around the fire Dog was coaxing into life. She looked at her companions and managed a faint smile.

'She was much thinner,' Shea whispered. 'Is she ill, Tika?'

'No. She is weary of her long life.' Tika hugged her knees, resting her chin on them. 'I'm not sure how hard she'll try to defend herself against Kahn when he decides to attack her. She's had enough, given up I think. I hated having to lie to her.'

Essa stretched out her long legs, Cerys on her lap. Tika had handed the cat to her when she'd gone to speak with Gremara. 'You could do nothing else but lie, Tika. If you had told her how her sister had spent so long as a small cat called Khosa, when she believed she had protected her, she would fall into a madness beyond anything she's suffered before. Your lies gave her a little comfort, Tika, and in spite of everything, I do not begrudge that poor creature a crumb of comfort now, so close to her end.'

Tika watched heads nodding around their tiny fire and

was grateful for Essa's words. Onion looked across at her. 'Khosa didn't want you to tell Gremara how she had suffered too, did she? You did the right thing Tika,' he told her.

'You did.' Kija mind spoke the company. 'She was correct, daughter. Finally, Gremara really sees herself, she sees what terrible things she's done. I hope she can also remember the good things too, the healings she did, and when she saved Vagrantia. Make no mistake, Vagrantia could have been destroyed if she hadn't taken the action she did.'

Those who had witnessed those events nodded their agreement.

'As the Elder of the Iskallian Treasury, I will tell you. I felt that even Thryssa neglected to thank Gremara for the pain she suffered then. I have heard not a word of gratitude for her destruction of those creatures who so nearly succeeded in ruining all of Vagrantia.' Kija's eyes flashed, just a hint of red in their many facets, indicating her very real anger at what she felt was an injustice.

Tika felt guilty. To be quite truthful, she hadn't considered the cost Gremara had paid at that time. Her concern had been focussed only on Fenj and Lorak. 'You're right,' she said aloud. 'None of us did. I didn't, for which I'm ashamed now. Certainly I never heard any Vagrantian thank Gremara for coming to their rescue.'

'It can't be very nice, living with that one who stared at you, my Tika.' Farn's mind voice betrayed a hint of uncertainty and worry. 'She hit him and knocked him over didn't she?'

Tika reached back to stroke his face. 'She did, Farn, but he is nearly as tall as her now and he will be far stronger than her all too soon,' she replied.

'Why do those children grow so very fast?' asked Ketro. 'I can't make any sense of that. They are really still very young are they not?'

'I've tried to think why that might be,' said Tika. 'I suspect it has something to do with whatever Namolos did to Gremara. We know he altered the length she and Khosa might live, and changed their physical bodies. Perhaps something he did, mixed with the Gijan Elder's blood and simply speeds up the children's growth?'

'Their father did such things to them? He was a mage?' Ketro asked.

'No. Khosa called him a scientist. Captain Sefri, in Green Shade in Wendla, she said scientists were highly regarded in her world. They studied many things.'

'We met another scientist in the City of Domes in the Qwah Desert,' Navan put in quietly. 'He was cruel, an unpleasant man. So was his sister.'

Tika shivered as she recalled Kertiss, his sister, Orla, and all the animals in cages lining the room where they did their "experiments".

'Sefri did say that most of them were honourable, decent people. It was scientists, she said, who invented the ships that fly through the star fields, made many medicines for every disease they had, They made the machines they used to speak to each other over great distances and make the pictures and maps,' Dromi suggested.

'You're saying that the three we know of, who arrived here, were just unfortunately three particularly unpleasant ones?' Tika smiled faintly. 'Just our bad luck?'

The atmosphere among them relaxed a little as her friends saw Tika was not as distressed by her meeting with Gremara as she had been previously.

'Will we stay here tonight?' Fedran asked her.

'I think so. We could stop to visit Troman in Strale, then call on Queen Tupalla. I was thinking a while ago, in the winter, that I haven't visited Tarran or Jerrad since we signed the treaty. We could travel home that way? Do any of you need to get back for anything urgent?'

'No,' said Dog. 'It might be nice to go somewhere with a lovely big library?'

Laughter greeted her suggestion although Tika had a suspicion Dog was only half joking. When people moved, beginning their usual routines when setting up a small camp, Tika resolved not to let Dog out of her sight, in Chaban at least. She was fairly confident Tarran and Jerrad possessed no such thing as a library, or if they did, it would be far too small to tempt Dog to try "borrowing" any books.

She looked at Farn and on impulse went to him, climbing between his wings. He lifted into the air at once.

'I didn't like that man, my Tika.'

'What man?'

'The one Gremara knocked over.'

'He looks like a man Farn, but he's younger than you really.'

Through their link, she felt two emotions from her soul bond: pleasure that he had her to himself, even if only for a brief time, and disturbance after the visit to Gremara. They didn't go far, just in a widening circle with their camp at its centre. Tika insisted he stay shielded although he'd taken them high into the sky. She saw no sign of even tiny farms or villages and she wondered yet again, why there was so much apparently ignored or abandoned land, both here and in the lands across the sea. Farn slowed into a glide, spiralling slowly down. 'Will there be more time perhaps, for us to just fly sometimes soon, my Tika?'

She leaned forward against his neck, her hand landing on the long scar that twisted down, bare of scales. 'Yes, Farn. I'll try to spend more time with you soon, I promise.'

Tika hugged him when she'd slid from his back then joined her company at the fire. They used some of their supplies to make a stew then sat around as darkness filled the sky, talking of various things that didn't involve Gremara or any of her children. Tika was smothering a yawn when Veka asked a question which fell into a momentary silence.

'Why do people always sit round fires?'

Tika blinked, her tiredness pushed away. She saw the others had all sat up a little more, frowning as they gave Veka's question their attention.

'To keep warm in the winter?' suggested Dog slowly.

'What about the summer?' Veka argued. 'Even when it's so hot, we still all sit near the hearth in the hall. Why don't we stay outside?'

'Many folk cook on their fires.' That was Ketro.

Veka conceded his point but still objected. 'Once food is cooked, like here, now, we still sit round the embers,' she said.

'Veka.' Dog sounded peevish. 'Be quiet and go to sleep.'

In the faint light, Tika saw Veka grin as she settled down, pulling her blanket round her shoulders. Tika smiled too. She guessed many of her companions would be mulling over the girl's question for a while before they slept. Just like she would be.

The following morning saw the company arrive above Gerras Ridge after travelling a short gateway. Looking down, they saw Troman's building seemed mostly completed. It was an unusual design though, unlike any Tika had seen before. She saw the small wooden cabin which had once stood where this large stone building now was. It was only a short distance away, nearer a barn she remembered from earlier visits. A long single storey building stood south of Troman's palace? Stronghold? She had no idea what to call the place.

As they drifted down to land, Kija sent a thought to Tika. 'I will look over the town, and see if he has changed it too much, daughter.'

Still quite high, Tika saw the Ridge stretching almost straight, east to west, its immensity now furred with trees except for a ribbon of clear ground threading along its top. There was something about it that nagged at her but she had no time to think now as Farn settled gently to the ground. They saw Major Rellak striding towards them as Tika's Guards moved beside her.

'Welcome Lady Tika,' said the major, smiling as he reached them. 'His majesty is speaking to the leader of the Meness clan, if you'd like to join them?'

'No. I don't wish to interrupt.' She indicated the small cabin. 'Is Tradjis content with his home being moved?'

'He wasn't at first,' Rellak admitted. 'But he seems happy enough now.'

They stared back at the building. 'It seems an unusual shape, now that it's nearly finished,' Tika remarked.

'Tayeuku explained it is how it has to be. He said if was built any differently, it would simply fall down, or worse.'

'Why would he say such a thing?' Tika frowned. 'Does his clan have buildings like that?'

'No. Very few clans have permanent dwellings. In some places they use caves for winter shelter and live in tents or simply constructed homes, smaller than Tradjis's cabin.' Major Rellak began to lead the visitors down the slight slope to the new building. 'Taysuku said the Ridge would be displeased.'

Tika stopped, peering up to see if the major was joking. 'Seriously?' She glanced back at the Ridge. 'In what way could the Ridge damage that house?'

Rellak shrugged helplessly. 'I didn't understand a great deal of what he told us to be honest, Lady Tika. He said it had to have the odd number of walls, the angles had to be a certain size, and the roofs at different levels.'

'That would be sensible,' agreed Onion, gazing ahead.

Everyone, including the major, stared at the engineer but clearly he'd said all he felt necessary.

Tika sighed and continued walking. 'How exactly would the Ridge destroy anything?' she persevered.

'Oh not the ridge itself. I don't think.' Rellak frowned in thought. 'No, not the ridge. Taysuku, and more particularly his wise one, Kutama, said there is something inside the Ridge. That's why they've been appointed to keep watch over it for many generations.'

'Something inside it?' Tika repeated. 'Stars forfend! What do they mean?'

'If they knew much more they haven't enlightened us, Lady Tika. The Ridge is enormous though.' Rellak smiled. 'Perhaps there's a huge army of ghosts or some such inside there,' he said.

'No, no,' Onion drew level with them. 'Something much worse.'

Chapter Twenty Nine

Ashri visited Endis to tell him she had met Ferag in the gods' space. Ferag had been astonished to find her there, but Ashri explained she'd been released from her charge as Sentinel and Endis was now in her place. 'Ferag may visit you, Endis. She has been much disturbed recently about several things she realised she has misinterpreted. You have my memories, my knowledge. You will know what to say but I wanted to ask a favour.'

Endis smiled. 'Of course. Anything you wish.'

'Do not be so quick to offer favours, child. This one is a small one, more personal perhaps, but I might have been about to ask you something terrible.' She laughed at his sudden frown. 'Ferag has been hurt, many times, by her siblings among the gods, and by humans she had come to trust. She has learnt to be wary, cautious, but she is easily wounded. I love her. Be kind to her, Endis. That is the favour I ask of you.'

He gave a sigh of relief. 'I will. I met her, in Sapphrea. She visits Lord Seboth and Lady Lallia to fuss over their children. She is very beautiful.'

'She is, Endis, and those two are kind to let her spend time with their little ones.' Ashri rose from where she sat on his doorstep. 'I see you've moved the libraries? Much more sensible to have them close to each other.'

Endis laughed. 'I had a moment's panic when I wondered if the building would take the weight of all of them in one section,' he told her.

Ashri shook her head, white hair tumbling round her face. 'You could put a mountain or two in here, silly boy. It will never collapse.'

'I did realise that,' he agreed. He noticed a certain look about her eyes and hesitated before asking if something was wrong.

'No, not wrong, Endis. It's a strange feeling, being me again, as I was so very, very long ago.' She wandered further into the garden.

'Are you bored, in the gods' space?' he asked softly. He thought she wasn't going to reply but then she turned back to him.

'I believe I am, a little. I have wondered if there is other work Mother could use me for, but I'll wait a while before I ask her.'

'You'd take human form, for another stretch of time that I still can't really imagine?' Endis kept his voice calm but he had mixed feelings about her suggestion.

Ashri smiled. 'No. I don't wish to repeat that.' She raised her arms and spun on the spot. 'I'd forgotten how wonderful it is to move without pain. I'd rather not experience that again.' She paused, a thoughtful expression on her face. 'I'm glad I *did* experience it though. I feel even more sympathy for the poor creatures because of it.'

'Will you tell me what you choose to do?' Endis asked.

'If you really wish to know, yes, I will. I am still a little tempted to return to Mother Dark.' Ashri smiled at his expression. 'I did say a *little* tempted, Endis. I am more inclined to continue, in some way, to serve Mother in whatever way she thinks I may be of service.' She walked back towards him and reached up to touch his cheek, her blue eyes warm. 'My visits here must be few, dear child. I *will* visit you, and I will come if you really need to speak to me, but being the Sentinel is a solitary task.'

Endis sighed, a reluctant smile on his lips. 'I do understand,' he said. 'I'm not really finding it difficult to be here alone. In fact, I think I'll enjoy it. It's just that you taught me so much and so I think of you, telling me what is now in my memories. I can't promise I won't continue to think of you.'

Ashri studied him, before nodding slowly. 'I am aware when you think of me. That is because we are linked through my memories. It will fade in time but it is still fresh, in your mind and in mine. You will find you become more confident, Endis, more aware of your abilities and strengths. Mother will speak more clearly to you and so your understanding will grow. You are so young in human terms, child, but my blood is changing you. You do realise that?'

'I didn't at first, but it has gradually come to me, knowledge of the changes you have made in me. I will do my best to be worthy of your decision to make me your successor.'

They stared at each other for a moment then Ashri gave a snort of laughter followed by an unmistakeable giggle. 'I'm sorry. Here we are, being terribly polite and complimentary to each other, almost like strangers. Let us agree to speak always as friends, Endis. Argue with me, as you did at first. Tell me of your decisions, opinions, rather than asking for mine. Yes?'

Endis had to smile. 'Agreed,' he said. 'But I do hope you will tell me if you think I have made a really wrong choice or overstepped my duties.'

Without replying, she was gone. Endis stared where she'd stood, shook his head and returned to his rooms. It would take a while to become accustomed to such abrupt appearances and disappearances, he thought. He sat in an armchair, a larger version of the Augur's chair, which had been one of his more successful manifestations, and leaned his head back.

Endis let his mind, his awareness, drift away across the world below, as he always thought of it now. He observed several areas, and people, who Ashri had marked of significance. He had, as yet, no full understanding of why those particular people were of interest but he observed them and listened to small snatches of conversations. He saw Lord Chevra in Harbour City, and with more interest, he watched Captain Zhora. He smiled, seeing Zhora's wife, Deema, raging up and down, clearly greatly displeased, but all seemed peaceful in the new town so his mind drifted on.

He saw a tower, hidden deep in the forests of southern Drogoya and the children who lived in its protective walls. Endis witnessed Tika's meeting with Gremara and when Tika left, he followed Gremara inside the domes. He found her sitting on a great heap of furs and watched as she reached for a leather pouch. She untied the thong and studied a small oval pebble in her hand, then carefully placed it in the pouch. She tucked the pouch under the furs on which she was seated. Then she stared at the wall, her eyes unfocussed, and Endis knew she'd retreated. Back to her so distant past, when she had a small sister whom she loved, for whom she would do anything to keep her safe.

Endis left her, seeking her son who'd he'd only glimpsed as briefly as had Tika. He was appalled and shocked by what he found: smaller children beaten, some nursing broken limbs, broken and torn wings, some unmoving in lifeless stillness. Endis found him, hurling objects around what seemed to be his own chamber, his wings half mantled. Yes. Soon this one would pit his strength against Gremara, and the outcome seemed plain.

Opening his eyes, Endis really began to understand what a huge change had been made to him. He wondered if it would have happened had the Asataria still existed, if his mother was still alive. Searching the vast quantity of information he now possessed, he saw that yes, this was the place he would have reached. He could not find the slightest hint of manipulation or interference and concluded there was an inevitability about his path through life. It was entirely due to the inheritance of his unknown father's blood line.

Deciding to make himself some tea, he began to rise, then sank back into the chair again. Surely he would be able to find out more about that man? There must be memories he could follow from Ashri's observations? With a sense of anticipation, Endis settled back and began his search.

An arms man marched up to Major Rellak, saluted sharply and told him His Majesty's meeting had ended but perhaps Lady Tika and her company would join him and the representatives of the Meness Clan for lunch? Tika nodded and the arms man hurried off. Rellak led them round the southern side of the building and they found a large paved area had been laid down, columns holding up a wooden roof above it but leaving empty spaces where walls might have been. Small rugs and pillows were spread across the slabs of stone and King Troman rose, Chief Taysuku and his shaman, Kutama following suit.

Tika offered a polite bow and apologised for arriving unannounced. 'We were in the north, majesty, and I decided to stop here. I'm sorry if it's inconvenient.'

'Not at all, not at all. You've met Taysuku and Kutama have you not.' Troman waved at the various pillows and mats.

Tika settled on the nearest, Fedran and Dromi to either side, and the rest of her Guards ranged behind them. 'Is all well on the Ridge?' she asked politely.

Troman nodded. 'As far as I'm concerned, yes it is. Taysuku is a little concerned but he's not sure what's causing his disquiet.'

'I am *not* sure, Lady Tika,' Taysuku agreed, smiling at her.

Although he smiled, Tika sensed far deeper unease than Troman suggested from both the chief and his shaman. 'Your building is a very interesting and unusual design, majesty,' Tika remarked. 'Perhaps my historian, Dromi, could have a look inside?'

Troman beamed, immediately getting to his feet again. 'Of course. I'll show you round right now if you wish.'

Dromi stood, Veka and Shea following him as he walked away with the king. After the briefest pause, Tika met Taysuku's gaze. 'Tell me,' she said.

The two clan folk exchanged glances, Taysuku nodding at the shaman. Kutama looked directly at Tika. 'What is within the Ridge is greatly angered. Not with this building, but we have been quite unable to discover what has caused the anger.'

'*What* is inside the Ridge?' Tika asked very softly.

Again there was a quick exchange of looks before Kutama continued. 'A very ancient spirit has lived within the Ridge since the birth of the world, even back in the time of mists. Our stories tell us the spirit made many helpers, their sole purpose to watch over those the spirit chose to protect.'

'Do you know who, or what in particular, this spirit chooses to protect?' Tika asked.

'We have always believed we were among those chosen. We understood we had to guard the Ridge, keep it safe. No

329

one was permitted to build upon it, or to dig in to it. In return, we would be sheltered from our enemies - the Black Clans, and occasional Kelshan or Stralanese farmers. This we have always done, Lady Tika. But in my lifetime we have been unprotected, left to suffer serious losses from the Black Clans.'

Tika felt chill fingers walk down her spine. 'May I ask if you have contact with this spirit?'

Taysuku sighed and Kutama lowered her head. 'It is many generations now since our shamans have spoken with the spirit. We redoubled our care, and still it has not seen fit to speak again,' Taysuku told her gravely.

'Is it male or female?'

Kutama shrugged. 'Either. Both. It is of the very earth,' was all she could say.

'You are more worried now though?'

Taysuku made a series of ritual gestures in front of his face, the meaning of which Tika could not follow. 'The sense of rage, increasing fury, grows stronger each day,' Kutama barely whispered the words. Her hands gripped each other in her lap and for the first time, Tika noticed the palms were stained red, as were Taysuku's.

The Meness chief saw her look and raised his hands. 'This means we are ready for bloodshed,' he said. 'We believe we will be punished for displeasing the spirit within the Ridge, or that we have failed in our care for it.'

'Could it be angered because all the trees suddenly grew?'

Kutama frowned. 'We did consider that, but for trees to grow there, seeds must have lain there once and covered it as they do now. Even as long ago as before our remembering of this place.'

Tika felt relief that the shaman didn't think any action of hers had caused the trees to appear. 'Is the circle known to you. The one that was in Tradjis's house?'

'There were ancient stories of such things, but it must have been long hidden beneath the earth until Tradjis cleared the ground for his cabin.'

'Is it connected to the spirit you say dwells within the Ridge?'

'No.' That was a very definite reply from both clan folk.

Again, Tika felt a surge of relief: for a moment she had been terrified that she had been mistaken to trust the circles if they were controlled by something as unpredictable as whatever was in this Ridge. She believed Taysuku and Kutama when they rejected any such connection so decisively. Tika knew she could probably probe the Ridge with her mage senses but she was reluctant to do so until she had far more information. 'Can you tell me anything about the spirit's helpers you spoke of? Have you seen *them*? What are they like?'

'The helpers have not been seen since the spirit ceased to speak to our shamans,' Kutama replied. 'I was told, in my apprentice years, they were small, ghostly shapes, barely visible. My shaman told me they were furred creatures, so he had been taught, but he was doubtful of that. It had been long before *his* training when they were last seen.'

Tika listened, nodding her understanding but giving no hint that her own suspicions were strengthened by Kutama's words. Her Guards had remained silent behind her, listening to the conversation. Although she said nothing, Tika sensed Essa's increased apprehension. Essa had limited mage powers but so did several Iskallians. Essa's powers were stronger than most and Tika's Sergeant was coming to similar conclusions as she was.

Tika glanced back casually and gave Essa the tiniest head shake before looking back at the two clan folk. 'I can offer no answers,' she said. 'I will think more about what you've told me but if you have no thoughts on what you might do, I'm not sure I'll be any help.' She felt relief from both chief and shaman.

'We understand, Lady Tika, but we would greatly appreciate you considering this situation. King Troman is a good man we believe. Unfortunately he has no strong belief in any form of spirit, or god, so it's a difficult thing to explain to him in any way that might convince him of our fears.'

Voices were approaching, the King strolling back with Dromi, followed by Shea and Veka. Troman sat down, smiling. 'I was explaining the Meness people advised on the design of the building,' he said.

'Is there a reason for the shape of it?' Tika asked.

Taysuku nodded. 'There must be eight sides,' he said. 'Each is aligned to the sacred directions. That offers the best protection against all manner of things.'

Tika felt there was far more he could have explained but he kept things simple for Troman. 'Well, it's most unusual but rather pleasant.' She chose to be tactful.

A line of arms men approached, bearing trays of meats, pies, loaves, fruit, a surprisingly large choice of foods, which they set on the floor among the guests.

'How is your plan coming for moving many of your administration offices here from Strale?' Tika enquired. From the corner of her eye she saw a large chunk of meat vanish into Cerys's travel sack which was lying beside Onion's leg. She was surprised he hadn't wandered off as he usually did.

'Better than I'd hoped,' Troman replied. 'Most will remain in Sarvental but a far smaller group will deal with anything I need here. Riders take messages back and forth fast enough and most of the council seem happy with this arrangement.'

The talk became more general as people ate but then Tika asked what this new building was called. Was it a palace, she wondered?

Troman laughed. 'No! I decided it can only be one thing. The Outpost. Tradjis has lived here so long, and he thought of his cabin as the last outpost of the Kingdom of Strale. So - it has to be The Outpost.'

Tika was eager to get back to Iskallia but politeness kept her there until early afternoon. At last she felt they could leave without seeming too hasty and she rose. 'Thank you for feeding us, majesty,' she said with a smile. She offered a bow to the Meness chief and his shaman. 'Thank you for speaking to me. I will think of your words.' Her comment passed Troman by, but Major Rellak glanced at her curiously.

Another major arrived requesting the king's presence elsewhere and Troman instructed Rellak to escort Lady Tika and her company back to the Dragons who reclined by the barn and Tradjis's cabin.

'Are the worries of the Meness something we should be concerned about?' Rellak asked Tika as they walked.

'I'm not entirely sure, Major. I would suggest you give serious consideration to any warnings they might give you. If necessary, get the king away, back to Sarvental.'

Rellak nodded. He lowered his voice. 'His Majesty is trying to do his best for everyone in Strale, Lady Tika. He is a good man, but he was never raised to be king. He struggles at times.'

'I know.' She smiled up at him. 'With help from men like you, and his new council, he could become a very good king as well as being a good man. He is indeed changed from our first meeting with him,' Tika agreed. 'He seems to have a great respect for Queen Tupalla, which has helped him I believe?'

'She is a sweet lady, and a shrewd and wise ruler,' Major Rellak replied.

Tika grinned up at him. 'She has remarked that she feels he regards her as a grandmother figure.'

The Major paused as they reached the Dragons. 'That is a fair description.' He returned her smile.

Becoming more serious as her Guards climbed onto Dragons, Tika met Rellak's eyes. 'Don't hesitate to send word to us if there should be any sort of disturbance concerning the Ridge?' she said quietly.

'It is more serious than His Majesty thinks?' he replied as quietly.

'I think it could be, yes.'

'It will be as you say, Lady Tika. Thank you for the warning.'

'I hope it is unnecessary, but better to give you a hint of possible danger,' she said, turning to climb onto Farn's back.

Major Rellak stepped back, and saluted, watching as the five Dragons rose, climbing high and fast. Kija mind spoke them as they rose. 'I saw only three new buildings, daughter, not large ones.'

Tika could see for herself when they reached a certain height and was glad to note very little had been changed in the small town. Kija opened a gateway for the short journey to Chaban and Tika mind spoke the company, telling them only Farn would land on the tower roof. The others should fly on, to the lower slopes of the Barrier Mountains, where she and Fedran would join them shortly.

Consequently, Zu Lan found only Farn, Tika and Fedran when she opened the tower door to greet them. The Queen's chief personal guard smiled as Tika slid from Farn's back. 'My dear lady will be glad to see you,' she said, leading the way down the tower stairs to the Queen's apartments. 'She is most grateful for the regular supply of salve you've been sending, *and* she has accepted the tea your healer sent. It does help her rest much better at night.'

Tika spent a while explaining a little of the Meness clan's concerns about Gerras Ridge but she kept her own much deeper concerns to herself. The Queen told them of several projects her new council had proposed and she expressed her pleasure at having such hard working and forward thinking councillors in charge of Chaban at last. After a time, Tika kissed the Queen's still beautiful, unscarred left cheek and made her farewells, promising a longer visit soon.

Farn lifted from the tower roof, arrowing to the south west. They soon saw the other Dragons sprawled on the slopes, enjoying the late afternoon sun. Her company had clearly set up camp so, in spite of Tika's sense of urgency in her desire to return to Iskallia, she said nothing. She realised those travelling with her needed a time to relax a little, after what had happened in Mertasia. So she sat back and let them talk, curbing her impatience to get home.

Dromi was made to describe more of Troman's new building and he gave very detailed accounts. All the ground floor rooms were either offices or reception rooms for any important guests visiting in the future. There were various comments about that as Guards wondered just who would want to trail so far out from Sarvental, which had far more to offer in the way of entertainments. He added that Troman had ordered the open paved area specifically for visiting clans folk, who believed all important discussions should take place outside.

'What's upstairs?' asked Dog. 'Is there a library?'

Groans and laughter greeted her question. Dromi smiled. 'More offices, and bedrooms. The king's personal apartment is very modest. He said he didn't like the rooms he had at Sarvental castle at all.'

'It doesn't seem to have occurred to him that he could choose any rooms he wanted,' Veka commented. 'He is the king after all.'

Tika yawned, then told them her plan for tomorrow. 'I'd like to visit Jerrad then Tarran, only a brief courtesy visit, then back to Iskallia.' She watched people nod then she settled back against Farn's chest, hoping they'd all sleep soon.

Into the quiet darkness, she heard Veka speak clearly. 'I still want to know why we sit round fires.'

Tika smothered a laugh as a chorus of complaints answered the poor girl.

Chapter Thirty

The small group of Iskallians duly paid calls first on Jerrad then on Tarran before returning home. As before, they all noted the stiffer, more formal welcome from the Elders of Jerrad in their main town of Kelsay. Tika sensed no ill feeling or animosity but the Elders were still cautiously wary. Flying on to Paxina, the main town of Tarran, the Elders there greeted them with delight and warmth. The Iskallians were urged to return for a longer visit so Lady Tika could see some of the work the Tarrans had undertaken along their northern border with Kelshan.

'It's not that we don't trust them, after they signed the treaty and all,' explained Elder Abeya. 'It's just that our people feel a little more secure.' She smiled, looking slightly worried as though she feared Lady Tika might be annoyed that Tarran had seen fit to reinforce their border at all.

'I'm sure your people remember too well when Kelshan arms men came and took your young men and your harvests,' Tika assured the Elders. 'Having clear, strong borders is a wise thing, and I'm sure it brings comfort to your people.'

They finally managed to leave Paxina and Brin opened the gateway to avoid the high chill of crossing the great Barrier Mountains. Tika went to each Dragon, as always, to thank them then she turned to Minyth who had been on the plateau as they arrived back. 'There have been no troubles, Minyth?' she asked the young Dragon.

'No, none at all,' he replied, his eyes sparkling. 'Skay and Heligg are along the valley,' he went on, in case Tika thought perhaps those two were shirking their duty. 'We've been checking those who are on patrol are quite safe.'

Tika nodded solemnly. 'That's very good of them. Whose idea was that?'

Minyth's eyes whirred rapidly. 'It was mine,' he said, his mind tone a mix of pride and modesty.

She hugged him gently. 'A good thought, dear one. Thank you.' She left him, entering the House behind the others as the lunch bell began to chime.

People waited after the meal to hear Tika's account of their travels. She made no mention of the three children in the Drogoyan tower, and spoke only briefly of Gremara. She stroked Cerys as she spoke, the cat having chosen to sit on her lap once Onion released her from her travel sack. Tika told of their visit to Gerras Ridge in the north of Strale, of seeing Queen Tupalla in Chaban, and lastly their brief stops at Tarran and Jerrad.

Her audience listened with interest, asked a few questions then went off about their usual day's work. Those at Tika's table also left except for Essa, Dromi and Onion. Werlan arrived and offered Tika a bow as he approached. He said nothing but Tika understood he had news of some kind although she didn't ask. It was clear he had no intention of speaking to anyone but her. She glanced around the table. 'If you have something you wish to discuss, come up to my quarters in a while, when you've taken your packs to your rooms,' she suggested.

'I'll get started on my report,' Dromi told her.

Tika was glad that all three had realised Werlan need to speak to her of something he deemed important and had left at once. 'What is it?' she asked when they were alone.

'I have had a letter from Lord Corman,' he said. 'He is greatly worried. About Lady Jian.'

Tika closed her eyes momentarily. Stars above, that was what she had feared above all since her talk with the Ancient Augur. She waited.

'Lord Corman reports her temper has become erratic. She had seemed so much better, back to her usual self this last half year. Now she deliberately provokes Lord Shivan, not teasingly as she used to do, but with a sharp edge, he says. The letter arrived two days after you'd left. He reports a huge argument between Lord Shivan and Lady Jian and she took Dragon form and left the palace. She has not returned. Lord Shivan is extremely concerned because Lady Jian repeated her oath of service to, erm, Youki, in defiance of being of the most high of the Dark blood lines.'

Werlan shook his head. 'Lord Shivan has had people looking for her, as discreetly as possible, but no one reports seeing her. Lord Corman is not even sure if she is still within the Dark Realm. If not, where could she have gone?'

'Would she have gone to the island in Ferris Lake?' Tika frowned as she thought.

Werlan shook his head. 'That was my thought then I realised Memek was Mother Dark's special place. Surely Jian wouldn't go there if she is forsworn?'

Tika stared at him. 'Forsworn?'

'That is what has been distressing Corman so much Tika. Jian is of the first blood of Dark. Lady Lerran's blood is in her. Jian is *of* the Dark, yet she has chosen to serve another. She made no allowance for dividing her loyalty.'

Tika looked confused. and Werlan explained further. 'She *could* have said she is born of Dark and serves Mother, but she might be willing to serve another - Youki for example - as long as her loyalty to Mother Dark was in no conflict with such a service. By refusing to qualify her oath to Youki,' Werlan paused.

'Go on,' urged Tika.

'By refusing to qualify her oath to Youki, she betrays Mother Dark,' Werlan finished.

'Betray is a big word.'

Werlan nodded. 'Indeed, but it is the *only* word Tika, the only honest and accurate word. Corman is distraught. He doesn't think Lord Shivan has grasped the full implications, but Lady Lorca has.'

Thoroughly alarmed now, Tika could only stare into Werlan's gold eyes. 'What are you *not* saying, Werlan? I know there's more to it than Corman being upset and Shivan being angry.'

'Tika there is one punishment for such a betrayal. Only one.'

Colour leached from Tika's quiet face as Werlan's words sank in. 'But she is Shivan's *sister,* the Lady of the Dark Realm until he marries and his wife takes that title. Are you *truly* suggesting Jian could be accused of such a thing?'

'She made it plain she serves only Youki, in front of

Corman, Lady Lorca, Shivan and Fenzir.'

'She has some mage powers. Surely they couldn't - destroy her? - is *that* what you're telling me could happen?'

'Tika, Shivan *could*. If he refused such a dreadful task, Corman would do it. Just because he is in the half death, as I am, people rarely understand his powers were once immense. Even in the half death Tika, those powers *remain* immense. Lady Lerran made him promise to stay in the world, to guard and guide Lord Shivan to become the ruler she foresaw he *could* become. That promise is all that Corman remains in the world for. He loved Lady Lerran beyond all. He will never allow any betrayal of her or of Mother Dark.'

They fell silent as the kitchen door opened. Sarila brought a tray of tea to Tika without a word, retreating back to the kitchens immediately. 'Tika, you *do* understand? Who Lady Lerran was?'

'She was the First Daughter of Mother Dark.' Tika sounded puzzled. 'That was her title.'

Truth suddenly dawned and she stared at Werlan in shock. He nodded.

'Lady Lerran was the first of all Mother Dark's creations.'

'But, but, she was human.'

'She wore human form, by choice, for nearly all of her long life, except when she allowed herself the freedom of Dragon flight.'

'She *wore* human form? You are saying - what? - she was a *god?* Like Simert, or Ferag?' Tika could scarcely say the words.

Werlan watched her, faint surprise on his face. 'You truly didn't understand that? Of course she was. She could have let the body she used, die, and then taken her original form, returning to the gods' space Mother Dark made for all her children. Lerran chose the finality of a complete return to Mother in the hope of a glimpse of her husband, Dabray.'

Tika's mind reeled. In a few moments, from the most unexpected source, she had learnt more of gods than she had yet discovered. 'Corman?' she managed to whisper. 'He's a god?'

'No.' Werlan smiled. 'Gods and lesser gods do not spend time in the half death. They choose to live or to return to Mother. I'm sorry Tika, I truly thought you knew all this.'

Tika shook her head slowly. 'So is Youki a god? A creation of Mother Dark?'

'No. I don't know a great deal, but I believe she was a spirit of some kind, of this world, when first Mother Dark was drawn here.'

Tika drank tea without noticing it was cold. 'I have much to think of at the moment, Werlan, but I'd like you to tell me much more when there is time.'

Werlan inclined his head. 'Whenever you wish. Meanwhile, how should I reply to Corman? He didn't say so outright, but I think he would like to speak with you.'

'I'll go to the Dark Realm tomorrow.'

Werlan stood. 'Then I will send word to Corman now.' Again, he bowed, then his tall figure strode from the hall.

Tika lifted Cerys to her shoulder, grabbed her pack from the floor and headed up to her rooms. Cerys was silent for which Tika was grateful right now. She changed out of her uniform, and had just sat down when there was a knock at her door. She wasn't surprised to see Essa enter and drop onto a pillow across from her. 'The Ridge?' Tika asked.

'Is that where she lives, do you think?' Essa asked.

'I have a bad feeling about it all,' Tika replied. 'I suspect it *is,* but its obvious something's happened to upset her.'

'Enraged rather than upset, I would say,' said Essa. 'When the shaman described the helpers, I just knew, but I thought Enki was such a one? There seemed only goodness in him from all I heard from Olam, Jian or Brin?'

Tika sighed. 'I don't pretend to understand, Essa, at least, not yet.'

'Is there anything I can do, help you with?'

'No. Not now anyway. I'm sure you'll be thinking as hard as I will. I have to go to the Dark Realm tomorrow.' She met Essa's pale blue eyes. 'Corman is worried about Jian. I don't know if I told you, Jian swore to serve Youki above all others.'

She watched Essa's expression grow increasingly horrified. 'But she *can't*. She is of Mother Dark,' she blurted. 'She cannot serve another, none of Lerran's blood can. It would be betrayal!' She stared at Tika. 'Mother Dark have mercy!' she whispered.

'Who knows how Mother Dark might feel,' Tika said with a rueful shrug. 'I have a suspicion I know how *Corman* feels.'

'Betrayed,' Essa said at once. She was born and raised in the Dark Realm: she would know and understand these things. Her father was The Bear, leader of his tribe. Her uncle was the shaman as was one of her brothers. Of course she would realise the deep implications of the situation Jian had brought about. 'Where is Jian?'

'No one seems to know. She and Shivan had a great argument. She took Dragon form and left. That was three or four days ago. I think Shivan's had people looking for her but no one's seen her apparently.'

Essa got to her feet. 'That's not good, Tika, not good at all.' When she opened the door to leave she greeted someone outside and Tika guessed Onion was her next visitor. She watched him walk to her small fire place and reach to touch each of the stone creatures Teyo had carved for her. 'I'm going along the valley for a few days,' he told her, turning to look at her. 'You're going to see Corman?'

How did he know that, she wondered. 'Yes. Tomorrow.'

'Hmm.' He wandered to one of the windows.

'Onion, what do you know of Youki? I had begun to think you served her?'

He looked back at her in astonishment. 'Me? No. I don't know much, except to keep clear.'

Tika waited but he said no more. He prowled along the book shelves then came to stand near the hearth again. 'You beware of that Ridge, Tika.'

She studied him. 'I will. Is it what I think?'

'Might well be.'

'You saw the pictures Endis shared,' she said suddenly. 'Of Enki, at the end. He was good.'

'Of course. He was Mother's,'

'*What?!* I thought he served Youki?'

'So did she!' Onion chuckled. 'Mother's been worried for a long time but she swore she'd never interfere.' He smiled at her then nodded and ambled towards the door. 'I'll be back whenever you want me,' he said casually and left her.

Tika looked at Cerys who stared straight back. 'Well? What do *you* think?'

Cerys was quiet for so long, Tika didn't think she was going to answer. 'I think she's too old now to make the creatures, which must mean her powers are failing. Perhaps like Sket?'

Tika caught her breath. Could that be possible? How would anyone be able to tell?

'I know you are fond of Jian,' Cerys went on. 'She has always been the wilder one of the two. Shivan *says* wild things, but Jian is far more unpredictable in fact. Lorca told me they were always in trouble at their school or whatever it was called, and it was always Jian's ideas and mischief which caused the trouble. I do not believe Khosa ever spoke to me of Jian. She told me much of Shivan, but not Jian.'

Tika sat, trying to sort out too many things in her mind when Cerys spoke again. 'That Ridge is a bad place, Tika. Endis knew that. That's why he got so sick,' she said. 'He might even know more, now he's training with the Ancient Augur person. Could you ask him?'

'I don't know how I'd contact him. He might know but I wouldn't think the Augur would appreciate him asking questions on my behalf.'

Cerys began a meticulous cleaning and tidying of her fur which had been sadly ruffled in her travel sack and Tika wondered about that strange, furred creature, Pesh, who had murdered Tarel. Where had she gone? If she was one of Youki's helpers, was Youki now annoyed because Tika had told Pesh to be gone and never return? Tika still felt a cold anger stir in her when she thought of that creature. Could Cerys be correct, that Youki's powers were waning, her remaining helpers becoming weaker as a result?

She rubbed her forehead, pushing those thoughts aside

and focussing on what she might face in tomorrow's meeting with Corman. Tika was extremely fond of Corman; she regarded him, in her odd way, as a member of the family she'd gathered for herself. Suddenly she got to her feet, hurrying out and down the stairs. Crossing the empty hall, she turned left, down to the forge. She was pleased to find Garrol alone in the rear store room, checking his stocks of iron. He glanced up with the beginning of a smile then straightened, smile gone. 'What is it?' he asked her.

'Jian,' said Tika simply.

'Let's walk,' Garrol replied, setting aside his list of supplies and joining her at the door.

Leaving the forge, they turned along the path down to the lake. There were a few people near the entrance to the tunnel to Port Maressa but it was clear Garrol and Tika were deep in conversation so no one bothered them as they reached the lake shore. They paused, looking over the water where thin sheets of broken ice still drifted, in the process of thawing now the days were warming up again. Tika had explained all that Werlan had told her and now she looked up into Garrol's face. His expression was grave. 'I blame myself, Garrol,' Tika said. 'I'm not sure Youki would have contacted Jian if not for me.'

Garrol pulled her against his side as she shivered. 'Oh I think she would.'

'I never asked you what you know of her?'

'Very little. Lady Lerran mentioned her once. She told me to beware.' He hesitated. 'The blood metal will protect you from her,' he said very quietly. He lifted her left hand and rubbed his thumb over the silver ring, one of two he had made for her. A dark band of blood metal circled it, with silver above and below. 'If Jian has let Youki enter the Dark Realm, there is danger for all. I am shocked and saddened that she would so betray Mother Dark, Lady Lerran, and her own brother.'

Tika shivered again. There was that word again - betray. Werlan, Essa, and now Garrol. The first word they thought to use. 'What happens if someone betrays Mother Dark?'

'Out in the world? Nothing. Within the Dark Realm, it is a matter of great seriousness. It was the cause of the Final Battle, Tika, when Lord Hanlif betrayed Mother Dark.'

Tika considered his words. 'What happens within the Dark Realm?' she asked.

'There is only one punishment.' His bright blue eyes, usually so warm and affectionate, were cold, bleak, as he repeated Werlan's words.

'They'd *kill* someone who chooses not to serve Mother Dark? Is that by Mother Dark's command?'

Garrol started walking again, towards the small grove of fruit trees. 'Not her command Tika, no. Lady Lerran's.'

Tika drew a sharp breath. 'Have many refused to serve? What happened to them?'

'Very few. Lady Lerran killed the first one or two. Then it became the task of the Sword Master.'

'Who were the ones who denied Mother Dark?'

Garrol stopped, frowning in thought then he shook his head. 'The earliest ones I really don't know. There were two when I was her Shield Master. Both men of the families who disagreed more with Lerran's rule rather than Mother Dark I believe. The last was the grandfather of Cyrek and Seola. Lord Favrian, Sword Master, he dispatched him.'

Tika remembered Favrian. She thought of the great blood metal sword he wore and closed her eyes at the thought of how he might use it to exact punishment. Leaving the grove of fruit trees, a chill breeze whisked around them and Garrol turned them to walk back. 'Suppose you changed your mind,' Tika suggested. 'Asked for forgiveness?'

The muscular man beside her gusted a huge sigh. 'Can you *truly* see Jian asking forgiveness, of anyone? Especially when she made her announcement in front of Shivan, Corman, Lorca and Fenzir? Can you imagine *they* could forget that, and continue to trust her?'

They began the climb back up the long path to the plateau in silence. 'Is there *anything* that could change this dreadful situation?' Tika asked when they reached the forge.

344

Garrol's work hardened hand cupped her cheek. 'No. If Jian has any sense left, she will stay far from the Dark Realm for the rest of her life. There is nothing you can do, Tika. If you try to persuade them to a different decision, I believe they will resent your presumption. By all means, listen to them. I'm sure Shivan will rage and rant to hide his grief. Listen, but do not try to change things.' He watched the small figure walk slowly up the final slope and stop as a donkey hurried towards her. Disturbed and sad, Garrol went into the forge and resumed checking his raw materials.

Tika stared at the donkey heading in her direction but she was surprised when Chichi slowed. Tika braced herself for the raucous shriek she usually had to endure, but it didn't come. Chichi's ears waggled but there was a very different expression in the liquid brown eyes today. Chichi lowered her head until her brow butted gently against Tika's shoulder. Feeling close to tears suddenly, Tika put her arms round Chichi's neck, burying her face in the warm grey brown hair. They stood for a moment then Chichi stepped back, watching Tika carefully.

'Thank you,' Tika murmured. Chichi snuffled, accompanied by renewed ear waggling and Tika fully expected the usual shrill bray but the donkey moved to walk to the House entrance, her head brushing Tika's arm. Reaching the door, Tika stared into the brown eyes and hugged her again before she went inside. She looked in to Fedran's office. 'I'm going to the Dark Realm tomorrow,' she said. 'Just a quick visit.'

He looked up, nodding. 'We haven't seen Lord Shivan lately,' he remarked.

'No. He's busy reorganising that Academy he hated so much.' Tika managed a smile and went back to her rooms. She was too worried and upset to sit still for long and paced round and round until Cerys suggested she stop.

'There is nothing you can do, Tika.' The cat's mind voice was gentle, she was all too aware how upset Tika was. 'I've been trying to think where Jian could hide. I can only come up with one place.' Her green gold eyes were enormous as she watched Tika at last come to rest behind her low table.

'You mean Gerras Ridge.' Tika's words were flat.
'That's what I've been wondering. If we're correct, I see no
way of reaching her. Even if I could, what would I say to
her? Help her hide somewhere else? She can't spend the
rest of her life hiding. Can you imagine Jian agreeing to
that?'

'You didn't know Jian very well before, did you?
Before she fell through time? Khosa said nothing of her,
although she spoke often of Lady Lerran, Shivan and
Corman.'

Tika chewed her lip. 'She was much changed when she
was returned,' she said slowly. 'She spoke to no one for half
a year or more. Then she changed again and we all thought
the old Jian was back. Then I showed her the letter and
pictures Endis gave me.'

'And then she met Youki and she changed again,'
Cerys's voice was a whisper in Tika's mind.

'I thought you were in awe of Youki, cared for her,'
Tika said with a frown.

'She was very plausible,' Cerys replied. 'I think she lets
people sense or feel what they want to believe.'

The bell chimed for the evening meal and Tika went
down to the hall. By the time she returned, Cerys was
asleep, or at least, refusing to talk any more. Tika slept
restlessly, tossing and turning as thoughts jangled and
twisted through her head. At last dawn sent fingers of light
through the eastern windows. She rose, washed, dressed
and went down to the hall where Farn waited, his eyes
flickering with pleasure.

When she'd eaten a small amount of breakfast she went
straight outside, Farn ready and waiting for her. As he rose,
heading east, she told him only that there was some trouble
concerning Jian. She asked him to only listen, make no
comments. They could talk when they came back.

'I will listen, my Tika,' he promised solemnly.

It was a short journey then Farn circled above the
terrace set high on the Karmazen Palace, before settling
gently on the black stone. Tika walked towards the arched
entrance, Farn close at her heels. In the shadow of the arch,
she saw Corman and her heart nearly stopped. He looked

stricken with such grief she could say nothing, simply walking on and hugging him, as tight as she could.

Chapter Thirty One

Corman held her a little away and reached to caress Farn's face. 'Do you mind if I take Tika to my study, Farn? The corridor is too narrow for you I'm afraid.'

'Not at all,' Farn replied, pacing on to recline by the large hearth in the throne room.

Tika pulsed affection to him, leaving their mind link open so he would hear all conversation.

'Shivan and Lorca are still away,' Corman continued. 'I believe they have almost reached the tribal lands in the north but they have found no sign of Jian.' He spoke as he led Tika along a corridor from the throne room which was indeed narrower than most of the passages Tika had been through here before. Opening a door to their left, Corman ushered her inside.

The room was full of papers, scrolls, books, lit only by a narrow line of windows high in the northern wall. Three rather worn armchairs were set in front of a wide desk and Tika sat in one when Corman moved behind the desk to his own chair. 'I blame myself,' Tika said as Corman sat down.

'No, not your fault, child. Don't you remember, Youki came here once before, when Lady Lerran brought Farn back from the Dark?'

Tika shook her head. 'I don't remember much of that time except how terrified I was.'

'Several of us, the oldest of us you understand, were much alarmed. Lady Lerran would have ordered her gone, but she could not do so then.'

Tika's eyes brimmed with tears. 'Lady Lerran was so desperately ill because of me and Farn, so we *are* to blame,' she insisted.

Corman watched her than shook his head. 'Let's not lay blame child.' He reached down to the side of his desk. There was the click of a lock releasing and he lifted a large file onto the desk. He slid it across to Tika. 'Read it,' he said softly.

Tika frowned, but lifted it to her lap. Opening it she stared at the topmost paper. She recognised the writing but instead of tremulously formed letters, this was written in a firm, confident hand. Clearly Lady Lerran had been quite well when she wrote it.

"Continuous report on Jian, daughter of my brother, Peshan and his wife, Abella. By my personal command and supervision, Lerran, First Daughter of Dark."

Below those words was Lerran's signature and the seal of the Dark Realm, an ivory oval with a black wing extended across it. Tika brushed her fingers over the signature, as though she might touch the woman who'd written it, then she turned the page and began to read. She was astonished how thorough and detailed each report was, although she didn't recognise many of the names of those who had submitted them. Each report was signed by its author then by Lerran, making it apparent that Lerran had taken a very close interest in each one.

The morning passed and Tika read on. She was only half aware when Corman left the room, returning with a tray of refreshments for her. Tika reached a section where Lerran's signature vanished, replaced by Corman's. She knew that must have been seven years or more ago, when Lerran lay so lost and dying. She closed the file and put it back on the table. 'There is very little about Youki in there, or exactly *why* the Dark seems to have always been wary of her,' she said.

Corman retrieved the file and put it back, the click of a lock seeming loud in the quietness of the room. He rose, crossing to a book shelf from which he selected an unimpressive looking slim volume. He handed it to Tika and resumed his seat. There were few pages inside this book, perhaps twenty five at most. It detailed some of what Tika had already learnt of Youki but she found nothing new and indeed, there were a couple of points they *didn't* mention. Whether those were deliberate omissions, she was unable to tell

After skimming through the brief pages, she laid the book on the desk. 'Werlan told me of your concern, Corman. He said deliberate betrayal of Mother Dark is the greatest crime here.'

'So it is.'

'He said there is but one punishment.'

'So there is.'

'Jian has the same father and mother as Shivan. Peshan, Lady Lerran's own brother. How *could* you destroy her? W*ho* would do such a thing?'

Corman pulled a pile of papers stacked to one side of his desk and removed several. Again, he handed them to Tika in silence. Tika drew in a breath as she read, then glanced across at the Palace Master. 'They *knew?* Have they known all along?'

'Since Jian went to the Academy when she was twelve, yes. They may have had suspicions, worries, before, but it was then that Lady Lerran spoke to them officially.'

'Did Lorca know?'

Corman was slower to reply. 'Lady Lorca is a very intelligent lady. I believe she might have guessed. She was the elder of the two at the Academy. She has said to me recently that she was always puzzled why Jian always wanted to spend holidays at Lorca's home and never at her own home. Lorca never visited Jian's home until these last few years when she's gone there with Lord Shivan.'

Tika looked back at the letter she held. 'This is signed by both Peshan and Abella. Jian's father and mother. Do they really, *truly* think this way? They write as if she is already dead, Corman.'

'In their view, she is, Tika. Even though Peshan chose a quiet life, away from the court, he was still Lady Lerran's brother. I remember him as a child. He adored both Lerran and Dabray.' Corman's eyes, like old gold coins, met Tika's. 'If Peshan believed his own arm had done Lerran any wrong, he would have cut it off himself. There could never be any question of Peshan's disloyalty to Lerran and Mother Dark. Abella too. Since Lady Lerran returned to the Dark, Peshan regards Shivan as Grandson of Dark first, his own son second.'

Tika thought for a while. 'Can they *truly* think that? Abella gave birth to them; can she truly turn her back on Jian?'

'I imagine it has caused both of them great anguish, Tika. But they are *of* the Dark, completely.'

'I'm not convinced any mother could turn her back on a daughter, Corman. I do understand what you're saying; I'm just not sure it's right or true.'

Corman nodded. 'It is the way of the Dark nonetheless. Many aspects of life here have changed since Lord Shivan became ruler, but there are still codes of our laws which he has adhered to. The one most important to us all is loyalty to Mother Dark. I gave him the report you just read. He was shocked and distressed but after consideration, he calmed.' Corman stared at Tika. 'I believe he is beginning to fully come to terms with his position, Tika. If he finds Jian, he will not treat her to any display of temper. He *is* the Lord of this Realm.'

'Do many others know of this?' Tika asked.

'Word has spread, inevitably. Neither Lorca nor I can think of any who would hide Jian. She will have a life, if she has left the Dark Realm, but she will know only death awaits if she returns here.'

Tika found herself drinking cold tea again. 'Suppose one of the Dark Lords found her if they travelled beyond this Realm, as Shivan has travelled? Would they hurt her?'

'No. They might try to bring her back here. Otherwise no, they will not hurt her in any other land.'

'What of Jian's mage powers? Surely she could cause considerable harm should she be cornered?'

Corman steepled his fingers in front of his face, tapping his lips. 'Her powers are not as strong as I suspect you think they are, Tika. She can shield well, yes, but mostly her abilities are of the showy kind. By that I mean she can strengthen her appearance to *appear* larger, stronger. She can call air, wind, to blow around her or someone near to her, but not for long. She has a superior manner.' Corman smiled. 'I know, you think many Dark Lords think they are better than most other folk. Shivan has never cared *who* people are. I mean, he will talk to the cleaning staff exactly the same way he speaks to you and me. He has never, from a young age, paid attention to who people are, which families they came from.' He considered what he'd just said. 'There are times, when he is very unsure of a situation, when he will wear the superior mask, but those times are increasingly rare. Lorca has a similar attitude.'

Tika sighed. 'Shivan really believes he will be able to - what? Witness Favrian killing his sister?' A look of horror crossed her face. 'He won't be expected to do it himself, will he?'

'No, he won't. Lady Lerran would have done so, no matter who the traitor was, but she allowed Favrian to take on the task later.'

'From all those reports about Jian, Lady Lerran felt there would be trouble from her many years ago. Why didn't she take action then?'

'Shivan loved her. As Jian has never loved anyone. Until she met Enki.'

Tika rose, pacing round the armchairs, pins and needles in her feet reminding her she'd been sitting too long. 'I will not question your laws or argue, Corman. It is your Realm, your way, not mine.' Seeming to change the subject, she spoke of Strale. 'Did Dromi tell you the clans in the north of Strale and Kelshan followed Youki?' She waited for Corman's nod. 'We were wrong. The Meness clan said their eternal task has been to guard *against* her.'

Corman sat forward, his gaze fixed on Tika. '*Against?* What do they know of her? Would they share their knowledge with you?'

'Perhaps. They offered hints but I chose not to press them further.' He nodded, accepting her judgement.

'You said Lorca had gone with Shivan to look for Jian?'

'Yes. She is a very good influence on him. Strange as it might sound, so is Lord Mim.'

Tika thought that over then she smiled. 'No. I think I can understand that.'

'Lorca liked Dessi and there is another, here, in Karmazen town, with whom she spends much time.' Tika waited. Corman gave a grunt of amusement. 'Gossamer Tewk.' In spite of her worries, Tika laughed. 'I have heard,' Corman continued. 'Lady Lorca even has a fondness for Drengle List.'

Their brief moment of a lighter topic quickly faded.

Tika sat down again. 'Jian is well liked by many,' she began.

'No, Tika. I know you mean Olam and Riff. They knew her when they all fell through time. They met Enki and perhaps that's when anyone saw the best of Jian. Otherwise, she has never been popular with her classmates, never had friends but for Lorca.'

'You are sure of Lorca's loyalty?' Tika couldn't imagine Lorca would betray the Dark but she felt she had to ask.

'I am completely sure of Lady Lorca,' Corman confirmed quietly. 'Lady Lerran told me she thought she would be a most suitable match for Lord Shivan long ago.'

Tika rolled her eyes. 'I'm not sure I agree with trying to plan people's lives for them,' she remarked.

'Indeed,' Corman agreed. 'There were no "plans". It was simply a remark Lady Lerran made to me once. It is quite coincidental that they have become friends now.'

Tika looked sceptical but said no more.

'Perhaps we should rejoin Farn now? He must be feeling forgotten,' Corman said as he stood.

Tika looked up at him. 'I will not search for Jian, Corman. I doubt I could locate her if she is deliberately hiding, but I have no wish to be involved.'

'I knew you would not, Tika. I am just grateful you came to see me.' He paused. 'It is a consolation to me to speak with you.'

Tika felt the depthless sadness in the man before her and simply stepped forward, her arms tight round his waist, offering wordless comfort. Corman stooped, his cheek against the top of her head. 'Thank you,' he murmured.'

'Family?' Tika whispered back.

She heard the smile in his voice when he replied. 'Family, child.'

They moved apart and Corman opened the door. They returned to the throne room to discover Gossamer Tewk and Snail of all people, chatting to Farn. Well, Snail was chatting while Gossamer was sketching on a large sheet of paper. Snail struggled to her feet and managed a curtsey. 'We saw Farn arrive, Lady Tika, and Gossamer wanted to make a picture of him, if you don't mind?'

Farn was clearly highly delighted with the attention and Tika smiled. 'If he doesn't mind then why would I? How are you, Gossamer? I haven't seen you for a long while.'

She received a baleful look and belatedly remembered that, by a freakish accident, Gossamer was also in the half death. She didn't take kindly to enquiries about her health. About to say she thought Gossamer was looking well, Tika managed to bite back the words. Instead she looked at Snail. 'How is the business these days?' she asked brightly.

Snail had been an embalmer in Kelshan and had a side line keeping some of those who found themselves in Gossamer Tewk's unfortunate position, looking presentable. When she, Gossamer and Drengle moved to the Dark Realm where the majority of the population were extremely long lived, Snail started a dye business. Now she beamed at Tika. 'I'm astonished how many people come for my dyes,' she told her. 'They use a lot to make paints and coloured pencils you know, so there are several other small shops set up nearby since we've been here.'

Tika looked at the short, plump woman, light brown hair in an untidy knot on top of her head. A figure of fun some might think, but Tika knew how kind she was, how unjudgemental and how very quickly she'd found a new place here in Karmazen.

'Farn was telling us how much he likes honey cakes,' Snail went on, patting Farn's cheek.

'Oh yes, I do, very much,' Farn agreed. 'Gossamer is very popular, making pictures of people, my Tika.'

Gossamer glanced up and rolled her eyes. 'I don't know that my likenesses are always accurate, but people are certainly ready to part with coin for them.' Her smile reminded Tika of Dog's expression when she was planning something devious. 'I've been trying to contact Jian,' Gossamer went on, apparently unaware of Tika and Corman suddenly staring at her. 'She asked me to make a picture of her, some time ago. I left it in her apartments but I also left her bill. I hope she remembers to pay me soon.'

Tika looked helplessly at Corman. 'I'm sure your account will be settled very quickly,' he said.

'Good.'

'We are just about to leave, I'm afraid,' Tika told them. 'Perhaps you can make a picture of Farn another time.'

'Oh it's all right. I've made enough sketches to work with,' Gossamer replied.

'I'll see you off.' Corman followed Tika and Farn out to the deep archway lined with the tiny flowers Lady Lerran had so loved. 'Again, I thank you for coming, Tika,' Corman said. 'Now I shall go and pay Gossamer her coin.'

'I hope it's a good likeness.' Tika smiled sadly and left the shadowed arch to climb onto Farn. He said nothing as they flew west over the mountains separating the Dark Realm from Iskallia. Once in Iskallia he curved to the left and settled on a high ledge bathed in sunlight. The air was still chill up here, but Tika knew Farn wanted to talk of what he'd heard. She was surprised by his first words though.

'Mother was always suspicious of Jian, my Tika.'

'She was? Then *why,* by all the stars, didn't she tell me? Or *you* could have told me.'

'It was nothing definite, my Tika. She just said she felt uncomfortable when Jian was with us.' Farn's eyes whirred in agitation. 'I heard all Corman told you. I don't really understand about being disloyal though. We are loyal to mother, our Treasury, to you, my Tika. Why would we turn against you? Why has Jian turned against the Dark?'

Tika leaned against him, her arm across his shoulder. 'I don't really know, Farn, but a thought occurred to me while I was reading the reports Lady Lerran ordered made. I wonder if Jian is, quite simply, jealous of Shivan?'

'Why would she be?' Farn was confused. 'Shivan told us he was always in trouble. His teachers told him he was stupid. You think Jian wanted to be like that?'

'Yes but he *wasn't* stupid, was he? He just thought about things differently. He told us he visited Lady Lerran quite often too, she encouraged him to talk to her. He didn't say Jian was invited as well.' Tika paced round Farn, partly because she was thinking, partly because she was beginning to freeze. She halted again in front of Farn. 'You remember the Gathering, soon after you hatched? Fenj cast out Nula and those other two Dragons who followed her, for killing

355

Krea and trying to kill us? He didn't *kill* them.'

Farn's eyes whirred anxiously. 'No, he didn't but Tika, mother said he *should* have done.'

Tika stared at him. 'Kija would have done that, in a similar situation?'

'I believe she would.'

Tika threw her arms round his neck. 'Oh Farn, why must there always be such worries to deal with?'

'I don't know. I still don't understand people very well.' Farn sensed how cold Tika had become. 'I'll take you home, my Tika. You missed a meal so perhaps Kastin or Sarila will have saved you something.'

Tika gave a choked laugh and scrambled onto his back. 'Let's hope so, my dear one.'

Endis had settled into some sort of routine as he had found himself wandering around this apparently endless building. When he discovered he was cooking what he'd thought was an evening meal early one morning he had determined to regulate his days better. He had realised that a part of his mind was now aware of the world below at all times, like an old song stuck in one's thoughts, buzzing away all day in his mental background. Now, he spent his mornings investigating new rooms, rearranging things to his liking. In the afternoons he tidied his garden and prepared a meal for later, and the evenings were for reading Ashri's countless journals and notebooks, and writing in his own.

Endis had become aware he slept less, but he also noticed it made no difference to him. In his previous life, he knew he would have been yawning over his desk in the Asatarian Academy. He observed a sudden unreasonable flurry of tremendous storms north of Ledgroda but after checking Ashri's memories he discovered Menan Kelati was no more. He made no attempt to overlook Pakan Kelati, but he knew Pakan had finally realised Menan was gone. Pakan's storms raged over the lands, battering Ledgroda and the tiny village of Iglurk, but the inhabitants were well used to such weather, merely hunkering down and waiting for it to pass.

Otherwise, Endis considered the various lands and

peoples of the world were relatively quiet and peaceful in the most part, needing no specific attention from him. Reading Ashri's notes and records, he was learning how difficult even she had found the command not to interfere. That thought had been in his mind all day today and when he'd cleared away the dishes after his evening meal, he called shadows to him.

'Mother's only command is not to interfere and yet I believe you did so in Mertasia,' he said aloud. He sensed an odd chittering in the base of his skull. Were the shadows discussing how they might reply, he wondered.

'People there unchangeable too long.' That was the eventual reply he received.

'But it was still an interference,' Endis pointed out again.

Again, a pause. 'You gave no order *not.* We are Guardians. So decide.'

'Are you not bound by Mother's decree?'

'No.' That was very definite.

'I thought *all* her creations were so bound?'

'We can use judgement of ours.'

Endis pondered the shadows' words. 'Suppose *I* commanded you to leave Mertasia alone. Would you disobey my order, the *Sentinel's* direct order?'

The pause was far longer this time. 'Would speak, explain why you were wrong.'

'Do you often decide actions on your own?' Endis asked curiously.

'No. Few. Ashri speak rarely us. So we forgot. Ignore world. Ignore humans. Remember now. Serve.'

'Serve Mother?'

There was the pause Endis was becoming used to. 'Serve Sentinel first. We are Guardians.'

Now it was Endis's turn to fall silent while he thought. 'May I ask you to speak to me, if you feel something needs to be done in future? If you could explain your reasons for believing such a serious action as you took at Mertasia is really necessary? I will listen to your reasons but I would like to know *before* you take action rather than after.'

'You argue then forbid?'

'No.' Endis was thinking hard. 'I promise I will listen. I will tell you if I disagree but I will still leave any decisions up to you to make. As long as you can assure me you have only the care and the protection of this world and all who live there, animals, plants, everything. Can you agree to this?'

Endis was surprised when the shadows replied. There was an unmistakeable tone of respect in the reedy voice. 'Agree. Sentinel seems much wise. Will discuss. Sentinel might speak more to shadows?'

The last words suggested a hopefulness. Endis agreed at once. 'I look forward to speaking with you. Can I ask if you can overlook the world the way I seem able to do now?'

'Same yes, but not.'

Well, thought Endis, perhaps that wasn't the best start. Deciding on another subject which had puzzled him, he asked: 'Where do you get my food?'

'Find.'

Endis sighed, settling more comfortably in his armchair.

These conversations might take some time.

Chapter Thirty Two

Tika decided she would visit Kelshan Citadel. Lady Ricca had been pressing her to visit and see the house for wounded soldiers for some time. Tika felt it would be a timely break from the various worries that beset her and about which she could do nothing. After her return from the Dark Realm, she had told her closest friends and advisors of what she had learned from Corman. Some were shocked but Tika noted several seemed unsurprised. They *were* all surprised that Lady Lerran had kept such a close watch on Jian for so long. Some voiced the same comment Tika had made - why had Lady Lerran not taken decisive action herself?

When Tika announced her plan to go to Kelshan Citadel in a day or two, one of the first to offer to accompany her was Dog. Tika glared at her suspiciously. 'I really don't know if they have a library there, Dog, and if they do I don't want you anywhere near it.'

Dog looked deeply hurt but said no more as others round the table laughed. 'Is General Falkir in Kelshan?' Tika asked Dromi.

'Yes he is. General Parrak recommended another officer take over in Mertasia. A General Makkus. Also, Major Bars returned there, as the general's second in command.'

'So everything is calm at the moment?'

'It is,' Dromi agreed. 'Shall I send word, to tell them you intend to visit?'

'Yes please. Say in three days from now?'

The informal meeting broke up and Tika remained in the hall as usual, in case anyone wished to speak with her. She was about to go up to her room when she heard steps she recognised and sat down again warily. Essa's twins trotted into the hall and sat opposite her. Their expressions were serious, earnest, and Tika waited.

'Mama says you're going to see Ricca's wounded

soldiers,' Ama began.

'*Lady* Ricca,' Tika corrected automatically.

'Why can't *we* come and see where *Lady* Ricca lives?' Etto gave her a winning smile.

She studied them. They hadn't yet given up long winter trousers for shorts, and wore sweaters in eye watering colours. Coming to a decision she sincerely hoped she wouldn't regret, Tika nodded. 'If you can find proper clothes, official looking, I see no reason why you can't come.'

Two pairs of pale blue eyes stared at her in disbelief. '*Really?*' said Ama.

'We *can?*' said Etto.

'I will need your most solemn promise that you will be on your very best behaviour.'

'Oh yes. We will!'

Tika found herself pushed back on her chair as they hugged her tight before dashing away. Kija had seemed asleep by the hearth but now her golden eyes gazed at Tika. 'What have you done, daughter of my heart? Do you really think Kelshan is quite ready for those two?' Kija's tone was hugely amused.

Tika chose a dignified retreat. 'I'm sure they will behave perfectly well,' she retorted and escaped to her rooms.

The following day, Dromi gave her a report from Wendla. Apparently unseasonable storms had caused havoc on the small farms around Ledgroda. Emperor Kasheen had sent ships with grain and other food stuffs as an indication of Wendla's willingness to be helpful. 'Storms of snow and ice,' Dromi pointed out. 'Not sea storms.'

'There's been no trouble on the coast of Malesh?' Tika asked as she thought of the other Kelati, who Penda had far sensed during the winter.

'Shashina seems to have little contact, if any, with the other two,' said Werlan. 'The Ledgrodans, or rather the Zeminat people, told you of the Sea Mother who sends warmer waters north at the end of winter to banish the ice.'

'Endis might know more but I don't know how I might contact him.'

People left to go about their usual duties but Sergeant Essa lingered. Tika observed a slightly stunned expression on her face. 'Are you *sure* letting my two travel with us is a good idea, Tika?' asked Essa.

'Ricca has been curious about them, Essa. *They* have asked a lot about *Ricca*. Let's see what happens, shall we? Surely nothing drastic can come of it?'

Essa snorted in the face of Tika's apparent ignorance of just how disruptive her children might be.

'Have you warned them we'll be visiting Ricca's house for wounded soldiers?' Tika asked. 'Ricca has said some of the men are badly disfigured.'

Essa nodded. 'I have. They're as prepared as they can be. No one will let you forget it if this visit ends in chaos though, Tika.' Essa stood. 'They told me they needed special clothes so they've been pestering Kastin and Sarila.' A faint look of hope crossed the Sergeant's face. 'If they don't look respectable enough, you can order them to stay here,' she suggested.

Tika laughed. 'They'll be tidy enough I'm sure, Essa.'

Shaking her head, Essa strode off to join Fedran.

Later, a message arrived from Kelshan suggesting the Dragons land in the large interior courtyard next to the building Ricca had taken over for her soldiers, instead of on the roof as they usually did. Tika asked Kija's opinion. 'I think I know where they mean,' Kija agreed. 'Brin is visiting Fenj but there will be five of us. There is room in that place I believe.'

Tika tried to relax in those few days but she was deeply disturbed by all she'd learnt of Jian, of Lady Lerran's doubts about her. She heard no more from Corman and, as far as she knew, Shivan and Lorca were still searching over the Dark Realm. Tika took time to visit the medical school where Konya and Palos were welcoming the new students. The donkey, Chichi, made a point of walking with her, snuffling quietly when Tika talked to her. Tika also spoke to Minyth.

He asked if he would be able to travel with Kija and the others sometime soon.

'Would you like to then, Minyth?'

His dark grey eyes flickered. 'I would Tika. Pearl tells me of many of your journeys.'

Tika sat down on the grass beside him. 'You understand sometimes people want to come close, make a fuss of you all? That wouldn't worry you?'

Minyth thought a moment. 'No. I don't think so. Heligg would be a bit worried I think but she really likes the valley here, and the port. I think she'll be glad to stay here, guarding Iskallia with Flyn and Twist and Skay.' He shifted his weight slightly, his wings rustling against his back. 'She was very frightened before we fled from our Treasury,' he confided. 'Could I come with you this time? Please?'

Tika thought quickly. 'Have you carried a person on your back yet, Minyth?'

'No, but I would like to.'

Tika got to her feet and stroked his face. 'I will ask Kija if she approves but I'm happy for you to join us.' She went back into the House, knowing Kija had heard her conversation with the young Dragon.

'He can come, daughter, but let Ashoki come down and fly with him for a while now. Ashoki has spoken with him quite often. I think they will be comfortable with each other.'

Tika hugged her. 'I'll go and find her. Will you warn them all, keep them calm? Many of Ricca's men had bad injuries.'

'I have already spoken to Pearl and Genia and Farn. You know Farn is the likeliest to be upset.'

'I know. Ricca says she's told them all about how wonderful you all are. I think that's why she's asked us to go to that courtyard.'

'Of course it is.' Kija closed her eyes, suggesting Tika go and find Ashoki and leave the gold Dragon in peace.

Tika watched as Minyth rose from the plateau. There was the slightest wobble as he adjusted to Ashoki's weight behind his shoulders then he steadied and curved away along the valley. Her mind link with Farn told her he was somewhere along the valley with Pearl. They were busy investigating something so she left them to whatever it was.

The morning arrived for the visit to Kelshan and Tika,

362

in uniform, found Fedran and seven Guards also in uniform when she went down to the hall for breakfast. Dromi wore his usual brown jacket and trousers. The hall soon emptied, leaving the small group ready to depart when Sarila and Kastin came from the kitchen with a large covered basket. 'Cake,' said Sarila. 'For Lady Ricca.' She handed the basket to Veka and then both women seemed to linger.

Tika was about to ask if Essa's twins had changed their minds when the kitchen door opened again. Tika stared. Two small, sturdy children stood there, holding hands. Iskallian blue jackets and trousers, black boots, faces a little pale with nervous excitement, they walked straight backed to Tika. In the sudden silence, Tika felt a stab of pain. Sket would surely have been so very proud to see them thus.

Before anyone could say anything, Garrol walked into the hall, a small, leather wrapped bundle in his hands. Tika held her breath. He stopped in front of the twins, then went down on one knee. He unrolled the bundle, revealing two knives forged of blood metal. His deep voice was steady when he spoke. 'These are your first true weapons, to be carried only in service to Iskallia. They are forged of my blood and my heart. Blood will feed them. Carry them with honour.' Carefully, he slid one belt round Ama's waist, the knife encased in a black sheath, embossed with the silver Dragon of Iskallia. He repeated the action with Etto then stood, gazing down at them 'Carry them with honour,' he repeated, then turned and left the hall.

Tika risked a quick glance at Essa and saw the rigid set of her jaw, the glint of tears in her eyes and looked away. She cleared her throat. 'Ama, you travel with me. Etto, you're with Onion. Let's go.'

People began to move, Ama and Etto exchanged a look then Ama went to Tika's side and Etto moved to Onion. Tika lifted Ama onto Farn's back then swung up behind her, followed by Fedran. Almost at once, Farn lifted into the air above the plateau and then took position behind Kija. Tika kept her arm around Ama, telling her they would soon enter a gateway which might look strange but was nothing to fear. Almost as she spoke, Kija opened the way to Kelshan but Ama twisted to look into Tika's face.

'These are special knives, Tika.'

'They are, Ama. You heard what Garrol said - that they are carried only in service to Iskallia. They are most definitely not everyday toys.'

Ama was shocked. '*Course* they aren't! He knelt down, like it was *really* important.'

'Yes, Ama. Making the blood metal is immensely important to Garrol. You understand that blood metal weapons are given only to those Garrol considers worthy?'

Ama nodded, only then seeming to notice where they were. 'Why is it all spidery?' she asked, peering over Farn's shoulder.

'You think it's spidery? I think it's more like ashes,' Tika replied just as they emerged into a clear sky.

Before Ama could say more, Tika gave her a squeeze. 'Don't forget, you promised to behave.'

Ama stared down as the Dragons approached the huge Citadel, flying above Kelshan City which clustered around three sides of the great building. 'So many houses,' Ama marvelled. 'How many people live here?'

'Far too many for me. There's Lady Ricca and General Falkir,' Tika added, watching Kija lead the Dragons down. She watched Ashoki and Minyth, who was following Pearl. She sent a thought to the young Dragon but from his reply, she knew he was more excited and eager than anxious. Genia followed Minyth and then Farn drifted down onto the paving of the courtyard.

Tika saw at once, a lot of men looking from windows, seated on benches close to the house, and in wheeled chairs outside. She set Ama down and turned to greet Lady Ricca. That Lady was beaming with pleasure. Tika stooped to kiss her cheek and straightened, nodding at General Falkir. Ricca paused, looking at Ama who had been joined by Etto, and stood at attention beside Onion. There was a hint of apprehension on the twins' faces then Ricca smiled. 'I'm glad you've come,' she said. 'My soldiers say they wish they saw more children. Will you come and talk to some of them?'

For once Ama appeared speechless but Etto nodded. 'We would like to, Lady Ricca.'

Ricca frowned. 'Your name is Etto?' He nodded again. 'And you are Ama?' Ama also managed a nod. Ricca shrugged. 'Then you should call me Ricca if you want. Come.'

With a helpless glance at Tika, Etto gripped Ama's hand and they trotted in Ricca's wake. Before either Tika or Falkir could say more, Kija rose, pacing carefully towards a group of men sitting in wheeled chairs. She reclined gracefully, lowering her head to look at them before speaking so all could hear her words. 'I am Kija, Elder of the Treasury of Iskallia. Greetings to you.'

Tika watched the younger Dragons, even Storm and Minyth, move closer and also begin to talk with the men on the various benches. She saw Onion disappear inside the house behind the twins and knew he would look after them. Veka approached General Falkir and handed him the large basket she'd carried. 'Cake,' she explained. 'For Lady Ricca, from Kastin and Sarila.' Then she joined the rest of Tika's small party, casually chatting to the men outside.

Looking at perhaps thirty to forty men, Tika saw many had crutches beside them, or sticks, and many had limbs missing. She saw one young soldier reach up to Genia, his fingers tracing lightly over her long face, his eye sockets a ruin of scar tissue. 'To be honest, Lady Tika, they didn't believe you would really come.' Falkir spoke softly even though the increasing chatter meant there was little chance he'd be overheard.

'I rather expected that. Would you mind if I see where the twins have gone? They asked to come and they *swore* they'd behave but.....'

Falkir grinned. 'Of course.' He walked beside Tika, who gestured to Fedran there was no need for him to go with her, and took her into the house.

'Why is it so dark?' were her first words.

'Small windows,' Falkir pointed out.

Through a door to the left they entered a long room lined with beds, less than half of which were occupied. She saw Onion sitting on one empty bed, the three children on other, occupied beds. Onion was talking, waving his hands and everyone was listening to him. Choosing not to interrupt, Tika left the room and pointed across the hall. The opposite room was laid out the same way. 'Is it the same upstairs?' she asked.

'Yes, but there's a room further back, like a sitting room, where some men play cards and so on. Here.' Falkir took her down a corridor. 'These smaller rooms are rooms where healers treat the men,' he added.

Tika glanced into another dark room which had rather tired looking armchairs scattered around and then she turned sharply at the sound of fast pattering footsteps. She dropped to her knees as she caught Ama who clung to her, sobbing. Falkir hauled Tika to her feet, burdened as she was, and took her into one of the smaller rooms. Tika sat on a couch, holding Ama close. The sobs began to slow when the door opened. Falkir stepped forward in an attempt to hide Tika but then he stopped. Lady Ricca and Etto moved past him, Onion towering over them all. Etto leaned against Tika's knee but Ricca reached for Ama's shoulder.

'What was it, Ama? What scared you?' she asked, sounding genuinely concerned.

Ama turned in the safety of Tika's arms, her brow one line of indignation above her wet cheeks. 'Not *scared*,' she retorted, wriggling round to face Ricca squarely. Etto immediately reached for her hand. '*Sad*. Why you make them be there in the *dark?*' she demanded. 'Windows too small they can't even see the *sky*.' Ama swivelled to look at Tika. 'Why can't Nia and Nemali come and paint pictures all over? Teyo could make big windows. All that *gloom* makes them sad. Didn't you feel that?'

'I did.' Onion was leaning against the door. 'They've no plants here either,' he added. 'It would give them something to do, filling up boxes with flowers.'

Tika was beginning to see what both Ama and Onion meant when Etto spoke up. 'The men that can't get *out* or even *up,* they might like a cat or something, to talk to or something.' His ears turned scarlet as everyone looked at him but Ama leaned forward, her brow resting on his chin.

'Exactly,' she agreed.

Ricca hoisted herself onto the examination couch next to Tika. She looked thoughtful. 'Painting on the walls?' she repeated.

Ama squirmed round to look at her. '*Yes*. Nasty dark grey walls. *We* put rugs and pictures and colours on the walls in our rooms in Iskallia,' Ama told her firmly.

Onion slid down the door to sit on the floor looking up at them. 'Perhaps some of your soldiers can draw or paint pictures,' he said.

'You could move the poor ones in beds, nearer to the windows,' added Etto. 'Then they could see outside.'

Ama leaned back against Tika, scowling in thought. 'Aifa!' she exclaimed, sitting up and nearly toppling from Tika's lap.

Ricca grabbed her arm to steady her. 'What about Aifa? She's the blind one who mixes the herb remedies isn't she?' Then her eyes widened. 'Oh. Yes. Some of my soldiers could do that.'

Ama nodded vigorously. 'Doesn't matter they can't see. Aifa knows all the plants by how they smell and how they feel.'

'You could grow quite a lot of them here,' Onion agreed. 'You could grow fruit trees in big pots too. And vegetables. And flowers.'

Falkir met Tika's eyes, his bright with amusement. 'Why don't you go and ask some of them what they think?' he suggested.

Ricca jumped down then lifted Ama to the floor. She headed towards Onion who unwound himself and stood up. Ricca stared up at him. 'You know all about plants,' she said.

'Oh yes. They talk to you if you listen,' Onion replied.

Tika held her breath. Ricca studied him, decided he was perfectly serious, and led the way back to the dismal dormitory rooms. Tika let out a long sigh. General Falkir was grinning. 'I have never seen Lady Ricca as she was with your twins then. Personally, I'm delighted, even though it looks like a possible source of some disruption.'

'Shall we go out and talk to some of your men?' Tika proposed. 'Lady Ricca seems in control in here.' She had a sense General Falkir found it all most amusing. She also doubted that he understood just how determined small children could be.

'The twins are younger than Lady Ricca aren't they?' he asked as they returned to the courtyard.

'They're five years old, but you know their mother is Sergeant Essa. They take after her in build. Lady Ricca will never be a very big person I don't think.' Tika paused, glancing up at him. 'Just because they look older, don't forget they're not.'

Outside she muttered something Falkir was fairly sure was a curse, and he followed her gaze. Farn reclined among a group of men and was regaling them with one of Brin's stories. After a moment, Tika recognised it as the ice cave adventure and groaned quietly. Then she let her mage sense drift over the men. Most had injuries she could do little for after too long a time since they were inflicted, but she could ease some.

Tika saw Jagamar, the healer in charge of this place, standing near the young man who was still sitting with one hand on Genia's shoulder. She focussed on him, and flinched. He suffered constant pain, and yet he wasn't bitter, angry. She was astonished by the gentle patience she felt from him. Without a word, she left Falkir, threading her way around chairs to reach Genia and the blind boy. The other soldiers fell silent, watching as she dropped to her knees beside him. She reached for his free hand. 'What is your name?' she asked. 'I'm Tika. I think I can help take some of that headache away.'

He smiled shyly. 'I'm Timmon. I'm used to it. Help the others, I'm fine.'

Then, to some mutters of alarm, he fell asleep, slumping back in the chair.

'My daughter is healing him. She makes him sleep to stop him feeling any pain.' Kija's mind voice was a soothing murmur to the men.

Tika was shocked. When this injury had occurred, the surgeons had removed the boy's shattered eyes but they had left pieces of bone, so many of them. She settled back on her heels and concentrated. Dog and Essa moved beside her, then Essa looked over the gathered men. 'Jagamar?' she asked.

'Here. I don't know what Lady Tika might need,' he said, bringing a towel and a bowl of warm water. 'Oh.' He had clearly thought Tika might reopen the scar but she was simply kneeling, her eyes closed.

'Essa,' Tika whispered.

Taking the bowl and towel, Essa leaned closer. 'Yes, Tika, I see.' She reached to the boy's face as a small thin sliver of bone protruded just above his cheekbone. It slowly worked free and Essa gently wiped it away.

'Bone splinters,' Jagamar said, clearly astonished.

It took some time until Tika was satisfied she'd found all of the splinters, then she opened her eyes. 'Jagamar, if he complains of headache again, send for me. I hope I have all of them out but I'd rather you let me know if he has further pain.' Tika got to her feet, complaining about pins and needles, and then saw she was the centre of attention.

'When will Timmon wake up,' one older man called.

'Oh. Now.' Tika roused the boy with a thought and her audience watched Timmon sit up looking slightly puzzled. Then his mouth opened and closed, his hand lifted to his head. 'It's gone,' he exclaimed.

'Yes. I want you to promise you'll tell someone if it hurts anymore though.' Tika told him.

She had already sensed many of the men had various aches and pains but none as serious as the boy's. Before she could offer any suggestions to Jagamar, Lady Ricca appeared with the twins and Onion. Falkir told Lady Ricca quickly about Timmon's pain being eased and she smiled. Then she looked around. 'I want any one of you who can paint or draw or make wooden boxes for plants or who like growing things to tell me. We have come up with some new ideas for you all.'

Listening and watching as Ricca pulled the twins among the soldiers, Tika was touched. She saw how these damaged men truly did care for their small Imperatrix in Waiting.

Chapter Thirty Three

The Iskallians returned home, all impressed with Lady Ricca's determined efforts to improve the lives of wounded soldiers. Onion immediately vanished in search of seeds and plants which he thought would do well in the Citadel. The twins clamoured for supplies of dyes and paints to be sent to Lady Ricca and, for the sake of peace, Tika agreed to order quantities from Snail in the Dark Realm. A few days after their visit, the tutor Rumak, made his way to the hall after breakfast to speak to Tika.

'Please don't tell me you want to go back to Kelshan, even though I'm sure things are far better organised there?' Tika smiled, waving him to a seat.

He returned her smile. 'No. I love it here. I'll be happy to stay as long as you allow me.'

'Good. Then how can I help?'

'I just wanted to say how excited all of the children are. They've all been making things since Ama and Etto told them about Lady Ricca's soldiers. They want to send their pictures to the Citadel, to use for decorations. It's inspired everyone. I wondered if perhaps we could have some boxes, like Volk made for the medical school? There are thirteen children here at the moment. I thought they could have a box each and choose what they'd like to grow?' They could learn how to keep the plants and so on, draw pictures of how they look, keep notes on them. There are so many other things they can learn just doing that.'

Tika spread her hands. 'Do as you wish, Rumak, it's up to you entirely. Did you want me to speak to Volk and Onion? Neither of them will bite you, you know.' She smiled. 'It sounds a good idea but really, you don't need to ask me. You have a free hand where teaching is concerned.' She paused. 'You have no problems with any of them?'

'No, none. I decided not to make them work to a timetable, as I would usually do in Kelshan schools.'

Tika looked blank.

'In Kelshan schools, they know what lessons they have each day and in what order. Perhaps numbers, then writing, then history, and so on. I've found these children might start talking of something, then the others join in and it leads to other things. They learn what really interests them.'

Tika frowned. 'I'm not sure I like the sound of - what did you call it? A timetable? Doing the same thing, every day?'

'I've long had my doubts about it myself,' Rumak agreed. 'But it's the way schools have always been organised, I was told when I suggested I might try a different way.'

'People mostly don't seem to like change, or trying something new. I've often wondered why.' Tika smiled. 'It's one of the many things I intend to investigate properly. One day. When I have time.'

Rumak smiled back. 'If you really don't mind what I do, I'll go and see Volk.' He got up.

'You don't punish them?' Tika asked suddenly.

'If you mean hit them, *no* I do not. I talk to them.' He spoke the truth, she knew.

She watched him walk out and turn right to the main entrance. She saw Teyo come in as she was about to leave and sat down again.

'You heard the twins suggested cats for the soldiers?' he asked without preamble.

Tika frowned, thinking back. She nodded. 'I'm sure there must be cats in Kelshan. Why does it worry you?'

'It doesn't *worry* me, but I haven't heard *any* mention of cats in the Citadel? We had them *everywhere* in Hallaven. All the Stone clans had a few. Like Cerys. Are you *sure* the Kelshans have them, treat them with some respect as we do?'

'I could ask Falkir.'

'If they don't understand about cats using mind speech as we did, what do you think we could do? Send out parties to just *catch* some? They'd be terrified.'

Alarmed now, Tika nodded. 'It was a good idea of Etto's though. If Kelshan doesn't have cats, what do you suggest?'

Teyo grinned. 'We could ask for volunteers from Hallaven? There are always kittens around in one clan or another.'

'You really think any would offer such a big thing? Moving from their familiar homes in Hallaven to an unknown place?'

'It's an excellent idea.' Teyo and Tika twisted round to look at Cerys on the windowsill. Her mind voice sounded faintly surprised which made Teyo scowl. 'You should look among the Granite cats,' Cerys continued. 'They are regarded as the best. Quite rightly of course.'

Teyo hooted. Cerys's green gold eyes narrowed to slits. She fluffed out her black fur and turned her back in affronted dignity.

'Perhaps it would be best to find four or five cats who are used to humans. I'm inclined to agree about cats in Kelshan. I think any that offer to come, should be promised they can go home if they hate it.'

Teyo reached over and poked a finger in Cerys's back. She spun, claws extended and hissing. He laughed at her. 'I could go myself, now?' he suggested.

Tika shrugged. 'If you like. Take someone with you anyway please.'

He nodded. 'I will.'

When Teyo had gone, Tika walked down to the forge. Garrol's new apprentices were all busy so she waited and watched. She saw the intense concentration on their faces and was glad Garrol had such eager students. Tika didn't spend much time here when there was work going on because she found the noise made her head hurt and her ears ring, but she watched today. At last Garrol called a pause and the clanging and banging ceased. The apprentices listened to his instructions, then Garrol left them to clear up as he joined Tika, wiping his face and hands on a ragged towel. They stepped outside to talk, Garrol breathing deep of air which still had a bite of coldness to it.

'I haven't thanked you for the knives you made for Ama and Etto,' Tika began.

Garrol sighed. 'There is no need to thank me. I knew I had to make them for those two. It is early for such a gift but the time was right.'

'How do you know when the time is right?'

'Sometimes it's just a dream, over and over. Sometimes Mother Dark tells me directly.'

Tika leaned against him. 'All I could think was how proud their father would have been,' she whispered.

'I believe he would,' he agreed.

They stood in silence for a few moments, both lost in memories then Tika changed the subject. 'You're pleased with your apprentices?'

'I am indeed. They are keen to work. I believe Folan will work best with Mekla. He has a delicate touch for silver work.' He grinned. 'Jacina is small but, Dark stars! She can work iron well!'

'Have you a lot of work right now?'

'We got all the repairs done, for the villages, during the winter. Now we're getting a supply of things ready for the Port. You've heard no more from Corman?'

Tika shook her head.

'It can't end well, Tika, you do know that?'

'I do. I can't say I understand all of it or why it must end that way, but it's none of my business. I still feel I'm to blame, at least in part.'

Garrol smiled sadly. 'It is *not* your fault. Did I see Teyo and Nia go through the circle a while ago?'

'They've gone to Hallaven in search of cats for Ricca's soldiers.' Tika laughed, leaving Garrol looking slightly confused, and returned to the House.

She had spoken to the young Dragons to see how they'd felt after the visit to the Citadel, and been intrigued by their reactions. Minyth admitted he'd been distressed at first at sight of the men but then he'd begun talking to them and found them interesting, he told her. Genia felt more or less the same way. Pearl made little mention of the scarred faces and missing limbs but had much enjoyed talking with them. Storm had gone straight to Port Maressa. Lastly she'd spoken to Farn. She'd asked him to take her to the little cottage high on its ledge.

He curled round her, sheltering her from the brisk breeze. 'Were you worried by those soldiers, Farn?'

'I was, my Tika. Then one of them reached up. He had one arm missing. He touched my neck where the scales don't grow.'

Tika turned so she could see his face just above her head.

'He asked me about it so I showed him some of the pictures, my Tika.'

She caught her breath. As far as she knew, Farn had never done that before. 'What did he say?' she asked.

'Well, there were several men sitting with him so they all saw the pictures.' Farn stopped. 'One of them had only one leg but he got up, with those stick things.'

'Crutches?'

'Yes, those. He gave me a hug, my Tika. They asked how old we were and I said I'd come from my egg less than half a year and you had seen fifteen summers.'

Tika studied his face.

'My Tika, he *cried*.'

'He did?' Tika was astonished.

'He said he was given coin to fight other soldiers but he didn't know if he could ever fight those things we had to fight.' Farn bumped his chin on her shoulder. 'Another man asked me if it still hurt or bothered me. I told him no, it doesn't but.....'

'But what, dear one?'

'I told him I was too easily upset and frightened of things.'

Listening carefully, Tika was truly astonished at how open Farn had been with these strangers. 'What did they say?'

'The one who hugged me, hugged me again, and he said soldiers are usually afraid just before a battle, and lots of them have bad dreams afterwards.'

They sat in silence before Tika sighed. 'So you feel better now, meeting people who have been hurt so badly?'

'It still makes me unhappy, my Tika, but it doesn't frighten me I don't think. I'd like to visit them again you know. Could I go, even on my own?'

'I don't see why not but I'll be visiting again soon. The twins had some ideas to cheer the men. The rooms they live

374

in are very dark and gloomy.'

'That must make them sad,' Farn agreed.

Tika shivered. 'I wanted to be sure you weren't upset,' she told him.

'No, I don't think I was upset, my Tika. But you are cold. I will take you back. When will we visit the Citadel again?'

Tika climbed onto his back. 'In a few days. We have to collect some things Ama and Etto told Ricca we would take to them.'

Farn had agreed to wait until they all travelled to Kelshan before perhaps going there alone and had gone instead to visit Fenj. Tika was relieved that none of the younger Dragons had been too bothered by the large number of wounded men, and particularly Minyth and Farn were calm and accepting of the visit.

In the days since then, there were several reports from Strale which were a little confusing but not worrying, at least, so Dromi and Werlan concluded. A message came from Harbour City. Chevra seemed in a cheerful frame of mind, speaking of a meeting he'd had with Zhora of Sea Town.

'I hope it stays peaceful between them. I see no reason it shouldn't,' said Tika. 'There is so much empty land around them both, they surely have no reason to fall into dispute.'

Werlan checked through the pages. 'You saw Chevra has sent men out to gather in some cattle, closer to Harbour City? He says there is more land under cultivation too.'

Dromi nodded. 'He thinks this year will be the first since the devastation that there will be a good surplus from their farms. Let's hope no storms cause any damage.'

Later that day, Ama and Etto appeared with Onion. 'We've found *lots* of seeds, and baby trees, and some blubs,' Ama announced with satisfaction.

'Bulbs,' corrected Etto and Onion in unison.

Ama scowled. 'Onion says it's a bit late to plant the *bulbs*, but we should take them anyway.'

Tika glanced at Onion. 'They must have gardeners there who can offer some help?'

'I'm sure there are. I'll tell Ricca to put one or two of them in charge of that part of the Citadel.'

Tika coughed gently. 'Perhaps you could *suggest* rather than *tell, Lady* Ricca?'

'That's what he just *said*,' Ama informed her.

'Oh. I see. Well, depending on whether Teyo gets back tomorrow, the day after that we could take everything? I hope you're sending boxes and plants through the circle? The Dragons can't carry everything.'

Onion nodded. 'Essa will do that.'

Tika wondered if he'd actually *told* Essa of this plan but the three left before she'd decided whether or not to enquire.

It was well before dawn when Tika sensed the circle was in use. She scrambled into clothes and hurried downstairs, Cerys ahead of her. Standing at the main entrance she watched two figures solidify on the great circle. Teyo held three cats in his arms and Nia held two. Teyo headed towards her, grinning. 'All volunteers,' he announced.

'Greetings, my dears. Come inside. I hope your journey didn't alarm you.'

Judging by the slightly wild eyes staring at her, the cats *had* found it a little stressful. In the hall they found the Dragons awake and interested. Cerys went to sit primly in front of them. Teyo set his three down, followed by Nia's two. They walked towards Cerys and sat in a semi circle in front of her. Tika sensed the faint buzz in her mind which told her mind speech was being used and she sincerely hoped it would a friendly meeting. She remembered Khosa's rather ferocious meetings with cats in Wendla.

'Sit down,' she suggested to Nia and Teyo. 'It will soon be time for breakfast. Is all well in Hallaven?'

'Yes it is. Grandfather sent you his greetings.' Teyo stretched his legs out.

Tika studied Nia. The girl looked a little unsettled. 'What is it?' she asked. 'Did you feel ill, travelling the circle?'

'No, no. It's just, erm, this.' She delved into her jacket pocket and produced a ruffled kitten.

Green eyes, far too big for the tiny face, stared at Tika.

'I wanted to come but they said I couldn't.'

Tika stared back. 'Why wouldn't they let you?' she asked, amused by this determined creature.

'Because he's too small and he's not sensible enough.'

Tika saw two of the new arrivals were staring back at her. Ignoring them, the kitten continued. 'I'm *not* too small. I can get into places those fat ones can't,' he said smugly.

Torn between amusement at the rising sense of annoyance from the older cats and sudden sadness as she recalled Khosa saying something very similar, Tika raised a calming hand. 'Why do you want to go to Kelshan?' she asked him.

'I *don't*. I want to be *here*.' He had left Nia's lap and moved closer to Tika.

Cerys stalked across the hall and jumped onto the bench beside Tika. Again she felt mind speech from which she was excluded as Cerys clearly interrogated this small puff ball of a kitten. Teyo was chuckling as they waited, then Cerys glanced at Tika. 'He can stay,' she announced and, pinning him firmly, she proceeded to give him a thorough wash.

Tika looked at the other five who were clearly talking to Kija. She thought they were all probably quite young cats and all were furred in mixtures of brown, greys and blacks. She looked back at the one enduring Cerys's close attention. He was pale brown with black blotches, as if someone had picked him up with sooty fingers. 'What is your name, little one?' she asked.

'Seren.'

'Then welcome to Iskallia, Seren.'

When people began to fill the hall for their breakfast, they discovered five cats watching them with close interest. Those who usually sat at Tika's table discovered another cat. He was physically small but it was quickly clear he had a large personality. Tika chose to retreat to her rooms after a brief wait when breakfast ended. No one wanted to speak privately with her due to the general coming and going of large boxes slowly filling the entrance. Raised voices, Sarila's and Kastin's, convinced Tika it would be far wiser to stay out of everyone's way.

Cerys clearly felt the same way although Seren protested he'd like to see what was happening. His ears were boxed with a swift black paw then he found himself lifted by his scruff and carried upstairs. Tika was careful to pretend nothing was amiss and went straight to her table, sitting down and drawing some papers towards her. Unfortunately Seren had other ideas once he was released from Cerys's grip. Tika kept a discreet watch as he investigated her rooms. Cerys strolled past him, leaping lightly onto Tika's bed.

Seren sat down, considering its height. Tika put her hand half over her face to hide her amusement when he began climbing, clinging to the bedspread with determined claws. She began to concentrate on the papers she was looking through until, some while later, Cerys joined her. Tika stroked her back. 'He does seem very young, Cerys. Should he not be still with his mother?'

'He should but she died. I knew her. He is eager to learn. He's probably already cleverer than those five downstairs.' Her tone implied a lack of enthusiasm for those cats. 'They will enjoy being fussed over by the men in Kelshan though.'

Farn had told Brin how well received the story of the ice caves had been by those men so Brin had decided to join the company on their next visit to the Citadel. Teyo, Nia and Nemali also travelled with them while a huge pile of boxes went with Essa through the circle. Once in Kelshan, it all had to be carried from the circle room down to the courtyard. Some Iskallians stayed there to help with the work they'd suggested and Brin and Pearl also stayed. The rest of Tika's party returned to Iskallia in a state of utter exhaustion to everyone else's amusement.

Tika went to bed early and found Seren already snoring softly half under her pillow. Cerys asked how the new cats had been viewed. 'Apparently Kelshans don't have much to do with cats,' Tika replied. 'They think they're useful to keep mice away from food stores but they don't talk to them or look after them. They were surprised at first but I think they're rather pleased already. What have you been doing?'

'Seren wanted to look around everywhere and meet

everyone. He'll be quite all right here.' Cerys sounded content with his arrival so Tika settled in bed, careful not to disturb the sleeping Seren.

It was a morning a few days later. Tika was about to leave the hall when a man walked in. For a moment she didn't recognise him, he looked older, more mature. And serious. She held a hand out, smiling welcome. 'Endis! How are you? Have you come to visit Fenj and Lorak?'

He took her hand. 'No. I've come to see you. I need to speak with you.'

Tika felt her heart give a lurch, then she got to her feet. 'Come up to my rooms,' she said.

He climbed the stairs beside her in silence and waited until Tika dropped onto one of the scattered floor cushions. He sat across from her and met her gaze. She saw she hadn't imagined it before - the gold flecks in his hazel eyes *were* more noticeable she realised. But his eyes also held pain and sorrow and then she knew. She lost her breath suddenly. Cerys rushed to her, her paws kneading Tika's leg. Seren, unsure what was wrong but aware of distress, climbed up Tika's shirt front. Her voice was barely a whisper as she stared back at Endis. 'Gremara. Tell me.'

'I can show you,' he replied softly. 'Only if you wish to see.'

Tika nodded, unable to speak. She noticed at once Endis's way of showing pictures was different from the way she saw pictures from the Dragons or others. It was more immersive, as though she was actually there herself, not seeing through his eyes. It began in sunshine, just outside the domes. Kahn paced back and forth, wings flaring and folding. Then he turned, striding inside and through labyrinthine corridors.

Tika was aware of a silence, the only sound the click of Kahn's talons as he walked. He paused at an open door space, staring in. As if looking over his shoulder, Tika saw Gremara cross-legged on a heap of furs. She turned her head, silver eyes gleaming and a so tired expression on her scaled face. Gremara stood, a movement so swift it registered only as a blur. 'Is it time, then, child?' she asked quietly, head tilted to one side.

'More than time.' Kahn's voice was harsh, guttural. He walked forward almost casually, his arm rising.

And Gremara smiled. Her achingly beautiful smile lit her face even as Kahn's claws raked through her throat. Blood gouted and Kahn became frenzied, slashing and hacking even as Gremara's body was still upright, and then when it slowly toppled back onto the furs. Kahn ripped and tore, shredding flesh and feathered wings. He dropped to his knees, lapping at the blood. Through her tears, Tika still noted the blood was red, still human blood then, even after all this time, after all the physical changes Gremara had been subjected to, still red.

Kahn rose to his feet, his arms and face bloody, his wings fully extended. Tipping his head back, he began a long ululating cry announcing his victory. Victory, when Gremara had made no attempt to defend herself. Then others pushed past where Tika appeared to be standing, hordes of them, winged and scaled, and completely inhuman. After a moment, Kahn's cry ceased, he stepped back, snapping his wings closed. And Gremara's ruined body vanished under a heaving mass of snarling, squabbling children, unmistakeably gorging on their mother's flesh and blood. The pictures ceased and Tika felt Endis's hand on her shoulder.

Her tears blinded her and sobs shuddered through her. Then, gripping Seren to her chest and a startled Endis by the hand, with Cerys running ahead, Tika stumbled for the door, down the stairs and out to the plateau. Dragons stood, towering up, wings extended to hold them steady, and the heart wrenching song of farewell soared up to the mountain peaks. Gradually more and more people emerged to witness the Dragons' sorrow and their Lady's grief, a murmur spreading that it was Gremara they mourned.

At last, the Dragons fell silent, lowering themselves to recline on the plateau. Tika went to each one, thanking them, then returned to Endis. 'Thank you for showing me. I am so sorry it ended that way for her, but I trust she is at peace now.'

Astonished by the Dragons' lament, Endis touched her

still wet cheek. 'She is, Tika. She is.'

Chapter Thirty Four

Endis stayed for the rest of the day, meeting the two new Dragons and avoiding questions about his training as a Seer. People soon gave up asking things and simply accepted his presence here again. 'Are there cats where you live?' Seren enquired after lunch was finished.

'No cats. There are birds though.'

Seren sat back against Tika, considering why someone would have birds and no cats. Tika's closest friends had been quiet over lunch, their feelings mixed about the death of Gremara. Those who had been with Tika when she'd visited the domes the last few times, understood why she had been so horrified and distressed. Kija had shared all she'd seen through her link with Tika's mind with all in the vicinity of the House, so no one needed to question her. When the hall had nearly emptied again, Tika asked if Endis was staying the night.

'I'd hoped to visit Fenj and Lorak,' he replied. 'If you don't mind?'

'Of course not. I hoped you'd be able to come back sometimes.' Tika smiled. She was still pale, smudges under her eyes, but she was calm. It still hurt her that Gremara had to endure such an ending but it had at least been swiftly done.

Neither Tika nor Endis mentioned Youki during this visit. Endis had half expected her to question if he'd learned more of Youki but she didn't, her thoughts all of Gremara. In the middle of the afternoon, Endis stood. 'I'll visit Dragons Rest for a while before I return to the Augur,' he said.

'Is she well? Truly? She seemed so old, so frail.'

'She is,' Endis replied, feeling a twinge of guilt at misleading Tika.

'Do you watch us?' she asked.

Endis smiled. 'Occasionally. But there is much to watch in this world.'

Before she could ask more, he stepped back a pace and disappeared. Seren, forgotten on her lap, gave a squeak of alarm. 'Where did he go?'

'Ask Cerys to explain,' Tika told him, and lifted him up beside the black cat lying on the sill.

She went back to her rooms and out to the tiny garden. Sitting beside the two graves, she quietly told Khosa that her once beloved sister was gone, at peace at last. The mood was still subdued that evening but Tika went to bed early and, to her surprise, fell asleep quickly. She woke to find Seren and Cerys peering anxiously into her face, moonlight poking fingers through the windows.

'You were dreaming,' Cerys said, worry edging her mind tone.

'Yes.' Tika sat up and both cats climbed onto her.

'Fire,' said Seren.

'Yes,' said Tika again. 'I've dreamed it before.'

'Hands in the flames,' said Cerys. 'Reaching for you.'

'No, I don't think it was me, but I don't know who else it could have been.'

Tika lay against her pillows trying to recall everything in the dream, stroking both cats. Seren began to purr, a purr loud for such a small creature but which vibrated through his whole body. Eventually he fell asleep, but Tika and Cerys remained awake a long time.

In the morning, Dromi and Werlan discussed reports from Gaharn. Captain Rassu gave them a far more honest report than he had previously done regarding Rajak, elder son of the Iskallian printers, Torgen and Rinda. Captain Rassu admitted that his earlier reports had been less than truthful. He understood how worried the parents must have been by the boy's behaviour. Rassu was now pleased to tell Lady Tika that a corner seemed to have been turned. Rajak seemed genuinely to have changed his attitude. The captain stressed that Rajak was still going to be closely watched but he, Rassu, was cautiously optimistic that the boy had changed.

Rajak was sent to Gaharn to serve in the town guards for two years and Rassu hoped, by the time the boy was fifteen, he would decide to remain as a guard. As usual,

Rassu had enclosed a separate message for Torgen and Rinda. Tika read the main report and returned it to Dromi. 'That will be some comfort to them, I hope,' she said. 'I'd rather wait a little longer before I'm convinced though.'

Dromi agreed. 'I know Torgen would like to see the boy, but he and Rinda understand it is best to leave things as they are for now.'

'Captain Rassu seems a fair man,' Werlan remarked. 'He is also a good judge of people. I hope he is correct in Rajak's case but I agree more time is needed.'

'Still nothing from Corman,' Dromi added quietly. 'I'm sorry, Tika.'

'I don't feel I should visit or even write to ask about Jian. If Shivan is still away, perhaps he wouldn't want Corman discussing such a personal matter with an outsider.'

Werlan nodded. 'You realise Lord Shivan uses anger to hide his hurt quite often?'

'I know. I can't help, but I do wonder where Jian could be. Surely she would be noticed wherever she's gone?'

'She is of high Dark blood, Tika,' said Werlan. 'She is not greatly mage gifted, but she can take Dragon form and she is intelligent. There is a whole world where she could hide herself.'

Tika sat back, thinking over Werlan's words. 'How long could she survive though, alone, with no shelter, food supplies? *Could* she deal with such a situation?'

Werlan considered her question. 'For a while, I would guess, in temperate lands where the weather is not harsh, but only for a time I believe. She has spent her life in some comfort, with servants to care for her. I'm not sure how she might fare alone.'

'Should we warn Seboth?' Tika was suddenly alarmed. 'Would she seek shelter with Olam and Riff? They grew close when they fell back through time.'

Werlan regarded her sadly. 'I think not. Corman will have sent word, to Lord Seboth, Lord Chevra and Emperor Kasheen, that alas, Lady Jian is forsworn and should be offered no assistance.'

Tika stared at him, only now truly realising the enormity of Jian's predicament. Guessing her next question,

384

Werlan pre-empted her. 'Jian will know. Word is always sent out in such a serious matter. For most of the time that the Dark ones hid within the Realm, word went to all the villages and clans folk. Now they have rejoined the wider world, word must go to all their allies.'

Tika shook her head. 'It is a sad mess, and I still feel to blame.'

When Werlan and Dromi left her, Tika wandered outside. The sky was filling with heavy clouds, suggesting rain would arrive soon, although the air was warm, no hint of chill underlying the breeze. She strolled along the plateau path to Volk's caves and found Chichi lying half asleep in front of the entrance. Tika paused, looking down at the donkey, then left her to her doze and looked into the central one of the three caves Volk occupied.

There was always a sense of calm in here and Tika appreciated that more than usual today. Volk was sewing a button onto a shirt but nodded her to an old chair as she entered. 'Chichi has given up yelling at me lately,' she said with a faint smile.

Volk looked at her in surprise. 'Well, she gets tired,' he replied.

'She does?'

'Her baby is due any time, so she's uncomfortable and tired.'

'Baby?' Tika stared in disbelief.

Volk bit the thread he was using and tossed the shirt onto the table. Eyes dark as treacle glinted at her. 'I'm sad that you of all people, didn't notice,' he said.

At a complete loss for words, Tika could only sit. Volk laughed, a rumble deep in his burly chest. 'I didn't think you'd noticed,' he said.

Finding her voice, Tika asked if everything was well with the donkey.

'Course it is. Last two days, she's stayed close so I'm guessing her baby will be here soon.'

'I've helped with human births but not other creatures. I'll help if you think she needs any help.'

'Not much different.' A flash of square white teeth in the dark beard speckled with grey as Volk smiled at her.

'Farn might be interested. He wasn't too keen on the new goatlings, but I think he might like Chichi's infant.'

'I have never understood his passion for babies,' Tika admitted.

'Aaah. So he hasn't told you about the new wolf cubs down by Romaby?'

Tika groaned.

After a time of comfortable quiet, Volk spoke again. 'Although the Dark ones change to Dragon form, they are not Old Blood. Shivan has no problem with us nor Lorca or Werlan or Corman. Jian hated us when she discovered what we are.'

Tika shook her head. How well had she really known Jian, she wondered.

'She learnt of us because you make no secret that you accept all people. I've never hidden what I am, nor has Rivan. Not since we've been here. No more has Dromi.'

Tika thought back but couldn't remember any occasion when she'd seen Jian in conversation with any of those three. 'Volk, how did Old Bloods come to be? You didn't come from another world, did you?'

Volk laughed. 'No we didn't. Long as I heard tell of, we kept ourselves hidden away, so we didn't even tell our children stories about our history. Less chance of letting something slip to folk who might wish us harm.'

'Do your people follow any of the gods? There were once many gods in Kelshan and Drogoya I think?'

Volk shrugged. 'The stars always meant safety to us, and the Dark. I don't know if Old Blood people ever lived freely, Tika, but we often had to leave places, and it's usually safer to move at night. In places like Blue Lake, where there have never been many "ordinary" folk, my people have been more settled.' He sat thinking. 'I suspect perhaps there was a connection far in the past with Shadow.'

Tika said nothing, just nodded. She had long suspected there was such a link. She rose to leave.

'If you're concerned that we care for Youki, put that thought from your mind, child.'

She turned back to him.

'She keeps well away from us. I don't know why.'

'Why do you think Jian didn't like Old Bloods?' she asked.

'She *hates* us, Tika, it's not dislike.'

'Has anyone else shown any aversion to any of you here?'

'No, never here, but I don't think you truly understand what an unusual land you have created here.'

Tika stood at the open door looking out at Chichi. 'Tell me when her baby comes?'

Volk moved behind her. 'I'll tell you. That little cat, Seren? Tiny as he is, he has the heart of a Dragon Tika. He told me he will protect you better than any Guards!'

Tika wandered off towards the look out rocks at the end of the plateau path and sat staring unseeing at the long valley stretching to the east. She was surprised to find herself grieving so deeply for Gremara, but the greyness of the day seemed to accentuate her sense of sadness. Gremara had indeed done some terrible things, but she had also done some good things. Her father persuaded her to let him alter her, physically, among other things. She had agreed to his experiments on condition he left her precious baby sister alone.

The centuries she spent isolated, in Dragon form, had seen the beginning of her madness, with the briefest intervals of lucidity. Tika thanked the stars that Gremara did not know her father had lied, doing similar experiments to that sister. Tika knew Gremara welcomed death, a release from her depression, her loneliness and her periods of madness. But to die at the hand of one of her own children seemed a harshness beyond endurance.

The first drops of rain left dark splotches on the rocks around her and Tika rose, turning back to the House, unaware tears mingled with the rain on her face.

Endis spent time with Fenj and Lorak who had been delighted to see him. He was made to sit and tell them all his news, which was in fact very little but he did tell them of Gremara's death. The old gardener and the ancient Dragon were both saddened by the manner of her demise but both said the same as Tika: surely now, the poor creature must be at peace. Endis was plied with food until he suspected he wouldn't be able to move, and given all the gossip of Dragons Rest.

The girl who had lost so many babies had at last produced a healthy daughter at the end of the winter and there had been much rejoicing. He was told of the plans to try growing new crops on one of the small fields this year and of the last, successful harvests. The evening wore on, Endis aware of how tired Fenj and Lorak were. He hugged them both and then sat down again. 'You sleep, my dears,' he said. 'I'll sit here awhile and then I must leave you.' He waited, the cave warm and cosy, as the pair fell asleep then quietly rose and stepped outside.

There was now a wooden bench set to the side he saw, and was glad the villagers bothered to make such extra efforts for Lorak's comfort. He sat there, staring out over the moon and starlit scene. There was something about this place Endis found wonderfully comforting. Lula leapt onto the bench beside him. Endis stroked her gently. 'Are you content here, little one?' he asked softly.

'Oh yes. Why do you watch us when Lorak and Fenj sleep?'

Endis stared at the small cat. 'You know when I overlook you?'

Lula blinked. 'Of course I do.'

'Do you mind, or do you think I'm spying on you?'

'I wondered at first then I saw you watch because you care.'

'I do care, Lula. You were all so kind when I needed time to begin to understand what had happened to me. I like to make sure you are safe. Would you prefer I didn't?'

'No. I don't mind.'

Endis stood and moved a few paces away. 'Take care of them for me, Lula?' He stepped back and vanished.

Lula blinked again. 'I always do,' she thought before trotting back inside to snuggle close to Fenj.

Endis returned to his rooms beyond the dark garden and sat down with a sigh. He had been unsure whether he should show Tika Gremara's death but he felt it had been the right thing to do. He had been astonished by the

Dragons' reaction; he'd had no idea they were capable of such song.

For the first time, the shadows spoke to him first, without his summons. 'We did not know of her.'

The whisper sounded in Endis's head. 'Gremara? You didn't know of her?'

'No. Told you. We forgot too much until Ashri called us again.'

Endis didn't reply. The voice sounded more thoughtful than he'd yet heard it. 'Did Tika's Shadows tell you of her life?'

'Yes.'

'Where did you go? What were you doing all the years Ashri left you to yourselves?'

'Forgot why Mother made us. Drifted. Nothing.'

'You saw the death of the creature Gremara, which I showed Tika?'

'Yes. Surprised.'

'What was it that surprised you?'

'Dragons and Tika and people there. They forgave. Their grief was real.'

Endis drew a deep breath. 'Yes. They forgave her. That surprised you?'

'Yes. Much different from humans we remember.'

'Do you regard that as a good or bad thing?' He saw the pale spindly figures wavering against the stone of the hearth.

'Neither. Just surprised.'

'Have Tika's Shadows told you of the things that you seem to have missed?'

'Some. They must. We command.'

Trying to sort out precisely what they meant was proving less easy, Endis decided, and asked nothing more. He spent half the night writing a report of his visit to Iskallia then he went to bed. He was quite unaware that shadows watched him carefully as dreams began to wind through him.

Endis drifted in the great darkness between the stars, and far ahead of him he saw the tall figure he'd seen once before. Somehow, he made himself slow his movement to a stop, drifting above a small cratered world that spun slowly to his right. Olekatah. How had he known his name? Or that he was in such pain? Endis watched as the figure moved further away and he had to fight an urge to follow him.

He had the strongest sensation of loneliness and regret as the man, if man he was, grew smaller with distance. Ashri had spoken briefly of Olekatah, but Endis longed to know more, to understand what he was. Whatever crime Olekatah had committed, for Mother Dark to cast him into this endless infinity, Endis wondered if there was no possibility of his forgiveness or rehabilitation. How many countless centuries had Olekatah wandered alone?

Endis floated back, a scatter of brilliant lights flashing around him, some so searingly bright he flinched, closing his eyes against their glare. He woke, tangled in his blankets, to find one of the long grey figures hovering beside the bed. 'I was dreaming,' he managed to mutter.

'Yes.'

Endis sat up, rubbing his eyes. 'Do you know him?' he asked. 'The man I saw?' He sensed agitation from the shadows.

'Yes.' The faint rustling voice sank even lower and Endis had to concentrate to hear. 'Knew him. Friend. Miss him.'

Endis was so astonished he could think of nothing to say and then was aware the shadows had left him. That was another thing he wondered about: *where* did they spend their time? He lay back, knowing he would sleep no more as he pondered their claim that Olekatah had been a friend whom they missed. Thinking of the little Ashri had told him, he wasn't sure she'd say more if he asked her. He quailed at the idea of questioning Mother Dark herself. Would Ashri have written anything of Olekatah? Endis thought of the numberless notebooks. Whatever had happened so long ago, he wondered if she had even recorded it.

Endis rolled out of bed, washed and dressed, mulling over how or where he might find the information he wanted. He worked in his garden as the light grew brighter, tidying and weeding. Later he climbed all the stairs to the top floor and the room with the spacious views of Ashri's needles. He walked slowly from window to window before sinking onto one of the couches. He worked through a section of Ashri's memories then spoke a name in a tone of command within his mind. Then, he waited.

Endis sensed the boundary of this place being breached, a slight twitch in his awareness, and a man stood before him. Endis wasn't sure what he'd been expecting but this plump man looked like a middle aged farmer or merchant. He wore rough spun trousers, a baggy shirt with a grubby waistcoat wrongly buttoned over it. His pleasant face wore a frown as he looked out of the window then at Endis.

'Welcome,' said Endis.

'Ashri is gone?' asked Simert, sitting on an adjacent couch.

'To the gods' space, yes.'

'I have rarely visited here. I presume you are now the Sentinel?'

'I apologise. I am Endis and yes, I have taken on Ashri's duty of service.'

Simert studied him. 'You are young for such a task.'

'Time will correct my age,' Endis replied calmly.

Simert laughed. 'That is true,' he agreed. 'Why did you call me, Sentinel?'

'I have had dreams of a man. Twice. His name is Olekatah. I wish to know of him, whatever you might be able to tell me. Please.'

Simert watched Endis then he came to a decision. 'Olekatah was much loved. He was one who took joy in his existence. He was loved, as I say, by all of us, except Hanlif. Olekatah adored Lerran and Darallax.'

So far, this was what Ashri had told him but Endis remained silent, hoping for more.

'I left soon after his banishment, sent by Mother to gather the souls of the human dead. I thought of Olekatah and I wondered if it had been planned by Hanlif. As we all learned much later, Hanlif was the one to be unfaithful to Mother, and to all of us. I once suggested this to Mother.' Simert shook his head. 'I believe I spoke to her too soon.

She was still enraged and hurt by what had happened and dismissed me from her presence.'

'You didn't try again?'

'It occurred to me through the years, but I had my task to fulfil. Humans seem to go through cycles of unspeakable violence and then I am so busy. I have never returned to the gods' space. I see Ferag sometimes. a few of the others who still live below. Ashri used to visit me quite often until she was appointed Sentinel.'

'I visited Tika yesterday, to show her Gremara's death. Did you take her spirit?' Endis frowned. 'What do you *do* with all the dead?'

'I saw the poor creature too.' Simert's tone was full of sympathy. 'The dead? I have a place, a realm if you like. I take them there. They are often confused, sometimes belligerent. They can choose to return to Mother, to oblivion or rebirth. Some dither and stay in my realm for some time. Others become ghosts and have a partial return to the world they knew. Gremara,' he paused. 'So you did not see the end?'

'The end?'

'Mother herself took her.'

They sat quietly for a time then Simert glanced out again at the view of clouds and spires. 'Youki took Tarel unfortunately. Tika destroyed his body but his spirit was taken as soon as the boy was killed. The boy was wrong, but I'm afraid to think what has become of his spirit.' Simert stood. 'I must return to my work. They get argumentative if I leave them alone too long.'

Endis also rose. 'Would you visit me again?'

Simert cocked his head then nodded. 'Ashri gave you her memories and her blood too. That is most unusual. I will come again. You could always visit me occasionally if you wished.' He grinned and his plump figure faded from sight.

Chapter Thirty Five

Kija alerted Tika in the middle of the night. Tika dressed and hurried down to the hall and out to Volk's caves. The cave further along had its door ajar and lamplight shone across the path. Tika entered quietly. There was the usual smell of hay, hens and goats, the air warm from the animals' bodies. Volk knelt beside Chichi, murmuring softly. The donkey's head hung low, her sides heaving and a rear hoof stamped suddenly. Tika moved closer. A dark brown eye rolled and Chichi's skin rippled and grew still again. Tika's mage sense checked and found all was well. She saw the baby was large for the relatively small Chichi and sent her strength as well as easing some awareness of pain.

Time passed with no apparent change then everything happened fast. Chichi gave a groan and her son slithered free, landing on the straw Volk had spread ready. Tika checked the baby then Chichi as Volk began to rub the newborn clean. 'Clever girl,' Tika crooned, stroking Chichi's face. 'Clever girl.'

Chichi snorted and turned to look at her child. He was bedraggled but already struggling to sort out his legs. Tika moved closer to Volk and they watched Chichi nuzzle him, encouraging him with soft whickers. Dawn was breaking when the newborn succeeded in standing, unsteadily but definitely standing. 'We look like proud grandparents,' Volk whispered and Tika laughed.

Chichi moved a little and her son found where he could feed. She looked at Tika. 'His name is Dijel.' It was the first time Chichi had mind spoken her.

Tika gave her a gentle hug. 'Dijel sounds a good name,' she replied.

'It means "safe". You won't take him away, will you?'

Tika stepped back a little, shocked. 'Of course we won't.'

'Five other children I had. All gone. This one I can keep safe.'

Tika left them and headed back to the House, the air cool and fresh. People stared, wondering where she'd been so early. She smiled. 'Chichi has a new son,' she announced to all.

Several people hurried out to check and Tika hoped Volk wouldn't let Chichi be bothered by crowds of visitors. Sitting at her table as kitchen staff began serving breakfasts, Tika saw most chairs had emptied. Veka smiled across at her. 'Poor Chichi. She'll get tired of everyone rushing to see her baby. I'll visit later.'

'Volk is there so he'll throw them out soon enough. How are your plans coming on for the markets?'

Veka swallowed some toast. 'Very well. The villagers are all pleased with the plans so far.'

Farn bustled into the hall in great excitement. 'Chichi's baby is very small, my Tika,' he exclaimed. 'He walks on his very tiptoes.'

Veka grinned. 'He is very small,' Tika agreed. 'He is also very new, so I'm sure he won't want too much excitement for a while.'

'Oh no, he won't, but Minyth and I will watch over them. That's where I'll be, my Tika, if you need me.' He hurried out again and Tika groaned.

'Even Kija doesn't know why he's so entranced by babies,' she told Veka as people came back chatting and cooing over Iskallia's newest resident.

Tika remained still in the hall at midmorning, listening to different descriptions of Chichi's son until Fedran appeared. Tika was aware a gateway had opened even as he entered the hall. Shea was still with her. 'Go and fetch Dromi and Navan, please Shea. Shivan is on his way.'

Shea raced up the stairs as Tika and Fedran walked outside. Two enormous Dragons swept along the valley, one gold and white, the other silvery grey. Tika felt a sense of relief that Lorca was with Shivan. She had a great respect for Lorca's steadiness, her calming influence over Shivan's wilder ideas. In the present situation she had no idea what the Lord of the Dark Realm's mood might be. The grey Dragon landed, shimmering in a cloud of cinnamon scented air into Lorca's human form. The gold and white Dragon settled immediately after, transforming into Lord Shivan's tall figure. They both wore the black uniform of Dark and strode towards Tika.

Shivan's gold eyes met Tika's, his face thinner, expression bleak. He bowed slightly. 'Tika.'

She returned his bow. 'Shivan.'

'I would speak with you.' Shivan looked over her head at her advisors and Captain Fedran who stood close behind her. 'In private, if you would agree.'

'Of course. Do you wish to come to my quarters, or walk along the plateau?'

'Walk.'

Lorca met her eyes, giving the slightest nod, as she moved past to join Tika's advisors. They headed back into the House and Tika began to walk towards the look out rocks. Shivan said not a word until they reached the flat boulders and Tika sat down, quietly waiting. Shivan stood for a moment, staring along the Valley then he gave a deep sigh and sat next to her.

'There's no sign of her, Tika. Where could she have gone?'

'I've tried to think too Shivan, but I can't imagine there's anywhere you haven't already looked.'

'Does this Youki have a realm, a place like Ferag has?'

Tika thought. 'She must have somewhere, yes, but not like Ferag's. Youki, from the little I understand, is earth bound, completely of this world.'

'So she *could* have some sort of stronghold somewhere?'

Tika looked at him helplessly. 'I don't *know*, Shivan.' After a while Tika looked at the tall, thin man beside her. 'What would you have done, Shivan, had you found her?'

'I would do what Aunt Lerran should have done long ago.'

Tika caught her breath, eyes locked with Shivan's. 'You would do that?' she whispered.

'I finally understand that I *am* Grandson of Dark, Tika. I must do what is right, for my people, my Realm and for Mother Dark. Do you think Aunt Lerran wanted to continue, once Dabray was entombed as he was? She understood she had to continue her service to Mother Dark rather than surrender to her personal wishes. Dabray remained in that appalling imprisonment when he could have released himself back to Mother Dark, because he served and loved Aunt Lerran. It has fallen to me to serve and I *will* serve, to the best of my ability.'

Tika drew a breath. 'You know Corman showed me Lerran's reports?'

'Yes. I believe she left Jian alone because she thought her loss would distress me. She never *spoke* of it to me though, Tika.'

'You are greatly attached to her, she *is* your sister.'

Shivan rose and paced across the small space between the flat rocks. 'Tika, I scarcely knew her until I joined your company. I was at school when she was born, then at the Academy. She never came home during holidays, always stayed with friends. In the last few years I got to know her more.' He sat down again.

'I found her intelligent, interesting, but she was always a little sarcastic, as if she thought I was really stupid compared to her. When she came back through time, so distressed about Enki, I was desperately sorry for her, and she seemed, I don't know, more real? More genuine? Then she withdrew again and argued all the time.' He shook his head.

Thinking back, Tika recalled times when Shivan had indeed seemed wary of Jian. 'Shivan, I regret deeply telling Jian of Youki. I believed Enki, who Jian seemed to regard so highly, was Youki's creation. Endis told me he was of Mother Dark. I don't pretend to understand how it could be so. When Enki was killed, it appeared that Youki was there and *she* believed he was *hers*.'

'Endis is training with this Ancient Augur?' Shivan looked interested. 'Corman spoke of him. He said he'd been surprised the boy had been chosen for such a task.'

The thought crossed Tika's mind that perhaps Corman knew the Augur was in fact the Sentinel, appointed by Mother Dark. She wondered if she might ask him at some future point. Pushing that thought away, she returned to the subject of Jian. 'You've searched all of your Realm?'

'All of Kelshan, and Drogoya too,' Shivan told her. 'I

will go next to Sapphrea, and search those lands. Favrian and Corman will have command in my absence, although all the Dark blood families are aware of Jian's betrayal and will keep watch for her. I doubt she will return to our Realm.'

Tika nodded. Personally, she didn't think Jian would have gone across the ocean to Sapphrea but she said nothing. Shivan needed time to fully accept Jian's departure and a fruitless search would do no harm. 'I am sorry Shivan.'

He gave her a faint smile. 'Reading Aunt Lerran's reports, I suspect something would have led to this sooner or later. Corman kept collecting information after Aunt Lerran returned to Mother. He thinks Jian might have tried to take my place.'

'I am truly so sorry, Shivan. Your parents must be sad.'

'But they've known, Tika. Lerran told them, right at the start. Jian hasn't been back to see them for years. They feel ashamed, angry, but not sad. Not now.'

Tika said no more. She found it difficult to believe Shivan's parents could really turn their backs on a daughter; that any parent could do so. Not being a parent herself, or remembering having a mother or father, she abandoned her attempt to understand.

'Lorca will come with me to Sapphrea,' Shivan added.

'Did she never notice something wrong?'

Shivan rose, pulling Tika up with him. 'She was intrigued by Jian's strange ways, then Aunt Lerran spoke with her. Lorca realised from the time she was fifteen that Aunt Lerran must be keeping watch on Jian but she, Lorca, was the only one who tolerated Jian's behaviour. You remember, Jian had ignored Lorca for a year or more until she fell through time? Then she chose to renew their friendship.'

Tika nodded as they began to walk back to the House.

'What's going on?' Shivan asked, watching Farn settle close to Volk's caves next to a smoky grey Dragon.

'He and Minyth are watching over Chichi's new son,' Tika said.

Shivan gave a reluctant grunt of amusement. 'Two of

them interested in babies now? Oh dear.' Reaching the
entrance, he paused. 'Let Corman know if you hear
anything, Tika? Lorca and I will be away a few days.'

'I will,' she told him.

Lorca had little chance to speak to Tika until Essa
arrived and engaged Shivan in brief conversation. 'She isn't
in Sapphrea, I'm sure, Tika, but Shivan insists on checking.'

'How long did you know of Lady Lerran's doubts?'

'Nearly ten years I suppose. Don't worry, Tika, Shivan
was furious and hurt at the damage Jian has done to their
mother but he is in control now.'

There was no time for more as Shivan glanced towards
them, preparing to leave. The two transformed and
disappeared into a gateway while Tika, Dromi, Fedran and
Navan watched. 'Did Lorca say much?' Tika asked.

They returned to the hall, Dromi explaining what Lorca
had told them. 'She said at first Shivan was just ordinarily
angry then Corman showed him the reports. Lorca read
them too and she realised she'd been reporting indirectly to
Lady Lerran through an older cousin who worked in the
palace. She said Shivan has finally come to understand
what it means to *be* a ruler of a realm.'

'Can their parents truly accept that their daughter is -
what? - a traitor?'

'I believe so, Tika. Don't forget Peshan was brother to
Lerran. Remember how he attended her in that last dreadful
illness?'

Ketro came into the hall, offering a scroll case. 'It
arrived as I was walking past,' he said and put it on the
table.

Tika lifted it, checking the seal as Ketro left. Three
jagged peaks were embossed on the seal. 'From Seboth.'
Snapping the wax, she drew out the message. Seboth was
much alarmed by a very formal letter from the Dark Realm.
It had warned him to offer no assistance to the former Lady,
Jian, who had been declared outcast from the Dark. It gave
no detail of why she had earned such punishment and
Seboth begged Tika for more information. After reading it,
she passed it to Dromi. 'Could you and Werlan deal with
this, please? Tell them all we know, but perhaps you should

make it quite clear it is a matter for the Dark Realm alone to deal with.'

Dromi read it quickly, nodded and went off to the archives. Fedran rose. 'Is there going to be trouble?' he asked quietly.

'I suspect so, Fedran, although I can't see where it will arise. Not yet, anyway.'

'Will you be involved?'

She met her Captain's gaze. 'Again, I suspect so.'

Fedran nodded. 'I'll start arranging Guard rotas,' he said, striding out of the hall.

'Do you have any idea where she is?' Navan murmured.

'I'm beginning to wonder, yes.'

'Gerras Ridge?'

Tika's brows rose. 'Why do you suggest that?'

Navan shrugged. 'Just a feeling. Is that where you think she might be?'

'The Meness shaman said they *guarded* the Ridge. That could mean they regard it as a special, sacred, place, so they keep people away, or, they consider it a dangerous place. I've begun to wonder which is more likely.'

Navan brushed tangled hair off her forehead, a gesture she remembered from her earliest days and later, from Captain Gan who had died in her service. 'I scanned the Ridge, Navan. I looked into it. It seemed solid, with no deep tunnels or anything, but I wonder now. I didn't seek *strongly*. I wasn't considering anyone or anything being inside really.'

'So it could have been shielded? That could be where Youki is, you think? Would she have offered Jian shelter?'

'That's not what I'd have thought but then, Jian would be a good servant, don't you think?'

'Because of her status, sister to the ruling Lord, you mean?' Navan considered the idea, nodding slowly. 'Surely it would have been better for Jian to stay close, well behaved, able to persuade Shivan to her views, whatever they might have been. What could Youki *want* with the Dark Realm, Tika?'

'That's been bothering me but I'm beginning to think Youki is weakening. Oh, make no mistake, she still has powers I'm not sure I understand. Strong powers in certain areas. I heard from Corman she was forbidden entry to the Dark Realm. When Jian swore to serve her, and *only* her, that gave her the chance to get inside at last.'

'You're saying Youki is no friend to Mother Dark?' Navan frowned, trying to understand.

'Apparently not.' Tika leaned closer. 'It was one of Youki's creatures who killed Tarel. I don't know if it was by Youki's order, but Youki did not punish the creature.' Seeing Navan's confusion, Tika elaborated. 'Endis told me the creature is no more. I didn't ask, but I think the Augur destroyed it. Navan, it spoke to me. It said Youki ordered it to watch over me, protect me, from my birth.'

Navan scowled. '*Protect* you? Wasn't too good at that, was it? Why do you think it was destroyed?'

'It visited me a couple of times, in my rooms. When Endis took me to see the Augur, she said it was no more.'

'It *visited* you?' Navan looked furious.

'Yes. Its name was Pesh. It thought I'd be pleased that it had killed Tarel. I told it I never wanted it near me again. I realised I was wrong to take Tarel in with no questions, but no one deserved to die as he did. Pesh spoke of it with pleasure, seemed astonished that I was sickened rather than delighted with her. Navan, Pesh *played* with him. Every bone in his body was broken while he was deliberately kept alive.'

Navan stared into her face. 'And you chose not to tell anyone that you knew this? Tika, you don't have to keep everything to yourself. Surely you know that by now?'

Before she had to reply, Fedran returned bringing scroll cases from Harbour City and Vagrantia. They asked much the same questions as Seboth, Lord of Far, had asked. Tika read them and gave them to Navan. 'Ask Dromi to send similar replies, would you?' She sighed. 'If we hear from any other lands, just do the same. I don't plan on travelling anywhere for a while.'

Fedran and Navan left her and Cerys slid off the window sill to Tika's lap. 'Why haven't you spoken of the fire dreams?' she asked. 'The Dragons haven't sensed them, not even Kija.'

'I'm not sure, Cerys. Do you really think they're important?'

Seren fell off the window sill to join Cerys. 'They're nasty,' he said. 'And it feels like it's close.'

She was thinking of a reply when Liekke wandered across, sitting politely, staring up at Tika.

'Are you well, Liekke? You seem to have settled in the kitchens - I rarely see you lately.'

The small orange cat glanced at Cerys then sat up straighter. 'It is nice here but I would like to be with Endis,' she announced.

'Oh my dear, I'm not sure how to reach him. I promise I'll tell him next time he comes here. Would that be all right?'

Liekke blinked. 'I would like that. Thank you.' She turned back to the kitchens and Tika felt guilty. She'd barely thought of how Liekke might view Endis's departure.

The following days Tika visited various people within the House and also went to Port Maressa. Farn remained utterly entranced with Chichi's baby, telling everyone in the hall each evening how amazingly fast Dijel could already run. And every night, Tika dreamed of fire.

Endis too found himself dreaming of both fire and Olekatah. He wandered through the apparently endless rooms of this impossible place and realised Ashri had never told him what she actually called it. Perhaps he should give it a name himself, he wondered, gazing out over the pastel clouds writhing slowly round Ashri's needle spires. Watching those clouds in their gentle swirls, he smiled. Clouds. He would just call this place Clouds he decided. He had no idea if he was somewhere actually in the clouds or deep in the ground; it was simply a construct of Mother Dark he thought. Ashri had changed it to suit her and he had begun to alter it too. Yes, he thought, Clouds it would be. He made his way down the many stairs, returning to the garden courtyard. There were always things to do there.

When he was restless, as he was lately, gardening soothed him. He sat on the doorstep later, contemplating the flowers, aware all the time that thoughts of fire, flames, and the dark silhouette of Olekatah, lingered in his mind. That night, as he feared, dreams again featured fire, but they were different, worse. He tossed and turned, waking to find shadows hovering around him. Shakily, he stumbled to the hearth, putting the kettle on the stove. He made tea and slumped in his chair.

'It was different,' he said.

The shadows blurred around him. 'Earth fires,' shadow agreed. Endis frowned. 'Ashri showed you. Pictures.'

'Earth fires?' Endis pushed himself up a little. Did they mean those pictures she'd shown him of volcanoes? Hills exploding? Land ripping apart? Were the dreams a warning that such things were going to happen again? But who could foresee such events? Ashri had told him the future was an unknown. Mother Dark didn't know what might come to pass. From all he had pieced together, Mother Dark watched certain people, considered their ancestry and lineage, and hoped they would reach certain potentials. Then he froze. Ashri had told him, not once but several times, Youki was of the earth, somehow an intrinsic part of this world since its beginning. Were these dreams of fire leaking from Youki?

'Yes.' The shadows clustered round his chair. 'Lord of Dark's sister betrays him and Mother. With Youki.'

'This is bad?

'Very bad. Youki much less now, but still has strength.'

'What can I do? I thought I must not interfere?'

'You are earth mage.' The shadows spoke as if it was perfectly obvious.

Endis poured himself more tea, his thoughts racing. He remembered making the earth retreat at his command so that he, Tokala and Liekke could escape the Asataria compound. Did that suggest he could *influence* the very earth, perhaps calm its restlessness?

'Yes.' The shadows reply was insistent.

'How?' he asked helplessly.

There was a flurry of movement from the shadows. 'Earth mage.' The words were a frustrated hiss.

If the shadows were frustrated and agitated, so was Endis. 'The Seniors in the Asataria said I had a minor talent

402

for earth magic but I was never taught how to use it,' he retorted.

The moving shapes froze to stillness. 'Not teach? Untrained?' Then all he heard was a chittering sound. The shadows were obviously much disturbed by this news.

'No, I have *not* been trained. Is there anything you can suggest?' Endis spoke sarcastically but the shadows gathered around him again.

'Look at world. Look deep. See where it is restless.'

'I could do that,' Endis agreed. 'If I find a place that is "restless" as you put it, what am I meant to do then?'

More chittering ensued. 'Speak to earth, to fires within. Calm them.' A pause then further comments came. 'Persuade earth to take fires elsewhere. Under ocean. Away. Away from human places.'

'Oh well, wish me good luck with that,' Endis snapped, then shook his head. 'I'm sorry. I'll look as best I can and I'll try to do what I can. More, I cannot promise.'

Endis spent the day scouring the world he'd been appointed to watch over. He sensed heat in several areas but it was a steady heat, deep and quiet, unthreatening. He was growing tired when he found the place. Something, or someone, was irritating the fire in the earth, tempting it up from far underground. And the fire was answering, surging ever closer to the surface., growing angrier as it rose.

Chapter Thirty Six

Although Endis had located the place, he knew he was too tired to attempt anything then, so he chose to make himself some food and then to write his report. He hoped, by keeping to his usual routine for a while, he might sleep better and be refreshed for the following day. He was briefly tempted to call for Ashri's advice but steeled himself not to: he was to be tested in the next days he understood, and he determined he would prove himself worthy of his new position. Accordingly, he went to bed and fell asleep quite quickly.

He dreamed, but the dreams were calmer, not so urgent or violent. Fire surrounded them but it was muted, held back, while he watched the dark figure of Olekatah turn to stare at him. This time, Endis noted his appearance more clearly because, instead of the huge figure of his first vision of him, he now seemed only a little taller than the Asatarian Discipline Seniors of Endis's childhood. He saw dark hair which fell below the man's shoulders, a narrow face, dark skinned and beardless.

Endis caught the glint of eyes reflecting light from the worlds spinning around Olekatah as he appeared to drift in the infinity. He found himself calling helplessly, wordlessly, towards Olekatah, but he was not aware of any response. Endis woke as usual just as the light was brightening in the garden, and he rose. Eating his breakfast, he decided he would go up to the top room to make his attempt to persuade the earth fires back to quiescence.

'Protect you but cannot help,' the shadows murmured in his head when he reached the high, wide windowed room.

Settling on a couch, Endis smiled. 'Thank you,' he thought back. Watching the clouds roll across his view, they reminded him of the ocean, waves breaking gently on a shore as the clouds fragmented against Ashri's needles. He wondered if he could convince the fires that water was advancing on them, as well as earth. He closed his eyes and sent his mind out over the world, to Gerras Ridge.

Tika stood at a window in her room, staring down at the circle of coloured stone slabs. She had believed it was made by Youki but now she knew, in the very core of her being, that Youki was not the maker or the giver of the circle. Tika had continued to dream of fire each night but last night she had seen the tall shape of a man watching the flames from a distance. She had struggled to see who he was, his outline had suggested Shivan but somehow she knew it wasn't him. Corman had not sent word that Shivan and Lorca were back from Sapphrea and Tika had prowled restlessly around the House and plateau, unable to settle to anything needing concentration.

This day passed like the preceding days, although Farn had torn himself away from his devotion to Dijel long enough to suggest she might feel better if he took her for a flight along the valley. Tika had thanked him with a smile and told him she was busy thinking. Tension grew in her throughout that day. By the time the evening meal was served, Tika's stomach was in knots and her head throbbed. Those sitting at her table kept up conversation while watching her push food round her plate until she gave up and moved the plate away.

She stayed in the hall for much of the evening, her thoughts obviously far away. Eventually she said goodnight and went up to her rooms, oblivious of the concern of her people and of the Dragons, heaped by the hearth. Cerys and Seren accompanied her, Seren struggling to keep up. Tika was silent, pulling off her clothes and sliding under the bed covers, both cats pressing close. She slept at once and the cats waited. Tonight Cerys's mind was linked to Kija down in the hall. Cerys had finally told Kija of the repetitious dreams Tika was having and Kija had been alarmed that she had been unaware of them.

Soon after Tika slept, the flames began to fill her mind, not quite so powerfully as before but licking closer, accompanied by a hissing roar. She stirred, then lay still again. She saw a person beyond the flames again, the man she'd glimpsed before, closer now. She suddenly sensed the earth shivering and recognised Endis's mind signature. She realised he was trying to work with earth round the fire and she woke in sudden urgency. Shadows were muttering in her head. *'Now! Go! Quickly! Help him!'*

Tika rolled out of bed, grabbing clothes at random, stumbling across to where her sword hung by the hearth. By the time she reached the hall, Guards were gathering, alerted by Kija, buttoning jackets and still buckling on swords. The Dragons were already pacing out into the night as Tika arrived in the hall, barely aware of the people there. She did notice Garrol, his great axe across his back, blue eyes hard as he strode towards Brin.

Farn rose as soon as Tika and Fedran were on his back, lifting into the star filled sky among six other Dragons. Brin flew north east at speed, taking them into a gateway before they'd left Iskallia. Behind Tika, Fedran watched the wingbeats of the Dragons, noting how rapidly they were moving. Usually the wind against his face gave him an idea of their speed but that didn't happen within the gateways. He'd never seen Tika so focussed, so unaware of the people around her. He spoke to her, not sure she would hear him, let alone reply.

'Where are we going, Lady Tika? What do we face?'

His formal tone pierced her thoughts. 'Gerras Ridge. Youki. And fire.'

When he made no reply, she half turned. 'You remember the pictures the ship, Star Flower, showed us? Of mountains exploding and fire and hot melted rocks pouring out?' Fedran nodded. 'Youki is trying to do that at Gerras Ridge, draw the fires from deep in the earth up to the surface.'

Fedran stared down at her in utter horror. 'The damage will be.....!'

Tika nodded, turning to look ahead again.

'Can you stop her?' he managed to ask.

Tika gave a humourless laugh. 'Endis is already there, using his earth powers. I hope mine will be enough, with his, to defeat her.'

Fedran looked across at the other Dragon riders. Should he have allowed Essa to come? Her children had already lost their father. Nia, Nemali, Veka. They were so young. How could he have refused them though? They had just arrived in the hall, alerted by some means that they were called upon to serve. And how did you begin to fight fire of the kind Tika spoke of?

Tika felt the journey was endless although in fact it was much briefer than usual. The Dragons emerged into a sky barely hinting at dawn and Kija took them on, over the town towards the looming presence of Gerras Ridge. Kija and Brin split the Dragons into two groups, flying alongside the Ridge in opposite directions. Tika sensed heat rising although she made no attempt yet to seek below the surface. Farn followed Kija to the west, the longer stretch of high ground, and the sun rose behind them. Kija swung round to circle as those following caught up and the riders stared back along the Ridge's length.

The only sound was faint birdsong and rustling of the multitude of leaves that now cloaked the land. The Dragons and riders watched in silence. Faint steam rose in almost delicate wisps. It could easily be mistaken for dew being burned away by the rising sun, but Tika knew better. So did Fedran, staring over her shoulder. He looked along the many miles of the Ridge and could not see how even his Lady Tika could deal with this.

'Back to Troman's new place,' Tika said aloud. To the Dragons she added: 'Don't fly above the Ridge, my dears, none of you.'

'The air near the trees feels warmer, my Tika,' Farn observed.

'It is, dear one. Keep away from it please.'

Dragons landed near Tradjis's small cabin and Guards moved quickly to Tika. Major Rellak hurried towards them, expression worried. 'Lady Tika.' Rellak saluted as he arrived. 'Are you here because of Endis?'

'Where is he?' Tika asked urgently then saw him, walking towards her. She felt something move in her jacket pocket and swore. Rellak's brows rose. Tika drew a ruffled kitten out of her pocket and glared at it. She dumped him in a surprised Veka's hands. 'Keep him safe.' She turned to Endis, noted his anxious face.

'They won't listen, Tika,' he said at once. 'I've told them they must leave, pull everyone back right to Sarvental.'

'You think that would save them if we fail?' Tika's voice was low, meant only for Endis but Rellak and her company heard her.

Endis's smile was sorrowful. 'I must try anyway. I do not ask you for help, Tika. You can leave if you wish.'

Tika scoffed. 'Don't be ridiculous. Promoted high as you may be, you can't do this alone.' She straightened her shoulders. 'Where shall we work?'

'It doesn't matter where, you know that.'

She nodded and looked at her Guards. Her friends. Her much loved family. She swallowed past a sudden hard lump in her throat. 'You all go with the Dragons. I don't want any of you closer than a mile. Is that clear?'

No one moved. No one looked anywhere but at Tika then Onion took a step past Essa. He stroked Tika's cheek. 'Silly child. You go and do what you must. We'll be right here.'

Tika met the gaze of each one of them. 'Keep back at least,' she managed, walking blindly towards Endis. He caught her hand, drawing her away from the small cabin nestled beside the barn, and out onto open grassland. They walked a short way, then Endis paused. 'This is as good a place as any,' he said, sitting down, tugging her beside him. 'Tika, don't think of them for now, only what we must do.'

She nodded, letting go of his hand. She put both her hands on the earth to each side, her fingers digging into the soil. Closing her eyes, she let her mage sense sink down. Her Guards settled in a semi circle a little behind the two still figures and the Dragons reclined around them. Kija was mind linked to Tika and the company watched the earth deeper and deeper below where Tika and Endis sat. They were both far down in the earth and were separately aware of how disturbed that earth was. It spoke to each of them, complaining of heat, of pressure, of being forced to move against its will. Tika realised Endis was speaking to the earth although she heard no words. She had only feelings, sensations to go on. Drawing her left hand free of the ground, it seemed as if the soil, the roots of grass, clung to her fingers, begging her to stay. Once freed, Tika's hand went to the egg pendant that always hung against her chest. Its familiarity brought her comfort.

The earth was so mighty and yet, to Tika, it now felt fearful. It was being *forced* to do something it had no desire to do here. Suddenly she was enraged. This was *Youki*, the creature supposedly of this earth, who she had believed *protected* the earth, and here she was - hurting it. Tika struggled to control her temper and focus its energy. As she forced her fury to do her bidding, ice began to form. The grass around her whitened, grew brittle, leaves on the trees covering the Ridge shrivelled, branches groaned. Tika's mage senses followed Endis as he went deeper down to the churning molten rock that fought against pressure from below and above, thrashing back and forth in ever wider tunnels of its own making.

The pendant she held was ice, her fingers stuck to its surface, but Tika was oblivious. The noise was deafening here, the roar and crunch of the fire, the grinding as rock was ripped and crushed. The ice around her melted, hissing and spitting, but her anger only increased, and slowly she saw the very edges of the viscous, scarlet rock coagulate into a jagged black fringe. Tika had always drawn strength from the earth when she used power. In this instance, she didn't dare make it any angrier. She sought help from the air instead, knowing Endis was trying to calm the earth, smooth its torment.

Lost in concentration, Tika heard the sudden howl of frustrated hatred as Youki finally realised what she and Endis were attempting. Ignoring Youki, as she fought to wrest control over the earth, Tika felt Endis making headway. The earth was listening to him, at last recognising him as mage born, friend to earth. Tika dared send a mind probe in the direction of Youki's scream even as most of her focus was on cooling the distressed rock. Then she saw Jian. She was alive, just, surrounded by advancing molten rock. Tika's rage peaked, ice smothering the fires nearest her but she had no idea where Jian was within this place. It felt as if Jian was distant while Youki was nearing Tika and Endis. At last Tika glimpsed her.

The silver grey fur was dark smeared and burns marked various places. The beautiful eyes Tika had admired, of no colour yet all colours, glowed a yellowish red as Youki's gaze locked on her. *'Traitor! Betrayer!'* The words were screamed through the vast length of the Ridge.

Somehow Tika found strength to reply. 'Yes. I was. I betrayed Mother Dark, but never again.' Another wordless shriek echoed around her. 'Release Jian to me!' Tika called again, near the limit of her power. Then she had another brief sighting of Jian, being engulfed by the swirling, near liquid rock. Tika felt her control slipping, her full anger pushing to be freed. And everything went black.

King Troman, his officers and troops were sitting with Tika's company, watching through Kija's mind link with Tika in horrified silence. They were all cold, their breath a fog around them. When the pictures in their heads stopped abruptly, everyone looked towards Tika and Endis. Tika was sprawled on her side, Endis toppling backwards, then darkness swept like a vast black wing over the Ridge and the air seemed to expand then press down tight.

Storm snarled, half rising as Endis and Tika vanished beneath that dark wing but Onion turned to calm him. 'Hush, they are well,' he said, his voice deep and sure. 'Just wait. Be calm.'

'Is it all going to explode, sir?' asked one of the troopers.

Onion looked across at him then at the now hidden Ridge. 'No. The Dark has quietened the fires. It is done.'

'Lady Tika and that lad,' King Troman said as he got to his feet, shuddering with cold like everyone else. 'Are they really all right? Why can't we see them?'

'They are protected,' said Onion calmly. 'We will wait here for them.'

'Major Rellak, see to the comfort of Lady Tika's company. The rest of you men, about your duties.' Troman shook his head, such visions as he'd witnessed today quite beyond his comprehension.

When only Rellak remained, Garrol rose, stamping his feet and swinging his arms. 'The frost is going, at least,' he said.

'Does that mean Tika is safe or not?' snapped Dog, heaving herself up with a groan.

'Onion said she's all right,' said Fedran.

'Then where is she? Simert's balls, it's cold.' Dog glared around. 'Would it be safe to make a normal fire? I hope someone remembered to bring some tea?'

'I always have some in my pack and I keep my pack ready all the time,' said Veka, earning a scowl from Dog and smiles from others.

'Are we *sure* Tika and Endis are safe?' Nemali asked.

'Farn is calm. Kija has said nothing to contradict Onion's words,' Essa pointed out.

The company looked at the Dragons who were all unusually silent although watchful. Navan sighed. 'Looks like most of the day is gone.'

'We will bring you food,' Rellak put in at once.

'I'm not sure how hungry most of us are right now, Rellak, but thank you,' Navan replied.

'Tika often needs food after she's used so much power,' Fedran reminded him.

'I'll see to it,' said Rellak.

'I'll help if you like,' Shea offered. She and Jarko hurried away with the Major while the rest of the company gathered round the tiny fire Onion had lit. They were as silent as the Dragons, casting frequent glances to the blackness shrouding the Ridge and all sign of their Lady and Endis.

Tika sensed the earth murmuring but its anxiety and panic had gone. All was dark yet she knew she was being carried. Strong arms held her easily, cradled against a chest. She knew whoever carried her was walking, striding somewhere through total blackness with a sureness of where they were. Her thoughts were fuzzy, her body cold. She still clutched the egg pendant but she felt no danger, only safety. Tika became aware whoever carried her was no longer walking but they were still moving. Her eyelids were too heavy to open, she felt total exhaustion. Did she sleep? Was she, in fact, lying on the grass beside Endis and dreaming of being

411

carried?

The sensation of movement ceased, she was moved higher, against a shoulder. A warm hand closed over hers as she clung to her pendant. A man's voice spoke above her head, warm, like honeyed velvet. 'I didn't know you were so cold. Is that how you tried to quench the fires?'

Tika managed a mumbled affirmative. Gently her fingers were pried away from the pendant and warmth began to seep from his hand to hers, spreading through her whole body. She felt her brain begin to function again just as whoever held her became utterly still. 'Where did you get this?' The words were a mere whisper.

Tika struggled to see in the total darkness but could make out nothing at all. 'I found it, in Fenj's treasure cave. In Sapphrea. Do you know what it is?'

The man holding her grunted. 'Of course I do. I made them for my sister to find. I hid them, some on their own, some together.'

Tika's hand moved up, touching warm skin, lips, a cheek. 'Who are you? Who is your sister?'

The following silence might have been brief; it might have lasted days. Tika was unable to tell.

'I am Olekatah, first of Mother's creations. My sister .....'

'Was Lerran,' Tika finished for him.

'You knew her?' There was surprise in the voice.

'Not for long enough. She died to save Farn.' Tika's words ended in a wail and she wept as she had never before, not even when she'd first known of Lerran's death.

The figure began to move again, fast, and there was suddenly soft lamplight. Struggling against the tears, Tika turned her head and saw a very ordinary looking room. Turning back to look at the man who carried her, she caught her breath. He was so very like Lerran. The same sharp cheek bones, straight nose in the narrow face, broad forehead. Where Lerran's skin had been pale as snow, her eyes golden, his skin and eyes were dark, but Tika saw Lerran in him and could only stare.

He returned her stare then set her in an armchair, giving a rueful smile. 'My first visitor,' he said softly.

Tika tried to comprehend what he'd said. He must have existed thousands upon thousands of years. Alone? 'I broke Mother's law and was cast out,' he said, reading her thoughts. 'Then recently a boy has been calling to me.'

'Endis.' Tika knew beyond any doubt.

The man - Olekatah - shrugged. 'He kept calling me, then he was asking for help. He said I should return. I thought perhaps Mother had at last decided to destroy me but I found him and you, dealing with that monstrosity who tried to sneak into the gods' space.'

'Youki. Is she gone?' Tika asked.

'No. I saw her slinking away like a rat. She is much weakened. She will not cause such trouble again. I expect I could find her, if you like?' he offered.

'No, no. Erm, I'm here. Where is Endis? Am I dead?'

His smile was beautiful to Tika who could only stare at him, transfixed. 'No, you are not dead. Endis is in Ashri's palace. I'm not sure how he got there.' He frowned, considering, then nodded as though he understood.

'Why did you bring me here? Wherever here is?' Tika asked.

'Your power was greatly diminished. It is a greater power than I have seen from humans. I was intrigued that you would set your strength against the angry earth.'

'Someone had to do something,' Tika retorted, then faltered, remembering. 'I could not save Jian. How will I tell Shivan?'

Olekatah looked puzzled. 'Jian? Shivan?'

'Shivan was named by Lerran as her heir. He is the Lord of the Dark Realm now. Jian was his sister but Lerran didn't trust her.'

'But what of Lerran's two children? Where are they?'

Tika shook her head. 'I don't know. She said once that her son died but her daughter had survived although she was lost.'

'And you, child, did you grow up in the Dark Realm?'

'I was a slave. My mother was captured far gone in pregnancy with me and died soon after I was born,' she said her tone flat. 'In Sapphrea.'

Olekatah stared at her, his eyes widening. Tika thought

he was about to argue but all he said was: 'I must take you back.' He lifted her and they plunged into darkness again.

Tika had no idea of time then she knew Olekatah was walking on solid ground. Ahead, she saw the Dragons, all suddenly alert and staring at her. Her company were on their feet, watching the stranger carry their Lady out of the dark cloud still covering the Ridge. It was Navan who walked forward when the stranger stopped. Navan who held out his arms to take his burden.

Olekatah bent his head, staring into Tika's eyes. 'We will talk again, child.' He hesitated then his lips brushed her brow and his voice lowered. 'You have your mother's beautiful eyes.'

Before Tika could react, she was in Navan's arms. Olekatah gave a slight bow and seemed to melt into the dark cloud which, in turn faded away to nothing.

Navan carried her to the fireside and Tika realised the sun had already set. For once, she wasn't hungry and wondered what Olekatah might have done that she was so quickly recovered. 'Where did you go, my Tika? Farn pressed close round her as she sat down.

'I have no idea where I was, dear one, but I was quite safe.'

'We saw most of what happened in the Ridge,' Kija said. 'When the dark cloud came down, we sensed you were gone but you felt safe.'

'Who was he?' demanded Dog. 'He vanished the same way certain other people do.'

'Ferag and Simert, you mean?' Tika smiled as Dog flinched at the names. 'He is Olekatah, first of Mother Dark's creations.'

Essa frowned. 'I have never heard that name.'

Disregarding these remarks, Tika looked around. 'If you saw what happened, you know Jian is gone. I have to tell Shivan.'

'I think he will know.' Onion sounded thoughtful.

'How?' asked Tika.

'Olekatah.'

Tika nodded slowly. If, as it seemed, Mother Dark had at last chosen to allow Olekatah's return, he may well see it as his duty to speak with Shivan. 'Can we sleep here tonight and go home in the morning, please? I'm tired and need to rest now.' Tika felt guilty but she had no wish for discussion of Olekatah right now. She wanted to think things through privately.

'What about Endis?' asked Veka.

'He's safe with the Augur,' Tika replied, settling down against Farn's side.

He lowered his head close to hers. 'You are quite well, my Tika?' he murmured on a single mind thread.

'Yes Farn. Quite well.'

'Will that man visit again?'

'Oh I hope so. I really do hope so.'

The story will continue........

Books in the 'Circles of Light' series

The Story will Continue in 'Beragia'

Printed in Great Britain
by Amazon